The Soledad Crucifixion

The
SOLEDAD
CRUCIFIXION

Nancy Wood

University of New Mexico Press | Albuquerque

This book was funded by a literature fellowship from the National Endowment for the Arts.

All events and characters depicted in this book are fictitious. No crucifixion of a Roman Catholic priest is known to have taken place in New Mexico.

LIBRARY OF CONGRESS CATALOGING-IN-PUBLICATION DATA

Wood, Nancy C.
The Soledad crucifixion / Nancy Wood.
    p. cm.
ISBN 978-0-8263-5128-9 (pbk. : alk. paper) — ISBN 978-0-8263-5129-6 (electronic)
I. Title.
PS3573.O595S64 2012
813'.54—dc23

                    2012014862

Design and Layout: Melissa Tandysh
Composed in 11/14 Minion Pro
Display type is ITC Mendoza Roman Std

Denver-born Veloy Vigil, 1931–1997, was an abstract expressionist painter specializing in horses and western scenes. A painting from his acclaimed Cristo series appears on the cover of this book.

For Robert "Foxhole" Parker,
and for Michael T. Kelly.

ACKNOWLEDGMENTS

I began this novel in 1974. It is a work of the imagination, steeped in my love for New Mexico history and mythology. It went through fifteen drafts, four agents, and eighteen publishers before it was accepted by the University of New Mexico Press.

During the time I wrote this book, many people gave me their support. Evan S. Connell, novelist and NEA judge, recommended funding. (He and others on the NEA panel thought I was a middle-aged Hispanic male.) He later became my friend and literary critic. Robert "Foxhole" Parker helped with editing during the many revisions, offering insight and suggestions. John Whickerbill, Anna Sekora, and the late Richard Erdoes were kind and patient critics. Marcel Legendre of the First National Bank didn't give me money, but he gave me strong support. Thanks also to Stella Davidsen, computer guru, who worked her magic, and to Bonnie and Chris Alexander for being good friends and neighbors.

At the University of New Mexico Press, I wish to thank my editor, Clark Whitehorn; director John Byram; genius copyeditor Amanda Piell; designer Melissa Tandysh; and also Kat MacGilvray, Beth Hadas, and Elise McHugh. Also at the University of New Mexico, I'd like to thank Mike Kelly, associate dean of the Center for Southwest Studies at Zimmerman Library, for his kindness. My lawyer, Ben Allison, was meticulous in the legal appraisal of the manuscript; lawyer Steve Natelson was responsible for securing use of the cover image from the Veloy Vigil family. Sunflower Elliott turned in perfect copy, as always. My brother Bob Clopp and his wife Prudence Clendenning were my fiscal guardian angels, as were India Wood, Paul Mandel, Chris Wood, and Lucy Piety.

PART ONE

Camposanto, New Mexico Territory, 1897

ONE

ON THIS, the last day of his life, the priest found himself thinking about birds. A canary he had taught to sing in Batwing, Texas, while listening to the cries of his mother in the room overhead. A chained eagle he set free that summer in San Angelo when the carnival came to town. A robin, half-frozen, that the woman he loved had hidden under his friar's cassock, meaning to startle him when he awoke. And now there were the ravens, large and black, circling above him as he hung on the cross, arms outstretched, feet fastened to the little block of wood that the mute boy had put there to help absorb a little of his pain.

"La Luz," murmured the priest, thinking of the bittersweet song of a mourning dove and the gracefulness of its pewter-colored wings.

Through a haze of pain and remembrance, Lorenzo Soledad looked for her in the crowd below. He saw nothing but a smudge of dark-robed figures against the muddy ground. La Luz had not come—although she had promised him she would—to see him one last time. In this isolated village called Camposanto, high in the mountains of New Mexico, he was alone. He recognized this now. A smile flickered across his dry and swollen lips.

The people who waited nervously below him in the cold were called the Calabazas, an impoverished tribe never officially recognized by any of the territory's three governments since the sixteenth century. They gazed sadly at the contorted figure of the priest, tied fast to the cross made from the stout limbs of El Abuelo, their sacred cottonwood tree. While the women wept, the men stood quietly, their hands clasped behind their back. *What good will come of this?*, they wondered.

Although it was early April, spring had not yet come to the high country. The clear air was cold. Patches of crusted snow lay on the slopes between the sturdy ponderosas. A lacy fringe of ice clung to the banks of the river where the redbud trees had begun to unfold. From the snow-shrouded mountains high above the village, a bitter wind tore down the valley and crept up the ice-blue knots of veins clotted in the padre's strong legs. Soledad shivered and sought to cover himself with the blanket that hung from his shoulders, then remembered. His hands were tied to the crosspiece; the stiff leather thongs cut deeply into his flesh. Long ago, another crucifixion had taken place here, so it was hallowed ground, where redemption emulated dreams.

Facing south, the priest imagined he was able to turn his body to catch the warm rays of the morning sun as it emerged briefly from the clouds. The pale heat brushed his cheek and made it tingle. For a moment, he considered the approaching spring and how he would not hear the red-winged blackbirds or the meadowlarks again. Nor would he see the field of wild irises blooming on the hill above the village. And the pasque flowers, dainty and obscure, that he had discovered the week before. He had pressed a pasque flower between the pages of his Missal, inhaling its faint, sweet scent, fingering the delicate purple petals and the fuzzy, slender stem.

Tears rolled down the padre's hollow cheeks. The pain was exquisite. He felt removed from his body, suspended in a weightless layer between life and death. He was not afraid, merely filled with regret that all he loved he would never see again. He yearned to touch the gold cross that hung from his neck for the reassurance it always brought him. He had treasured this cross ever since his ordination twelve years before, but now he was able to touch this holy object only in his mind.

"Water," the priest whispered through cracked lips caked with spittle and the bitter taste of blood. Into the padre's open mouth came the sour water drawn from one of the shallow village wells. It tasted of earth, mold, and a decidedly human flavor. The priest sucked at the sponge, nonetheless wondering at this late date about germs. A stream of water dribbled down his grizzled chin onto the matted hairs of his chest, behind which his lungs were slowly collapsing.

The bony fingers of an old man wiped him off and tugged gently at his cross, noticing the resemblance between the object and the man. "If you want cerveza, Padre, I will get you cerveza," wheezed El Comanche, the oldest man in the village. The transparent layers of life lay upon his sun-weathered face; two beady eyes peered out of the dermal ridges of a scabrous countenance forged by years of adversity. The old warrior expelled his pungent breath, heavy with garlic and the thick taste of old age. He teetered on the ladder, which was set at an odd angle to the cross so that the Calabazas could climb up easily as they came to say good-bye to the sad-faced padre who had been in their mountain village not even a year. They wished he had stayed longer, but it could not be helped.

"Not now," said the priest, feeling a hot arrow of pain shoot down from his shoulders to his feet. Soon he would become unconscious, and then death would fall upon him. *It is God's will,* he thought, as the old man gently wiped his face with a cloth. He had agreed to this sacrifice for one reason, and he remained stead-fast in his belief that it was the right thing to do. "Vita breva est," he said as the old warrior rubbed his forehead with sage and offered a prayer to the spirits for his safe journey into the next world.

"Open your eyes and take one last look," the old man said. El Comanche was more than a hundred years old, a renowned war-rior who had fought in every important battle of the nineteenth-century West without receiving a single scratch. *I have survived three governments, two wars, seven wives, gonorrhea, and boils,* he thought as he tried to keep from falling off the ladder. *I can survive whatever happens next.* He waited until the padre's eyes fluttered open, and then he spoke in a voice wrinkled with experience.

"We will miss you, Padre," the old man said, his false teeth clattering against Father Soledad's ear like a pair of castanets. One of his wives had ordered his teeth out of a Sears Roebuck catalog, and they had never fit him properly. He wheezed, "It is up to me to keep a battle going between the opposing sides of life." El Comanche remembered his long years in the War of the Locomotives and how he had fought against the Atchison, Topeka and Santa Fe Railway line. Throughout the West, El Comanche was known for his bravery and his cunning, his ability to materialize history.

"Thank you, El Comanche," murmured the priest. The old man, with his hawklike nose and his deep-set eyes, resembled Soledad's ancestors, the small, persistent ones from the Mexican jungle, who had passed down to the priest the ability to make the most of dreams.

El Comanche regretted the turn the padre's fate had taken, but it could not be helped. "We are your friends," he said. "Remember that the next place you go." By this he did not mean heaven or hell, for he did not believe in them. He meant a battlefield. To him, life was eternal war; death was only a respite for the next ordeal. "We will remember you," he said, resolving to shoot off at the moment Soledad took leave of this world the souvenir cannon he'd borrowed from the Union army at Glorieta Pass. The cannon resided in the courtyard of his house, pointed at Luis Madrone's horse pasture. When the priest succumbed, he would point it toward the sky and conduct an honorary blast. The old man took out the store-bought teeth with the bright pink gums, put them in his pouch, and began to sing a death song. It sounded like the cry of a wolf.

"Do battle in the name of truth," the priest rasped. But his words were lost in a rush of wind. Pain spread from his shoulders to his feet.

As El Comanche felt the ladder begin to sway beneath him, the old man grasped the priest around the waist and clung to him for dear life. He swayed in the air, back and forth like a clapper, until at last he fell to the ground with a thud, accidentally yanking the bright blue blanket from the padre's shoulders.

Soledad realized that now he was completely naked except for the cotton underdrawers that covered his private parts. The people gasped; they did not know what to do for their priest, hanging unceremoniously on the cross. One man reached up and wrapped his own blanket around the padre's waist. A woman came forth, replaced the ladder, and climbed up, intending to cover the priest with her shawl. But another man pulled her down. A woman's shawl was not meant to come in contact with a man. Soledad shivered, a spasm of dying and discomfort that made his body, fastened to the cross in three places, twitch like a snake. In two days it would be Easter, but for him, there would be no resurrection. He alone knew why. He let out a hoarse, deep cry.

Beneath the cross lay El Comanche, crumpled in a heap on the ground, his long braids wrapped around his neck like a muffler. He looked dead as a stone. His two wives, Hermosa and Tomasita, rushed to him and began to massage his head and feet, weeping all the while. Even at his advanced age, the Custodian of War was still a lover to them both. While the rest of his body had aged, the sexual part of his anatomy had not. "It's a miracle," the priest had said when he heard about it. "No, Padre, determination," the old warrior had replied, flexing his shooting arm.

"Viva the struggle for justice!" El Comanche cried, his big fist raised to the sky where two ravens hovered. As he shouted the best of his battle cries, two men came along and carried him away.

"Tío," said one, "you will be better off in bed."

"As for justice, you know how it is," said the other. They wore pistols strapped to their middles, and ammunition belts hung from their shoulders like necklaces. In this high, remote village called Camposanto, men had been armed for ten generations against a common fear.

Soledad squinted down at the plaza where the Calabazas had gathered to witness this spectacle, a gesture of their esteem, as well as a manifestation of their complexity. They had lived deep in the mountains for sixty years, ever since disease and the steady incursion of the outside world drove them from Pecos Pueblo where they had lived forever. The blood of the Calabazas was mixed, their customs mixed, as they themselves were mixed—part Hispano, part Indian, part Anglo, part animal. Some observed the ancient customs of their Pueblo Indian forebears; a few enjoyed certain customs of the Catholic faith. Crucifixion was one of them. They performed it every thirty years to remind themselves of the courage it took to preserve obsolescence.

"If we are dead, then we might as well do whatever we please," the Calabazas said. They clung to their rugged land in the mountains, isolated at eight thousand feet, and looked backward into time, as if to pluck from the past the fortitude of their ancestors. They tried not to think that the land they were living on had recently been made part of the forest reserve. Or that they would be moving to a new home in the desert before long. The government had claimed their land.

Now fewer than two dozen dilapidated adobe houses nestled on a slope near the edge of the forest, wisps of piñon smoke curling from their chimneys. The houses looked like part of the earth, for they were made of the earth. In the open fields, where the remnants of sagging juniper-stave fences separated one man's land from another, a few bony horses grazed, along with half a dozen dried-up cows. Behind the houses, goats, burros, and pigs meandered; a handful of listless chickens pecked in the sodden dirt, chased by matted dogs too tired to kill them. The soft cries of the animals, anxious to resume a normal life of eating, mating, and caring for their young, could be heard in the hushed stillness of morning.

A sense of resignation had settled over the people of Camposanto. The priest understood them, though he'd tried to plant his religion in their heads. And they had introduced him to some beliefs of their own. So all in all, it was an even exchange.

The little knot of people huddled inside their blankets and their shawls, waiting for the ordeal to be over. The women could not control their tears, but the men were more pragmatic. They walked up and down, discussing whether to bury him along the river under the spreading branches of El Abuelo or at the edge of the alfalfa field, where the view was better. Father Soledad had been a good priest, though unreasonable at times. Something deficient in his character had led him to his end on the cross, though the Calabazas had not crucified him against his will. No, it was not that at all. The people whispered about his good intentions, the way he'd tried to turn them into dutiful Catholics, just as the Spanish friars had done more than two hundred years ago. But the holy crucifixion could not be stopped, no matter how they might have wished it. So their memories of him began to take form. He had saved the life of a child. Danced their animal dances. And loved the fiery woman who was part jaguar.

From the anonymity of the crowd, a thin, morose man, overcome by apprehension, stepped forward and stood at an odd angle to the cross. Maimed at an early age when he had jumped from a cliff when his heart was broken, Juan Talamantes had only one good leg to stand on, and he used it like a pillar. Juan stared up at the priest, an ache expanding in his heart.

He cleared his throat. "Padre," he began, but he could not go on. The padre had turned him into a mathematician. He had helped him acquire a wife. Still, it was not enough. Unresolved, yet with a certain vision in his heart, Juan Talamantes spoke with a nervous little laugh that stemmed from his fear of a commonplace life. He dropped his watery eyes to the muddy red earth of the plaza, where over the years, so many memorable events had taken place that he saw a dark impression of history everywhere he looked. He shifted uneasily and put his weight on his wooden leg, which he'd had for so long it had acquired all the aches and pains of the real one. "Padre," he said, "is there anything we can get for you?"

"I am cold," he said hoarsely, dissolved in a throbbing pain that augured through his body. A raven, dipping lower to have a better look, cast a deep shadow across his face. The others fluttered above him in a whirling vortex, creating a somber turbulence that the people sensed as a warning.

Juan Talamantes limped away and came back with a dark blue woolen blanket he had taken from his own bed in the little adobe house where he lived with his wife, Ermina. Of all the men on the council, only he and his cousin, Narciso Ortega, had voted against the padre's crucifixion. "Are we still barbarians?" he'd asked. The rest of the men had raised their hands. "We do it because we love him," they said. "We do it because he has proved himself to be the worthiest among us. We do it in hopes that our village will be saved from the American *pendejos*." They had spent all night talking about what Father Soledad had given them. Already he was being woven into their folklore by Luis Madrone, the storyteller, who at this very moment was taking mental notes about the way the padre looked and what he said and who was climbing up the ladder to see him.

Juan Talamantes eased himself up the ladder and draped the blanket around the padre's sagging shoulders, noticing the marbleized blue color of his skin.

"Bless me, Padre," said Juan Talamantes in a barely audible voice.

"Be done with it," whispered the priest. He felt nauseated, as if his stomach had wrung itself out into a twisted cord. But he knew he would not vomit. Nor would he flinch or cry out. He would die in a way he had never lived.

Juan Talamantes could not stand comfortably on his one good leg, so he held onto the cross above the priest's tousled head. "I wish to acquire wisdom," he said. "So bless my determination to succeed."

The priest moaned. "Bless your determination, Juan Talamantes."

Juan looked into the priest's ravaged eyes. "Do not forget us," he said as he cautiously made his way down. "Wherever you go next."

Beneath the cross, the priest heard the soft, hopeless bleat of what sounded like an animal. He knew that the mute boy beseeched him. "It is all right, Sotero," the padre said, smiling through his pain. "You will always be my friend."

Sotero Madrone, the twelve-year-old mute son of Luis Madrone, stood helplessly at the base of the cross, a fine wood carving in his hands. He had finished it only hours before, the stately figure of a man meant to be Saint Francis, with birds perched on either shoulder and two rabbits curled at his feet. Because of the way he felt about the priest, Sotero had turned Saint Francis into a replica of this man. His mouth fell open, but no sound came out. He kissed the padre's blood-crusted feet. "Certium est quia impossible," he heard the padre say. Something new began to form in the boy's awakening mind. He worked his lips back and forth.

Luis Madrone, a short, squat man who looked like a bear, had been waiting his turn at the base of the cross, absorbing the details of how the thawing earth smelled on that early spring day, the way the people looked, huddled in their sorrow, and how the padre behaved under pressure. He also observed the way his boy Sotero was trying to remove the leather thongs from the padre's ankles, using the sharp blade of his wood-carving knife. A great wave of love surged through Luis's heart. "Cada quien es como Dios los hizo," he said. Everyone is the way God made him. All his life he had tried to teach the child something, for he knew he was different. Sooner or later, if he went to the outside world, people would exploit his innocence. Sotero would always be as he was, and he wondered how he would protect him.

"That is enough, my boy," said Luis Madrone, gently leading the child to his mother, Catarina. "The padre will not last long," he said to her, wiping a tear from his eye with the back of his hand. "Why are we doing this thing?" he asked her.

"Look, Tío," Juan Talamantes said in alarm, pointing a quaking finger at the wing-shaped stain that rushed out across the plaza and lapped at the base of the cross. The people stepped back, as if to avoid a rattlesnake. This sign had appeared to Juan twice before, once when the last man was crucified, and again when his beloved Florita Lobo floated up to the heavens on a long, red sash.

Luis frowned. To him, the stain looked like nothing more than a large puddle left by the melting snow. But he said nothing. Juan Talamantes had been peculiar since the day he was born and fell out of bed, still tethered to his umbilical cord. His mother, Maria White Wolf, crawled after him, remaining attached to this burden for two days until his father, Majestico Talamantes, came home and took a hunting knife and sliced them neatly apart. "Come down now. You are seeing things again," Luis scolded. "Like the time you said butterflies turned into pigeons and dropped two inches of shit on the gringo governor when he came to visit." Luis never forgot any tale, no matter how insignificant.

Luis climbed halfway up the ladder and turned so he could examine Father Soledad's body, wrapped in Juan Talamantes's blue blanket. The priest's dark head had dropped to his chest; his brooding eyes were closed. A thin bead of saliva trickled from the corner of his half-open mouth onto a corner of the blanket. Only the slightest twitch of a facial muscle indicated he was still alive. People thought him handsome, but Luis wondered what his daughter, the beautiful La Luz, saw in such a man. And why she had ruined her life for a priest who believed he could create God out of bread and wine and the words of a dead language.

Steadying himself on the ladder, Luis Madrone gently pulled the blanket across Soledad's shoulders. He heard a terrible rush of air come from his mouth. *The padre has not learned anything useful, but he has acquired character*, Luis thought to himself as he smoothed back a wisp of hair from Soledad's tortured brow. He was sorry to see him go, but some things could not be helped. He shoved his round, pensive face up against the priest's ravaged one. He was feeling quite bold, knowing that the others watched him.

"Padre, I am the Teller of Stories. Through me, our village lives, year after year, with delusion. We survive through our imagination, believing we are as we were when Bears took human form," he swallowed. "Well, Padre, do you still believe in God, eh?"

It was the sort of rhetorical question the priest knew he should answer, despite his circumstance. He tried to moisten his lips, but he felt only a crusted dryness. He must choose his words carefully. "I believe in Beethoven," he said.

Luis supposed Beethoven was a politico or a pope. "Believe in nothing, Padre," he said in a voice filled with resolution. "You will be better off."

The priest, swallowing what tasted like ashes, said, "Bless your imagination, Luis, for it is a true and lasting gift." He would miss this great, round rock of a man, who had helped to teach him the truth about himself.

As they stood watching this frightening spectacle, the Calabazas shuddered. Now and then, as if to reassure themselves, one or two people stepped forward and, reaching as high as they dared, touched a toe, an ankle, a leg. They craned their necks to look upward into the priest's face. Once there had been weakness and fear in that visage. Now there was a disturbing gratitude. *So he is truly brave*, they thought. With a wave of shy regret, they dug their feet firmly into the ground, as if to plant themselves anew. They spoke to Soledad, in their old ruined Calabaza language, about the secret life of trees and how a man could ride to the moon on the energy of clouds. Something primordial began to stir in their blood, and deeper still, the stories the people began to tell when they emerged from the sacred lake.

The oldest woman in the village pushed through the crowd. She carried a red-eyed, palpitating rooster in one hand and a breathless white hen in the other. "The egg is greater than the chicken, Padre," she called to the priest in a high-pitched voice. "The egg is the germ of life. Whether it came first or not is unimportant." She wore a long, loose coat made of softest doeskin, with chicken feathers of different colors sewn to the surface. Through her chickens, Ana Coyote believed she was connected to a mystery as basic as what made the moon come up each night. *The Great Spirit pushes it up from the bottom of the sky*, she thought.

Soledad's eyes fluttered open. "Dominus vobiscum," he murmured.

"Aha," the old woman said, as if she understood him.

The mute Sotero tugged at her sleeve, his mouth wide open. A red anger surged across his face as he struggled to make her notice him. With a muffled cry, he broke one arm off the statue of Saint Francis and threw it into the mud. The boy was her great-nephew, and though she had tried to make him speak using her various potions and herbs, he remained mute much of his life. She dropped him headfirst from a cliff. She held him under water and made incisions in his tongue. Nothing worked. "Be still," she said to the child she delivered during a full moon while six white wolves made a circle outside his mother's door. The wolves stole the boy's voice and in its place left a wind that howled like a baby.

White-haired, beady-eyed, and with a birdlike inquisitiveness, Ana Coyote handed the chickens to Luis Madrone and carefully made her way up the ladder holding a tin cup of water in one hand. When she reached the top, the old woman looked at the priest and shook her head. In the distance she heard coyotes singing the "Song of Changes." She placed her mouth against the priest's own puckered one and expelled her hot breath. Working swiftly, she forced his lips apart and shoved something hard into his mouth with her fingers.

"This is to help you in your suffering, Padre," she said. "Chew slowly to get the goodness out." She waited to see if he would gag on the peyote button that she had gotten from a lice-ridden tribe from Chihuahua.

The priest received the peyote button as if it were a Holy Communion wafer. The button tasted dry and bitter, but in his present condition, he could not tell the difference between one thing and another. "Thank you, Ana Coyote," he whispered. He remembered trying to baptize her and how she had knocked the holy water from his hand and shouted, "Water will not cleanse the soul, Padre! Only the union of a man and a woman can do that." How he'd gasped at her blasphemy. Now, he understood that one had to look beneath the surface.

The old woman saw that Soledad's facial muscles were beginning to relax; she hoped that the healing touch of Father Peyote would plunge him into a world filled with ecstasy. Whatever troubled him would soon be gone.

"I am the humble Keeper of Chickens, Padre," she said, breathing into his ear. "Through me, a man can become a chicken, but a chicken cannot become a man." She shoved another button into his mouth and offered him a little water from the tin cup. He could not swallow; the water dribbled down his chin onto his blanket. Then she said, "Bless me and all my chickens. They offer a path to understanding."

"Bless you and all your chickens," Soledad croaked. "The hens especially, for they are mothers, too." How he hated to leave this world, with all its beauty. He wished he had explored mountains. Oceans. The mystery of anemones. Tears solidified in his eyes and dropped to the ground where people later said they became butterflies, which flew off in search of spring.

Despite their differences of opinion, Ana Coyote did not want to see him go. She remembered how he had built for her a new, improved chicken coop, one with a narrow little gangplank too small for a coyote or a dog. "My hens will pray for you." She wiped his face with a cloth and saw that an impression had been left on the cloth of a man with an open mouth. Later, the Vatican would place great significance on this eventually holy relic.

As the Calabazas huddled together, they realized they needed to give something to the priest. One by one, they went down to the river and embraced El Abuelo, the magical tree that had always guarded the village. They said a little prayer, their faces pressed into the tree's deeply ridged bark. They scooped up dirt from around its mighty roots, as big around as Luis Madrone's fat legs, and rubbed it all over themselves. A certain energy began to form. In this energy was the endurance of stones, the relentlessness of water, the tenacity of trees, and the immutability of mountains. In a deep, subconscious way, this energy had enabled them to survive, clear back to a time when they climbed out of the sacred lake to establish a new life in the Middle World. This was when songs and stories began to form out of trees and rocks, clouds and animals and birds. Ten thousand years of adversity had forged an indestructible vein of energy created from their earliest connection to the natural world.

The Calabazas willed this connection into the dying priest. The beat of a war drum played by an old man sitting on the flat roof of his house echoed to the top of the mountains, among the lonely rocks. The words of a familiar hunting song rang out and nudged the dormant leaves toward unfolding. Then came the imitated cries of all the Animal People: the howl of the Wolf, the wail of the Coyote, the growl of the Bear, the whimper of the Fox, the short laugh of the Magpie. These cries were uttered by Narciso Ortega, the Custodian of Amends, who only did them on special occasions, like the time that El Comanche claimed victory over the Confederate army at Glorieta Pass and when Luis invented a story that made them forget their hunger and when the dead Florita dropped roses down from her home in the sky. The priest lifted his head.

On a hill above the village, a dark-skinned man in a baggy white suit reined in his magnificent black horse. He seemed to be at home in this place, though no one recognized him, dressed as he was in attire suitable for the tropics. The Stranger watched what was happening, yet he made no effort to stop the ghastly crucifixion unfolding on the plaza. *What courage he has*, the man thought as he rested one leg over the pommel. The Stranger decided to wait a little while longer.

Soledad had been on the cross for an hour. The worst of his pain had passed, and he felt only a spreading numbness, from his head down to his feet. An unfamiliar peace began to filter into his brain. "Michelangelo," he murmured, seeing, in his last moments, the masterpiece that had haunted him all his adult life, ever since he saw it reproduced in a book in seminary. Now, however, he felt a living part of the Sistine ceiling. In his oblivion, he saw himself as the condemned sinner, locked between the avenging angels and the rebellious damned, wrapped around by a pair of swarthy devils built like wrestlers. Looking up, he saw the muscular Christ, right hand waved in condemnation; Saint Lawrence with his gridiron; Saint Bartholomew flourishing his knife; Saint Simon was there with his saw; Saint Catherine of Alexandria with the fragment of her wheel; the untamed Adam with the fierceness of the Old Law written across his features. There, too, was the frightened Blessed Virgin, stripped of her foregone authority. And Saint Sebastian, pierced with arrows, yet courageous in his suffering. Beneath the bloody crust of his body, Soledad felt a new self forming.

"Ubi nulla est redemptio," he said. His head dropped forward.

With a feverish cry, Sotero shook the cross upon which the padre had been hanging for so long that the boy could not remember the time before it. With dark, wide eyes, he was determined to awaken this man who had tried to teach him something. He opened his mouth and tried to speak. "Ah-ah-ah," he said, trying to reconcile his thoughts with his tongue.

"Confiteor," murmured the priest.

The boy's face brightened. After a lifetime of silence, the words of the Latin Mass started to loosen his tongue. Had he not assisted the priest at Mass, even though he couldn't utter the responses? "Misereatur tui omnipotens Deus," he replied. This was the first sentence ever to drop from his mouth.

"Oremus." The lips of the priest were purple, and they barely moved.

"At long last he speaks!" shouted Luis. He tried to drag the boy away, but Sotero stubbornly clung to the base of the cross, hoping that the priest would eventually come down. He shook his arms upward, trying to make himself understood. "Domine," he sobbed.

Soledad squeezed shut his eyes. "Domine, non sum dignus," he gasped, his voice but a shred. "Bless your wasted innocence, Sotero."

The boy, still clutching the one-armed statue of Saint Francis, squatted at the foot of the cross. The padre had opened a new channel to his brain. All those months of assisting him at the altar had amounted to something after all. Perhaps the words the padre had taught him might now induce him to come down. "Et dimissis peccatis tuis, perducat te ad vitam aeternam," he said carefully.

"You have given us a miracle, Padre," Luis shouted up at Soledad. "But it is in Latin. No one speaks Latin around here." He hugged the boy to him. "Ah, what does it matter?" Remembering the promise the priest had made, Luis Madrone climbed up the ladder again. The gold cross gleamed. Luis curled his fingers around it, feeling the vertical crack. "You promised him this, if he ever spoke." Carefully, he lifted the cross over Soledad's drooping head and gave it to his son. "In honor of a miracle, Padre." Without his cross, the priest felt naked, but he was in no condition to argue.

A beautiful young woman, heavy with child, pushed through the crowd, her shoulders drawn together as if to protect herself. La Luz had been watching the spectacle since dawn, when Soledad came out of the church and embraced her for the last time. She had begged him to think of their unborn child. "Leave me, woman," was all he'd said. Now, as she made her way toward the dying priest, she felt the disapproving looks of the people. She was part Apache. They would never understand her, no matter how long she lived among them. "You are a whore, La Luz!" someone shouted. She stopped and turned around. "Oh really?" she said crossly. Arching her back, she slowly made her way up the ladder, stopping often to catch her breath. Her whole body ached; her legs were swollen, but soon the child would come, and she would offer its spirit to her dead lover. Tenderly, she wiped the priest's forehead with the hem of her shawl, noticing how his suffering had deepened the lines in his face. With the tip of her finger, she touched his brow, his lashes, and his crusted mouth. "I loved you," she sobbed and felt the child pounding on the inside of her womb. "Now your son will come into the world alone." Impulsively, she leaned forward and pressed her mouth against the crusted saliva of his lips; his breath smelled foul. How cold he was, how stiff and lifeless. "Go with God, Lorenzo," she whispered.

His eyes fluttered open. "La Luz," he said weakly. So she had come to him after all. He felt his arms slip around her, even though they were fastened in place. He prayed for the memory of love to go with him. At last, he was at peace.

In her hands, the woman held a wreath made of the thorny leaves and bright red berries of the native kinnikinnick plant. She had gathered them on the south-facing slope above the village, selecting only those that were the most beautiful and suited to her purpose. "This wreath I give you is made of pure gold," she said as she placed it on his brow. "Believe it." The finality of the situation was something she had not prepared herself for. She looked at the thongs holding his hands in place; they had cut nearly to the bone. The blood had oozed from his wounds and coagulated on the earth beneath the cross. His skin was dry and taut—the color of wash water—for the blood no longer flowed in the veins beneath it. She thought she would be sick as she looked at him and realized that nothing could be done. "I wish I could have saved you," she cried.

The priest's voice was barely audible. "You made me live," he whispered. Nothing remained in his senses except the imprint of her lips.

She gazed into his eyes, the color and consistency of ashes. Nothing was reflected in them, not even the fragments of love that he had bestowed upon her with the passion of a man who was no longer a priest, but a creature of passion and will.

In his receding consciousness, Soledad wondered if she would remember him. "Pax Domine sit semper vobiscum. You are free of me," he gasped.

Her dark eyes flashed the way they did when he used to try to teach her the catechism. "I have always been free," she said. "I loved you, that's all." As she descended the ladder, La Luz understood that, in the end, not even her love had mattered—nor had God, nor the principles of his Roman Catholic faith. What drew Soledad into the abyss went much deeper than that.

Luis Madrone called to her from the crowd. "You have ruined our family name!" he said loudly, to bring her to her senses. "We have lost our reputation as a people who know how to control themselves."

La Luz only laughed. "One true thing happened here," she said. "Do you know what it is?"

By this time, Rafael Madrone, La Luz's husband, had come out of the house where he had been taking a nap. He had escaped from the *pinta*, but he was not glad to be home. He had wanted no part of this crucifixion. Because of his wife's involvement with the priest, he was happy to see him die. He rubbed his eyes and looked around. Then he walked resolutely toward the cross and looked up at the unconscious Soledad. "You loved her," he said bitterly. "She was my wife. I loved her as well." La Luz felt the pressure of her husband's hand on her shoulder. "I want to talk to you," he said roughly, grabbing her by the hand. "The priest is dead. And I am leaving you, La Luz." His bag was packed.

By now, a dark, spreading warmth enveloped Soledad completely. In the realm of his dissolving dreams, he saw a curtain of brilliantly colored flowers, reaching from earth to sky. He heard the passionate anguish of Beethoven's music and wept because he would not play it again.

A murmur rippled through the knot of people. "The padre has power," they said. "He will save himself yet." They were greatly troubled by all that had happened. As their storyteller would remind them years later, the sky became filled with silver moths. Along the river, the fish jumped out and danced. They noticed tears falling from the moon. They were filled with remorse. Why had they allowed such a terrible thing to happen?

Now, the ravens extended their wings from one horizon to the other, and then one bird swooped low for a better look. His wing made a deep, red gash across Soledad's face, as neat and clean as a surgical knife. This meant that the birds had accepted him into their sacred circle, but he did not know that he had passed through. He saw only a great dark hole above the mountains that the ravens had pecked out. The padre drifted off into unconsciousness. He dreamed of the canary and of his mother, who told him there were two sides to every truth. He dreamed of the chained eagle and the fat lady in the carnival who told him he always would be deluded by love. He dreamed of the robin and of the woman he loved, who told him that passion would become his religion, *per omnia secula seculorum*. He dreamed of La Luz. He said her name over and over, like the Gregorian chants of his seminary days.

A low moan coursed through the crowd. They sensed the ordeal would soon be over. The people formed a circle and began the "Song of Passage into Another World," scraping their worn moccasins against the ground. Even the Stranger, who waited patiently on top of the hill, heard it and smiled. The song went on for some time, all the ancient verses learned through the centuries and improvised with verses about their own lives that evolved out of stories that Luis Madrone had told them.

Lorenzo Soledad was released from his tether to the world, as completely as if someone had snipped him loose. The color red rose before his eyes; a great bloodred wave poured down from the sky and washed over him like rain. Soon he felt a tingling in his fingertips and toes: no pain, no fire, no fear—only an exchange of substance for an incredible, expanding glow.

"Look. The padre shines like the moon," said Luis Madrone, nudging his son. At this, the boy dropped the statue of Saint Francis in the dirt. "Ete, missa est," he said with a stifled sob. He knew now that the priest would never come down. His heart felt broken, and he buried his face in his father's broad shoulder. He dared not look up at the priest. Luis Madrone clasped the sobbing Sotero to his bosom. "You were his friend," he said tearfully. "He was your friend. Is not that all that matters, my boy?" Sotero shook his head and refused to speak any more Latin. He held onto the padre's cross and pressed it against his cheek. He would never part with it.

Juan Talamantes had other things on his mind. He stood in the sun and squinted toward the opposite ridge. He had noticed the Stranger, dressed all in white, patiently waiting in the trees on a giant black horse. He frowned. Who was this man? What did he want?

El Comanche made his way to the middle of the plaza, dragging his three-inch cannon. In his Overland trunk, carried to the plaza by his two wives, he had a hundred and forty-six rounds for his Henry, ninety-one shells for a .45, two bear traps, and fourteen arrowheads, plus the sharpened head of a tomahawk. "Adios, you bastards," he said, loading the cannon and aiming it at an unseen target a hundred and fifty yards up the hill. As Rafael dragged La Luz across the plaza, El Comanche swung his cannon around and fired. Instead of cannonballs, a fusillade of potatoes soared through the air. "Death to the locomotives!" he shouted.

Juan Talamantes let out a cry. He had seen something else in the distant trees above the village. The glint of rifles. A number of horses and men. "Do something, Luis!" he gasped. "They have come to arrest us." A sickening dread swept over him. *We will all be implicated*, he thought. *Myself included, because I was part of the plan.* He saw himself spending the rest of his days in prison. *I will never see my wife again. Nor hold my baby child.* He grabbed Ermina's arm and began to propel them both toward home. If he had but an hour more to live, he would spend it making love to his wife. In the distance, the posse started down the hill, their guns drawn.

A dark, wrinkled hand passed in front of the padre's face. It was Juan Lobo, the cacique and chief of the Calabazas, who had waited to the end to perform the necessary rituals. "Are you comfortable, Padre?" Juan Lobo asked. He was an old man who looked connected to metamorphic rock and ancient seas; he had a high, sloping forehead, a nose bestowed by a red-tailed hawk, and eyes that reflected the tenacity of his ancestors. Around the padre's shoulders he draped his own chieftain's blanket with a wide, red stripe running down the center. He would bury the padre in this blanket after a suitable ceremony using the natural expressions of the Indian's ancient faith.

A trickle of blood oozed from the padre's mouth. The wreath of kinnikinnick had slid across his eyes and fallen to the ground. The two eagle feathers in his hair went with it. His slumped upper body hung almost at right angles to the cross. The people turned away. No one had thought it would go this far, that he would actually die like the real-life Christ so long ago.

"You are all barbarians!" Ana Coyote cried. She strangled a hen in plain view.

Juan Talamantes limped up. He shook his wooden leg. "I had nothing to do with it, Padre." The priest managed to open his eyes a little. "No," he said. "It was not you."

Juan Lobo pressed himself closer to the padre and whispered, "Remember me, Padre. I am the cacique of the Calabazas." The old man's face was painted with the diagonal red, black, and yellow stripes of his Turtle Clan. His body was covered with charcoal with which he'd rubbed himself into a color that was like the inside of a chimney. He wore a plain buckskin shirt and leggings; two weasel skins dangled from his braids. As he sang the ancient "Song of Passage into Another World," he began to prepare the priest for his journey by rubbing a white powder across his brow.

His face impassive, the old man reached out and, with a strong arm banded with many bracelets, forced his fingers into Lorenzo Soledad's mouth. He jerked out his tongue and spat something yellow onto it. He gazed into the priest's glassy eyes and noticed a reflection of the fiery comet birthmark on his cheek. He ran his hand across the padre's forehead, rubbing a certain medicine into his brain. The birthmark dimmed but did not disappear. Juan Lobo saw that the birthmark was duller but still glowed like the sunset. So he rubbed his magic into it, too. "I want it to leave you," Juan Lobo continued. "It is evil."

"Now, Padre," Juan Lobo said, "you will be able to walk into the next world without interference." He inserted his fingers, gnarled as the roots of an old tree, into the padre's ears. "What you hear next will be the voice of dreams. Do you have any last words?"

Suddenly, the priest opened his mouth and croaked a response. No one heard the words except the old man. Then Soledad felt himself being borne away on the wings of an enormous silver bird, part eagle and part raven. He opened his arms wide to encompass the moon and stars. He felt the light of a million suns pass through him.

At last, he had come home.

The comet, which had been there since his birth, hurtled across the sky.

AT THE MOMENT Lorenzo Soledad passed from one world into another, the Stranger rode out of the trees and across the plaza. He rode effortlessly, as if he were weightless, his baggy white suit billowing out like a cumulus, his wide-brimmed hat shoved securely down on his brow. As the Stranger approached, Juan Lobo stepped forward to confront this grotesque figure with no discernible features. The eyes of the black stallion were red, and his coat glistened with an unnatural shine. The cacique felt a sensation in his chest as if his breath were gone. The old Indian stood defiantly below the cross, his arms folded across his chest.

"You cannot come here," he said. The Stranger reached the base of the cross and stopped. He looked up at the lifeless form of the priest and uttered a few words in a strange language. Then, as Juan Lobo watched, the Stranger dismounted. He turned his face to the people, who gasped at the sight of him. "He is not among the living," they murmured, and drew back, afraid to confront this apparition. The Stranger nodded. The ragged opening that was once a mouth opened and shut, but no words came out.

Just then, four men rode down the hill, the long barrels of their rifles gleaming in the sun. They stopped and stared at the bizarre scene near the plaza. The deputies had not expected to find a crucifixion, but a fragmented tribe they would escort out of the mountains to Arizona Territory, where a certain amount of desert had been made into a reservation for them. The men looked closer. They recognized Father Soledad, his body twisted at odd angles to the cross. "Madre de Dios," they muttered, and crossed themselves. The murder of a priest was like the murder of Christ Himself, an affront to fifty generations of respectful Catholic religion. The lawmen kicked their horses' flanks and called out, "Hola!" to announce themselves. So grisly was the scene that they were not certain what they should do next. Their hands went naturally to their revolvers.

Trailing along behind the lawmen, riding sidesaddle on a horse, was a middle-aged Catholic priest, beneath whose long, black cloak showed the pink trim of a monsignor's robes. His eyes were wide with horror as he slid off his horse and clasped his hands in prayer. He was totally unprepared for what he saw. "I am Monsignor Canopus," he said, but none of the Calabazas paid him any attention. He walked stiffly to the base of the cross and kissed the cold, blue feet crusted with a layer of blood. The leather thongs that held Soledad's feet in place also had cut deeply into his ankles.

"No, no, no," the monsignor wept, falling to his knees. Soledad had been his friend for fifteen years. For a number of years, he had been Soledad's confessor as well. He knew Soledad's sins better than anyone, understood the complexity of his soul, forgave his perversity, and prayed for him every day. But this?

"This was not the only way, dear friend," he whispered as he gazed at the lifeless figure on the cross. He shuddered, mindful of the probable scandal that the death of Lorenzo Soledad would cause. *A martyr*, he thought. *Soledad is truly a martyr.* And then the possibilities of this reality began to filter into his head. "Martyr," he said aloud.

The mute boy gazed up at the monsignor, momentarily arrested from his fit of grief. "Gloria Patris, et Filii, et Spiritus Sancti," said the monsignor, making the sign of the cross in front of the buckled, discolored knees. In a small, almost inhuman voice, the boy answered, "Sicut erat in principio, et nunc, et semper, et in saecula saeculorum." He tugged at the monsignor's cloak, thinking to engage him in Latin conversation, the way he had tried with Father Soledad. A trickle of hope spread across his wide, innocent face, clouded until that moment with grief. Sotero thought he had found a substitute for his crucified friend. But the monsignor scarcely heard him. He held a small bundle containing the sanctified host and the ointments necessary for Extreme Unction, the last of his Church's holy sacraments. He started to climb the ladder when the man in white laid a decisive hand on his shoulder.

"No," the Stranger said. His face was faceless.

"You are the Devil!" the monsignor said, stepping back.

Afterward, the monsignor would describe it as being as if ice water had run through his veins, keeping him from moving at all. Then, the Stranger climbed the ladder with a lightness of step not lost on those who watched. Gently, he touched the priest on the cheek. "I have come to take you home," he whispered, and with an anguished little cry, he drew Juan Lobo's blanket around the padre's blue shoulders.

What happened next would be debated for many years. Those

standing closest to the cross said that the Stranger lifted Soledad in his arms and carried him down the ladder. Lifted him as though those three tight thongs that held him in place were nothing more than pieces of string. Others said the thongs, dangling in the air, stayed in place on Soledad's lifeless body. Who was this apparition with the smell of leaf mold?

Juan Lobo stepped forward to block the Stranger's way, and what he saw was enough to make him recoil. "It was Death," he would say later. "Death looked into my eyes and frightened me." He darted behind a tree and peered out.

Others claimed that Soledad's eyes fluttered open and he smiled at the man in white. Sotero Madrone indicated in his crude sign language that the priest spoke to him in Latin just before the Stranger took him away. El Comanche leaned against a wall of the church and aimed his Henry at the Stranger as he came toward him. He called out for him to halt, to leave the body of Soledad lying on the ground, but the Stranger kept coming, as resolute as a river in flood. For the first time in his life, El Comanche put down his rifle. He rubbed his eyes. "There are no locomotives," he said.

La Luz felt the Stranger brush past her, carrying Soledad in his arms. She pulled at the man's sleeve. The sensation she got was of an electrical current passing through her body. "Instead of flesh," she would say later, "I felt fire. I got blisters on my hands."

Carrying his lifeless burden, the Stranger mounted his stallion and gently laid Soledad across the saddle in front of him. Then he trotted off through the trees in a southerly direction. The marshal and his deputies tried to stop him, but the Stranger's horse might have had wings. It seemed to rise over the steep, rugged trail and disappear. The deputies said they saw Soledad and the Stranger rise to the clouds with red-ribboned ravens on either side, forming an honor guard. A deep unrest fell across the village of Camposanto. "Father Soledad was a holy man," Juan Lobo said fearfully. "And we killed him."

Luis Madrone made up a story for the authorities when they rode through the trees and reined in. "You should have seen him," he said. "Like Christ Himself. Just hanging there. He was not afraid. I myself would have been afraid." He talked very fast, hoping they would not understand his native Calabaza language and take him to jail. "The Apache did it."

The monsignor had seen a miracle. It was not every day one saw a crucifixion, and one such as this—well, it had implications. He rode down the mountain. He blessed everything he saw, even the squirrels and chipmunks. A whole new world was opening up, and he himself was at the center.

THE STRANGER RODE steadily south. He crossed the river when it was night to avoid detection by the *federales*. When he got to the other side, he stopped to drink a little water. He held a cup to Soledad's mouth, but the water trickled down his chin. "You can never go back," the Stranger said. "You will not remember your old life, except perhaps many years from now."

Soledad's eyes were closed, his body stiff. The stigmata of his hands and feet had turned a hideous red. And they were swollen. The Stranger bathed them with water. The priest seemed to feel nothing. "I am all the lives you have ever lived," the Stranger said, lifting Soledad onto the saddle again. They rode slowly through the saguaro and the greasewood until they came to a beautiful village by the sea, and there the Stranger left him.

TWO

ONE DAY, when the leaves were beginning to turn, Monsignor Canopus strode into Juan Lobo's cell and sat on the edge of the cot. The old Indian had aged considerably. More white hair. More wrinkles. A sadness in his eyes. "Much is happening," the monsignor said. "A newspaper found out about the crucifixion. Stories went out all over the world. People came from everywhere." He laughed. "They expect to see a miracle. Perhaps Soledad rising from the dead." The old man's face did not change expression. "La Luz had her baby," the monsignor went on. "Black hair and eyes like Soledad. She calls him 'El Mundo.' The World. Not even a saint's name, mind you. She refuses to let me baptize him. If he died with original sin on his soul, he would go straightaway to limbo."

Juan Lobo did not believe in limbo, whatever it was, nor in any of the other things the religious said were true. "I will take care of the child," he said. "Soledad's son. Part lion and part hawk. I know already." The old Indian assumed a crouching position on the floor, lost in thoughts of how he would teach El Mundo to become a warrior, a member of the Turtle Clan, like himself. He would hunt with a bow and arrows, like the old days. Luis Madrone would tell him stories to keep him in touch with his long and noble history. Everyone would do his part, as they had always done.

The monsignor had to get back to the rectory. Let the old man rant. "Did Soledad perform any miracles?" the priest asked. "Because if he did, there's still a chance you can stay where you are, in Camposanto. I shall have to go to Rome and convince the Holy Father to intercede with the authorities in America. But I need to know certain things first."

Juan Lobo hesitated. He was not anxious to impart such information to the religious. They were the ones who, several centuries before, had given their own names to his ancestors who were living peaceably in Pecos Pueblo, people known as White Hawk and Blue Willow, Running Bear and Clay Pipe. Spanish surnames made it easier for the religious to keep track of them and to enter them in the holy register of baptized communicants.

"The mute boy began to speak Latin when Soledad was crucified," the cacique said slowly. "You were there, Padre. You heard."

The monsignor nodded excitedly. "Go on," he said.

"When the dwarf Papita died, Soledad brought her back to life by Getting Together with her," Juan Lobo said. "She grew as much as my middle finger." The old priest wondered what "Getting Together" meant, but he decided not to ask. "The first day he came, Father Soledad took off his cross and shoved it in the ground," Juan Lobo said. "He told us it would bring rain, and it did. Rain, after seven years of drought. Imagine!"

The monsignor was a dull sort, not given to curiosity or adventure. What Juan Lobo was telling him was a lie, anyone could see that. But it was a way for him to advance his career. It was possible he could be elevated to archbishop of Philadelphia if he played his cards right. "Do you want to get out of here, Juan Lobo?" the priest asked. The old man nodded. For six moons he had been locked up in this wretched jail. It was time to go home.

"I need what is called an affidavit, attesting that two miracles happened," the monsignor said, rising with difficulty from the cot. "You see, if Soledad were to become a saint, Camposanto would be on the map."

"It's already on the map," Juan Lobo said. "A graveyard."

RICHARD CANOPUS SAW to it that Juan Lobo was released from jail and escorted home, where tourists, alerted by the newspaper *stories, swarmed all over the village, disturbing everything. A handful of American troops stood around with their rifles, wondering when orders would come from headquarters to move these dirty Indians to Arizona Territory. They'd heard these savages had crucified a priest last spring. Well, so what? Several soldiers picked at the cross where the priest had supposedly been crucified. They forgot his name.*

Juan Lobo started toward his house, then saw some soldiers were stationed there. They sat on his porch holding their rifles. They were smoking cigarettes and feeding bread to the squirrels.

The cacique did not like what he saw. Armed troops were stationed all over, waiting to move the Calabazas out. The matter had not been settled while he was gone.

Why had Soledad died then, if not to save the land and its people?

WHEN HE GOT back to his office in the Santa Fe cathedral, Monsignor Canopus lost no time. He wrote a letter to his cousin who was on the Committee of Saints at the Vatican. I believe we may have the first American saint, *he wrote.* His origins are cloudy, but he died a martyr's death. He performed two miracles. He converted a heathen Indian village to the Holy Faith of Rome. The natives helped him build a church. He conducted baptisms and weddings. He taught them to read and write, to do mathematics, to live as devout Catholics. A mute boy learned to speak the words of the Latin Mass. I must have an audience with the Holy Father to discuss Father Soledad's canonization. Please arrange a meeting, dear cousin. My next posting in Philadelphia depends on it.

Within the Catholic Church, things move at a glacial pace, in matters of canonization especially. Monsignor Canopus readily saw that his project was going to take time. A lot of time. That fall, the monsignor made a trip to Rome and waited. And waited. And waited. He amused himself by feeding the pigeons in Saint Peter's Square. He tottered into the Sistine Chapel and was awed by its grandeur. He fasted and contemplated; he prayed for all mankind. He became a humble man. Finally, after ten years had passed, he was granted his heart's desire. The Holy Father himself cut through years of red tape because he saw the benefit of naming Lorenzo Soledad, a wanton, murderous priest, a saint. Communicants worldwide would easily identify with him. Slowly, the wheels began to grind. Cardinals came and went, offering advice. The Holy Father sat on his throne, listening. A white dove perched on his right hand close to the glittering papal ring. It had been trained not to crap.

Despite the long wait, the monsignor was determined to remain calm. The canonization of Lorenzo Soledad de Camposanto would be his lifetime achievement. Before long, he would be promoted to archbishop of Philadelphia. But the ambitious monsignor did not live to enjoy his victory. He slumped over dead at the supper table, a glass of Chianti in his hand.

By that time, Father Antonio and Father Bartholomew, the two Vatican representatives, were on a steamship, headed toward America. They were not looking forward to their assignment. They hung over the railing of the ship, sick as dogs. "Do you think we will succeed, Bartholomew?" asked Father Antonio, who was forty years older than his colleague. His personal goal was to become a member of the Curia and perhaps to be elevated to the papacy.

AMERICA WAS HIDEOUS. *No real food. No real wine. Only a few people they met on the train from New York to St. Louis and then south to Austin understood what they were saying in their broken English. They pressed their faces against the dirty window of the train. They could not eat the food that was brought to them. They became smelly and unkempt. Desolation. Misery. Texas was barbaric. They saw a colored man hanged from a tree in Batwing, their first stop on their terrible journey. They stepped out of a carriage in front of a two-story house that pretended to be Victorian. They went to the door and knocked politely. A beautiful middle-aged woman in a red velvet dress answered.*

"I am Muy Contenta," she said, extending her hand. "Welcome to Morning Glory's."

Father Antonio gazed long and hard, then he kissed her hand. Father Bartholomew looked away.

"A pleasure, Miss Contenta," the old priest said. She looked like a Rubens painting. He reminded himself of the job he had come to do. His vow of celibacy. His age. When they were seated in the parlor, he drank his tea, inhaling her lavender scent. "Why did Soledad become a priest?" he asked.

"Well, Father, it was like this," she said, looking at him with interest.

PART TWO

Texas and Mexico,
1879–1885

THREE

LORENZO SOLEDAD DID not enter seminary for the usual reasons. He had not had a call to vocation, a vision in which Jesus or Mary or one of the principal saints directed him toward a celibate life in the service of God. His heart was far from pure. When he was sixteen, he seduced a girl named Rosella, the pretty young daughter of a shopkeeper. He coaxed her to the top of the barn, tore her drawers off and entered her from behind. Shameful, and yet he could not stop. He did it again and again. Girls seemed to like him with his thick black hair and flashing dark eyes. In a little West Texas town called Batwing, he became a girl chaser. He loved kissing and touching, rare moments of intimacy where he felt a girl's breasts against his knobby little chest. He'd unbutton his trousers and watch his member grow. The girl would giggle and cover her face. Even then, he knew his sins were great. When he went to confession, he didn't tell the priest what he did to the girls. The secrecy of his life grew deeper. "I am the son of a Spanish duke," he boasted to his classmates. "We have a castle. A room lined with pure gold."

In fact, he lived in a house of ill repute. It was called Morning Glory's, where the Vatican priests would find themselves years later. His mother worked there, first in the kitchen, then in the laundry, then upstairs. She had a large, airy room on the third floor. He watched the bankers and the lawyers and the civil engineers come and go. He knew what they did. He knew what she did. He hated her clients. He hated her. Why couldn't she be like other mothers in town? Sixteen years old and he thought he knew about sex. He peered through the keyholes or watched Johnny Fogg's swinging balls as he ran down the hallway. He took a kitchen knife and tried to cut the man's testicles off, but Johnny ran. Soledad dropped the knife on the floor and went to his room. He picked up his violin and played a squeaky tune. He was a bad violinist, but music calmed his nerves. A German immigrant named Herr Leiber had taught him. He said he showed great promise.

Soledad was ashamed of Henrietta, that much he knew. When he made enough money, he would take her away from this awful place. "How can you do it, Mama?" he'd ask. "Those men are all over you, and you don't even know who they are. They give you *money*. Five dollars one time. Isn't that true?" Henrietta was beautiful, with large brown eyes and long lashes and high cheekbones. She had nice rounded breasts that men stared at and touched, as if they had a right. He was protecting her, he told himself, but deep down he was doing something else.

Soledad punched out a balding architect from Chicago. He pushed the railroad engineer down the stairs. Soledad was small for his age, but he was strong. Muy Contenta, a sturdy Dane who owned Morning Glory's, threatened to throw them both out.

"Goddamn it, Lorenzo," she said. "This is a respectable place. The governor himself comes in. The president of the bank. The newspaper publisher. I give them the finest champagne. We have musical soirees. Poetry readings. My girls are clean and smart. Just shut up." He looked up at the ceiling. The chandelier had crystal prisms that sparkled in the sun. A canary sang in a corner cage.

"Yes, ma'am," he said. He thought of Rosella waiting for him in the barn. He ran down the street to find her. He was a man, after all. He proved it again and again.

There were three other bastard children like himself. Amos Filigree. Porky Arbuster. Fat Jane Stokes from Atlanta. They were all there for the same reason. Their mothers were doing it for money. But some day, in the not too distant future, they'd run away and live on a little ranch. Just the three of them. They'd raise chickens and milk cows. They'd have a vegetable garden. Jane Stokes sucked on her hard tack and thought about it. She could almost see the place. She'd make gingham curtains for all the windows.

Lorenzo Soledad wasn't going to stay around. Let them have their pigs and cows. He was meant for a good, high purpose. Henrietta said his father was dead. She didn't say his name. She only said, "My father was angry because I didn't have a husband. So he threw me out, just like some common parlor maid. He gave me enough money to get this far. When I got off the stage, with you in my arms, here was Morning Glory's, the nicest house in town. I knocked on the door. Muy Contenta answered. She was from a good Baltimore family, but she'd gotten herself in some kind of trouble. So here I am, Lorenzo. It's not so bad."

"It *is* bad, Mama," he'd said. By the time he was ten, he knew what went on there. He'd push his eyeball to the keyhole and watch the girls, their legs in the air, letting some fat old man lie on top of them. Downstairs, champagne flowed. A canary sang. Someone played the piano. It didn't make any difference. "Your Mama is a hoor-lady," a classmate said. Soledad gave him a bloody nose.

Lorenzo Soledo grew up in a high-class bordello, way down in southwest Texas, where white people were streaming in by the thousands. The Texas Rangers had pretty much wiped out the Comanche by the time the boy was old enough to realize what was happening. He saw Indians shot in the bushes where they had taken refuge. He saw them wandering along the roads, begging for food. He took a small boy in his arms and gave him a strip of dried meat. A Ranger shot the boy. "You bastard," he heard himself saying. The Ranger raised his pistol in his direction. Soledad backed away. He hated the Texas Rangers from that day on.

It was around this time that his sympathies began to drift toward the plight of the Indians, though it would be many years later before he was able to confirm his feelings in a real way. He looked for signs that the dirty, ragged Comanche were less than himself with their red skin and filthy clothes. He looked at them. They looked at him. There was nothing he could do. Indian corpses lay all along the road. They were covered with flies. He threw up.

HENRIETTA WAS SITTING at her dressing table, brushing her long chestnut hair. He sat on the edge of the bed, watching. She had fine lines around her eyes. Brown spots on her hands. She was thirty-four now, he figured. He handed her the two ivory combs she used to hold her hair in place. "The Comanche are dead," he said, holding back his tears. She smeared lipstick across her mouth. A clock ticked on the wall. A breeze blew in the open window. In the street below, wagons clattered by.

"They're not like us, Lorenzo."

"Why not like us, Mama?"

She smelled of rose cologne. He laced up the strings of her corset, listening to her breathe in and out, a quiet, reassuring sound. She had fine skin with small pores, thick hair, strong arms.

"God created some people better than others. The darkies, for instance. The Civil War didn't change anything. My father freed the two hundred darkies he owned, but they're still slaves. Understand?"

"No," he said. The town of Batwing had about eight hundred people. It was thriving with speculators, railroad men, real estate hawkers, and people building cabins where recently the Comanche had been. Indians were whipped in the town square. A Comanche family hid in a cave along the river. He took them food at night. When he went back the last time, there were only the cold ashes of a fire to indicate where they had camped. He found their bodies by the creek. "I will make it right," he said to himself. "I swear I will."

He had one last encounter with Rosella before her family went back to Cincinnati. They lay together in the barn on top of fresh hay. Animals made soft bleating noises. He felt her small breasts. "I'll never forget you, Rosella," he breathed.

"I'll never forget you, either, Lorenzo. Write to me."

"Oh, I will." The spasm that shook his body was heaven itself. "Marry me, Rosella." Boys his age got married. He'd go to work for the dairy. Maybe the livery. He'd escape Morning Glory's and never come back. His future lay to the north.

"I wish I could. Mama would kill me. I ain't even fourteen, Lorenzo."

"I love you," he said. He liked the sound of the words. "I love you," he said again.

He ran to the graveyard and lay in the rich section, where doctors and lawyers and engineers were buried. "You better amount to something, boy," they said. He thumped on the graves. "Tell me what to do!" he cried. But the dead had nothing to tell him.

HE LIVED IN a whorehouse, and his mother was a whore. Like it or not, that's the way it was. A two-story frame house on Main Street with a porch across the front was where Carmina and Babette, Francine and Henrietta rocked on muggy summer nights, waiting for Johns to stroll by. They looked enticing in their tight bodices and full skirts and ivory fans. They were immune to the law because Judge MacIntosh came there almost every night. He was a fat man with a toupee and a silver cane. When he passed Soledad, he called him "boy" and threw him a nickel. "You can sweep my office," he said. "Another nickel." He had a tinny laugh.

There were others, too. Big Jack Cochran owned fifty thousand acres west of town. He ran Texas Longhorns where only a few years before the Comanche had run buffalo. Lincoln Farwell's company was putting in the railroad from Kansas City. It had almost reached Batwing. Up and down the stairs they went, these animals of fear and degradation.

Soledad stayed in his room and read, but one night he heard a commotion, and he got up from his bed and went up the flight of stairs to the third floor. There was Henrietta, her chestnut hair loose, cowering in the bed. And there was Jack Cochran, smashing his big fist into her face. "You are my exclusive property," he said. "Say it."

"I'm not anyone's exclusive property," she said. He hit her again. She screamed.

The rancher's .45 was on the table in its holster. Soledad reached for it, pulled the safety off, and fired. All the rest of his life he would tell himself he had aimed for the rancher's broad back no more than five feet away. But when the smoke cleared, Jack Cochran was still standing. Henrietta was lying in a pool of blood on the bed, her eyes wide open. Soledad dropped the gun and ran down the stairs, the rancher after him.

"You done killed your ma," he said. "You are in one heap of trouble, boy."

It was an accident, Soledad tried to tell himself. He thought of Henrietta's fine hands that played Chopin and Beethoven, her long, chestnut brown hair that she brushed with an ivory-handled brush. And the dresses with their bodices cut away.

Judge MacIntosh heard the case. Only two nights ago he had been at Morning Glory's, having a time with Dorina. Now the judge stared straight ahead. He asked Soledad to step forward.

"Matricide," he said. "Did you do it on purpose?" Soledad shook his head.

"It's up to me," the judge said. "I can send you up to prison for the rest of your life, or I can send you to a place where you will learn repentance."

"Where is that, sir?"

"A Franciscan seminary not far from here. You will give your life to God, Lorenzo, or you will give it to the State of Texas. What is your choice?" He tapped his fingers on the bench. "Well, boy. I'm waiting."

Soledad was not a Catholic. He wasn't anything. He lacked faith, and he knew himself to be an undependable boy, easily distracted by matters of the flesh. A priest or a convict? He had a choice, but it wasn't much. He swallowed.

"A priest, sir." The judge banged his gavel. He wore a ring with a large, red stone.

"If you try and run away, the Rangers will hunt you down. Do I make myself clear?"

"Yes, sir." It did not occur to him to wonder what right a judge had to sentence him to a religious life.

Soledad packed his valise and took a wagon to the next town where the seminary was. He noticed a flock of crows flying overhead. He saw a Comanche family shuffling along. They looked emaciated. He dug in the pocket of his cotton trousers. He found a handful of coins. He threw them out on the ground. But the Comanche did not stop to pick up the money. They kept on walking. What use did they have for money?

The driver went up a long, curved driveway. The high, iron gate swung shut behind them. Bells chimed. Young novitiates in white robes walked across the grass, chanting in Latin. There were a number of brick buildings with tile roofs. Chickens scratched in the dirt. Goats chewed on the sparse grass. A rooster crowed. A half-naked Mexican lad ran out to greet him.

His life had truly ended. He got out of the wagon and looked up.

"God is a blackbird," Soledad said.

FOUR

FOR THE NEXT six years, at a seminary with high brick walls and strutting pigeons and an air of cloying religiosity, Lorenzo Soledad tried to submerge his guilt, the doubts behind his vocation. He tried to reconcile the opposing sides of his nature, applying himself with exemplary diligence to the study of Greek and Latin, theology, the complex laws of the Church, and the memorization of the Latin Mass. His nagging doubts he likened to the transgressions of Saint Augustine, a wayward man like himself, beset by temptation much of his earthly life. Saint Augustine had found what Soledad had yet to find—unity with the grace of God, a deep and lasting faith in Holy Mother Church. He was exhorted by the teaching friars to trust, the way his twenty-seven seminary brothers did, and to hope he might acquire—after only a year or two of prayer and contemplation, receiving Communion, and turning himself over to the Lord—a profound faith. But his sins had not yet been washed away by the Lamb of God. He heard the friars reproaching him each time he knelt for matins or vespers on the hard tile floor of the chapel. A voice would say, "You are a fraud, Lorenzo Soledad. You are hiding behind the sanctity of the Church." So Soledad would pray harder and wonder what he had to do in order to achieve peace within himself. *Thou shalt not kill*, he thought. But he had killed the woman who gave him life. There was no forgiveness.

At one point, he fasted for forty days, like Christ in the desert, but at the end of that time, he felt no closer to God, only a terrible weakness and thirst. Whither do we go? To the Truth. By what path do we go? By Faith. Whither do we go? To Christ. By what path do we go? By Christ. For He Himself hath said, "I am the Way, and the Truth, and the Life." Soledad prayed with all his heart to understand these axioms and, failing that, to achieve acceptance of his guilt.

One fine summer day, a robust young girl scrubbing the floor of the seminary kitchen caught his eye as he shuffled past, reading his breviary. He had been there five years. During all that time, he had not looked at a woman. But there she was, a girl with the radiant beauty of the Madonna. The same dark and shining eyes, the same inquisitive expression and raw sensuality that kindled a small flame in his heart. "Pax vobiscum," he said, without looking up. He walked slowly, the soles of his sandals sticking to the wet floor. He dared not turn around.

Maria Isabel pretended not to notice him, as he pretended not to notice her, crouched on her hands and knees, the soapy water spread out in a puddle on the tile floor. He inhaled a scent that had nothing to do with strong lye soap, honest sweat, or the wet clay odor of the tiles. This was something else, and he tried not to think about it as he went about his duties, a long-dormant desire rising in his loins. He saw her next in the orchard, picking apples. Her long skirts clung to her legs and thighs. He saw she had nothing on underneath. Obligingly, he held the ladder so she would not fall. He followed her to the chicken coop and helped her gather eggs in a basket. Her blouse was undone at the top. Her breasts were large and brown; her nipples looked hard and pointy. Soledad thought he would faint; flustered, he dropped two eggs and stepped on them.

Maria Isabel was very young, no more than fifteen, with tiny feet and hands and a shy, inviting smile. Though he wished to do more, he merely kissed her in the chicken coop, feeling an indescribable joy at the touch of her soft, full lips. He resisted the impulse to pull her down on the straw, there to ruin his life, and hers as well. "I am almost a priest, Maria Isabel." He wrapped his arms around her. "Soon I shall belong entirely to God." Solemnly, she nodded and pulled away.

"Why you no marry me?" she asked.

"Because I am married to God," he said. "Do you understand?" She stared at him. "God a man. You a man. Man no marry man." He laughed uproariously. Surely, something this innocent could not be wrong. So he kissed her again, harder this time. Soledad's happiness lasted about an hour. Then the pendulum swung back and crushed him.

Prior Sena, his confessor, was not surprised at Soledad's confession. Temptation was common among novitiates, especially in the last years. Sometimes, if their hearts were not right with God, men left the order days before their final vows. The prior granted absolution and imposed a harsh penance after Soledad told him about Maria Isabel. The elderly friar had been concerned about the young man ever since, shortly after his arrival, he had confessed to killing his mother. "I was raised in a brothel," he said. "I'd watch her go upstairs. She was beautiful. One day, I had enough. There was this gun on the table. I aimed it at him, but Mama fell dead." He wept but the prior was not moved.

"It's still a mortal sin," the friar had said, amazed to find a murderer in his midst. "Why are you not in prison?"

"Because no one would believe me," Soledad had replied. The novitiate revealed a deep torment that the older man hoped prayer and fasting would finally assuage. "Trust in God," the prior kept saying. "The love of God calms the most wretched of sinners." But he wondered if anything could calm Soledad. He had heard of his scandalous behavior, lying with whores and, face down, listening to the dead in graveyards. The police in Batwing, Texas, had a report of such things. "The upstart boy bears watching," a policeman had said. "He thinks he hears dead people talking to him. Belongs in an asylum, if you ask me."

Soledad had yet to repent of these sins, defying logic, canon law, and Holy Writ.

"Sometimes I think I am not fit for the priesthood, Prior Sena," Soledad lamented one day as he and the administrator walked around the grounds of the seminary. He turned his face to the bright sunlight. He listened to the birds, chirping a happy song. He inhaled the scent of apple blossoms. He looked at the sky, remembering the brilliant sunsets of his youth.

"My heart is elsewhere," Soledad said. "I wonder about things. I have disturbing doubts." His eyes traveled to a child begging outside the gate. "Why do we not bring the child in and feed him?" he asked. "There is plenty of food." The prior pressed his hands together. "We do not feed him because it is the will of God that this child go hungry."

Soledad stopped in his tracks. "But Jesus said, 'Suffer the little children to come unto me.'" The novitiate shook his head in amazement. "Surely you believe in the Gospel, Prior?"

The old prior sighed. "Saint Augustine said, 'For what is believing, but consenting to the truth of what is said?' So my prayers are with you, Brother Soledad, that you may enter into the body of Christ and thus embrace the love of our Lord Jesus Christ." Prior Sena was a chubby, short, suspicious Andalusian. He hated the crude roughness of Mexico, the indolence, the grinding poverty, the petty crime, and the corruption of those in office. He had taught hundreds of novitiates the fine points of theology during his long tenure at the seminary. But none had struck him as less inclined to Holy Orders than Brother Soledad. Then, too, Soledad's comet birthmark blazing on his cheek made him uneasy, quivering the way it did during lectures and at matins and vespers. Yet the prior had a duty to send new priests into the world, even ones as troubled as Brother Soledad. God knows the Church was terribly short-handed all over the hemisphere. Had not the Holy Father himself issued a plea for more novitiates in his latest encyclical? So Prior Sena had kept Soledad in seminary, despite his doubts. "May God bless you and let you die soon," the prior would whisper each time he blessed Soledad after confession. He wished him swift entry into heaven, that he might be spared further temptation in his mortal life. And that the prior himself not be disgraced by Soledad's further misadventures.

Soledad paused at the wrought iron gate, fished a centavo out of his pocket, and gave it through the bars to the beggar. "God bless you," he said as the child scampered off. The prior frowned, visibly agitated. "You must learn obedience, Brother Soledad, as part of your final vows. Do not give money to the peasants. Holy Mother Church will take care of them."

Soledad bowed his head. Something lay heavily on his mind. "I have been reading in the library an account by Father Bartolomé de las Casas, who came to Mexico during the Inquisition. He speaks of great cruelty to the Indians because of their refusal to become Catholics. So the Europeans strangled and then burned them. They took everything in the whole country. And in South America as well. In other books, I have read how thousands of Indians were killed because they refused to build churches, plant crops, or cut timber for the padres. The women were raped by the soldiers. Is this true?"

The prior had read these books himself, as part of his education; he, too, had had compassion for these unwashed souls until he realized the impediment to Holy Mother Church they represented. "Oh ye of little faith, Brother Soledad," he chided, smiling his yellow-toothed smile. "We must learn not to judge others, lest we ourselves be judged. Look around you. This once savage country is now a peaceful land, filled with those of the one true, holy, and apostolic faith. The end often justifies the means, Brother. You must remember that."

Soledad, nearly speechless, stopped and looked at him. "Nothing can justify the murder of thousands, millions of innocent souls, Prior Sena. Why doesn't the Church make reparation for its sins?"

Prior Sena's face turned red. "How dare you question Holy Mother Church, Brother Soledad?" he demanded. "How dare you interpret Church history by yourself! One more episode, and I will dismiss you from seminary for gross insubordination! Now leave me in peace!" He hurried down the path toward the chapel, greatly agitated. Certain chapters in Church history had to remain closed, for the good of all concerned.

But Soledad remained unconvinced. He prayed for under-standing of the prior's logic. He prayed to believe what he had been taught in this cloistered seminary, with beggars at the gate and beautiful girls with sensuous lips trying to tempt him. His chronic weakness perched on his shoulder like a greedy vulture ready to devour his soul. He prayed for the unwashed souls of the heathen Indians who had been murdered in the name of Christ all across this poor country in which he found himself. At last he began to understand what the price of Christianity was all about in the New World. *I will never be able to accept such a price*, he said to himself. Yet what could he do to change centuries of religious belief?

Then, as if through divine intervention, everything changed. For a time, Soledad felt happily connected to the sacred mystery of the Blessed Trinity. He was aware of the divine grace of Christ. He slept but a few hours a night, staying awake to study Holy Writ in his airless little monk's cell near the stables—the works of Saint Augustine, Saint John Chrysostom, Pope Pius IX, Saint Cyprian, Saint Thomas Aquinas, and Cardinal Newman. He drank strong black tea in order to stay awake until dawn, when the brilliant tropical sunrise frequently caused him to fall to his knees in a sort of drugged ecstasy.

Perhaps to deny the doubts raging within himself, Soledad came to love the magic of Church pageantry and ritual, the incense and flickering candles! He loved the holy silence of the chapel, the way the place reeked with ancient authority. The transubstantia-tion of Christ at Mass awakened in him a positive, humbling faith. Nothing else mattered: not his silly attraction to women, not the altar wine he felt compelled to drink whenever God deserted him, not the heavy burden from a past that bound him to his guilt.

Not even the sight of the nubile Maria Isabel scrubbing the kitchen floor aroused him anymore. He would barely acknowl-edge her as he went by, secure in his faith; he was winning the war with the Devil at long last! He did not notice how the girl rubbed her breasts where he had touched them and ran her tongue around her delicate, pink mouth, nor the way her dark eyes followed him whenever she encountered him tending to his clerical duties inside the cloistered walls. Safe in his newfound piety, Soledad was blissfully unaware of Maria Isabel's innocent plans for his future.

But he could never quite put the massacred Indians out of his mind. Again and again, he returned to the library and pored over the old volumes, making notes on his discoveries. He spent his annual leave in the Biblioteca Nacional de México in Mexico City, where he learned even more. There, in that vast repository of knowledge, Soledad sat at a table and wept. Deep inside, a tiny spark took hold. Aztecs, Olmecs, Toltecs, and Mayas slaughtered by the tens of thousands—a sea of blood flowed across Mexico. *I will spend my life in reparation*, he thought. *Where do I begin? What shall I say to them?* He heard their cries coming out of the earth. Saw their spirits drifting among the trees. He saw their accusatory eyes in the middle of flowers.

With a contrite heart, Soledad went forth into the hilly countryside around the seminary whenever he could, to visit the sick and dying. It was scrubby land, hilly and dry, washed with a rich gold-green light that softened the harshness. There had been scant rain for several years, and the animals and the crops were failing. In one poor village, he found a thin, terrified woman hiding in the ruins of an old mission church, nursing a sick baby. The roof was gone and the sun poured through. Gaunt cattle wandered in and out, making thirsty, hollow noises; pigeons cooed fitfully among the broken beams.

The *federales* had shot her husband, the woman said, because they thought he was a notorious rebel. She had no food, no money. From the sound of her cough, he knew she had consumption. "What am I to do?" she asked pitifully. "Can you help me? I am hungry, Padre. My baby is dying." The sight of this woman aroused Soledad's compassion. Nothing could be done, and he knew it, yet at this moment, he decided to speak from his heart. "Come," he said, and took her hand.

The altar had been mostly destroyed, but gently he drew her to it and bade her kneel in the dirt. The church was still sanctified, after all, and served the purpose, no matter what condition it was in. "Trust in God," he said, and he touched her hair. Though technically not yet a consecrated priest, he blessed her and offered words of encouragement. He baptized the fitfully crying baby with dirty water drawn in a bucket from an old cistern. Sunlight cascaded through the broken window, creating a dusty halo. "God loves you," he said with a self-righteous air. "The Church is your everlasting mother."

"The Church is nothing," she said bitterly, looking around at the ruins. "Three years ago, my husband and I were married in this church. The priest said the same things you did. Trust in God. Well, Padre, I trusted in God and look where it has brought me. I no longer believe in God, only the peace of death."

Soledad bent closer to her and whispered, "Good woman, do not despair. God lives in that pigeon overhead. He is in that apple tree blooming outside the window. God is in every living thing. And I say to you, there is no heaven, no hell, only this short time upon the earth. Make the most of what has been given you." He actually believed those words.

Soledad hurried out of the ruined church with a sense of unease. *I am two different men*, he thought wildly. *One a priest, the other an agnostic.* He knew he was obligated to confess his apostasy to the prior, to pack up his things and leave the order for a life without reward or promise. But he did not. What he had said to the tubercular woman he would say many times again, and each time he would lose a little of his foothold in a conventional religious life.

As Soledad trudged along the road in the heat, old people scowled at him from their dirt yards. Grimy children with a look of hunger in their eyes stood in his path until he fished a centavo from the depths of his pocket. He inhaled the putrid odor of human excrement and rancid oil and food gone bad in the hot, tropical sun. Great swarms of flies buzzed in the streets. A mangy dog hobbled across the street and tried to lift its leg on the hem of his seminarian's trousers. An old woman looked at him listlessly from her window and crossed herself as he passed by.

Ah, how can I change any of this?, he wondered. *The world is filled with suffering. In a hundred years, it will be the same as it is now. How can God permit such misery?* At the seminary, he flung his body down in front of the altar and prayed with his whole mind and heart and soul to ease the suffering in the world. But he knew that his prayer had not made a dent in the world's misery.

Struggling between his natural sympathies and his intellectual certainties, Soledad again buried himself in the seminary's sacred volumes, written in Latin and Greek, to try to forget the sorry tragedies unfolding beyond its walls and to banish the constant spectre of his own squalid sins. In the book of Job, he found a measure of consolation: "Even so are the ways of all that forget God: and the hope of the hypocrite shall perish." Soledad realized that after his disaster, Job begat a new family, re-created his flocks and herds, and lived on. *So shall I live on*, he vowed with an imperious air. *I will sow the seeds of love. I will bring to those without hope the gift of faith*. His commitment was never stronger, more idealistic, or more impossible. And he still could not get the massacred Indians out of his mind. *Cortés was evil*, he thought. *Murdering. Plundering. All in the name of the Church. How, then, can God be love?*

One day, while reading the Gospel according to John under a eucalyptus tree, he looked up. An old, wrinkled face peered down at him from among the shiny foliage. "Where were you when I created the world?" it asked. The face was benign, and despite its age, an aura of newness emanated from it. Soledad sank to his knees and crossed himself. These were the words of God to Job, and they tore at the very fiber of his being.

"You are God," he whispered, with a deep bow of his head. "And I am not worthy." The face began to weep. "You are the worthiest among them," it said. "Believe what you truly are, as this tree believes it is not a stone instead." Then the face disappeared.

Soledad rubbed his eyes. Maria Isabel stood next to him and touched his shoulder as if he were a holy icon.

"I also saw the vision, Padre," she said in an awestruck voice. "You are a very great man already, no?"

Shaken to his core, Soledad hurried to the chapel and prayed through the night, yet nothing would ease the premonition that hung over him. He told no one of his extraordinary experience, except the prior, who declared him mad. But each time he saw Maria Isabel, she nodded in silent conspiracy. "I have seen God," Soledad said to himself, in a state of wonder and excitement that left him sleepless for many nights. He would wait all the rest of his days for God to appear to him again. Surely the vision eradicated the terrible sin that remained with him always. His soul felt clean.

When the day of his ordination arrived, Soledad, dressed in pure white, prostrated himself before the archbishop of Durango and repeated his holy vows. He thought himself at peace; his mother Henrietta's accusing face no longer haunted him. Women were in the back of his mind as a vague and flickering distraction. He wished only to serve God with all his heart. "Of Him are all things," Soledad whispered in his spartan monk's cell as he packed his few belongings for the journey northward. "By Him are all things. In Him are all things." He crossed himself beneath the crucifix that hung above his pallet. "God so loved the world as to give His only begotten Son." The ecclesiastical words rolled comfortably off his tongue. "God, my God, I am not worthy to come under Thy roof. Say the word and my soul shall be healed." From then on, whenever he prayed, the dear and comforting face of God would rise in his memory, as it had in the eucalyptus tree. He sighed. Before him lay a lifetime of mystery and miracles and obedience. He approached it joyfully. For a very short time, women were at the back of his thoughts.

The newly ordained priest felt a presence in his cell before he saw the man standing behind him. He was a barefoot paisano, stoop-shouldered and stocky, but he was dressed in a beautiful embroidered wedding shirt. "May I help you, good man?" Soledad said. The man's face cracked in a smile. His name was Carlos Diaz, he said, the father of Maria Isabel and ten other orphans left to themselves when their dear mother died in childbirth. Carlos Diaz removed his hat and held it in his hands, trembling. He had never spoken directly to a priest before, except in the confessional, during instruction for marriage, and during the baptism for each of his children.

"My daughter tells me you love her," he blurted. "She tells me she loves you. She says you have seen God in a tree. This makes you a very great man. As soon as the banns are read, there will be a wedding in the church, yes?"

"No, no, Señor Diaz, you have it all wrong," protested Soledad. "I am a priest." He sat down on his narrow, uncomfortable cot, somewhat dazed. "Priests cannot marry. It is against Church law."

In Carlos Diaz's native village across the mountains, priests had married girls who loved them. They had children. Some continued to celebrate Mass. The paisano had seen with his own eyes how happy these priests were. He was anxious for Maria Isabel to enter a life better than the one that had killed his beloved wife. Life with a priest was better than life with a paisano. That much he knew.

"You have made it possible for my daughter to go on living, Padre," he said, his mouth set in a good-natured smile. "You will come to our little farm and live there, once you are married to Maria Isabel." Carlos Diaz was thankful for his anticipated good fortune. A prosperous son-in-law was as good as money. He said a prayer to the crucifix on the wall, hoping to make a good impression. "Even now, Maria Isabel and her aunts are making her wedding dress."

It took some time, but Soledad finally made himself clear: He could marry no one. He was married to God. He thanked Señor Diaz and said he would offer a Mass for him and his children. Then he took up his satchel and hurried toward the seminary gate, his friar's sandals stirring up the dust in the courtyard. He gazed at the cross on top of the archway and crossed himself. *As God is my judge, I renounce temptation in the form of female flesh. I humbly swear allegiance to Jesus Christ and to His Holy Mother Church, to the Communion of Saints, and to life everlasting. Amen.* He crossed himself again and walked toward the train station, an imperfect man, an uncertain priest, but one determined to make the most of his life, nonetheless.

FIVE

*T*HE INVESTIGATION HAD *hardly begun, yet Father Antonio knew it was time to leave Batwing. He was growing entirely too fond of Muy Contenta. He had allowed her to kiss him on the cheek. Father Bartholomew, ever watchful, gave him a surly look. The two Vatican priests were staying in a rooming house filled with cowboys and drovers and gamblers. Every day Father Antonio found an excuse to for them to go to Morning Glory's. It had a crystal chandelier. Tiffany lamps. Velvet covered settees. He was treated to vintage wine and French cuisine. He toasted her. "Ah, Muy Contenta, you are a fine woman."*

Father Bartholomew looked up. "Hold your tongue, old man," he whispered. He had had enough of the barbarians. He'd witnessed two shootings and hurried by the bodies lying in a pool of blood on the street. He'd made the sign of the cross over them and did not look back. Batwing was penance for his sins.

The two Vatican priests were finished with their research. Their bags were packed, and they were ready to go. They stopped by Morning Glory's for a last farewell.

"Were you really baptized with the name Muy Contenta?" Father Antonio asked as he sat in the parlor, sipping his tea.

"Claudia Hortense," she replied. Father Antonio stirred. He was eighty-one years old. He had only had a woman once in his life, when he was sixteen. A whore in Amalfi, which didn't count. Sometimes the gap in a man's years was nothing at all. Sometimes

he felt reborn, even when he was old. He smiled at her. Father Bar-
tholomew leaned forward.

"Do you think Soledad deserves to be a saint after his upbring-
ing here?" Antonio asked. *She offered him a plate of sweets. She told*
Dorina to stop listening at the door.

"Everyone deserves to be a saint, Padre. Evil makes us good. Good
makes us evil." *He moistened the tip of his pencil and wrote down*
what she said.

"Did he mean to shoot Henrietta?" *the old priest asked. She shook*
her head. "It was that bastard Cochran he was after. I ran him out
of my club a couple of times. A troublemaker. He always came back."
She looked at the priest in his brown cassock. He was very clean and
tidy. He spoke with a thrilling Italian accent. He was educated and
debonair. "Would you like one of our girls, Padre? One just arrived
from Memphis. Peony Flowers. A blonde."

Embarrassed, the priest got up. He glanced out the window.
Father Bartholomew had gone out and was now standing close to the
gardener, punching his bare arm. "I am an ordained priest, madam,"
Antonio said. *This was his first stop in his investigation of Soledad's*
worthiness for canonization. He had many other places to go. He
kissed the hand she extended. She wore many rings. She smelled like
fine soap. "Thank you for your time," *he said breathlessly. In a way, he*
was sorry to leave her. He was certain he would never see her again.

"Not at all," *she said. He had a lot of white hair. If she didn't know*
he was a priest, she would have invited him to stay a while. She pulled
the drapes aside to see which way his carriage took him. She glanced
at the piece of paper he'd given her. So that is where he is going next,
she thought.

FATHER ANTONIO TOOK *the rattling stagecoach from Batwing,*
thinking of Muy Contenta the whole way. An interesting woman who
aroused his curiosity. And something else. But now he was to interview
the aged prior about Soledad's character during his seminary days.

"Did you see signs of Father Soledad's propensity for sin, Prior
Sena?" *Father Antonio shouted in the prior's ear.*

The aged cleric rested standing up, like a bird, except he used two legs. His head dropped to his chest, loud snores emanated from his mouth, and he appeared lost in slumber. Father Antonio shouted the question again, waited, and then turned to leave, when Prior Sena roused from unconsciousness. He turned his milky white eyes heavenward; he drooled onto the cassock that Maria Isabel changed for him every morning. "Nothing but sin!" Prior Sena shouted back. He collapsed into a chair.

More sleeping, more snoring. A deep, rumbling belch. Then suddenly Prior Sena reached out and grabbed Father Antonio's wrist with his claw-like fingers. "Holy Mother Church has lasted two thousand years. Why? Nothing can ever change. Do you understand?"

"I see," Father Antonio said, slowly. "Change is dangerous, eh?"

The prior nodded. "All must stay the same," he murmured. "Holy Mother Church was founded by Christ. To insult the Church is to insult Christ, you see?" He had a lengthy coughing fit and then resumed. "Soledad made his own laws. I never believed he saw God in a eucalyptus tree. He saw the Devil and that's what possessed him!" He collapsed onto his hard, narrow bed and appeared to die. Just to be certain of his fate, Father Antonio administered last rites, though the ancient cleric was to last for many more years.

"He is not right in the head," Father Antonio said. Next, Father Antonio interviewed Maria Isabel Diaz, now head housekeeper at the seminary and guardian of the sacred eucalyptus tree. She was a plump, weary, middle-aged woman, a spinster who had devoted her life to God and to the rearing of her ten orphaned brothers and sisters, and their numerous children and grandchildren. Though technically not a virgin, thanks to a traveling beeswax salesman, Maria Isabel was pure in heart; every day she dusted the statues of the Blessed Virgin and tended to the shrine out under the eucalyptus tree. As she uttered the beatitudes on her knees in the chapel, she felt the state of her sanctifying grace expanded until now she thought of nothing except her upcoming trip to heaven, where she believed she would be reunited with Lorenzo Soledad at long last.

She had heard he'd been crucified in Nuevo México by some

Indian savages and was soon to become a saint. Every night, she prayed to him for the strength and guidance she would need to let go of this world and move into the next. Her faith in this holy man was indestructible. It was she who had been the only witness to Soledad's visitation from God, she who the Mexican hierarchy had interrogated for days on end about what had happened, she who was responsible for the unusual shrine under the miraculous eucalyptus tree.

Now Maria Isabel Diaz, with a certain air of importance, waited in the kitchen for the two Vatican priests. She had received a letter about their arrival. She was too nervous to do anything except pace up and down and say her prayers to the Virgin of Guadalupe. She wore her Sunday dress, clutched six new rosaries to be blessed, and fussed with a silver comb in her hair. Her knees shook so hard she had to sit down and could not get up when Father Antonio and Father Bartholomew arrived. The older priest gave her a miraculous medal blessed by the Holy Father, took her hand, and offered a blessing to her goodness. He noticed all the children. He closed his eyes. That was the goal of the Church, was it not? A bounty of children. God would provide.

"Father Soledad was a saint in the making," she said, breathlessly. "I was there the day he saw God in the eucalyptus tree. I saw Him, too, then never again. Come, I will show you."

Father Antonio would never forget what he saw in the garden. Not even in Italy, where bizarre religious manifestations often took place, had he seen anything quite like the scene before him. All manners of religious objects of glass, ceramic, metal, or painted wood were fastened among the shiny green leaves like Christmas ornaments. Votive candles flickered from banks of candelabras on the tables. Dozens of crutches, wheelchairs, splints, bandages, and medicine bottles littered the ground.

Pilgrims from all over Mexico, young and old, healthy and infirm, stood in line, saying their rosaries as they waited their turn. Two strong seminarians kept order among the worshippers. The priest was moved beyond words. There was Soledad's glamorized portrait, done in flagrant oil, propped up on a table next to one of a wise and ancient man who looked like Abraham.

"Well," whispered Father Antonio, crossing himself. "This is truly something."

"It means they have great faith, Antonio," Father Bartholomew said. He moved closer to a young man leading a burro. He touched his bare arm.

Arizona Territory,
1885–1896

SIX

THE PARISHES THAT Soledad served after his ordination melted one into another, with little to distinguish them except their individual poverty. Ortiz, Los Gatos, Ramos Canyon, Valentino. For eleven years, he moved from one end of the Southwest to the other, confronted by a blur of faces, stoical or sad, devout or devious. Each asking for what he could not give: understanding of why God had conferred such burdens.

"Please, Padre, tell us what to do. My wife is sick. There is nothing left to eat. I cannot pay the rent. Only yesterday the milk cow died. I have ten mouths to feed." What could he say? His innocuous sermons were about obedience and grace, acceptance of their fate, and how heavenly reward could not be attained without suffering. He dared not speak the truth. The only thing that comforted him was the violin he'd learned to play when he was twelve. Occasionally, he played a few bars of a Beethoven minuet, then threw himself wholeheartedly into his work, administering the sacraments, celebrating Mass, tending to the sick and dying, performing marriages that he saw as the gateway to more misery, and on and on, until the end of life.

Will faith truly save them?, he'd asked himself at Los Gatos. *Does free will exist here among people too poor to get out of bed in winter because they have no warm clothing to wear?* Two hungry children came begging at his door one evening when he was eating a supper of beans and tortillas. He'd shared what he had, but tomorrow the children would be hungry again.

He'd looked at young women, pregnant for the seventh or eighth time, who lived in one-room, dirt-floored shacks with their families, and he thought to himself, *No matter how deep their faith in God, they will always be poor and hungry. And there will be too many children.*

"What shall I do?" he'd written to Monsignor Canopus in Santa Fe, who wrote back, enclosing a letter from the Holy Father in Rome: "Overcome your difficulties through devotion to the Blessed Virgin. Love God with your whole mind, your whole heart, your whole soul. Pray to the Blessed Lord Jesus Christ that His flocks may increase tenfold." Soledad crumpled the letter and threw it away.

Deep in the desert at Ramos Canyon, which lay between the towering sandstone monoliths of the valley, Soledad blossomed. In this vast country, the Navajo tended flocks of sheep that grazed on almost nonexistent grass, they rode wagons for miles to draw water from the village well, they clung to traditions older than the Church herself. The Navajo had a way of looking at life that touched him deeply. From the very first day, he was happy among them, riding horseback from hogan to hogan to comfort the sick and dying. In the desert, he exchanged his bulky cassock for the shirt and trousers of a working priest, so he was not always recognized as a cleric at the far-flung trading posts. He bought a black felt hat with a wide brim and a pair of lace-up boots, and he rode out across the huge expanse of desert, feeling like an ordinary man for the first time in many years.

Now, when he dreamed, he seldom saw Henrietta's accusing face as she fell over on the bed, but instead a sea of blowing pink sand, drenched in sunlight, that lifted him in the air. He believed he had almost forgotten about women, too. Only once in a while did he think of the silky smoothness of a girl's thigh. He told himself he was free and that God had forgiven him at long last. When the Indians invited him to their dances, he went, moved by these heartfelt expressions of a simple, outlawed faith. He was supposed to report these pagan dances, with their animal skins, rattles, and primitive drums, to the monsignor. But he did not. Instead, he absorbed the wild, thumping music; he listened to stories about magical beasts who could cure sickness and relieve pain. He learned about the sacred Four Directions and the birds and animals and colors that went with each of them. He spent many pleasurable afternoons with old Ansawaka, the medicine man of the Parrot Clan, and from him he learned about a mystical village, far to the tropical south, where certain great men of wisdom were, like himself, blessed with a red comet birthmark on their cheeks. The old man looked deeply into Soledad's eyes as if he could read something behind them.

"Someday, my friend, you will make the tracks of the badger," he said. "That is what the people of that village became when they went north to escape the evil of the men from across the sea. They became badgers. Known for their cunning and ability to survive."

Soledad looked at the old man, seated cross-legged in his hogan. "I am a priest, Ansawaka. I have been sent here to preach the Gospel. Nothing more."

The old man nodded. "We hear your Gospel. We do not believe it. It makes the white man feel good to have answers. Who are we to tell him there are no answers, Badger Man?" He asked Soledad to sit beside him while he played his red willow flute and sang the "Song of Passage into Another World," for he was soon to die. The priest felt the tears running down his cheeks. So simple. So shorn of dogma or hyperbole. Just a natural profession of faith in something greater than Church dogma and authority. This was not the first time that Soledad had questioned the validity of his Church's teachings, but it was the first time he realized that all men are essentially the same, bound by the same set of natural laws and limitations. The music filtered into Soledad's heart and stayed there.

When Ansawaka died, the priest was holding his red, rough hand. The ointment of Extreme Unction lay upon the old man's forehead and the cornmeal and pollen of his old religion as well.

There you have it, Soledad thought, as he closed Ansawaka's eyes. *One way offers a faultless return to nature. The other, false hopes of everlasting life.* The old man's reward from God was not based on any last-minute conversion to the Catholic Church, but on his ties to a faith far beyond present human memory or experience.

Soledad thought about these things night after sleepless night. Could the Holy Church of Rome coexist with a religion that believed in the power of the natural world? For four hundred years, no unity had been possible. And that became his goal, one moonlit night, when he climbed to the top of a two-hundred-foot-high rock. He would do what no priest before him had done. What was forbidden for him to do. He would integrate these two faiths in a lasting, meaningful way. All that had happened before at the hands of the Holy Church of Rome would be forgiven and forgotten. It all seemed so simple at the time, and so foolish when he looked back on it in later years.

After that revelation, the strange young priest stopped trying to convert the Indians. He merely took care of what was already there. No mission church had been built to replace the one that had burned down years earlier, so he said Sunday Mass in one of the ramshackle government buildings, where a dozen Indians showed up to warm themselves by the stove. They watched the ceremony with curiosity, waiting to see blood magic come out of the chalice that the priest held aloft, intrigued by the round, white wafer he claimed was the mystical Body of Christ. Then, from beneath the folds of his chasuble, he took a stone fetish that Ansawaka had given him and laid it on the altar. He turned and raised his arms. "See," he said. "Your way and my way are one and the same."

For the remaining months of his tenure at Ramos Canyon, Father Soledad learned what he could. The Navajo waited for his comet birthmark to fly off, the way Ansawaka had said it would. Small children rubbed it, thinking it would disappear. The Navajo built him a new church and a school, but they refused to accept the religion he brought. "Bad medicine," they said. An old Indian woman had clutched not her rosary beads but a flower when he administered the last rites of Holy Mother Church. "Because we are all flowers," she had said as he drew up a colorless quilt around her dark, still face. She was conditioned not to dying but to an acceptance of life's simplicity. "I will take the memory of flowers with me," he said, turning away, embarrassed at his acceptance of her pagan piety, yet finding himself in secret agreement. A new vision of God—not the Holy Trinity, but a wilted rose that he'd tucked into the folds of her burial gown—was beginning to form in his troubled mind.

There was an old man, lying in the hushed stillness of his hogan, his three wives weeping at his bedside, who taught Soledad still another lesson. "Life is a song," the man said, his breath coming in spasms. Soledad brushed his hand across the old man's eyes and began to anoint him with the precious oils of final absolution. At this, the old man turned his vision in the direction of the sacred mountain, blue and indistinct in the distance, outside the hogan.

"Up there," the old man whispered to the priest, "the spirits are pulling the mist from the mountains to turn them into stories. These are the stories I leave behind, blowing across the sand, blowing there in the circle of the mountain." The old man closed his eyes and breathed his final song.

At the man's funeral, Soledad had listened to the chants of all his sons and grandsons and had witnessed the three wives pulling the spirits from the sacred mountain to turn them into stories that would bear his name. He'd known then that faith was a result of consciousness itself and that no amount of preaching, dispensing of sacraments, or authority and holy laws of the Church could possibly replace that which had always existed in the human heart.

Sometimes, in a burst of joy, the awakening priest would sing a passage from the Mass in his off-key tenor. The Indians would watch with amusement as he climbed a mesa and stood there, his arms outstretched to the searing blue sky, singing his newfound epiphany. And in spring, they watched him remove his clothing and his boots and, wearing nothing but his union suit, wade into the swiftly running creek for an impromptu baptism in his adopted faith. "Badger Man," they would say, laughing. This was the name the Navajo gave him, and it followed him to his crucifixion. Shyly, the Indians filed in for Mass in the new church and stood in the back, watching for signs of transformation in the priest. "The comet-faced religious make good medicine now," they said. And they turned themselves over to him to be blessed.

Finally, the day came when his tenure at Ramos Canyon was over. The monsignor had a new assignment for him: another desolate mission somewhere in the Southwest. Though he had begged to remain where he was, the Church's policy was to rotate priests every two or three years so they did not become too attached to their parishioners. On the day he left, the priest sat in the spare, cool interior of his little house. He felt not a little sad to be leaving. The half-breed servant girl, Maya Begay, brought him fruits and sandwiches on a tray as an all-encompassing weariness settled over him. He did not care whether he ate or not, nor if he ever left the narrow safety of the room with its whitewashed walls and its ceiling made of branches and its floor of tamped earth. He liked it here, with him living at one end of the house and the girl at the other. He liked her flowery fragrance, her luminous half-formed beauty, and the sound of her voice when she sang the old songs of her people as she scrubbed and cooked and cleaned. Yes, a woman in the house made him feel happy.

For three years, his own resolution and the saltpeter in his food had repressed his sexuality, creating a hollow place where passion might normally have been. But his experience in the desert moonlight had opened a new channel to his heart. He suddenly wanted to share with this girl nothing more than the joy that filled him at this moment.

"Maya," he said softly, "please put down the tray and talk to me." He wanted to tell her how the old woman with the flower had made him feel, how she herself had stirred something long forgotten the day she arrived in her father's wagon, a slender girl of eighteen with large and brooding eyes. "More than a year has passed," he wanted to say, "and still our thoughts have not connected, our hearts are as empty as ever." She trembled when he took her hands in his and pulled her into the chair beside him. He had not slept in several nights, and his eyes were red. "Tell me," he said, "what you most deeply believe." With the tips of his fingers, he touched her cheek. How he had missed the physical connection of himself to another breathing soul. She was dressed in a plain white hand-me-down blouse made of a thin material and a gathered skirt that hung to her ankles. Though he had tried to introduce her to shoes, she preferred her own handmade deerskin moccasins.

"I—I believe in my mother and my father because they gave me the breath of life," she said, her hands folded discreetly in her lap. Without a word, he picked up the tray and carried it into the kitchen. She followed him along, wondering what he wished of her. "I believe in my grandmother and grandfather because they are old and very wise," she said. She was not sure she knew the words he wanted her to speak; she had only been converted to the faith a few months before and had yet to be confirmed. She curled her hands into fists when he pulled her closer, pressing her head against the rough material of his cassock.

"It's quite all right to believe in one's family, Maya," he said, "for they are God's creations." She reached back and felt the cold hardness of the sink, piled high with the dishes she had yet to do for the day. She felt her face grow hot, but she did not try and draw away from him. "Oh, Maya." He ran his fingers through her hair and brushed his lips against its raven blackness.

"I believe in our land, Padre, for it is beautiful here." She turned her round, dark face upward, and he saw a peacefulness in her eyes that he coveted. "I believe in beauty," she said, "for it makes me feel good inside."

"What of God?" he wished to ask but could not, for he was overcome with an emotion that reached deep into his bones and cleansed him. "Come," he whispered, and from around his neck removed the golden cross he always wore and lay it on the table; by this small gesture, he believed he absolved himself of whatever he might do next. He led her gently from the kitchen, scarcely aware of what he was doing, only that it seemed natural. "Dear child," he said, "the glory of Almighty God exists in all that you speak of. It is here in my lonely heart as well." He squeezed her hand. "Yes, Maya, even priests get lonely. Do you believe that?"

In his room she stood, her face burning while he flung open the window to the wondrous beauty of the desert beyond. He saw the great shimmering land stretching all the way to where the rose-colored mesas arched toward a bright blue sky.

"I know that I do not believe in your God, Padre, not even after all you taught me," she said, looking over her shoulder as if she expected someone to come along and save her. Lorenzo closed the door and cradled her in his arms. Perhaps, he thought, he could express in words the raging desire within him that he had vainly struggled to suppress. But he feared that such honesty would only confuse her. A holy peace descended on him as Maya took off her clothes, her back to him, and lay down on his hard, narrow bed. She stared up at the ceiling, as he lay down beside her and covered them both with a sheet. Her smooth, taut body quivered at his touch. She squeezed shut her eyes; she seemed to be saying her prayers. Now he could not stop and threw himself upon her with a passion out of control. How blessed were her wide, full lips. How tender her shy embrace, how filled with a woman's sweet resistance she was. How precious that moment of deep and expanding light, when his whole body felt infused as if by the Holy Ghost. With the sun pouring through the window and the warm breeze lapping across his bare torso, he thought he had never known such happiness before. For one brief moment, it seemed he had died, so great was his sense of time having stopped.

"Surely you believe in Almighty God now," he whispered, holding her close, feeling the throbbing of her heart beneath his gentle fingers on her breast. "For He lives inside you, Maya, as proof of your own existence." *And mine*, he thought, for he knew now that God directed his actions, for good or for ill, for some reasons yet unknown.

"I have been in this house thirteen moons," she said, getting up on one elbow to look at him. "And not once did you notice me. Until now." She had only given herself to one man before, Hosa the sheepherder, but he had been killed in Gallup, and now she was alone. She looked into Soledad's dark eyes with sudden insight, remembering a similar look in Hosa's eyes the afternoon they climbed to the top of the mesa and made love in the sunlight, speaking of the children they would have and how he would soon own many sheep. She pulled away from Soledad with a sharp little cry, remembering the fragility of those dreams. "I have wished for this moment," she said, brushing the hair from her eyes. "But now I do not know what it means."

"It means," he said, stroking her cheek, "that you and I have shared in God's love." So young, so beautiful, reminding him of the old woman's flower; reminding him, too, of other women he had loved and left behind. As he lay enveloped in a deep and spreading joy, he knew, with a terrible, blasphemous certainty, that sexual love was a sacrament as pure as those he offered in the name of the Holy Trinity. *As I offered this one*, he thought, seeing the transitory shadows of himself and Maya cast on the wall, knowing that this blessed moment of peace and fulfillment would just as quickly go.

Hearing a wagon pull up outside, he reluctantly got out of bed and slowly dressed. As he waited for her to finish dressing, a stabbing pain shot through him. *What have I done?*, he wondered, seeing the stricken look on the face of the beautiful half-breed servant girl. "I am sorry," he said. "Someday you'll know what you meant to me." Picking up his cross and his lizard fetish, he kissed the cross before putting it around his neck. Then, without thinking, he pressed his lips to the fetish before he stuffed it in the pocket of his cassock. Maya Begay stared at him, intuitively aware of the significance of the gesture. He glanced out the window at the waiting wagon. He hoped to get to Chinle by nightfall, and the afternoon was almost gone. He touched Maya gently on the shoulder. "Do not hate me," he said. "I'm an imperfect man, trying to do God's work. Perhaps someday I'll be back." The room smelled of their lovemaking; the rumpled sheets were evidence of his unchecked passion.

Maya Begay pulled away. "If you come back, Padre, it will not be because you love me. It will be because you cannot live with people of your own kind." She brushed past him on her way to the kitchen. Her body throbbed. The smell of him wafted up from her crotch. She was different now. She would never be the same. Maya Begay felt touched by God in all His infinite glory. She drifted out the door and across the sand. She belonged to the priest in a lasting, holy way. *He has to marry me*, she thought. *I will have his child.*

The Stranger sat on top of the mesa, looking down. She did not notice him. But he took note of her and raised a ghostly arm. The priest was headed for trouble. That much he knew.

SEVEN

*T*HE PRECISE MOMENT *at which Soledad's loyalties began to shift away from Holy Mother Church to the pantheistic religion of the Indians was never discovered by the Vatican priests. Father Antonio, with his mania for detail, never learned when his nemesis priest began seriously to consider the Indian way as legitimate, shoving aside the faith of two thousand years of authority and reward. He suspected it was at the poor mission church at Ramos Canyon, where Soledad had been sent for a three-year tenure. He hadn't collected any money. He had only baptized two souls and these out on a rock mesa, nowhere near the church. A funeral was held with a Navajo medicine man. Chanting. Drumming. The body wrapped in a blanket and laid in a grave. The Vatican priests had to grudgingly admit that the land was magical, the people serene, if you overlooked their paganism. A man could see things that weren't there. He could lose perspective of all that he held dear. Certain influences could take hold. Devil influences, perhaps? Then a man would have to ask forgiveness. Did Soledad?*

Father Bartholomew listened to Maya Begay's confession in her bedroom with the door closed. He absolved her and told her to say ten Hail Marys. "You should not have been tempted by a priest, my daughter. His fall from grace began with you." He knew it wasn't true, but he persisted. "He had God's work to do, but there you were, interfering." Doubts were interfering with his own vocation, but he could not confess to Father Antonio. Not yet.

Maya looked at the dirt floor. It wasn't that way at all, *she wanted to say, but she could not argue with a great man from the Vatican.* "Coffee, sir?" *she said. He nodded. A girl of about thirteen came in with two cups. The priest looked at her. She was beautiful.*

"Who are you?" *he asked.* "Kneel down, and I will bless you." *The girl obeyed.*

"She is Elizabeth Mary," *Maya Begay said.* "Father Soledad's daughter."

The priest spilled his coffee down the front of his cassock. It burned clear through to his private parts. "Dear God, have mercy," *he said, hurrying through the door to the wagon where Father Antonio was waiting. As they moved across the desert, the older priest noticed a herd of antelope. Clouds in the shape of sheep drifted overhead. He rubbed his eyes. He longed to talk to Muy Contenta, but she was miles away. He could not get her out of his mind. In his pocket was a letter written in her elegant hand.*

"Do not forget me," *it said.*

EIGHT

FATHER SOLEDAD NEVER gave Maya Begay another thought. She was just a girl who had satisfied his desires. Now she was gone. He rode confidently on a swaybacked gelding toward his new parish of Valentino, a small farming village along a muddy river. Fruit trees were in bloom, the alfalfa grew tall. The air was sweet with the smell of wet earth. As he rode along, dragging a pack mule behind, he inhaled the sweet, fresh air. Acequias carried water to the fields from the deep vein of the mother ditch that ran from the meandering river to the east. A sandstone bluff rose from the desert to the sky. A sea of red cactus flowers burst across the sand. He turned his head to look at everything.

"See? There is a God, Torreon," he said to his horse, and pointed to the cactus flowers. Nowhere in seminary had he been taught that God was anywhere except in the mystery of the Blessed Trinity. But was God not also in this swaybacked chestnut gelding? Affectionately, he patted the horse's mane. He had bought him from the livery for a dollar.

"Because you are a horse," he said, "they can make you into coyote bait. While I, who am no more worthy, am promised immortality. Think of it, Torreon. My Church does not even acknowledge that you exist! They say you have no free will, but how does anyone know?" The priest turned things over in his mind.

The doubts that had always been there began to surface the

more he considered the predicament of the horse's brief moment upon the earth.

As he rode toward Valentino, the sun at his back, Soledad wondered if he was unworthy, as so many people in his past had said. He threw his head back to the wide, blue sky and dug his heels into Torreon's flanks. "Agra somnia!" he cried. A sick man's dream. Yes, perhaps he was a sick man. He felt God most deeply not before the altar of his Church but here among the natural elements of the desert.

For nearly two years, Soledad felt at home in Valentino. A dry wind blew the desert sand from one longitude to another, back and forth, year in and year out. Except for the irrigated fields and orchards, the scoured landscape was desolate yet serenely beautiful, drenched with untold centuries of dreams. The people trusted him. A farmer named Ramón brought him a live chicken in exchange for the padre's intercession during his wife's sickness. A boy named Chico moved into the padre's house and slept on the floor. The boy brought him water and strong yucca soap. These people believed in him, and they waited patiently for him to perform miracles.

One Palm Sunday, he put aside his usual sermon on forgiveness. Stepping down from the pulpit and wearing tattered vestments that had belonged to an earlier priest, he stood among the people and raised his arms. "Listen to me, good people. It is no longer a sin to limit the size of your family," he said. "The Lord has changed His mind about allowing you to have sex solely for the procreation of children. Go and make love whenever you want, but take precautions. The *curandera* will tell you what to do."

The people sat in shocked silence, then slowly drifted out of the church. *What does it mean, this permission?*, they asked themselves. It took some time before reality sank in. Then one by one, the couples of Valentino began to relax and enjoy one another in ways they had only dreamed about before. They did not have to confess their sins. Soledad had decided to do away with confession. The confessional was dismantled and chopped into firewood.

Because of Soledad's alarming benediction, the conception rate went down in Valentino, thanks to the use of herbal contraceptives prescribed by the *curandera*, who had never dared to offer them since the Church began ruling their lives. Lusty young men, whose agony had been observed by young girls anxious to love them in return, soon went around smiling and relieved. All over town, people talked about their young, brash priest, and how he had, with the help of God, been able to take their minds off the harshness of their lives. They wondered what he might do next.

Because of the social change he had brought about, Soledad began to enjoy certain advantages of his holy office. He liked the deferential way that people spoke to him whenever he strolled down the dusty streets, his hat pushed back on his head. He handed out holy cards to children when he prepared them for First Communion, and they kissed his right hand. He was given the best table by the window at the Tecolote Café so that he could see who was coming in or out. People sought his advice on everything from whether to buy a mule or when to plant corn in a field he had blessed, to how a bride should behave on her wedding night. They loved his laugh, his handsomeness, the way he could recite whole verses of alabados taught to him by the Penitentes, the flagellants who spent their nights in the morada seeking forgiveness from Jesus Christ.

His somber appearance in his plain brown cassock knotted with a cord at the waist caused people to treat him with respect. The cross he wore around his neck set him apart from ordinary men; the blazing comet birthmark on his cheek reminded them of old stories about a wise man who would come bearing solutions to their problems. Because they liked and respected Soledad, they gave him a special chair when he came to watch the school Christmas play. They left gifts of food at his door and remembered him on feast days with packages of sweets. They named infants after him, but they were too embarrassed to invite him to their dirt-poor homes for supper.

On a hot, stormy summer afternoon, the padre was lying in his bed, reading Rousseau, when a tornado struck Valentino, tearing the modest belfry from the church that had stood in the plaza more than a hundred years. From his meager collection funds, Soledad bought the materials to rebuild it. The people supplied the labor and a three-piece band. When the work was done, they brought a roast goat, tortillas, salsa, beans, and raisin pies for a fiesta. And a great deal of cerveza.

Working in the boiling sun, his little dishpan hat perched on his perspiring head, the padre became very drunk. He did not know when he had enjoyed himself more. His hands were blistered from stirring the adobe mud with a long wooden paddle. His cassock was ruined, and he had rolled up his sleeves, so his forearms were sunburned. His black, curly hairs glistened in the sun. From time to time, because of the heat, the priest yanked up his cassock, so that his bare, well-muscled legs showed.

Working beside him was a lovely, dark-skinned girl with enormous eyes named Maria Villanueva, who he had watched longingly ever since his arrival in Valentino. She was sixteen—not much older than Maya Begay. She could not help but notice Father Soledad's hairy forearms and legs and his rich, earthy smell. She giggled self-consciously whenever he turned and smiled at her. The priest drank a toast to the girl, and then another and another. *You are beautiful,* he thought. *My heart aches for you.* With a crooked grin, he asked her to dance, and she, blushing to the roots of her dark hair, yielded to his open arms. All around the plaza, the people stopped whatever they were doing and watched the way the priest danced with the beautiful Maria. "He holds her too tightly," they whispered.

Father Soledad had only danced part of a slow waltz with Maria Villanueva before the earth began to spin and he slumped to the ground. Two men carried him home. One poured a dipper of water on his head. The other removed his cassock, noticing his ragged underdrawers. They remarked about the padre's fine, hard body, and on the strange comet that turned to throbbing scarlet on his face. They wondered aloud if he was *camandulero,* sexually experienced. They had seen the way he looked at Maria Villanueva. The way she looked at him. The two men glanced at one another.

After the fiesta, people began to avoid the priest. Those who had been his friends were cool to him now. *What have I done,* he wondered, *except dance with a pretty girl?* As if they could read his mind, many of his parishioners stopped coming to Mass. They asked for his help only when someone was dying and they needed last rites. He noticed that young couples went to the next town to be married. And that men who had promised to help him build a new school were nowhere to be found. *I will pray for patience,* he thought. *Sooner or later, they will see that I mean no harm.*

One day, after he had finished his breviary, written his monthly report to Monsignor Canopus, and read from a book on Saint Thomas Aquinas, he went to the closet and took out his violin. Lovingly, he ran his fingers over the smooth, polished wood and pressed the instrument to his face. He found his bow, and though several of its horsehair strings were missing, it would serve his purpose. The priest had not played in months, and his fingers were rusty, but somehow he managed a lively minuet by Mozart. His heart soared to the heavens as he played, utterly absorbed in the joy that music afforded. Then he played a Beethoven rondo.

The mellow sound of the violin drifted out the open window and fell on the ears of Maria Villanueva, who was on her way to see him. She had been strangely moved by her encounter with the priest at the fiesta, but that was not what she was coming to see him about. He was a priest, and therefore untouchable, while she, the uneducated daughter of a herdsman, merely wished advice from a man she trusted. Her heart thumped as she approached his little, whitewashed house, with a lacy pink tamarisk tree offering shade on the south side. The truth was she had not stopped thinking about this man for weeks. The way the sunlight fell on the hairs of his forearms, especially.

On a mild May afternoon, as Father Soledad stood in his living room playing Mozart, Maria Villanueva stood outside listening. She had never heard classical music before, only the alabados of the Penitentes and the off-key hymns that the Church choir tried to sing. No, this was different. This was like sunlight. Or rain coming down in long, silver threads. The kind of music a priest would make. She smiled and went around to the front door and knocked loudly. Finally, she opened the door and went in. Father Soledad had his back to her, now playing Beethoven with a deep and wondrous passion. Maria Villanueva drew in her breath and coughed. The priest turned around.

"Dear child!" he gasped. "What do you want?" He could not help but notice how much she resembled Maya Begay.

She had come for advice about a boy from the next village, the son of a sheepherder, she said, eyes on the priest's long, graceful fingers. The boy wanted to marry her, but he wanted to sleep with her first in order to prove his love. Maria Villanueva sat in the chair opposite the priest, twisting her handkerchief. She lowered her eyes to the plank floor.

"I do not know what to do, Padre." She could not bear to look into his darkly handsome face, so similar to her own. Her luminous eyes were downcast; her hands held almost in supplication before her breasts. She had the most beautiful face he'd ever seen. "Is it right to give myself to him now? I have never had a man before."

"Do you love him, child?" the padre asked, searching that innocent face for clues to her behavior. She had not confessed fornication to him, so he assumed she was still a virgin. Her sins as recited in the confessional were mild. She had lied to her mother. She was disrespectful to her father. She had taken the name of the Lord in vain. Nothing troublesome. He closed his eyes, basking in her presence. As always, whenever he was nervous or afraid, he rubbed his cross between his thumb and forefinger.

Maria Villanueva nodded. "He is kind and gentle and hardworking, Padre. He will make a good husband and father."

"Do you wish to marry him, then?" he said, resting his hand gently upon her knee.

She trembled at his touch, but she did not push his hand away. "I do not know, Padre, if I am ready. Marriage may be out of the question for many years. With my mother dead, I have six brothers and sisters to care for."

He pulled her to her feet. "Come," he said impulsively, "we will dance." She stared at him incredulously. "I was unable to finish our waltz at the fiesta," he admitted.

At first, she was rigid with apprehension, then he felt her small body begin to relax. He hummed some familiar music. She picked up the edge of her skirt and twirled in front of him, laughing, her lovely face beseeching him. "Do you approve, Padre?" He looked at her with longing. Slowly, he removed his cross and kissed it. Then he laid it on the table. "Come with me," he said, huskily.

Later, he remembered the silkiness of her hair as he loosed it from its ribbon and buried his face in it. He remembered how her small breasts felt pressed against his hard torso. He remembered how she turned her face up to his and how he kissed her softly, tenderly on her full, soft lips, tasting faintly of the mesquite twigs she used to keep her teeth clean. He would never taste anything sweeter again.

"I love you," Lorenzo Soledad blurted into the astonished face of this butterfly as she lay in his bed with nothing covering her smooth, taut body except the flowers he'd taken from the table and laid across her breasts. In all his life, he had spoken these words only to women in Batwing. He touched Maria's face and her body, marveling at her loveliness. She stared at the ceiling, her great dark eyes wide open.

"Do not be afraid, dear Maria," he said soothingly. "God wishes me to do these things. In the eyes of God, we will always be married because of this. Do you understand?" He had been overcome by a passion he knew to be as fruitless as all the other passions he had known. "I love you," he said again, soberly. Then, aware of his own nakedness, he slid off the bed and dressed quickly.

As she sat up, Maria Villanueva looked down at the dark red stain appearing on the sheets and, suddenly realizing its significance, broke into a shuddering sob. "I was engaged to be married," she wailed as she hurriedly dressed. "Now you have ruined my life." As she ran from the rectory, Soledad watched her go with feelings of both sorrow and panic. This meant leaving Valentino, he knew. But with Maria, he had felt something profound. What of his sacred vows? He felt himself torn in two by the conflict between his vocation and his passions so deep they seemed to transport him to another world.

Only because he was a priest was Father Soledad not slain by Maria Villanueva's father, who arrived with a ragged posse, every one of them armed. He stood against the wall in silence as they crowded into his house, muttering the things they would do to him. The grim, determined men, some of whose confessions he had heard only the day before, pressed around him, armed with knives, guns, clubs—even a bag of cacti—with which to flay him alive.

Felix Villanueva, his face dark with loathing, held a razor-sharp knife to the padre's throat. A drop of blood appeared on the blade. "You have twenty minutes," he said, "to gather up your things and leave. If not, we are going to kill you ten times over."

Lorenzo Soledad left without saying good-bye. Maria Villanueva had been hidden from his view, and people had turned away in disgust as he walked slowly through town, carrying one small bag. A bean farmer picked him up and drove him to town in his wagon. They did not speak. At the stage stop the farmer fished in his pocket and gave the priest some coins.

"Adios," he said. He had never seen a priest up close before.

"Adios," Soledad said and raised his hand in blessing. There was a thrill in it.

What would he say to the monsignor? He was his confessor, but some things could not be confessed. No, they were included in the general absolution. Richard Canopus frowned as Father Soledad drew up a chair and sat down. His office in Santa Fe was grand. It overlooked the plaza where people were walking about. Years later, he would propose this young priest for sainthood, but now he felt only anger. "If the authorities should get wind of this," he said, "you will be defrocked, Lorenzo. I am sending you to the worst place I can think of. Hopefully, you will not come back." He rang a little bell to signal the meeting was at an end. Then he bent his head to his papers.

NINE

*F*ATHER ANTONIO HAD *been in Valentino several days and knew very little more than when he had arrived. He was drinking a warm cerveza at the kitchen table. Flies buzzed around a plate of empanadas. He smelled the stench of sheep. "Did you think he was God?" he asked Maria Villanueva, who was cutting the hair of a young boy. "When he came here as a priest?"*

"I know he was God, Padre. He lie down with me, and I feel fire in my belly. Then nine months later, a baby come."

"Where is it?" the Vatican priest asked Maria Villanueva, now a pudgy widow. He glanced at Father Bartholomew. The younger priest hated it there. He was thinking of ways to get out.

Maria Villanueva took her time answering. "I drowned him in the well, Padre." She looked up, aware of the look of disapproval from the priest. "He looked like a badger, this baby. His teeth were strong. They tore my nipples off." She lifted her shirtwaist so the priest could see where her breasts had been, now two scars the color of plums. The padre crossed himself. "Murder," he said. "Make your confession, Maria." He took out his surplice, kissed it, and draped it over his shoulders. "Kneel," he said.

She shook her head. "Father Soledad ruined my life. He gave me a badger monster. I see it roaming the fields behind the house. He puts a spell on people, then they die. My Tía Sophia lost all her children that way."

Father Antonio said good-bye. He climbed in the wagon and drove through the sand with Father Batholomew beside him. It was a warm, pleasant day with a rain cloud or two on the horizon. The desert had a certain appeal, he had to admit. When they got to Destino, they would have a hot bath, a bottle of wine, and each other's learned company.

"The world is corrupt, Antonio," Father Bartholomew said suddenly.

"Only because we have made it so, Bartholomew. One wonders if there would have been a badger monster without so many rules and regulations. The Anglicans have a point, old Henry VIII notwith-standing." His eyes went to a herd of antelope racing across the sand. "Do you think those antelope listen to the Holy Father in Rome?"

"But they are four-legged animals. They do not have free will."

"I am a two-legged animal," the older priest said. "Do I have free will?"

Bartholomew nodded. "We have souls," he said. "We are created by God in his image."

"I am not so sure anymore," Father Antonio said. "I am slipping into mortal sin." He waved his hand. "In thought only, as of now." His cassock was torn and dirty. No matter. "I believe we are put here on earth to set an example. To follow our hearts, as it were. Suppose that's all Soledad was doing?" He crossed himself. "He showed us the way."

"Surely you don't think so, Antonio? Our mission is to show how unfit he was." The younger priest felt sand blowing between his teeth.

"Is it?" the old priest said. In his pocket was a packet of letters from Muy Contenta. She wrote of something he had scant knowl-edge of: love. He had read the letters so often they were falling apart. I love you, Buzzard, she wrote. Fifty years a priest and now Father Antonio de Crepizi y Montefiore of Florence felt something unfamil-iar in his bones.

He reined in the horses and the wagon stopped. He got out and knelt in the sand, breathing heavily, his hands clasped. "I want you to hear my confession, Father." He crossed himself. "I have sinned. I have sinned most grievously. In my mind I see myself making love to a woman. A fallen woman, mind you." Absolution made him feel better, for a time. He would not think of her again. He would not respond to her letters. But there she was in all the little towns he went to. There she was on the altar dressed in sacred blue like the Blessed Virgin. At night he dreamed of her.

"Were you ever in love, Bartholomew?" Antonio asked as they drove along again.

The younger priest hesitated. "Yes, for many years."

Father Antonio swung his head around. "Who was she?"

"He, Father." There was silence between them, and finally Father Bartholomew said, "He was the miller's son. I could not live without him. And then finally he—he drank a tumbler full of lye." Nothing more was said between them. There were many kinds of sorrow. And many kinds of love.

THE ELDERLY CLERIC shifted uncomfortably in his seat.

"It's hopeless, Bartholomew," he said. "We have months to go, traveling around this godforsaken place filled with snakes and vampires. I'm not sure I belong here. As you now know, as my confessor, I'd rather be with Muy Contenta." The modern world was encroaching, and he had no place in it. When he returned to Rome, he was to be transferred to Finance and Investments. But what did he know about handling the billions of dollars of the Vatican's money that went back to the plunder of the Holy Crusades?

"I agree we should call it quits," the younger priest said. "We don't belong here. I have my secrets as well."

Father Antonio pulled over to the side of the road. As much as he hated to, he urinated into the sand, thinking of deadly snakes and scorpions and lizards. He hurried to finish, dribbling a few drops of urine down his leg. A cassock was a damned nuisance sometimes, as awkward as a woman's skirt. As he turned to get back in the car, the priest thought he heard a voice calling to him. He turned swiftly. An aged Indian stood by the side of the road, his burnished face a map of wrinkled experience. He wore a plaid flannel shirt and leggings; his silvery hair was drawn back in a chongo and tied with a brightly colored ribbon. The old Indian stretched out his hand. "Take this," he said. "Bring you good luck. From Badger Man."

"Who?" asked Father Antonio, dazedly. The old man's fingers

touched the priest's; there passed between them the briefest flicker of understanding. Then the Indian was gone, walking swiftly across the rose-colored desert sand. Where had he come from? And why did the priest's right hand tingle where the Indian had touched it?

"What did he give you, Antonio?" asked Father Bartholomew.

Father Antonio uncurled his fingers. "An eagle's claw," he said, wonderingly. "What does it mean?"

Father Bartholomew drew in his breath. "Throw it away, Father. It is a pagan symbol."

Father Antonio looked out across the spacious, defiant land. What had the eagle claw done for the old Indian that the blessed host had not? "He said it was from Badger Man," Father Antonio mused. "Now who on earth is Badger Man?" He slipped the eagle claw into the pocket of his cassock. A strange place, this. It made people forget what they had come here to do. He began to hum a long-forgotten song from his youth. Overhead, a red-tailed hawk made a deep, slow arc. A skunk ran across the road.

"Nature is frightening," the younger man said. "I long to go back to Rome."

BARTHOLOMEW WAS AT the reins now, feeling ill from the heat and dust. They were at the southern edge of Albuquerque. They had perhaps an hour to go. The sun was sinking fast in the western sky. They did not want to travel in darkness.

"Hurry up, son," Father Antonio said. He had no watch; he could only guess the time by the position of the sun. He told Bartholomew to pull over so he could drop into an arroyo and quickly change his priest's clothes for those of a prosperous Italian merchant. He had brought these clothes along, just in case. He combed his hair and wiped his spectacles on his handkerchief. There, he was ready. His heart beat wildly as they drove into Albuquerque, a dusty town with low buildings and few trees. "How dreadful," he said.

Muy Contenta was waiting for him at the hotel. Had it really been a year since he'd seen her? She hadn't changed a bit; she was even lovelier than he remembered.

"Oh, my dear," he said, kissing her hand. "I have missed you a great deal."

She stepped back to look at him. "What's with the outfit, Antonio? A disguise?"

They drank a bottle of wine and ate a tough steak with gravy and pinto beans. Bartholomew sat watching them. The old priest needed to be taken to task.

"We need to go to Camposanto, Father," Bartholomew intoned. People in the dining room were watching. It made the younger man uncomfortable.

"Later, my boy. Later." Antonio took Muy Contenta's hand and led her upstairs.

PART FOUR

New Mexico Territory,
1896

TEN

IN THE STILLNESS of the hot, dry morning, the whistle blew, low and mournful, echoing across the wasteland of northern New Mexico Territory. The priest stared out the window. There had been little rain in several years; the grass was dry and yellow. Dust clouds blew across the cracked earth, waiting for rain. Half-starved cattle stood in the shade of the parched cottonwood trees.

A deep heaviness settled over him. This was his last chance, the monsignor said. Reports had come back from the parishes he had served. His conduct was unbecoming to a priest ordained in Holy Mother Church. He had been given a heavy penance for his sins. Camposanto was his final opportunity to redeem himself. If not, they would give him a clerical job somewhere and forget he existed.

Camposanto was up there in the vast Sangre de Cristo Mountains, filled with half-wild Indians who wanted nothing to do with the Church ever since they had been forced to accept Catholicism in the seventeenth century. They had revolted in 1680 along with the other pueblos, but their freedom did not last long. The Spaniards returned, and the Indians clung to a life that was half this, half that. No one ever came back alive, Monsignor Canopus had told him last night over dinner in Santa Fe. He wanted Soledad to take a revolver for protection, but the younger priest shook his head.

"I have God to protect me, Richard," he'd said. He hoped it was true.

As he rode along, back first, toward his destination, the priest clasped his white hands across his cassock stained with the remains of breakfast's eggs, coffee, and marmalade. The seat was extremely uncomfortable, the air was thick with dust and cigarette smoke, the heat welled up from the floor littered with twitching locusts that had blown in the open window. He got up and closed it, aware of the smell of his own sweat. Locusts clung to the folds of his cassock. The train rocked along the track. It passed little villages that had not changed much in a hundred years. There was always a plaza and a church and chickens scratching in the dirt. Children waved as the train went by. The priest automatically blessed them. "Better yourselves!" he called out, opening the window. Dust blew in. He sneezed and sat back down again.

The people who were sitting opposite him looked startled. They said something to one another in a language he did not understand. "I am Father Lorenzo Soledad," he said, pleasantly, tipping his dishpan hat. These people were obviously Indians, but what kind? They had red skin and black hair; they were small and defiant looking. The man wore a shirt made of a flour sack; if he turned his head sideways, the priest could see the words "Gold Medal 100% Pure." The old woman wore a yellow printed dress. He expected them to beg, but they did not. They stared at him in a disconcerting way. The priest turned to the window. He wondered where they were from.

When Soledad got on the train in Lamy, the two were already there in the last car, the one he usually preferred. In case of derailment, the last car stayed on the tracks, or so he'd always heard. Although the coach was only half-full, he deliberately chose the seat opposite them. They did not so much as acknowledge his presence when he hoisted his valise onto the rack above and sat down. They were not like the Comanche of his younger days; they were clean and well fed.

The woman, short and dumpy, perhaps sixty, returned his sidelong glance with an air of haughty amusement. The man, sharp-featured, coiled as if to spring out of his seat at any moment, stared out the window; scarcely a muscle moved in his body. An ugly scar ran down the side of his face. The priest shuddered, wishing that he could move away from them. But his habit was deep in him. He settled into his rut of feigned indifference, until, bored with counting locusts, he violated his own rule and spoke.

"*Buenos dias*," the priest said, smiling.

"*Buenos dias*," the old woman said without looking at him. She busied herself mending a pair of trousers. Minutes passed and still the old people remained almost as still as the alabaster statues in a church. Father Soledad studied them out of the corner of his eyes while pretending to read his newspaper with its frequently disturbing news. When he had read everything that interested him, he rolled up the newspaper and fanned himself with it. He glanced at the couple opposite. No use to talk to people such as these, no use to give himself a dyspeptic ulcer worrying about the impoverished state of their souls.

The old man sat on the stiff straw seat. He wore a pair of dungarees rolled up at the bottom, patched at the knees. His hair was black and parted in the middle, with two pigtails hanging long in back. His skin was burnished like an old saddle; it was smooth and covered his bones with no excess anywhere. His features were sharp, as if he had been chiseled out of rock. He sat quite still, his head turned to the window.

The old woman, on the other hand, was quick and birdlike. She had tiny black eyes that bore into the priest and made him uneasy. She was not the color of the old man. Her skin had an olive cast to it. Her hair had touches of white; it was drawn back in a simple bun. She wore a yellow printed dress. Her black leather shoes were worn down at the heels. Her hands were swollen and red. She had the look of a woman who had borne many children.

"*Buenos dias*," he said again. The old woman fished out a brown paper bag that lay under the seat. From it she took a piece of jerked meat, salted, black in color, and stiff as the leather of her scuffed and patched up shoes. She held it out to the priest, who took it between his two fingers and held it to his nose.

"What is it?" he asked.

"Dog," said the old woman. She smiled, and he noticed that her teeth were yellow and broken off. "He was old. We could not let him go to waste."

The priest slipped the meat into the folds of his cassock. "I am not hungry."

"Oh?" said the old woman, and she went again into the brown paper bag. She took out a dark green bottle, unscrewed the top, and offered this to the priest. "Drink, Padre," she said.

"What is it?" the priest asked again, noticing that some of the liquid had spilled and hardened down the side of the bottle like syrup.

"*Sangre de venado,*" said the old woman. "Dragon's blood." She had made it herself—a potion of deer blood, herbs, and pure mountain water. The mixture warded off colds, headaches, and boils, or so she'd always believed.

The priest felt nauseated. His head dropped back against the seat, and he closed his eyes for a moment. When he opened them again, the old man had turned around. His right ear was missing. There was only a red, ugly scar.

"Where is your ear?" he cried, sitting up straight.

The old man shrugged. His eyes were heavy lidded, and he lowered them so that only a small slit of his eyes appeared. He had but one ear.

"Where is your other ear?" he repeated.

For the third time, the woman went into the brown paper sack and held out to him a small wooden box with two brass hinges.

"Open it," she said. The priest shrank back against the seat.

"Mother of God," he murmured, feeling faint.

The old woman held the box in her lap and ran her fingers over it. "He was very brave in the old days when he went to join his relatives in Mexico," she said. "He had a uniform with gold braid. And a sword with a silver handle, plus two revolvers on either side. His horse was black with a white blaze, and he could run faster than any horse in the army. This is true, Padre, so why do you smile, eh? My husband was so brave he killed eleven men all by himself. Eleven!" She held up all of her fingers. "Plus one more. So there was a price on him because the eleven men were *federales*." The old woman stopped for a moment. "They said he was worth only twenty thousand pesos." The old man sat up with a jerk.

She continued. "One day, he was out riding ahead of the others, and he went down to the river to get a drink. The *federales* came out of the brush. But they could not kill him because he has a special power. No one can kill him, you see. So they cut off his ear instead. With his own sword." She laughed. The priest blinked and ran his tongue around the edges of his lips.

"Go on, go on," he whispered, fascinated. The palms of his hands were wet.

The old woman continued in a low voice. "After that, they took him away to prison. On the morning that he was to be executed, a strange thing happened. The sky was filled with a great many birds. They were black with huge wings, and they circled the prison where he was. They set up a huge cry. They created a terrible wind. These birds were my husband's people. They came to save him as if he were the Cristo." The old woman paused to look at the priest.

His dark eyes blazed. *They are trying to make a fool of me*, he thought. Were they not aware of his priestly garb, the look of kindness on his face? His golden cross he wore so proudly?

"That is—blasphemy," he said, tugging at his cross. "Only Jesus saves."

The old woman smiled. "You may think so, Padre. But I—"

The priest interrupted. "It is a mortal sin to speak as you do. Only God has such power. Only God flies about in the sky." He could feel his face flush.

The old woman laughed. "Oh, Padre," she said, "who is to say what God can do? Look." And opening the box with her thumb and forefinger, she took out what remained of her husband's ear. It was hideously brown and shriveled, like a dried apricot, only larger. She held it between her thumb and forefinger. "It was his

93

good ear, too." She closed her hand over the terrible thing. The priest was too shocked to speak. He rubbed his precious cross. He had rubbed it so often that some of the gold had worn away. There was copper underneath.

"My husband was standing with his back against the wall. His hands were tied together. The soldiers were all in a row ready to shoot him. But as I said, they couldn't have killed him anyway. He has a certain power. The birds were circling above, crying and flapping their wings. And all at once, one of these birds that had one white feather in his tail swooped down and dropped the ear at the feet of the comandante. You see, Padre, after the soldiers had cut off my husband's ear, one of them rode all the way to Mexico City with it to give it to the president as proof that he had been captured."

The priest leaned forward. "Then it could not have been dropped by the bird, could it?" His voice was sharp and breathless. "The bird did not fly to Mexico City and get the president to give him the ear." He felt foolish saying these words, but he could not help himself. "Furthermore, if the *federales* had cut off his ear, your husband would have bled to death. *Verdad?*"

The old woman had a serene look. She stared at the ear, which lay in the palm of her hand. "They took it as a sign," she said. "The sky was so thick with birds they could not see. The dust blew on a wind that was like a hurricane. And so they let him go. They gave him a horse and told him to go back where he came from."

She put the ear back in its box and put the box back in the paper bag. She turned her head to the window. "The country," she said, "it is hungry for rain."

"Who are you?" whispered the priest, fiercely rubbing his cross. He was sweating profusely now. Under his cassock, his knees stuck together. He felt a river of sweat running down his legs from his groin.

The old man turned and faced the priest. His eyes opened

wide. In a strong, even voice that astonished the priest, he said, "I am Juan Lobo, Padre. This is Maria, my wife." He bowed his head politely. "We are at your service."

The priest moistened his lips. "Where are you from?"

The old man did not answer right away. His eyes went off to the broad plateau that the train was moving across, trailing a long stream of smoke from its smokestack. The plateau was deeply cut with arroyos and was cracked and dry like the skin of the old woman. The lone cottonwoods standing in the creek bottoms were bleached and dead. The old man's eyes went to the bluish, high-ridged mountains west and north of the plateau, so indistinct that they seemed part of the sky itself.

"There is a little town up there," said the old man. "We call it Camposanto. The Place of the Dead. For that is where we truly belong. We have been there for sixty winters. Before that we lived along the river in a pueblo many stories tall. Coronado came here in search of gold in the Time of Weeping Clouds. No gold, just our spirits, which he did not get. Many winters went by. Most of our people died. A few of us ended up in Camposanto." He managed a short laugh. "Others went to Jemez, where they still are."

"Camposanto," gasped the priest. "It cannot be." That was the name of the new parish the monsignor had given him. He took a slip of paper from his pocket and checked. Ah, true.

"Yes," said the old man. "I have lived there all my life except for the Mexican wars. And my father before me. There were many of us then. Now only a few." His eyes met those of the priest. "What troubles you, Padre?" he asked kindly.

The priest belched once, tasting the frijoles from breakfast. The monsignor would kill him yet with his insistence on eating a diet that included rancid frijoles and gangrenous red meat with Madeira that turned to vinegar the moment it left the bottle. *So late in life, I am not up to challenges*, the priest said to himself, listening to the thunder of his intestines and for the queer ringing that had lately begun in his ears. He took out his handkerchief and wiped his face. He removed his hat and smoothed down his hair that lay in flat, damp strands across his head. Then he clasped his hands together.

"I am Father Lorenzo Soledad. I have come to be your priest."

The old man looked up in surprise. "But we have not had a priest for so long. We do not need a priest." He looked out the window, obviously troubled.

"Nonetheless, I have come. And you will see that it is a good thing." He smiled, hoping to make the old man like him.

Juan Lobo glanced at his wife, whose little black eyes were burning into the priest. "So you have come," he said. "We will make the best of it, Maria. He is no different from the last one." She gave her husband a dark look.

The priest leaned forward. He saw a mysterious face. "Will you be my friend?" he asked.

Juan Lobo pulled his knee away. "I will try, Padre. Friends are not easily made." The old man's black eyes fastened on the padre's face. *Another religious*, he thought.

"Have you forgotten the faith, good man?"

Juan Lobo hesitated. "No, Padre," he said. "The faith was never there to begin with."

"You are not Catholics, then?"

"We are tumbleweeds blowing in the wind."

The priest resolved to say nothing. Instead, he took from his cassock the little black book bound in leather, with gold along the edges of the pages. He folded down the still-new binding. Then he made the first entry in a shaky though decipherable hand. *I will succeed*, he wrote.

When the boy selling lemonade came by, the priest bought one lemonade for himself and two for the Lobos. They drank silently. The old man sang softly to himself, some sort of chant. The priest listened intently, but there would be no more of it. The train lurched on. Soledad looked down and saw that locusts were trying to nest in the hairs of his toes. He shook them out and squashed them with the sole of his well-worn sandal. The whistle blew, as mournful as a dirge. He would get out at the next whistle stop. But when the train stopped, he stayed in his seat. Maria Lobo was examining a scalp she took from her bag. Soledad leaned forward. He could scarcely speak. "Whose scalp is that, Maria?"

"A Cheyenne warrior who came to rob us, Padre." Her smile was tight. She balanced the scalp on her knee, stroking the coarse black hair.

The priest lay back in the seat. He prayed to God for mercy, but when he listened for a reply, God was silent. The priest got up. He lurched toward the lavatory. A man in black opened the door. He had no features.

"Do not waver," he said. And then he was gone into thin air. The priest closed his eyes. Who was this apparition?

ELEVEN

THE STATION AT San Sebastian was a flat-roofed adobe with the windows boarded up. When the conductor came through announcing a five-minute stop, the Lobos collected their things from the overhead rack and hurried down the aisle. The priest struggled with his bag. "Wait!" he shouted, but they got off the train without looking back. A wagon driven by a young man was waiting for them. They got in.

That same hot summer day, a warrior called El Comanche rode briskly toward San Sebastian, its rooftops shimmering in the sunlight. He was a ferocious sight, dressed in his war bonnet, which was given to him by his old friend Crazy Horse, his face painted in the diagonal gray-and-black stripes of his extinct tribe, the Wackamungas, slaughtered in Wyoming forty years before. It had been a long ride down the mountain from Camposanto, but he did not feel tired. His latest wives, Hermosa and Tomasina, had cured his fatigue by making love to him the night before he left, rubbing their sensuous bodies against him until he thought he would erupt through the top of his head. El Comanche was more than one hundred years old, and he still enjoyed the pleasures of the flesh. He was sure his sexual appetite was all that had kept him alive when other men his age had long departed for the World Beyond.

El Comanche rode through the trees, singing an old hunting song his father had taught him. He was the last of his old tribe: not a single one remained except himself and his progeny, some thirty-eight in all. He wondered how it might have been if the Calabazas had outnumbered the Spaniards, had they known about gunpowder, bullets, dynamite—and other tools necessary for human survival—when there was still time. Suppose the religious had not come and introduced the notions of heaven and hell into an otherwise balanced existence?

As the little town came into sight, the blood rose in El Comanche's veins the way it always did before combat. His finger itched for the trigger of his old, dependable Henry repeating rifle, encased in a scabbard hanging from his saddle. He could smell the hot metal of the locomotive stuffed with hot coal; he could envision the graceful plume of smoke curling above it, the iron wheels turning on shiny steel tracks with a clattering little sound. He wished he had brought his dependable three-inch field cannon, too—the better to blow the locomotive off the tracks. But now, because of the price on his head, he had to travel lighter than usual.

He looked carefully at the position of the sun. Soon the train would come puffing up the hot tracks from the east. El Comanche hid deep in the piñons until he heard the whistle of the train off in the distance, where it went over the trestle that he had blown up in '81. The train gave him the opportunity for the military precision that he loved. He removed his Henry rifle from its scabbard and gave it a final check, then he drew in his breath and dug his heels into the flanks of his pony as he shot out of his hiding place and rose, higher and higher into the saddle, as free and majestic as a bird.

El Comanche crippled the train with a lucky shot that severed a steam line. He could have shot the newly-arrived priest, too, staring open-mouthed as the warrior tore past. "Death to the locomotives!" he cried as Father Soledad pressed himself against the peeling adobe wall of the train station, certain he was about to be shot. As the padre raised his arms in grim surrender, El Comanche galloped toward the northern end of town. His wild antics made the people hide in their forlorn casitas. They were used to him by now.

The priest gasped and crossed himself. It was almost the twentieth century, but this old warrior, whoever he was, had a look of incipient decay, as if he'd just escaped from the battlefield of a long-ago war. He saw the Lobos disappearing into the trees in the wagon. "Wait for me!" he cried, but they went on.

Soledad picked up his valise, and walked resolutely down the platform. *Where were the San Sebastian authorities?*, he asked himself. He recoiled from the sight of one wall of the station house, pockmarked with bullet holes. He stared out at the vast, uninhabited landscape. To the south was a long, steep mesa, more than five hundred feet high and studded with junipers and piñons that emanated the same brooding quality he often felt in other lonely outposts of civilization. To the west, he saw the rugged summits of the Sangre de Cristo Mountains, snowcapped even in summer. Camposanto lay somewhere in that purple sweep of wilderness. But how was he to get there?

The padre started toward town on the far side of the tracks, shuffling through the dust with his battered valise. His shoulders ached. Dust stung his eyes and made them itch. His trunk he'd left with the woman who claimed to run the station. Somehow, he had to recover the trunk, hire or buy a horse and mule, and find his way to that mysterious place called Camposanto. With a sinking heart, he went to find a livery stable, his cassock flapping in the breeze. A man named Colonel Pazote rented him a sorrel mare and a mule. The saddle was extra, but Soledad didn't care. The monsignor had advanced him a little money.

Colonel Pazote invited him to stay overnight in the barn, but the priest said he had to be on his way. But he was hungry, so he followed the colonel inside his casita. It was cool and dark.

"Do not go up there, Padre," the old Civil War veteran said. "They are savages, not Catholics like you and me." He crossed himself. "The army should get rid of them."

Soledad had washed his face and combed his hair. He felt better. He reached for a tortilla that Colonel Pazote offered him and loaded it with beans. He ate his fill, then he went outside for some fresh air. He looked around fearfully. El Comanche was waiting for him in the shade of a tree, astride his horse, having galloped back from the north end of town. His Henry was aimed at the padre's head. Soledad raised his arms. "See here, I am a man of God."

The old warrior gave him a look of pure hatred. "All the more reason," he said. He squeezed off a shot, narrowly missing the padre's head. Then he laughed and was gone.

Soledad mounted his horse. His hands were trembling. The cerveza he had drunk with lunch made him dizzy. The sun was hot. Locusts sizzled.

TWELVE

Y EARS LATER, *when their inquiry into Father Soledad's qualifications for canonization was nearly complete, the Vatican priests got off the train at San Sebastian, just as Father Soledad had done when El Comanche was killing locomotives. The priests were not speaking. Father Bartholomew had had enough of the old lecher. Father Antonio had had enough of the prissy younger priest. They had only to investigate Soledad's tenure at Camposanto, then they would go their separate ways. It would not be soon enough. Antonio already knew what he would do.*

San Sebastian looked worse than it had some years before. In fact, its broken-down façade had been enhanced into further disrepair with chisels, hammers, and instantly peeling paint for the benefit of tourists who came to enjoy anything that had to do with the crucifixion. San Sebastian had become another Lourdes, with pilgrims leaving rosaries and miraculous medals at the train station, now more picturesquely decrepit than ever. A hand-painted sign said, "This is where Soledad got off." Another said, "Gen-you-wine soo-vin-neers, 25 cents up."

The Vatican priests walked silently to where Colonel Pazote once had his livery stable. He had lived in a simple adobe house behind his business, but no more. He had built a lavish Victorian mansion and filled it with antiques and portraits of Spanish nobility he claimed to be his own. Kings, princes, dukes. It was all there in oil paint and gilt.

"So, Colonel Pazote," Father Antonio said, making himself

comfortable in a huge arm chair. "You no longer have a livery stable. What do you do?" The warring Vatican priests sat at opposite ends of the table, each drinking a passable Chianti. They did not so much as look at one another.

Colonel Pazote was a few years younger than Father Antonio. His hands were gnarled, his face deeply lined. But a singular joy erupted from his being. "I sell mescal to the tourists," he said. "Good stuff, imported from Mexico."

A young woman, no more than twenty years old, emerged from a bedroom. "This is my wife, Luisa. We have three children, no?" She nodded.

The old priest stared. The girl was young enough to be the colonel's great-granddaughter. The children were young enough to be his great-great-grandchildren. He blessed them. What did it matter when all was said and done?

"I don't like the looks of this," Father Bartholomew said as he waited for a wagon to fetch him and Father Antonio up the mountain. The sun was hot, so he found some shade. "I'm glad this is the last place we have to go, Antonio. I have someone waiting for me."

"So do I," said Father Antonio. He had not stopped thinking of Muy Contenta. Their time in Albuquerque was all too brief. But it had opened the old man's heart.

A wagon driven by Luis Madrone finally came along. They got in. The storyteller had been expecting them for some time. He flicked the reins and the wagon lurched up the hill. The priests hung on for dear life. New Mexico Territory was a dreadful place with wolves howling in the distance and bats flying out of the trees, they thought. But devout pilgrims hurried along, dragging miniature crosses. The priests blessed them.

"Want to hear what happened when Soledad arrived?" Luis asked. They nodded. "It was the Planting Moon. We were all busy, and here he came. A fucking priest!"

The wagon dipped into a hole. The Vatican priests tumbled out. The storyteller laughed. It had been twelve years since Soledad's arrival. Much had changed.

THIRTEEN

SOLEDAD RODE ALONG, his feet dangling out of the stirrups. He had half a mind to turn back. So much effort, and for what? He would do his best in Camposanto, but the odds were against success. He was feeling sorry for himself and not a little concerned, as he rode through an open forest of ponderosas creaking in the wind. The cool air of high altitude was pure, scented with fragrant pine and the sensuous smell of warm earth.

As he came out into a clearing, the azure bowl of sky pressed down on the far horizon, pierced by snow-capped mountain peaks stretching north and south. He expected nothing in Camposanto. They would resist him, and he, in turn, would urge them to consider certain positive aspects of his religion. Not the old, restrictive parts that had enslaved them before and seen that they were dead before their time, but those that would give them a new outlook. The priest rubbed the horse's mane in a gesture of affection.

"Amigo," he said, "our work here will not be easy. *Absit invidia.*" Let there be no envy or ill will. The horse bobbed his head up and down as if he understood. "Why have I accepted this mission," he continued, "when I know already it will not go well? Why am I not a married man with children? A house? Work like any other man? I would be happier, Amigo. Don't you think?" The horse nickered.

He dug his heels in his horse's flanks and headed down the slope, trailed by his mangy mule. There, in a wide valley, the village lay gleaming in the sun, wreaths of smoke curling up from the chimneys of the small adobe houses. A deceptive serenity bathed the scene, a timeless beauty that made him gasp. Camposanto seemed frozen in time, trapped in obscurity and decay. People moved about. Dogs took their time. He heard a rise of voices. He imagined they were getting ready to shoot him.

As the priest approached, the Calabazas looked up. They were working in the corn fields, wringing the Elixir of Dreams from the yellow ears. This syrupy liquid, once fermented, sustained them all winter long, producing the kind of euphoria necessary to their lives. It was potent to the point of being almost explosive. They kept an eye on the priest as he rode steadily toward them. They could have killed him easily. Each man was armed with a knife.

They observed the way the priest rode, hunched forward in the saddle, his stirrups too short for his legs. They studied his face, handsome but troubled. They noted the scarlet comet emblazoned on his cheek and how awkwardly he dismounted, his long, brown robes flapping around his ankles. The men's fingers closed around their hunting knives shoved into the tops of their work pants. They looked to Juan Lobo for a signal, but he shook his head and gave them a look of warning. Last night in the kiva, when they had taken up the matter of the priest—whose arrival the monsignor had written them about—they had decided to do nothing, at least at first.

Maria Lobo sat quietly in the shade of a ponderosa, her strong hands rubbed raw from washing clothes in the river. She was more tired than usual. A pain in her chest had begun last month, when she and Juan Lobo had been visiting the American authorities in Santa Fe, bargaining to save their tribal land. The result was no bargain—just the news that the Calabazas did not own the land they had been living on for a long time. They were squatters, the federal magistrate had said. By the time of the Ripe Corn Moon, they would be gone, to the Arizona desert where she knew they would die. She had become ill then, seeing in her mind's eye the end of the long, unbroken line of the Calabazas, who had the blood of Bears and Eagles in their veins. Only last week, the *federales* had shown them where the boundaries of the forest reserve would go.

Right down the middle of their village. Along the ridge where they hunted. Across the river that was their umbilical cord to Mother Earth. Maria took a deep breath. Many things disturbed her nowadays, but the arrival of the priest was not one of them. He was young and inexperienced. He would teach them nothing. But they would use him to their ends. When she met him on the train, she knew what she and Juan Lobo would do.

She turned to Tomasina, who had been watching Father Soledad with interest. This thick-waisted, good-natured woman was the older of El Comanche's wives, the daughter of a chieftain from a southern pueblo who had admired El Comanche's battlefield skills and made him a present of his daughter. Tomasina had already formed an opinion. "This priest comes just in time," she said. "Perhaps he will save our land so we do not have to move to the desert."

Maria Lobo rubbed her face with tired hands. "You are too young, Tomasina," she said. "You do not understand. It is too late to save our land. Juan Lobo says we will make an example of this priest."

"I will not go," Tomasina said, with the sort of useless defiance El Comanche had taught her. "My husband says he will kill anyone who tries to make us go." She looked around for the old warrior.

El Comanche was sitting under an apple tree, his Civil War cannon beside him, watching intently. To the old warrior, the priest spelled trouble at a time when the Calabazas had more than enough. "I should have shot him when I had the chance," he muttered to himself. Despite twenty years spent fighting the War of the Locomotives, he had learned nothing about the futility of resisting change. His ancestors had resisted, and they were spirits now, urging him on.

The old man eased himself up and inserted his store-bought choppers that Tomasina had ordered from the Sears Roebuck catalog. "Kill him now!" he said loudly. The aged warrior was too old to care about what people thought. "Fuck the priests," he said, loading his cannon with its standard ammunition, smoothly rounded potatoes bought from a farmer in town. "I killed two religious with my old Henry rifle last year. There they were, praying in the trees."

Soledad stood uncertainly in the sun, trying to understand what was happening in the cornfield. He could hear voices and see people moving among the tall, green stalks. He'd seen some of the threatening gestures of the men with their hunting knives. His heart skipped a beat. "Please, come out so I can greet you," he pleaded in Spanish, a fixed smile upon his face. No one came forward at his greeting; the men continued to move up and down the corn rows. Nothing but the wind, the gritty taste of dust in his mouth, the rustle of the corn stalks as people worked among them. He ran his tongue around his dry lips, watching the people's movements out of the corner of his eye. He fanned himself with his dishpan hat; his dark, thick hair lay in damp strands upon his high forehead. He felt fifty pairs of eyes staring at him from the field and from the trees beyond. "God be with you," he said haltingly and raised his arm in benediction.

Juan Lobo stepped forward and stood, his moccasined feet slightly apart, fixing the priest in his unwavering gaze. Soledad caught his breath at the sight of him, with his high-bridged nose, his piercing eyes, his hair in two long braids. He recognized him from the train; he looked more formidable here in his own sur-roundings. "We met on the train. I am sorry you have come, Padre. This is our homeland," he said softly. "What you see is all we have." The cacique's heart ached as he said this, for he loved the moun-tains more than he loved life. They *were* life in the deepest sense. He would gladly give his own to keep his people here. "There is only one Catholic here, the mother of Luis Madrone. But look at all the possibilities. You have only to figure out how to convert people who are not interested in conversion. They have seen the damage the Church has done. My grandfather was sold to the Spaniards when he was twelve years old. Many generations ago, my peo-ple were burned at the stake by your so-called Church. And they expected us to embrace them. Hah!" He spat in the dirt.

The old man opened his arms wide to the sky, as if to implore the sun. He chanted something long and drawn out in his thick Calabaza tongue. His wife Maria was the first to answer him. Then the others, one by one. El Comanche began a chant about all the locomotives that had been blown up by his Civil War cannon. Together, the people came forward out of the field, each chanting his own version of Calabaza history. They were not very tall and the skin tones ranged from molasses to wheat. They were mostly old, but there were a few children, a beautiful young woman, and a few young men who looked drunk. How ragged they were! How poor! Yet they stood with a collective dignity, appraising him. He could not help but be impressed.

"Please, listen to me," Soledad said in a loud voice. But his voice was lost in the sudden deep sound of a drum that rippled out of nowhere. The voices of the people echoed higher and higher. The priest thought he heard laughter, but he plunged on. "I'm not here to change you. I simply wish us all to become brothers in the love of Christ."

A middle-aged man, his hair in a *chongo* with bangs like a Navajo, stepped forward and said, "Ah, Padre, we have had enough of Jesus Christ. Look at what Christ did to us. And we do not want to be anybody's brother either." Laughter swept through the little knot of people, obviously trying to unnerve him. Soledad blinked his reddened eyes, aching from the dust and the summer sun. He wished he could lie down and rest, drink a little wine, read John Donne, and play his beloved Beethoven on his violin. Civilized things. Lost things. He sighed.

An obvious half-breed with red hair said mockingly, "How did you find us, Padre? We are dead. That is why we live in Camposanto. We are ghosts."

Laughter echoed across the field.

"What . . . do . . . we . . . want . . . with a . . . priest, eh?" asked a dark-skinned man with circles under his eyes.

Someone else took up the theme. "We are savages, Padre. We do not need your Christ," said a man with a wooden leg. "Yes, we are good enough as we are."

Out by the apple tree, El Comanche wiped the tears of old age from his eyes, so he could aim his ancient cannon. "Adios, you fucking round hat," he said, but he could not get his igniter to fire. He aimed his Springfield, one of many rifles in his arsenal, but he had no ammunition.

Laughter shook the people so hard that they seemed to wave in the hot sun. *I must keep calm*, Soledad thought, aware that they were testing him. His head felt light. He should have stopped and eaten some of the bread and dried meat Colonel Pazote had packed for him. He should have rested better the night before rather than done what he did. He shouldn't have drunk so much cheap whisky in Santa Fe, trying to bolster his courage for the task ahead. From high above, he felt the weight of the sun. He pressed his fingers to his temples and ran his tongue over his parched lips. How much longer would this strange welcome continue?

A beautiful young woman, dressed in a tight-fitting blue dress, moved closer. "Hello, Padre," she said. "I am La Luz." She ran her hands suggestively over the bodice of her dress.

Ignoring her interest, Soledad persisted. "I am not an ordinary priest," he announced. "I believe in a loving God who accepts all people. But I also believe in the Indian way, taught to me by the Navajo in the desert." He heard laughter. "Do you find it strange? Well, I have discovered the hard way that there is no right path or wrong path. A man must live by his conscience and by tradition as well. Let me teach you our traditions, and you can teach me yours. Perhaps we can both learn."

The voices rolled over him like a wave. "We do not need a priest. We need food. Money. To be left alone. We want to stay on our land. As for the Navajo, they are our enemies," said the red-haired man, who waved a bunch of corn tassels in the air like a rattle. In his other hand, he held his hunting knife. "You should not be here," he rasped, pressing closer. "Go back to where you came from. We do not want any more priests. The last one made us build a church. We tore it down."

Soledad went on. "Please, just give me a chance! You will see, it will be a good thing." But he was not at all sure what good he could do. "Look at me. I am a sinner," he went on to say. "There is no greater sinner among you."

Just then, El Comanche finally got his igniter to work. The cannon's blast startled the priest but left him unscathed. He strained his eyes but could not see who had fired the shot. Around him, a scattering of potatoes attested to El Comanche's faulty aim. Soledad straightened his hat. He looked around for his horse, Amigo, running blindly in the direction of the village below, the pack mule trailing behind him. He would not show fear—they could kill him if they wanted, thus absolving him of all the sins of his past life. He faced them, his fists clenched. "I am happy to be here in Camposanto," he said haltingly. But he sounded unconvincing.

In the silence that followed, only the beautiful young woman called La Luz had the presence to respond. "We are happy to have you, Padre," she said. She liked the strength of his hands, the set of his jaw, the way he tilted his head to one side when he was listening. And she liked the strong body she sensed beneath his heavy cassock.

"Thank you," he said, embarrassed. "There are some things we must do together." He thought he saw someone loading the cannon again on the other side of the apple trees, so he tried to look nonchalant, even as he envisioned well-aimed potatoes battering his body. "The first is to talk about the true nature of God. And what you yourselves believe life and death to be." Lorenzo Soledad felt that he was talking to the air. "I am here to introduce you to the love of God—no more, no less. Please think about my words." His knees felt weak, but he could not sit down. He smiled bravely. "God is a spirit," he said.

"God is a moonbeam," said the man with the knife in his hand. He could not take his eyes off La Luz and how she was making a fool of herself with the priest.

"God . . . is a . . . river," muttered the dark-skinned man, lying flat on the ground because he had drunk too much of last year's Elixir of Dreams.

"God is a meadowlark, singing a love song!" shouted Juan Talamantes, the man with a wooden leg.

"God is a cannonball," roared El Comanche, as he again fired his cannon. This time, his potatoes blew the top off a corncrib that had stood in the field for twenty years. Hermosa and Tomasina ran to him and pulled him away from his cannon. Recently, their mutual husband had become so unpredictable he shot at trees. Not to mention the locomotives at San Sebastian he would not give up on, despite a price on his head.

"Do not let them frighten you," Juan Lobo said pleasantly. "It is their way of showing how much they appreciate your coming here." He turned his head so Soledad could see the hideous red place where his ear had been.

"Why do they want to kill me then?" Soledad stammered, scarcely able to keep standing. "What does it mean?"

"It means nothing, Padre," the cacique said, his hand firmly on the priest's elbow. "We are all your friends." He uttered some words in a language the priest didn't understand.

The dark-skinned man stared at the priest. "I saw . . . God . . . yesterday . . . in an . . . ant pile," he stammered. His eyes were glazed. "Do you . . . believe . . . me?"

The priest looked him straight in the eyes. "Yes, I do," he said.

The man with the wooden leg rubbed it, as if he still had feeling there. Because it was made of a tree limb, his leg was always trying to grow back into the earth. It had sprouted several branches and some leaves. "I have seen God in a kettle of stew," he said. "Do you believe me?"

"I do," said the priest.

The red-haired man stood with his arms folded across his chest. "Do you see that mountain, Padre? God lives up there. He turns into a deer and visits us when we need him. Do you believe it?" He took his knife out of his shirt and licked the blade.

"I believe that God is everywhere," said the priest. "In all things. I myself have seen God in a eucalyptus tree."

Juan Lobo smiled. He wondered what a eucalyptus tree was.

"We are not used to strangers," he said, and suddenly images of all the strangers the Calabazas had endured flashed through his mind—armored conquistadores, brown-robed priests, painted Plains Indians and fierce Navajo, tough mountain men, crafty officials from one government or another. He could not control these strange images that came to him in tense moments like this. He raised his eyes to the priest's. "Suppose we kill you," he said evenly.

"Life is short," said Soledad somberly. "It comes and goes in an instant. There is no heaven or hell, only what you see before you."

"I was once the governor of this miserable territory," a short, fat man spoke up importantly. "Elected by mistake by a drunken assembly. That was hell. I have lived here in Camposanto all my life. This is heaven. It is very simple, Padre. Heaven consists of a place where people think alike."

"It's true," the priest laughed.

In the shade of the apple tree, Maria Lobo watched the confrontation unfolding before her. The priest could not save them from what was happening. The good old times she had known were nearly over. Just last week, the gringos had come with their official papers. And a little pot of ink, which they'd set on a makeshift table in the plaza. Though most of the people did not know what the papers said, they signed them anyway, making their thumb prints on the paper and waiting for their little sack of silver dollars. But the *federales* said they couldn't give them money until everyone signed up, whenever that might be. Next week. Next month. Next year. The Americans had plenty of time. Hadn't the Great White Father said that all this land, stretching from mountaintop to mountaintop, belonged to the federal government now?

Juan Lobo had hired a lawyer in Santa Fe, who looked at the papers and decided they were legal. The Calabazas never had title to anything, he had said. So gringos could make their land part of the forest reserve, where people could come and hunt and trap and cut down trees. She remembered how Juan Lobo had stormed out of the lawyer's office and caught a train to Washington. There the *federales* had told him the same thing. They'd pulled out a map and showed him where the new Calabaza reservation would be. In the desert, next to their enemies, the Navajo. No trees. No streams. No familiar animals. No familiar birds. Just sand and misery. "We are not Snake People," Juan Lobo had said, and he had returned heavy-hearted to Camposanto.

Maria Lobo called to Soledad. "Can you save us from our fear, Padre? That is what is killing us. We never go to bed without it. We never get up without feeling it stuck between our teeth. Things are happening we cannot control. You and your salvation. Well, we don't want to be saved."

Soledad smiled. "I cannot save you from your fear, old woman." *I am a sinner and a liar*, he thought.

Maria Lobo nodded at his reply. Whatever his motives might be, she had begun to like him. She wondered where he was to sleep, and what he might like for supper.

The red-haired man stepped forward and thrust out his chest. "Make it rain, Padre!" he said boldly. "If it rains, we will accept your God. We will all become Catholics."

Everyone laughed and clapped. The man with the wooden leg touched his arm. "Yes, Padre, make it rain. The fields are burning up."

Soledad's next move was impulsive. Irrational. Sacrilegious. Even as he removed the blessed cross from his neck, he thought to stop himself, but it was too late. He wanted to make an impression before these ragged Indians, but he would later realize this was the first step in his undoing, just as, much later, it would become one stumbling block to his canonization. "Very well, I will make an offering for rain," he said. "Watch."

He planted his cross on a little mound of earth and blessed it. "By tomorrow it will rain," he said, "if our Lord Jesus Christ so decrees it." The comet began to throb so hard that it made his jaw ache. He looked up. He thought he saw the Stranger standing at the edge of the trees, shaking his head at such arrogance.

Flushed with anger, Juan Lobo faced the priest, his black eyes boring into Soledad's. "See here," he said. "We pray for rain our own way. Sometimes it comes. Sometimes it does not. This is not your way, Padre. It is ours."

"How long since the last rain, Juan Lobo?" The priest had seen the parched fields, the dry cornstalks, and the river reduced to a trickle. He felt the first twinge of fear as he stood there, not knowing if he would be killed on the spot.

"Nearly two moons, Padre," Juan Lobo said, remembering how the Corn Dances had not worked this year for the first time in memory. "Everything has been dry since early spring. But you can do nothing. You are not one of us."

"Very well then, let us pray for rain a different way." Soledad began to pray. "Our Father who art in heaven . . ." But it was a futile gesture. The deep thud of a drum again came out of nowhere, as if a giant, unmistakable heart had suddenly jolted to life. It was a signal of some sort. The Calabazas formed a circle and began to dance. Their voices rose in song, higher and higher, until at last the singing throbbed with a tangible intensity. The old man gripped the priest's right hand, feeling the tension in his muscles, the uncertainty of a man afraid of his new circumstances. La Luz took his other hand, and the three of them joined the dancers. She felt the smoothness of Soledad's skin, remembering most of the male hands she had held were rough and coarse. She blushed as the priest squeezed her fingers in a gesture meant to be a measure of his appreciation. La Luz took it otherwise. Her heart leaped. She liked this handsome, brooding man with the crimson mark on his cheek; she had not felt such excitement for many years. She wondered how she could get the priest into her bed.

When the dancing stopped, Juan Lobo lifted his head and spoke to the sun, then to the sky. Finally, with an enigmatic glance toward the priest, he prayed for rain in the low, droning tones of the Calabaza language. Almost as if they understood the cacique's entreaties, the clouds rolled over the mountains, blotting out the sun. Distant thunder echoed from the peaks, and a cold wind blew up the canyon. A few drops of rain fell on Camposanto, then more, until soft, brown puddles began to form between the rows of corn.

Just as suddenly as it began, the rain stopped. The puddles dried up. The thirsty corn was still thirsty.

"You see what happens, Padre, when you attempt things you do not understand," the cacique scolded.

Soledad blushed to the roots of his hair. He stared at his cross, stuck in the mud at Juan Lobo's moccasined feet. To retrieve it now would appear childish, uncertain. On the other hand, if he left it where it was and the rains continued, would they believe he'd worked his magic, too? Before he could make up his mind, the dancing started again. He breathed deeply, took La Luz's hand, and merged, almost against his will, with the hypnotic rhythm of the drum. He was soaked to the skin.

As he danced, the padre's hat blew away and rolled like a wheel on its edge, faster and faster. It rolled through the heaven-sent rain puddles, across the cornfield, and came to rest alongside the cauldron, where the corn was beginning to be transformed into the Elixir of Dreams. This was a one-hundred-proof beverage, drunk by every adult and sometimes children. The people lifted the padre into the air as if he were weightless. His feet no longer seemed to touch the wet earth as he spun one way, then another. For a time, he felt disconnected from himself, as if he were someone he could see from the outside, engaged in something totally foreign to his nature. The people spun him again, surrounded him with a throbbing, pagan joy, until he yielded to their ancient dance. Someone handed him a tin cup filled with the Elixir of Dreams. He drained it and laughed, the liquid burning all the way down his throat.

The Calabazas danced on, trying to dance him into the heavens, to separate him from the last vestiges of his mortal concerns.

FOURTEEN

EXHAUSTED FROM THE dancing, the priest climbed onto the seat of Juan Lobo's wagon into which jugs of the new Elixir of Dreams had been loaded. His cassock was torn and splattered with mud; his feet, encased in sandals, were dirty. He had not enjoyed himself this much since the ill-fated dance at Valentino, when he'd allowed himself to be seduced by Maria Villanueva. This time he'd allowed himself to notice the woman called La Luz. A smoldering beauty, if he ever saw one. He gazed longingly at his cross, still embedded in the mud; the Calabazas were laughing at him. Dare he climb down and retrieve his precious cross? Or would they kill him for removing the holy object that may have brought rain?

As he rested, someone handed him a plate of food: beans, chile, fry bread—all the greasy things he liked, but which gave him indigestion. He mopped up the watery juice with a piece of bread and sucked it. He drank warm water from a gourd, letting it trickle down his chin and loosed a long, deep sigh. Out of the corner of his eye, he looked for La Luz, knowing as he did so, that he had crossed an invisible line. The Calabazas knew he wanted her. They knew she wanted him. Later, when Father Antonio learned the circumstances of Soledad's arrival, he would say there was an inevitability about it. Soledad belonged in Camposanto, but on that day, he was far from certain he belonged anywhere.

As the priest chewed on the tough bread and drank the tepid water, El Comanche, decked out for battle, galloped toward him and reined in. The padre drew up his legs, nervously. "What do you want?" he asked.

"I want you to leave," the El Comanche said. He had a murderous look.

The old warrior smelled of gunpowder and animal skins, crusted perspiration and decay. In one hand, he carried a tomahawk and around his waist was a six-shooter with a mother-of-pearl handle; a six-foot-long war bonnet crowned his head. Soledad shuddered; he thought such attire had gone out when Crazy Horse died two decades earlier. "I am El Comanche," the warrior said in a deep, cracked voice. He gave the padre a piercing look. "I am the Custodian of War. I have killed eight locomotives, nine bridges, two water tanks, and eleven wagon trains. I am the father of sixteen sons—four for every direction—and two daughters. I have ten hectares of land, two wives, four horses, nineteen sheep, a pig named General Sherman, and a horse named Kit Carson." He glanced over his shoulder at his giggling wives. "I am more than one hundred years old. What keeps me alive is war. And fucking my beautiful wives within an inch of their lives."

The padre laughed uneasily at the old man's strange way of introduction. "See here, El Comanche, it's nearly the twentieth century. The Indian wars are finished."

The old man spat a wad of saliva across the front of the wagon. "Bah," he said. "Nothing is ever finished, Padre—not as long as I am alive. White men took our land. Killed our people. Religious like you destroy what we believe. So warriors like me fight. Death to the locomotives!"

"Why do you attack locomotives, El Comanche?" How immutable he looked.

El Comanche curled his gnarled old fingers around his tomahawk. His breath was foul. "So fucking progress will be arrested!" He waved a long arm toward the mountains, where unseen enemies lurked. "Bless me and all my ammunition, so I can fight forever!" In addition to his Henry, he had in his storehouse by the river the field cannon, nine Springfields with bayonets, thirteen muskets, two kegs of powder, four double-barreled shotguns, and a pair of matching revolvers, plus four hundred rounds of ammunition to fit his assorted weapons. When the day came, he would fight the U.S. Army as he had at the Battle of Glorieta Pass, after he had promoted himself to a Confederate major—two stars, epaulets, and all.

The padre, knowing nothing of the old man's arsenal, thought it an odd request, but nonetheless he obliged. "Bless you and all your ammunition, El Comanche," he said. He saw that the warrior's beady eyes were focused on something not in the present, but deep in the past, where old battles were still to be fought against enemies long departed. The old man seemed to take heart from what he heard. He looked around from the cornfield to the apple trees, from his adopted village baking in the sun to the great golden sweep of buffalo plains that he visited now only in his mind.

"Goddamn it," he said. "Used up freedom too fast. Now only memories left." He removed his .45 from its holster and shot it into the air as his horse trotted up the hill.

Emboldened by El Comanche's impromptu self-introduction, the man with the wooden leg waited for the old fighter to ride away, then limped toward the priest. Without looking directly at his face, he said in a whisper, "I am Juan Talamantes." He leaned on his one good leg and shoved the wooden one to one side. "I do not have children or even a wife—only a dog named Jesus Christ. I am the Custodian of Meekness." Blushing because he had said too much, the shy, hesitant man dropped his watery eyes to the ground. Though he was hopeful of a life that meant something, Juan Talamantes had been unlucky in love so many times that people had given up on him. "I wish only to find the right woman before it is too late." At this he glanced around, hoping a certain woman would notice him. "Bless me and my lost courage," he said softly. "Bless Jesus Christ, a fine and noble dog."

"I will never bless a dog named Jesus Christ. Why? It's blasphemous." Soledad reached out and touched the top of Juan Talamantes's head. What he saw in this man's eyes made him hopeful. "But bless your lost courage, Juan. May you find it again in your dreams." At this point, Father Soledad noticed that the people had lined up next to the wagon and were waiting their turn, like at a confessional. *How odd*, he thought, but he inclined his head to hear better. The red-haired man was next; the priest saw that he still clutched his hunting knife and that his look was murderous.

"I am Delfine Madrone," he said sullenly. "I am the Custodian of False Hope. What I want, I cannot have. What I have, I do not want." He glanced around and saw La Luz slowly moving toward him. His heart ached for her. *If she does not soon become mine*, he thought, *I will set her house on fire*. "She will never be mine, Padre. But she will never be yours either. Bless my false hope, for without it, I have no cause to live."

Soledad understood, having been in that position himself. "Bless your false hope, Delfine. May you find some other use for it."

How odd this blessing sounded, contrary to everything he had ever learned in seminary. Strange, too, that the Calabazas would even ask for one, since they had not been Catholic for a long time. Yet, a blessing was a blessing, was it not? He rubbed his eyes. *Where had Delfine's red hair come from?*, he wondered. *And the bagpipe he dragged along? A Scotsman must have visited.*

La Luz sauntered up to the wagon and stood alongside Delfine.

The Custodian of False Hope touched her bare arm. "You see, La Luz, the padre approves."

The priest shook his head. "I don't approve. I only know that God will help you, Delfine," he said.

La Luz made a face. "How will God help me, Padre?" she said, and she shaded her eyes with one hand. "Once I saw God in a vat of lye soap."

Soledad drew in his breath. She was close enough for him to see the bead of perspiration on her upper lip, to smell her earthy, woman's aroma. "I know you believe in animal spirits, which I do not condemn. But there is a greater spirit that connects us all." Even as he said these words, he knew they were not what she wanted to hear. Nor was he entirely sincere, since his mind was on the contours of her body and what he would have to do to keep himself in check.

La Luz raised her arms and raked her fingers through her thick, black hair. "I believe in nothing," she said angrily. "My husband is in the *pinta* until 1934 for killing an important gringo in Santa Fe so we could have money to buy food. My children have no father. I am going to grow old before my time because there is no man in my bed! Why do I need faith for that?"

Delfine Madrone turned to face her. "There could be a man in your bed, La Luz," he said with a hopeful smile. "If you wanted me."

"Why would I want you?" she asked scornfully. "I would rather sleep with a sheep."

Delfine stepped back and hurried off. He could see there was already something happening between La Luz and the priest.

La Luz adjusted her skirt, then swung it provocatively, aware that the priest was staring at her. "I am the Custodian of Desire," she said in a breathy voice. "Bless my desirability. It is what a man should feel for a woman, if he is ever to become a man."

He hesitated. His face turned red and his comet began to throb. "I cannot bless desire, La Luz," he said, recoiling slightly from her intensity. "I will bless your goodness instead."

"Bah!" she said, and strode away from the wagon.

He watched her walk briskly down the hill, her blue dress catching the late afternoon sun. "She is beautiful," he whispered. "And she is another man's wife."

Next to introduce himself was Juan Lobo's son, who approached the wagon with a crooked grin on his lips. "I am . . . Bonito Lobo, Padre," he said with a tinny laugh. "I am . . . the Custodian . . . the Custodian . . ." But he could not go on. He did not know what he was.

The priest leaned toward him. Bonito's skin was mottled, his mouth slack, the circles under his eyes as dark as flint. "Yes?" he said. He wondered what accounted for Bonito's strange appearance. And what these Custodians were that each villager claimed to be.

"I am the Custodian . . . the Custodian of . . . Unfinished Thoughts. That is why . . . I have not . . . slept in twenty years. . . . Bless . . . my insomnia, Padre! . . . If I were to sleep . . . the world . . . would stop." Bonito's hands were raw and lacerated from cutting down the corn stalks after the ears were harvested. He had worked hard for three straights days, and what he wanted now was to ride his horse over the mountains, but he could not remember why, or where he wanted to go.

"What has caused your insomnia, Bonito Lobo?" asked the priest.

Bonito Lobo stared dully into space. "I . . . forget," he said. He held a jug of the Elixir of Dreams to his lips. Whenever he drank, he felt better, though Juan Lobo, his father, never drank.

"Well, Bonito, I will bless your waking moments, and pray they give you the means to discover the benefits of sleep."

Bonito Lobo felt encouraged. Perhaps tomorrow he would ride to San Sebastian and sleep at long last with Elena Pazote, the livery man's beautiful daughter. He had been in love with her for years. *If the world stopped, so be it*, he thought. He stepped closer to Soledad. "Nothing is . . . what . . . it seems to be," he whispered in his ear. "Watch out."

A short, fat man with a mustache took his time approaching the wagon. Ever since morning, he had been soaking himself in the Elixir of Dreams. Now he was saturated with delusion. He clung to the side of the wagon and gave the padre a crooked leer; most of his teeth were missing. His thick, gray tongue darted in and out like a lizard's.

"Bless me, Padre," he said, "I am Peso Mondragon. Lover. Hunter. Warrior. Former governor of this flea-bitten territory." If he tried hard enough, he could imagine himself sitting in the rough splendor of the Palace of the Governors once again, training pigeons to open his mail. He thrust out his chest importantly. "I am the Custodian of Good Intentions. I tried to teach the curse of religion to schoolchildren when I was governor, but I saw that in New Mexico everyone thinks the same."

Soledad laughed. "Did you succeed in destroying the curse of religion, Peso Mondragon?"

"No, Padre, but I gave them something to think about. When I was governor, I tried to execute all the priests. I put a lock on the church so they could not get in. Or out. I took those little round white wafers and fed them to the birds." He removed his straw hat and bowed his head. "Bless my good intentions to wipe out the Catholic Church."

Soledad leaned forward until he was face to face with this unbalanced man. "I will never bless such heresy, Peso Mondragon! Think of something else." The padre's face was dark with anger. First a dog named Jesus Christ, now this.

"There is nothing else," said Peso Mondragon. "When we poor, starving, half-baked Indians get rid of the religious, the world will be ours again." He shuffled away to his spot under a cottonwood tree where he had left his jug of the Elixir of Dreams. He drank from it thirstily. In no time, he was out among the clouds.

Up the path from the village trudged a fat-bellied man who appeared to be dressed for a costume party. He wore the moldering uniform of a Confederate Civil War general, with stringy epaulets perched on either shoulder and a set of tarnished brass buttons spilling down the front of the double-breasted gray jacket. El Comanche had gotten it for him when he fought on both sides of the Civil War during the Battle of Glorieta Pass. The uniform was too small now, so the man held it together with leather thongs trussed around his middle, like a Thanksgiving turkey. Around his waist hung a long saber that had worn through the end of its scabbard; its point gleamed in the sun like a metal tooth. On his head he wore a long-plumed purple hat, moth-eaten and several sizes too big, left over from the days when the soldiers of the Spanish king had invaded the old home of the Calabazas along the Pecos River. He had come as fast as he could, and now, as he waited his turn to speak to the padre, he wondered what stories he would pass down about the visit of this sad-eyed priest. Would it be long or short? Bloody or clean? Would the Calabazas do to him what they had done to the priest before? His grave was down along the river. Coyotes dug up his bones and ate them. So people said. At night you could hear him screaming just like he did in real life when his scalp was being removed.

Now this man who looked like a refugee from a battlefield presented himself to the priest, holding a boy of about twelve by the hand. "I am Luis Madrone, the unfortunate husband of Catarina, the father of a nitwit, a murderer, a mute, and a vixen," he said. "I am also the Custodian of Stories." He looked around at his fellow villagers. Yes, all the Calabazas had listened to his stories and been changed by them, sometimes for the better. "Bless my imagination, Padre, for it is all that keeps us going in these difficult times." He winked at the priest. His round face was alive with mischief and a confused expression of happiness.

The padre liked Luis Madrone immediately, with his crooked smile and his ragged uniform, the way he cocked his head. "Bless your imagination, Luis," he said. "It is a useful gift."

Then he noticed the egg-headed boy who stood alongside his father, nodding excitedly at everything that was said, staring at the padre's sandaled feet, his large, wooden rosary beads, and the coarse fabric of his cassock. "This is Sotero, my youngest son," said Luis, with love in his voice. "He has never spoken a word, neither in our old mutilated Calabaza language nor gringo English nor the *pendejo* Spanish of the conquistadores. So we made him the Custodian of Silence. Is that not right, my boy?" Sotero Madrone's short-haired head bobbed up and down. "What lies inside this boy's head are unimaginable things," Luis said. "Bless his silence, for he hears the songs of the universe."

The priest examined the boy's earnest face. "Bless your silence, Sotero Madrone. Those who cannot speak shall see God. *Domine, non sum dignus, ut inters, sub tectum meum.*"

At the priest's strange Latin words of the Mass, the mute exploded. His silent laughter, his silent cries, and a curious bleating sound all converged. Sotero shook as if with palsy and threw his head back until it seemed his neck would break.

"Those words you said, he liked them, Padre. You must tell him some more," Luis cried excitedly. On the other side of the wagon, he saw his wife, smiling at Sotero's enthusiasm. His heart leaped to his throat. As frigid as she was, he was still attracted to her beauty. *Someday*, he thought, *I will have her again, and she will not get up for a week*. In his mind he made up a story of his wife as a virgin and how he would take her to some sweet, dark corner of the forest before winter settled in and turn her mind to love. There would be the right amount of protest, of course, as there had been before, but then she would submit to his love, whispered in her ear as ten thousand years of history.

Just then a rifle shot rang out, then another. Thinking El Comanche was on the warpath again, Soledad jumped to his feet and squinted toward the forest.

Luis laughed. "It is only Alvar Talamantes, Padre. He is the Custodian of Madness." As he spoke, a strange apparition—half horse, half buffalo—galloped toward the wagon. Thundering dangerously close to where the padre sat, the creature wheeled, shook its rifle at the sky, then galloped away, a cloud of fine dust obscuring its real identity. At the top of the hill, the dark, ominous figure stopped and turned around. It was a man on horseback, with a moth-eaten head of a buffalo on his head, curved horns sticking out of either side. Having stopped, however, the weight of the buffalo had unbalanced him, and he toppled from his horse with a muffled cry.

Standing nearby, Juan Lobo watched the spectacle, a smile of satisfaction on his face. "Alvar Talamantes wants you to notice him, Padre, and to bless his madness as you have blessed our other virtues," the cacique laughed. He knew from long experience what Alvar was trying to do. What each person, in his or her way, was trying to tell the priest.

Soledad covered his eyes. "Madness is not a virtue, Juan Lobo," the padre heard himself saying, "and I will not bless it." He sat down again, visibly shaken by the galloping apparition, and looked out over the valley.

Some of the people had drifted away to their sagging adobe casitas in the village below. There a few scrawny chickens scratched in the dirt; numerous goats and cows and horses, underfed and scraggly, wandered where they pleased. A sorry-looking milk cow chewed thoughtfully on the corn husks piled at the edge of the field. A small boy took a stick and slammed it over the head of a goat nibbling on a cabbage. What a run-down place it was, slowly sinking back into the earth from whence it came. Yes, the priest understood why the monsignor had sent him to this hopeless place. *He knows I will never come back. I will disappear like all the rest, and he will be rid of me at last. How would they do it? In my sleep? While I am saying Mass? Or something else entirely?* The priest shuddered.

On the hill above, Alvar Talamantes, older brother of the humble, one-legged Juan, shoved the rifle into its scabbard and climbed back into his saddle. The buffalo head was suffocatingly hot; it smelled of buffalo brains, blood, and mothballs bought from a trader. Inside the smelly old head, a part of his ceremonial dance costume, Alvar thought he could hear the voice of the buffalo telling him it wanted to return to the plains. Trotting down the hill again, he let out another bloodcurdling whoop, but Juan Lobo shouted a warning to him in the Calabaza language. Alvar called back in the same tongue: "Fuck you!" he rejoined, or it's Calabaza near-equivalent. "I will ride all night, if necessary, until this foolish priest knows who and what we are!" Finally, heeding the cacique's warning, he rode off into the forest.

"I am sorry, Padre," said Juan Lobo, with an effusive air that did nothing at all to reassure Soledad. The old man had climbed into the wagon next to him. "Sooner or later, you will have to bless Alvar's madness, or he will not stop riding his horse and screaming. At midnight, it can be very disconcerting." Juan Lobo smiled to himself; he had only to maintain this one-sided dialogue a little longer for the priest to understand he was in the wrong place.

"I don't care, Juan Lobo," Father Soledad said stubbornly. "I cannot bless Alvar's madness any more than I can bless Peso

Mondragon's desire to wipe out the Church." He stared at the old man. "You are a Custodian of something also?"

"Of course, Padre," Juan Lobo said, almost reverently. "We all are. These are our best true natures that have, in one way or another, survived. They reinforce our strengths. They allow us to overlook our weaknesses. That is what Custodians have done ever since the beginning of time. So we help them all we can. Madness is no different than silence, let us say, or imagination is as good a thing as war, on the right occasion." He waved his arm toward the hill where Alvar had ridden into the forest. "We judge nothing, therefore we are not judged. In that big book of yours, the Bible, it tells about it. I have not read it, but my wife says it is a good book, full of wonderful stories. Even though we are what you call 'pagans,' we have learned much from it, on the matter of judgment especially."

The look he gave the priest was deep and insistent. From whence had his wisdom come? Soledad was certain Juan Lobo had never gone away to boarding school like many Indians of his time, there to have tradition beaten from his soul. The cacique reminded him of the old Navajo men in Arizona who had made him think twice about the nature of reality. "What is your best true nature, Juan Lobo?" he asked with an uneasy laugh.

"I am the Custodian of Abundance," Juan Lobo said. "This is a special sort of medicine, taught to me by my father and his father before him, on back to the day we emerged from the sacred lake and learned how to survive. Through wars and floods and famines, through every sort of misfortune, through all the years of fighting the Spanish pigs and the Mexican whores and the gringo snakes, we survived because of the wisdom of our ancestors. That is the kind of abundance I mean. So I will ask you to bless these cornstalks, Padre, for in them lie the power that we need."

His face, stoical in its acceptance of things, was turned to the west as if to draw from the healing rays of the sun the sort of strength he needed for the difficult days to come.

What could be the harm?, thought Soledad. *Corn was essential to life, and had been for ten thousand years or more. The people depended on this crop for many things, including the Elixir of Dreams.* The priest looked at the cacique and felt something dark and mysterious happening. He breathed deeply and raised his hand, not certain which part of himself was emerging. "Bless your cornstalks, Juan Lobo. May you come to use them in the service of our Lord."

Then, from out of the forest, Alvar Talamantes made another ferocious assault, this time directly toward the wagon. The horse came at full gallop, with the mad Indian in his buffalo head astride him. Though horse and rider seemed about to collide with the wagon, Juan Lobo stayed perfectly still. But the priest jumped up, shouted, and waved his arms, and at the last moment, the apparition veered off. *What am I to make of these things?*, Soledad wondered. "Very well. I shall bless Alvar's madness, but only because I believe he has no power," he blurted. "He is possessed by the Devil!"

Juan Lobo waved his arm in some sort of signal and shouted something. Alvar Talamantes again disappeared into the trees. The two sat for a moment in companionable silence until Soledad became aware of a muted singing, seeming to come from beneath the wagon.

"What is that singing, Juan Lobo?" Soledad asked.

"It's only the dead Spaniards, Padre," Juan Lobo replied. "Buried here in the cornfield these many centuries. Whenever they are lonely or frightened or tired of being trapped in the earth, they sing the most wonderful alabados from their old morada days. Listen."

Soledad climbed down from the wagon, his heart racing. He put his ear to the ground. Yes, he heard singing—lovely ballads and laments sung in the old language of Cervantes, drifting out of the hard, red earth. "A long time ago, when I was a boy, I heard people talking to me from the grave," he said softly. "They gave me my first real lessons about life. So I believe you, Juan Lobo."

Smiling, the old man slid off the seat to the ground and was gone. Maria Lobo walked slowly up the path from the cornfield, wiping her hands on her dress. Solicitously, Soledad helped her into the wagon. She touched his soiled cassock as if to rub out the stains of the noonday meal he had spilled on it. A tired wisdom poured from her eyes, and an equanimity that he had seen before among Navajo women. Maria Lobo sighed. Deep inside, she felt a new world forming. "I am the wife of Juan Lobo, as you know, the mother of his children, the granddaughter of Elk Old Man, our last great leader, who was killed by Navajos. I remember when animals danced on two legs. I remember when the mountains were white hot and covered with snakes and fig trees. I remember the first time a woman lay with a man and taught him to be gentle with his hands. I remember when Buffalo covered the land and Eagles flew with sweet grass in their mouths. I cannot forget how it was when the Spaniards came to tame us. Or where our innocence went. We had ten thousand years of companionship with stars and wind. All gone. I am the Custodian of Memory, Padre."

There was about her the dark, ripe smell of moist earth and a hint of stewed apples. "For my memory, I select only the best things. Good hunts. Good harvests. A happy, healthy village. Times before the Spaniards came." For many years, Maria Lobo had taught Calabaza girls about their heritage, to prepare them to make the most of a difficult life. "Bless my perception of truth. You will find it very useful sometimes."

The priest frowned. He could not imagine a time when he would need such a gift, but he said, "Bless your perception of truth, then, Maria Lobo. It can do no harm." He squeezed her rough, red hand.

The old woman bit her lip, uncertain how to proceed. "I am old now, and covered with my life. When I die, memory will go with me. All that has happened, all that was said and done, will go with me. Twenty generations from now, an infant will be born with what I have always known and those before me knew."

"Surely other people have memories as well," he said. "Juan Lobo, for instance."

She shook her head. "His memory is of his medicine. El Comanche's is of war. La Luz's is of love. My son, Bonito, his memory is of wasted opportunity. Luis Madrone's memory is of stories he has told, also stories he has invented. Sotero, the mute, his memory is of unborn stars. Each person has a piece here, a piece there of the memory puzzle. That is what is passed on."

"And I?" Soledad said. "What does my memory consist of?"

She looked at him long and hard and took her time answering. "Your memory is your perception of truth," she said at last. "And it is a lie."

His heart beating fast, he bent toward her. "What do you mean, old woman?"

Maria Lobo held up her hand. "When the time comes, you will know. People will try and stop you. But stay on the path of acquiring a truthful memory, Padre. It is all that will save you here." And she climbed stiffly down from the wagon.

Soledad greeted the next woman with astonishment. She was a shriveled old woman with snow-white hair cut with bangs straight across her forehead. Despite the oppressive heat, she was dressed in a long buckskin coat with thousands of chicken feathers fastened to its surface, some of them fluttering off in the wind.

"I am Ana Coyote, Padre," she said in a creaky voice, climbing up next to him so she could see him with her cloudy eyes. She had a little, round face; a high-bridged nose; and small, near-sighted eyes. To him she looked like the scrawny rooster she carried by its neck. "I am Custodian of Oblivion," Ana Coyote said, smiling. Her teeth were chipped and stained. "Married the renegade Balthazar when I was sixteen. He died a hero's death fighting blue coats on the plains." With a disturbing clucking sound, she examined the muscles of the padre's forearm. *A man's strong arms of passion*, she thought, *not unlike those of Balthazar*. Dead for twenty years, and still she missed him. Every night she dreamed they made love in the same passionate way they used to, on and on, until Balthazar rode off and joined the last futile stand of the Lakota against the white man. With a bony, claw-like hand, the woman drew her coat of chicken feathers around her.

"My father was the great chief Croaking Frog, part Calabaza, part everything else. He looked like patchwork, so many tribes written all across his face. My father had no sons, all girls. Eleven.

Each had something to do. Scalping. Making baskets. Sharpening flints. Making arrows. Scouting for the enemy. Tanning hides. Dragging big loads tied to our shoulders like mules. Me and my sisters did it all. Even fight in battles against the Comanche. Kiowa. Navajo. Lakota. He treated us just like boys. 'Learn to do something useful,' he said. So, I took up with chickens. Always have eggs. Feathers. Stew." She shook the squawking rooster aloft. "This foolish bird does only one thing with his life. Rides the hens so they cannot walk. Like my own dear Balthazar. Bless me and my roosters, Padre. I dream of them as fertile warriors."

The blessing was strange, the way all of them were, but the priest obliged. "Bless you and all your roosters, Ana Coyote," he said wearily, making the sign of the cross over her white hair. "May you find in them the answer to your dreams." His words seemed contrived, but he did not know what else to say.

Juan Lobo, who had stood silently near the wagon, heard them and smiled. A small, round-shouldered woman with an unpleasant face was next to confront the priest. Soledad recognized her as one of those who had challenged him from the cornfield. "I am Pilar Mondragon, Padre," she said in a shrill voice. Her green eyes sent shivers down the padre's spine. "Daughter of Ana Coyote, the chicken woman, and Balthazar, the Dancing Fly. I have had two husbands, eleven lovers, and a dog. I am the Custodian of Witchcraft. Bless me and my ability to make the most of spells." Her lips were purple and thin.

"I most certainly will not bless witchcraft, Pilar," the padre said crossly. "A sin against the first commandment! You must replace it with the love of God."

"We have no word for sin. Explain sin to me, Padre."

He detected a certain malice in her voice; he instinctively did not trust this stoop-shouldered woman with a deceitful look. A witch look. Soledad took a deep breath. "Sin means you are not in a state of grace, Pilar. If you should die, you would not go to heaven, but to hell."

Even as he said these words, they sounded hollow, for he was no longer certain he believed in these concepts of his Church; in fact, he wondered if he ever did. *Hell is here and now*, he thought, *just as is heaven*. Pilar's green eyes and light brown hair gave away the fact that she was actually the progeny of a mountain man who had spent the winter when Balthazar had left to join the Taos Revolt in 1847.

"We do not believe in heaven or hell," she said. "We believe that God is in everything, even that caterpillar you are sitting on."

Carefully he felt under his cassock and found a crushed caterpillar. "I will bless you, Pilar Mondragon," he said, wiping his hands on his cassock. "And that is all I will do." He had had too long a day, and for several hours he had permitted himself to bless chickens and ammunition and cornstalks, and now he was asked to bless witchcraft, too. *What is happening to me?*, he wondered. *Am I too exhausted to think straight?* He closed his eyes. When he opened them again, a thin, nervous man stood before him, hands clasped in supplication. His shoulders sloped, his mouth turned down, his ears projected, and the edges of his eyes ran off into his cheekbones. He was nondescript, seemingly without character or grace, yet there was something wistful about him. When he spoke, his voice was the merest whisper.

"I am Narciso Ortega, Padre. A woodcutter who life passed by. Once I was happy. Then something happened and I could not be happy anymore."

Soledad noticed that Narciso was about his own age, that he wore a mustache, and that a long, diagonal scar ran down his cheek.

"I am the Custodian of Amends," he said.

The priest, observing the suffering in this man, lightly rested his hand on the other's, which was covered with the scars the axe and crosscut had left over the years. "What happened to you, Narciso?"

The shy, sad woodcutter drew away. He could not say what had happened to him. He could only tell the padre what kept him alive. "I have my niece Papita to take care of. A little dwarf with a mind like a child. She plays and sings and scampers about all day long while I am in the forest cutting wood. Bless my sorrow, Padre. May it return my poor, dead sweetheart to me."

Soledad shifted uncomfortably on the hard, wooden seat. He saw no harm in blessing sorrow, after so many improbable things. "Bless your sorrow, Narciso," he said. "But nothing will return your sweetheart to you if she is dead. She is in heaven now, with God."

"Not in heaven," Narciso said stubbornly, his voice rising. "Away for a while. Do you not see?" He turned and walked away to look for Papita the Dwarf, who had been chasing butterflies along the edge of the field. The strain of revealing his troubles to the priest had brought the ringing in his ears to a painful crescendo.

Soledad was exhausted. "No more blessings today, Juan Lobo," he called to the old man. "And I don't want to meet any more Custodians, either."

As if he had been expecting these words, Juan Lobo brought the horses from the shade and hitched them up. With the agility of a panther, he sprang into the wagon and picked up the reins. "You are also a Custodian, Padre, whether you like it or not. You are the Custodian of Poor Excuses. That red mark on your face proves it."

Soledad rubbed his cheek. "Why?" he asked. "It is only a birthmark."

"You have it because you have never accepted life," Juan Lobo said. "You are not a priest. You are a badger trying to dig a hole so you can hide. Like the badger, you will wear that slash on your cheek until you come out into the sunshine and accept your life."

"When will that be?" the priest asked.

"When you die," the old man said.

The seat of the buckboard was suddenly a plank of pain. The priest hung on as they bounced along the narrow road through the trees. Abruptly, the old man stopped and pointed toward the sky. "Look up there in the clouds, Padre. Do you see those horses running toward the east? Look, one is brown. The other black. Between them is a paint."

Soledad squinted. "The sky is perfectly empty. I see nothing."

The old man sighed. "That is because you are used to seeing only one way. Who sees a thing deeper than the spirits see? Within us Indians is the vision of all things. Trees. Rocks. Sky. Ancestors.

Animals and birds. Also, other times when we have lived, way back before there were humans. We were animals then."

Soledad nodded. When in the Arizona desert, he had begun to understand these concepts, and he had been touched by them. "I have been sent here as your friend, Juan Lobo. Not as a priest, but as a man who sees your difficulties and wants to help you."

"Then leave us now, Padre, before it is too late."

"What's happening, Juan Lobo? People are very nervous and afraid."

"They think you are here to cause trouble, Padre. You want to change us into something we do not want to become. That is why my people act the way they do." His voice was filled with the inherited suspicion of his ancestors whose spirits even now drifted among them, urging vigilance. All his life, Juan Lobo had believed in the old ways, not the new order that had descended upon the Calabazas. Their time was passing into history, but Juan Lobo was unwilling to accept it. He had made the long walk from the old pueblo with his family when he was still a young man. He had seen more change in the last seventy-five years than most people might see in two hundred. The future was unimaginable, with the sorts of machines he'd seen or heard about during his trip to Washington. There was a machine that ran along the road without a horse to pull it. A machine that talked. A machine that played music. A machine that made light. A machine that took pictures. His legacy was to keep the shards of the old ways intact. In a little while, he would be gone. What of importance would he leave behind?

"We do not care about the Catholic Church," he sighed. "We have other things on our minds." He glanced at the sun, which was in a different place now than it was the day before.

"What things?"

The old cacique shook his finger. "You ask too many questions, Badger Man," he said irritably. The sun's journey amazed him. Why did it not get tired and fall from the sky? The elders said it was because the stars kept it there.

Changing the subject, the priest asked, "Have you provided a house for me, Juan Lobo?" A house of his own was what he needed, a simple place where he could have his books and play his violin. *If I tried*, he thought, *I could live very well in this poverty, offering grace to the people.* The idea gave him some comfort. *My sins would be forgiven. I would no longer see my mother's face. Those women I wronged would forgive me.*

"We have little room for you, Padre," Juan Lobo replied. "We are full, like an inn in Santa Fe during fiesta."

Soledad squinted downhill. At the bottom was the village, glowing with the warmth of the late afternoon sun. "But there are all those houses down there, Juan Lobo. Surely one of them—" he began.

"Yes, there are many empty houses. Spirits live there."

"Spirits?"

"We count them among our number, for they are part of us forever. Grandmothers and grandfathers from way back. They are like children, they will not go away." He gave a short laugh. "That is why we appear to be many when actually we are few." After a moment, the old man relented. "However, I will see to it that Maria finds a house for you."

The wagon clattered along the rutted road until Juan Lobo reined to a halt at the edge of a hay field. When he turned around, his face was taut. "Do you like games, Padre?"

The priest sensed some kind of trap. "Yes, some games I like. Chess and bridge and backgammon. When I was in Arizona, an English doctor taught me cribbage."

"This is a different sort of game. Only you and I play, and the stakes are very high." Juan Lobo gazed steadily at the padre. When he spoke again, his voice was the merest whisper. "I mean your life."

"What?" said Soledad dazedly. "I come with love in my heart, nothing more. I am a priest, Juan Lobo. A humble man of God." He started to get out of the wagon, but Juan Lobo stopped him. His hands were amazingly strong, his gaze as cold as ice. *What is happening to me?*, the priest thought in alarm. *I am not myself up here*. Anxiously, he looked toward the sky. Great swirls of clouds exploded above the highest peaks. "Very well, Juan Lobo, what is this so-called game?"

"It consists of a wager, Padre. I believe that our religion is so strong that you cannot convert one person among us, no matter how hard you try. You believe you can. If you fail to convert one person in a given length of time, we will kill you for wasting our time." The old man stared ahead at a porcupine shambling across the road. He called to the creature in the Calabaza language, and it turned back the way it had come, into the chokecherry bushes.

The priest swallowed. His throat felt dry. "I am not here to convert anyone, only to make a bridge between your way and mine."

The old man laughed shortly. "The religious always try to convert." He paused and then continued. "You do not understand our way any more than those who came before. You never will."

"I understand. Better than you think. I once lived among the Navajo. I know they are a different people, but they taught me many things about the Indian way, so much so that I began to doubt my own faith."

For a long time, Juan Lobo said nothing. He watched the golden light play off the highest peaks. He watched an eagle soaring on the wind. So extraordinary was the look in his eyes that it seemed he could see what was happening on the other side of the mountains. He could see backward into time when the conquistadores came riding up the river, pretending to be friends. "Listen to what speaks to you, then. Why are you a priest?"

Soledad hesitated. "Long ago, certain things happened. Becoming a priest was a way of accepting guilt and of trying to help those in need. It hasn't always worked, though from time to time—"

"You are a selfish man," Juan Lobo interrupted, "filled with self-importance. You believe you are here to help us, but you are really here to further yourself."

"Your people matter to me," Soledad insisted, looking around.

"Nothing matters to you," the old man replied firmly. "Prove it to yourself."

"How should I do that, Juan Lobo?" Soledad asked, looking around with a sense of foreboding. In the late afternoon light, the wilderness was beautiful and hushed. It was also frightening, for Soledad knew he was many miles from help of any kind. Overhead, the eagle still circled. Soledad strained his eyes and craned his neck to see the majestic bird. "An eagle means freedom," the priest said in awe. "See how he flies, with such grace and power."

The old man sat perfectly still; his face like a rock. "No," he said. "The eagle does not mean freedom at all. When the day comes that you understand the meaning of the eagle, maybe you can help my people."

The old man emitted a piercing call—once, twice, three times. The eagle wheeled from its northerly path, circled over them, lower and lower, until it fixed Soledad in its unearthly gaze. Its head was golden; its dark bronze wings cast a shadow as wide as the wagon. A whoosh of air from its wings blew across Soledad's face. He knew the eagle was a sign, just as Juan Lobo's ability to turn the porcupine around had been. He shuddered at the implications of such power.

Soledad pulled his cassock around him. The air had turned colder, as it did every evening at nine thousand feet. "Tell me one thing, Juan Lobo, with respect to this wager, would you accept baptism as a sign of conversion?"

"In the old days, when we were all brothers along the river, that is what happened. A religious came and poured water over our heads. 'Now you are Catholics,' he said. Well, people liked the feel of water running down their backs. It was a hot summer. They thought baptism was a bath. They did not think that because of this water, they were better than they were before. Cleansed of what you call sin." The old man laughed. "In the first place, we do not believe in sin. In the second place, we believe water is for washing away dirt and feeding our crops. How is your belief in baptism different from my telling you the eagles are the spirits of our ancestors helping us stay on the true path?"

Soledad persisted, in spite of the logic of the old man's argument. "Revealed truth is not the same as superstition," he said.

"What makes it different?"

"One comes from God, the other from myth, arising out of fear."

Juan Lobo shook his head. "Your God lives in a church, like the one we burned down," he said. "While ours lives up there in those eagles, those clouds. Or that porcupine back there. It is a matter of conviction. Do you see that?"

"Yes, Juan Lobo, but it is also a matter of the task I have been sent to do."

"Yours is not a proper task, Padre. We told the last priest that."

Soledad stared deeply into the old man's eyes. In the last light of day, he saw huge wings reflected there. "Before you killed him?" he asked fearfully.

"Before we killed him," Juan Lobo replied and snapped the reins. As they rattled toward the village, Soledad reflected on the fate of Father Montez, believed to have perished in an avalanche. Or so the Calabazas had said when they presented his cross, his tattered cassock, and his shredded sandals to the monsignor, who had come to investigate why Father Montez had made no reports for more than a year. "What did you do to Father Montez?" he whispered.

The old man shook his head. "Someday, perhaps you will know." Juan Lobo braced his moccasined feet against the motion of the wagon and turned toward the priest, who saw in his face a ruthless passion. "Very well, Padre, here is the game. We will give you until the Snow Falling Moon to prove your religion is the true religion. We will wait for a sign. If there is no sign, then we will know that you are no different from the priest before you, or the one before him, on and on, back to the ones who made slaves of us. If you lose, you must submit to our method of death. If, on the other hand, you are able to make one person among us believe your ways, you will have won the game. We will all become Catholic at long last, for our world will be truly over. Do you accept or not?"

The priest was sweating in spite of the chill air. Why should he be afraid to die? His sins would at last be forgiven. He could not win against this old man's persistence nor was he a match for his power. "All these terrible things happened a long time ago. Why do you speak of them now?"

The old man gave him a deep and accusatory look. "Nothing is long ago," he said. "Two thousand years ago was yesterday. Time goes round and round. What happened before is the same as what happens today. Nothing changes. Everything changes."

"So this is why there are Custodians," the padre said slowly. "As a way of preserving the old ways. El Comanche believes he can turn back time by killing locomotives."

The cacique shook his head. "El Comanche does not want to turn back time. He believes he still lives in another century. He waits for time to come back to him."

The padre laughed. "And Peso Mondragon? He wants to kill me for things that happened two hundred years ago."

Juan Lobo was patient with the priest. "You must understand our ways," he said. "Peso remembers certain things in his heart, put there by the elders when he was a boy. So he believes it is still possible to win a battle we lost long ago. When he was governor, he wanted to set things right by killing all the padres, just like two hundred years ago when we killed those Spaniards." The old man chuckled, enjoying himself. "Time is round like the moon."

Soledad had to laugh, too, in spite of himself. "How did this murderous Indian, who can neither read nor write, become governor of the territory, Juan Lobo?"

"It happened this way, Padre. You see, another Peso Mondragon, a Mexican, was appointed territorial governor, and our Peso Mondragon heard about it when he was in Santa Fe, selling the Elixir of Dreams. So he had a good bit to drink, dressed in the clothes of a Mexican, then presented himself and said he was the new governor. The other Peso Mondragon, who lived in a remote village, had died. In those days, it took even longer than it does now for word to get around. So, Peso Mondragon, the Indian, was our governor for a while. He was going to give us back all our land!" The old man laughed. "And execute those who did not believe like us."

Soledad gripped the wagon seat as they bumped down the hill, and wished he were somewhere far away from this strange asylum in the mountains. "I'm sorry," he said. "I wish I could undo the past. But remember, the Bible teaches that what happened to you, happened also to Christ, who died to save the sinners of the world."

"No one saved us," the old man said crossly. "We have always been on our own."

"What do you expect me to do?" Soledad retorted.

The old man did not answer for a long time. "I expect you to accept our ways."

"Will you accept the word of Jesus Christ then, Juan Lobo?"

"It depends," the old man said, "on what Jesus Christ is. People say it's an eagle saving a rabbit from the fox. Others say it's Juan Talamantes's mongrel. You hear him calling, 'Jesus Christ! Jesus Christ!' And the dog comes." He laughed, but the priest thought it was blasphemous. "He is going to have to think of another name," he said.

"That is the dog's name," the old man insisted.

Soledad pressed his back against the seat as the wagon lurched into the plaza. By now, it was almost dark. Shadowy figures, wrapped in blankets from head to toe, moved silently past, watching this intruding priest. He wondered where he would sleep and eat.

As the wagon pulled to a stop before a darkened casita, the priest accepted Juan Lobo's challenge. "Very well. I will play your game, Juan Lobo," he said, slowly. In the back of his mind he saw Henrietta, lying dead; Felix Villanueva, grimly telling him to leave; the monsignor, coldly ordering his exile. But, in a nearer time, he saw the faces of the day: sweet Maria Lobo, hateful Pilar, shy Narciso Ortega, innocent Sotero Madrone. And the supple body of La Luz, with her shirtwaist undone.

FIFTEEN

AFTERWARD, SOLEDAD WOULD ask himself why he did not leave Camposanto the first day, after the Calabazas had tried their best to frighten him. The course of his life had changed the moment he confronted them in the cornfield, yet he was powerless to walk away. True, there was the matter of the monsignor's deliberate attempt to seal his fate. But there was, beneath the Calabazas' antics, also an ingratiating candor. He had the feeling that the wilderness had forged a fierce resistance in them that he could not break down. He had studied the map he'd brought with him: their lands stretched twenty miles north to south and ten miles east to west; within that vastness lived only this small tribe of inbred natives. And he had seen that there were encroachments within the federal boundaries: logging, mining, and frontier ranches where families ran sheep or cattle.

With a purposeful air, the priest set about cleaning out the little adobe house that Luis Madrone had given him. One room with a flat roof and a window to the south, where the sun streamed in and fell on his hard, narrow bed, which was covered with a ragged quilt. He had a few cracked dishes, one pot, two cups, a hook for his clothes, and odds and ends of dilapidated furniture. From his porch, he observed a few bony cattle and horses grazing in a yellow pasture; beyond the forest were the dark green mountains where— he had heard—grizzlies still lived. Deer, he knew, often came down from the forest and wandered through the village. The men did not kill these deer no matter how hungry they were; tradition dictated that the hunt be fair, their skills pitted against the cunning of the animal. When the deer stood uncertainly in the plaza, the people came out and greeted them.

Once he was settled, Maria Lobo brought him jerked meat, flour, sugar, coffee, and a prune pie sprinkled with granulated sugar on top. Catarina Madrone arrived with fresh bread, a can of lard, a sack of beans, another of apples, and a jug of the Elixir of Dreams. Even Pilar had left a crock of bumblebee paste on his steps, which she said cured warts. Ana Coyote presented him with a live chicken; she wrung its neck while he watched, and handed it to him to pluck. The priest whitewashed the walls, scrubbed the floor, and repaired the portal railing, and now he felt the place was his. But twenty times a day he looked out the window at the house where La Luz lived with her in-laws, hoping for a glimpse of her. When she came out, it was to chase the goat or to call one of the children—never to see him—though he waited for her to come. One morning, before he was out of bed, she trotted past on her pony and tossed a loaf of fresh bread on his porch. LA LUZ. With his finger, he drew her name in the dust of his table, over and over, until had used up all the spaces. He did not erase her name, but ate his food on top of it until the letters disappeared. *I will not make my feelings known*, he said to himself. She cast pleading glances in his direction. He could not meet her eyes.

Everything has two meanings, Soledad thought as he ate a chunk of bread and drank his bitter coffee. *This is what I'm learning here.* He had been in Camposanto less than a week, watching the people begin to prepare for upcoming winter. The women were drying fruit and wild vegetables, as well as strips of venison, on racks high above the ground. Some of them were tanning hides; others were making leggings to protect against the winter's cold. The men were putting up hay and hunting deer and elk in the mountains. Every day he heard the sound of their rifles, though Juan Lobo preferred to hunt the old way, with his bow and arrows.

One sunny day, La Luz knocked on the door. Soledad caught

his breath at the sight of her in a hand-me-down dress of blue muslin with a lace collar, her long hair loosened down her back, her face freshly scrubbed. She had brought him a pillow that Catarina had made, stuffed with lumpy sheep's wool. "Thank you," he said, his hand brushing hers as he accepted the pillow. His heart skipped a beat. She smelled faintly of pine and wet earth.

She stood back, appraising him. The padre was not a virgin; she could tell by his mouth, his eyes, the way he stood with his legs apart when he talked to her. But he was afraid of her, too. "You need more sunshine," she said huskily. "You are too pale." She stood on her tiptoes and touched his comet, hoping perhaps to see it move.

The priest grabbed her hand. "Don't do that," he said. She ran from his house, and he watched her go, admiring her fine, bare legs and her strong but narrow shoulders and the way her hair blew out behind her in the wind. He shook his head slowly. "God help me," he said.

Every day Soledad went up to the cornfield where he had impaled his cross in the dirt, and every day he stooped over it, but could not bring himself to touch it. A week had passed with nothing but the distant roll of thunder and a few hopeful drops that splattered on the hard, dry ground. "Will it rain again?" he asked Juan Lobo anxiously.

"When it decides to rain, it will rain," the old man said gruffly. "The Rain Spirit hears. Jesus does not hear. Jesus is as deaf as a stone." He was busy gathering corn husks from which he would make a sacred doll to use in the kiva. His eyes fell to where the priest had abandoned this great symbol of his Roman Catholic faith. The cross was covered with mud. The old man smiled. In just one week, the priest had made five mistakes. The cacique had marked them, one by one, on his kitchen wall.

One night at the beginning of the second week, as Soledad lay awake thinking about the rich purple-black color of La Luz's hair, a staccato of rain hit the roof. He sat bolt upright, then sprang from bed and threw on his clothes. A downpour! He ran outside, turning his face upward to feel the cold, stinging drops on his skin. He splashed through puddles, noticing Juan Lobo on his porch, his arms outstretched to the evening sky, pewter gray and heavy with rain. He dashed toward him. It was a downpour at long last. The priest smiled.

"Just because you think you made it rain does not mean you have power outside your Church," the old man said solemnly. "We had our own offering for rain and danced all night in the kiva."

The dripping wet priest looked at him incredulously. The cacique seemed taller than he had the day before, with a resistance to old age evident in the vitality of his hard, sinewy body and the deep, inward look in his eyes. Then it dawned on him. The Rain Spirit had heeded Juan Lobo's prayers, not his. *I have broken the first commandment,* he thought miserably.

Soledad, his face hot with shame, went up the two sagging board steps and felt the magnetism of this man surrounding him. "I feel nothing except the loyalty of these people to you, old man," he said quietly. "It is you who made it rain. I foolishly left my cross in the ground, as if it were medicine as strong as yours. That is blasphemy, Juan Lobo. What I did is forbidden, and I apologize."

The old man said nothing. He walked inside. Soledad followed, dripping water over the worn linoleum floor. Juan Lobo reached inside his blanket and handed the cross to the priest.

Soledad gasped. The beams of the cross had mysteriously cracked. "Lightning," the cacique said tersely. Soledad gripped the holy object. "Forgive me," he said. "I am a deceitful man." A pain commenced in his belly; his head began to swim.

Juan Lobo's look was long and dark. He shook his head. "You must be careful, Padre," he warned. "These mountains make men do strange and terrible things."

"I am beginning to understand that," he said, falling into a chair in Maria Lobo's kitchen. She was still asleep, but a fire blazed in the stove. "Perhaps I should leave."

The cacique shoved a cup of hot coffee in front of the priest, then he gripped his wrist. "Do you want to be a coward all your life?" he demanded. "Well, then, you may not leave. We have a wager. Even though I will win, you agreed to play the game."

In the morning, Soledad, sneezing and coughing, put on his workman's clothes and donned the high boots he had worn in the desert to protect himself against rattlesnakes. The day before, he had shoveled some of the rubble out of the church, broken and burned by the Calabazas during their last frenzy thirty years before. The labor had exhausted him, and now his hands were cut and blistered; his back felt broken. No one had volunteered to help him.

On this morning after the storm, he faced the strangely tilted cross that stood in the plaza. What made it go this way? He had tried repeatedly to shove it upright, only to have it tilt back to its old position. He knew the whole village was watching him as he tried once again to push the cross into place. He took a deep breath and put his shoulder to the heavy beam.

Luis Madrone leaned over the adobe wall and shook his head. "For many years the cross has gone the way it wants, Padre. You cannot change its mind. The cross is very stubborn." The look the Custodian of Stories gave him was one of scorn. "This cross is made from a fat branch of El Abuelo. It is an Indian tree. Very old."

"Help me," the priest implored, tiring from his effort. Luis shook his head.

"Not I, Padre. The tree is what it wants to be. Crooked yet strong. It will not fall down. I remember the last man who was crucified there. Quite a sight."

Stopping to catch his breath, the priest glanced at the wall. He gasped. A bone stuck out of the unplastered adobe. A human bone. Belonging to the foot, complete with ankle and toes. The wall was studded with gray-white bones! Why had he not seen them before? These strange human relics seemed to reproach him as he stepped closer and tried to dig them out with his fingernails. He saw them retract into the mud wall, as if they were alive.

Soledad took a few steps backward. "What on earth?" he stammered.

Luis merely shrugged and affectionately patted the bones.

"These are the feet of our ancestors. A long time ago, when the Spanish came to our old village, they tried to make the men work. Digging for gold. Building the church. Growing crops to feed the Spaniards and their families. After a while, the people got sick of working so hard. Their own families were starving. So, they ran away to the mountains. The soldiers rode after them and brought them back. They lined them up in the plaza and cut off their left feet, so they would never run away again. When the ancestors were mixing mud for the church, they took these bones and stirred them in, to leave something of themselves in the walls. When we left our old village, the cacique ordered us to tear down the wall and bring the bones along. When this church was built, the feet were buried in the wall. Leave them where they are. This is what we pay our respects to. Not your Catholic objects, but the feet of our ancestors!"

Soledad felt dizzy. He thought he heard the sun buzzing in his ears. "We must tear this wall down and build a new one," he said. "We'll bury the feet in the cemetery."

Luis frowned and shook his head. "We cannot do anything with these feet, Padre. They are our good luck charms. Through sickness, health, hunger, and plenty, we always remember them. Feet give us mobility. Attached to our legs or buried in this wall. They must stay where they are." He sighed. "When the day comes for us to leave Camposanto, we will carry the feet of our ancestors along. They will point the way."

Scarcely knowing what he was doing, Soledad raised his right hand and blessed the feet of the Calabaza ancestors, using the Latin words; later, he blessed them again with holy water while Juan Lobo watched and thought the padre had lost the wager. "And he does not even know why," the cacique said to himself.

"You cannot come in, Padre!" Catarina Madrone yelled when he knocked on her door, intending to speak to her about the infestation of mice in his house. "Luis is busy composing a story. La Luz is taking a bath. And I, the Custodian of Lesser Causes, am leaving to spend the day shaking piñon nuts from the trees."

As he went down the stone-lined path, the padre glanced over his shoulder. La Luz came out and stood on the porch, her back to the sun. She was dripping wet, a thin cotton blanket wrapped around her sleek, brown body. The priest caught his breath. Slowly she turned around, saw him, and threw back her head and laughed. Then she dropped the blanket and stood there, stark naked. Her breasts were full and magnificent.

"No," the padre said softly, covering his eyes with his hands. "Do not tempt me, La Luz." But she had already tempted him, again and again, in the weeks he'd been there. She was the last thing he thought about before he went to sleep, the first thing he remembered when he woke up. He didn't mean to, of course, but he often followed her to the river while she was washing clothes. Or gathering wild mushrooms and berries and nuts. Or stretching an elk hide over a frame of poles. His desire never went away, not even when he slept. When he heard her throaty laughter, goose bumps popped out on his arms. When she came to the door with a dish of chile, he could say nothing. His tongue was tied. "Everything is part of God," he whispered now, "including you." But by then she had gone back inside, her rich, dark mane of hair streaming down her back.

How beautiful she was! How she drove him to lewd ideas when he lay in his bed trying to sleep. *Lucifer is inside me*, he thought as he felt his stomach contract. His soul was an arena where the two enemies of spirit and flesh had met and collided. Yet there was no victory, only incessant torment. He was afraid to confront her, and when he saw her coming, he sometimes turned away. *I do not trust myself*, he thought. He drank the Elixir of Dreams to soothe his ragged nerves; it gave him a headache.

One morning, walking across the plaza, the priest saw the mute boy grinning at him from inside Luis's tool shed. "Ah, Sotero," Soledad said as he stopped to examine the carving of a bobcat the boy shyly held out to him. "It's very good. *Dominus vobiscum.*"

Sotero flung his head from side to side. The words seemed to touch a nerve.

"What wisdom lies inside your head, my boy?" Soledad asked kindly. "If only you could speak, what would you tell us about the world?" He bent lower. "Never confuse women with happiness," he said impulsively. "They are deceitful creatures put on earth to tempt men. To make men do things they would otherwise never dream of doing."

Excitedly, Sotero nodded his head.

"I have known a great many women, even though I'm a priest. But this woman who is married to your brother," he pointed to La Luz's house, "she is wicked. And I believe I am in love with her, which is what makes my heart ache, Sotero. *Varium et mutabile semper femina.*" Woman is ever a fickle and changeable thing.

At the sound of the Latin words, Sotero Madrone, the lifelong Custodian of Silence, began to bleat like a sheep. The sound had a strange, unearthly quality to it. Soledad, overcome with emotion, hugged the boy to him. "You must learn to speak," he said, "for without the power of speech, you will never leave this utterly mad, corrupt village. I shall pray to God for a miracle. I want you to utter one word I can understand. And then, yes, I will give you this gold cross, with its poor, sad, cracked beams. See how it shines."

He let Sotero touch the cross and saw him insert his fingernail in the lengthwise crack. Then Soledad crossed himself and hurried away. His mind on Sotero, he went to El Comanche's house, where the old man was cleaning his Springfield in his front yard. "God is a bullet," the warrior said pleasantly. Soledad hesitated. The warrior was so old he looked as if he'd been propagated from El Abuelo. His forehead was deeply ridged and dense as bark, his fingers like curled roots, and his skin appeared to have been baked in the sun for the whole long tenure of the earth itself. Soledad's dark eyes fastened on the old man's strong and nimble fingers. "What if God were also a spirit who lived inside you, El Comanche?"

The warrior stopped what he was doing and turned his face to the sky. "God is this Springfield, Padre. It can work miracles, just like that God of yours." He pointed to the cracked cross that Soledad now believed had lost its effectiveness.

The priest shook his head. "God creates, El Comanche; He does not destroy."

The old warrior rubbed his eyes. Out of the encyclopedias of his memory rose the outlines of the bloody battlefields of his life. He had tried hard to turn back the hand of history to the Stone Age, without success. "Listen to me, Padre. If you know what is good for you, you will leave now. A big war is coming, right here. Soon there will be soldiers on every ridge. Soldiers behind every tree. But I will kill them all! Every single one!" He loaded his rifle and aimed it at a tin can on top of a stick inserted in the ground a hundred yards away.

To Soledad's astonishment, the old man hit his target. *What a shot*, he marveled, his ears ringing. Even his old cowboy friends in Texas could not have done it.

The Custodian of War hobbled toward his house, the rifle slung across his shoulders. "Death to the locomotives!" he cried, waving his gnarled old fist in the air. "No one can kill me! Not the stupid gringos! Not the *federales*! I will live forever!"

Soledad was unaware that earlier that summer, Juan Lobo had led a hunting party to Black Lake, deep in the mountains on sacred land, theirs forever—or so they thought. There they found squatters building log homes in a clearing. When El Comanche shot an elk, the squatters opened fire on the Calabazas. The old warrior shot back, and two settlers fell to the ground, dead. The hunting party fled into the trees, leaving the carcass of the elk behind. El Comanche wanted to go back and kill all the homesteaders, but Juan Lobo stopped him. "Killing won't solve anything," he said. But the old warrior had closed his ears to reason long before.

Now, during the sweltering heat of July, the bureaucrats were meeting in their dingy little offices in Santa Fe, going over the complaints of the Black Lake homesteaders, who wanted the Indians jailed. The bodies of the two men had been carried to town in gunnysacks for the officials to inspect. As for finding the guilty Indians, they hadn't known where to begin. The area was vast, used as hunting grounds by a number of tribes. Yet these bureaucrats were paid to protect peaceful homesteaders, so they called out the militia to comb the hills.

Two Picuris and an Apache were taken into custody, then released. Excitedly, Bonito Lobo came back from a visit to San Sebastian to announce that there was a big reward for the killer of the Black Lake settlers. One hundred dollars. The village was apprehensive: El Comanche had gone too far this time, first killing the two homesteaders with two shots from his Remington, then attacking the locomotive and wounding the conductor. They begged him to hide deep in the mountains for the winter, but El Comanche only roared, "When the sun comes up in the west, when the moon falls out of the sky, when the stupid gringos get smart, then El Comanche will hide!"

Juan Lobo consulted the Raven flapping above his house, issuing its brittle one-note call. *What we need*, the cacique decided, *is to take our minds off things*. The Raven agreed.

That evening, Soledad sat on his porch drinking the Elixir of Dreams and watching the stars appear in the sky that had held them captive all day long. There was the Hunter. The Dog Star. The summer night was beautiful and not too cold. He inhaled the rich perfume of burning piñon and juniper. Around the village, the houses glowed with a warm, golden light. A couple of dogs barked, and off in the distance, he heard coyotes. The sheer, mystical beauty of the night calmed his soul. Only this morning he had said his first Mass amidst the ruins of the old church, and half a dozen people showed up. Perhaps he was not a hypocrite, as Juan Lobo seemed to believe. "Deo gratias," he said, rising to refill his cup. He had not eaten all day and was feeling pleasantly drunk.

Returning to his porch, he noticed several men wrapped in blankets that covered their heads, slipping from their houses and hurrying across the plaza. He heard them shout greetings to one another in the Calabaza tongue; they stopped and looked up at the stars. One man sang a short, shrill song. More men came from the other direction. Then still more. He stood up and squinted into the night. "Is that you, Luis? Is that you, Juan Lobo? Bonito? Hello!" The men fell silent and hurried to their destinations.

Something strange is going on, he thought. More blanketed

figures appeared. Soledad called after them, but they too hurried away without answering. He wondered if they were planning to kill him tonight, before he had been here a month. He wrapped himself in a blanket and stretched out on the sagging boards. He wanted to miss nothing, but drunk on the lethal beverage Juan Lobo had forced on him, he fell asleep under the stars with the lullabies of the Spaniards drifting down from the cornfield.

He dreamed of the persistent foot bones of the Calabazas' ancestors and the crooked cross, which rose like a dagger to stab him. Henrietta's accusatory face swirled out of the clouds, her mouth wide open. "I will never let you rest," she said. Lorenzo Soledad cried out in his sleep, "Don't you know I loved you too much to let you live like that! Do you know what they called you in school?"

In the darkest part of the night, Pilar Mondragon stood over him, listening to his deep, heavy snoring. She bent down and inserted something in his ear. "There. Now you will hear nothing but lies from now on." Pilar Mondragon stood up and turned her face to the moon. Her hands were covered with ashes; her body was smeared with blood, according to the rituals of the clan of witches to which she belonged. She hurried back to her house, but as she passed a certain ponderosa tree that was as big around as two men, she became a large, yellow dog with fangs, and cried at the door of her home. When Peso Mondragon saw the dog, he let it in, knowing it was his wife. His short tenure as territorial governor had prepared him to accept most anything.

Before dawn, the men returned home; they seemed to float across the chill, still plaza, anxious to beat the sunrise. From his porch, Soledad rubbed his eyes and watched. The figures were covered with their blankets. Whatever was happening, he wanted to know what it was. "Why did the men go out last night and come back this morning?" the padre asked Juan Lobo, who was working behind his house scraping the hide of an elk.

There were some things that Juan Lobo did not care to talk about, and this was one of them. "We have our customs," he said tersely, as the flint knife moved expertly over the hide, which had been soaking for three days in elk brains. "You have yours." He stopped his work and gazed at the priest. "If you try to learn too much, you may not live long enough to understand it." He gave him a cunning look. "Father Montez wanted to live, but it was his time."

Crestfallen, Soledad felt a strange ringing in his head, brought about by the tiny fetish that Pilar Mondragon had shoved in his ear. He felt nauseated, and all day long, he again ate nothing. But he continued to drink the Elixir of Dreams that stung his lips and coated his intestines. Feeling quite ill, the priest again sat outside that night and watched the men hurrying back and forth. *What is happening?*, he wondered, but he did not move from his porch until much later, when he decided to take a walk along the river. He saw dark shapes moving from house to house, heard low voices and laughter. "Who's there?" he cried.

"We are stealing a nighttime of happiness," Alvar said. "Do not interfere, Padre, or we will kill you."

The wonderful old custom of Getting Together had been revived among the Calabazas by popular demand. For centuries, their ancestors had observed this enjoyable custom, an antidote to loneliness and melancholy; it dispelled evil spirits and imparted warmth and good will to young and old. In troubled times, it saved them. Thus, as darkness fell, Juan Lobo entered Luis Madrone's house and disappeared into a room with La Luz. Shortly thereafter, Bonito Lobo arrived and, with a suggestive laugh, pushed aside the curtains to Catarina's room. No sooner was Catarina secure in Bonito's arms then Luis Madrone left the house and made his way across the plaza to the home of his mother, Coba Madrone, who waited eagerly to hear his stories the way she always did. Tenderly, Luis held the sick old woman in his arms and told her how the world was made from a kernel of Corn and how Birds were born from Stones and how Deer dropped out of the leaves of Cottonwood Trees. Coba Madrone spent the night listening to her son speak of wonderful, impossible things. When the sun came up, she fell asleep, dreaming of her girlhood, when she had swum in a turquoise sea, accompanied by Dolphins and Frigate Birds.

Juan Talamantes limped across the plaza and entered the house where Maria Lobo awaited him anxiously, as she always did on nights of Getting Together. She liked this troubled man, despite what he'd done to her youngest and most beautiful daughter, Florita. She still missed Florita, though she'd been dead for twenty years, yet she felt connected to her through Juan Talamantes's melancholy. They sat at the kitchen table where Maria served raisin pie and hot coffee and spoke to him of Florita's beauty and the children she might have had. After a while, wiping her eyes, Maria Lobo led him to the bed she'd shared with Juan Lobo for sixty years. Though the old woman remained dressed except for her shawl and moccasins, Juan Talamantes took off everything except a pair of ragged underdrawers. He unbuckled his wooden leg, tossed it in a corner, and buried his face in Mario Lobo's shoulder. "Dear Tía," he said, "I am in love with Ermina Madrone. But she does not love me."

Maria stared at the ceiling, with its thick beams cut from ponderosa trees. "You worry too much. Ermina Madrone is young and spoiled. She knows nothing about real life."

Juan Talamantes had a firm, lean body. The old woman ran her fingers lightly over it, remembering when Juan Lobo had looked like that. "It is good to talk to you, dear Tía," he said. He had brought her a bunch of purple asters, daisies, and paintbrush, and these he carefully placed in her hair, one by one, until she looked like a bouquet. When Maria stared at herself in the small, chipped mirror, she smiled with happiness. Juan Talamantes had turned her into the beautiful young maiden she thought she had forgotten.

Meanwhile, the mute Sotero Madrone, though just a boy, headed straight toward the house where the dwarf Papita Ortega lived with her uncle Narciso, who did not believe in Getting Together, so he shut himself up in his room alone. Papita Ortega was twenty-two years old, but inside she was still eleven, the age she had been when four hunters raped her in the mountains where she had gone to gather berries all alone. Narciso had sworn revenge, but Papita was unable to describe her assailants. She had only sobbed, "*Los malos,*

los malos," when Narciso carried her down the hill, his heart filled with a futile vengeance that gnawed at him all the rest of his days.

Frozen in childhood because of what had happened to her years before, Papita the Dwarf dreamed childish dreams that kept her from remembering the horrible event and played with her rag doll. She liked Sotero enough to allow him to make a carving of her while she rocked the doll to sleep. Then she made a place for them to rest together, outside in the stall where a pig, a goat, two sheep, three rabbits, and Juan Talamantes's mongrel, Jesus Christ, had already bedded down for the night. Papita dragged a buffalo robe from the house and covered them as they lay on two pillows filled with straw. The children dreamed with the animals and absorbed their wisdom into their subconscious. Peace wove itself into the fabric of their brains, and when they awoke, it was with the gentle nature of these creatures. No harm came to them, nor did they do harm when they were grown.

Before long, Delfine Madrone, his red hair slicked back with pomade, sauntered across the plaza to the house where El Comanche's wives, Hermosa and Tomasina, waited with sugar cookies and hard cider. They plastered him with kisses as he entered with his bagpipe. Delfine removed his double-breasted wool jacket; because of his Scottish ancestry, he was not permitted to wear a blanket like the other men, so he wore a kilt left behind by his father, a Scottish surveyor who spent the winter with Catarina when Luis went east in search of stories from the plains tribes. When the red-haired man snuggled between them on a mat, El Comanche's wives kissed his cheeks, his shoulders, his legs, his feet. "You are not as ripe nor as wise as our husband, El Comanche," Hermosa said to Delfine, "but you have the freshness of youth."

For a few hours, Delfine forgot his obsession with La Luz and allowed these two hearty women to set his mind at ease. "Ah, life is very good," he sighed as he fell asleep, an arm around each of them. He had spent himself in two short hours.

By this time, El Comanche had made his way to Isabela Talamantes's log house—a small, dark place at the edge of the forest. The fence had fallen down, and the yard was littered with tin cans and papers and the refuse from supper that the pig had not yet eaten. The beautiful young woman with large, expressive eyes kissed him on the cheek and served him apple pie with fresh cream. During his time with Isabela, El Comanche thought only of the satisfaction of her company; his rifle and his revolver he left in the kitchen, along with his store-bought teeth. Filled with good food, the old warrior fell asleep the moment he lay down on the pile of buffalo robes, but Isabela rubbed his head with a salve that Pilar had given her, guaranteed to ensure sexual prowess to the very end of life. "Ah, you have taught me many things, Tío," Isabela said. "How to live. How to die. How to put up with a brute like Alvar." El Comanche was snoring loudly, but it didn't matter. Isabela poured out her heart to him all night long, snuggled against his strong, old body. When morning came, she felt that she could face her life, no matter how badly her husband treated her.

Just before El Comanche arrived at the house, Alvar slipped out the door to find Ermina Madrone, who, because of the crowded conditions at her house, waited impatiently for him under El Abuelo, witness to many such assignations before.

Here the sleepless priest found them, lying together in the moonlight, when he walked down to the river to clear his head. "What are you doing?" he gasped when he stumbled over them lying on a blanket, entwined in each other's arms.

Alvar was a big, ugly man with a huge head and a voice like thunder. "You should not be here, Padre," he said. "Get out before I hurt you!"

Ermina Madrone hid her head in the thick fur of the buffalo robe and said in a muffled voice, "Leave us alone, Padre."

The priest stepped back. Into his mind raced pictures of himself. With Maya Begay. With Maria Villanueva. But here was a married man lying with Luis's only daughter, a shy virgin, or so she'd appeared to him these many weeks. Soledad shook his head. He did not understand.

"It is nothing, Padre," said Juan Lobo the next morning, licking a knife blade covered with the blood of a rabbit he had just shot for supper. "We call it Getting Together. You see, at night our *tasoom*—the spirit we live by—leaves us. It goes away to the far side of the moon and stays there until the sun comes up. We are naked as babies without our *tasoom*. Bad spirits are able to enter us at that time because we have no power against them. But if we are with someone whose heart is in the right place, we are protected. A very old custom. Surely you do not object?"

The priest leaned against the side of the house. The sun was warm on his face. He chose his words carefully. "I do object," he said at last, "to fornication between young girls and married men. You will have to stop."

The cacique expertly filleted the rabbit and laid it on a rock. He shook his head. "You have it all wrong," he said. "Getting Together is like a breath of fresh air. Love is new, every single time." His wrinkled face broke into a grin. "This is a beautiful custom, one we have had since the beginning, when people had four legs. Back then, they were afraid. So they would lie down and hold one another. Old to young, young to old. I always hold La Luz until she falls asleep. So no, we will not stop. If you think that, we will kill you twice over."

The priest felt the blood drain from his face. "You and La Luz?" he asked, stunned. "But you . . . you are an old man, and she is but a girl!"

Juan Lobo shrugged. "I told you, time means nothing. I am young in my heart. She is old in spirit. That is what matters. You see, Maria Gets Together with Juan Talamantes and Jesus Christ, the mongrel dog. What can she do, at her age, except listen to him? The mute Sotero Gets Together with Papita the Dwarf to amuse her. Luis Madrone Gets Together with his mother because she will die soon. And that lazy Delfine Gets Together with El Comanche's wives!" He threw back his head and laughed. "And you, Padre, you will Get Together with someone, too?"

Soledad's face reddened. "Never," he said. "I am a priest."

"So?" he laughed.

The priest had never felt more frustrated in his life. "You must stop Getting Together with La Luz, Juan Lobo," he said, trying to conceal his anger. "It's uncivilized." The thought of them lying in bed together nauseated him.

The Custodian of Abundance laughed. "When the four-legged animals develop one more, then yes, perhaps I will not Get Together with La Luz anymore!"

The next morning, the sleepless priest knocked on Juan Lobo's door. Maria answered it, wiping her flour-covered hands on her apron. She smiled at the sight of him—agitated, yet with a sincerity she found appealing.

"Maria Lobo," he said breathlessly, pushing into the house without being asked. "I must talk to you. Why do you permit Juan Lobo to Get Together with La Luz?"

Maria Lobo was very tired. Deep in her body, something had begun to grow. She could feel it pressing there, just as when she carried her babies inside. A hot, thick pain had decided to make its home in the space just behind her navel. She poured them each a cup of coffee before she answered. "What harm can it do, Padre? He is an old man filled with experience. She is a young woman filled with loneliness. Her husband is in the *pinta*."

He shook his head. "What do you do with Juan Talamantes when he visits in your bed? Do you cohabit? At your age, the Church considers it a sin."

She shrugged her small shoulders. "We talk about the way it used to be. He tells me he misses my daughter, Florita. They were going to be married, and then Narciso Ortega killed her in an argument with Juan. An accident. Juan has never gotten over it, which is why he is always sad. For a while, he wanted to kill Narciso, but then he went away and thought about it. Now he and Narciso are friends. They both loved Florita. We all loved her." She was silent.

The priest was aware of her tears streaming silently down her cheeks. He reached out and squeezed her hand. "Is Juan Talamantes your son?"

"Oh, no. But he is Alvar's brother."

"I see," he said, rubbing his forehead. But he didn't. "When Juan Talamantes spends the night with you, what else do you do?"

"I repair his wooden leg, since he has no wife to take care of him. I plant moss on it, and tiny flowers. Then we comfort one another in the night." This priest with the magic on his face would never understand the customs of her people. She could tell by the bewildered expression he wore. Maria cleared away the dishes and began to punch down her bread. She liked the smell of unrisen bread—the yeast, the flour, the bit of molasses she put in for flavor. She hummed softly, thinking how Juan Talamantes would enjoy the bread with the fresh wild plum jam she had made the week before.

"Maria, this cannot go on," he said quietly. He had to put an end to this foolishness, before he did anything else. "Juan Lobo may not Get Together with La Luz anymore. I will not permit it. And you may not call a dog Jesus Christ. It's disrespectful."

"You will have to talk to Juan Lobo about it," she said shortly. "The dog is happy with his name."

"But . . . but don't you see, it . . . it's . . ." He started to say "immoral," but he stopped himself. Who was he to judge? He was an immoral priest himself. He had made love to several women since his ordination. And felt a shameless satisfaction. He dreamed of women and their softness. Their ability to transport him to a sort of heaven. He swallowed. "Do you understand about shame, Maria?"

Maria Lobo remembered that concept from her convent school days. How hard it had been to suppress her traditional religion for one that was based in sin and guilt. "Shame is the invention of the Church, Padre. If everyone felt shame, everyone would want to be forgiven. To be forgiven, one needs padres like you. Since we do not believe in sin, we do not believe in shame. We do not believe in heaven or hell, either. That is why we have never needed a priest."

"Perhaps you need one now," he said. Looking around, Soledad noticed what was on the walls. A shaggy buffalo head with horns curved like quarter moons. A bow and arrows. A painted parfleche. A cluster of golden aspen leaves. A finely woven Navajo blanket. An eagle feather wand. A clay pipe. Simple things. Natural things.

Harmless things. Were these any different than the crosses and Madonnas he'd seen many times on the walls of Spanish Catholic homes? He began to understand the frustration of the early friars, trying to superimpose their complex dogma upon people who had but a single uncomplicated standard. Who was right? He was again torn between what he had vowed to uphold and what pulled at his heartstrings. "I bring you a way to connect both worlds, but certain things will have to change."

Maria Lobo shaped the dough into loaves. She shook her head. "That is not for you to decide." Her shoulders sagged. She needed to lie down. "What do you really believe, Padre?"

He rubbed his broken cross and looked closely at her. What a stubborn woman! "I believe in love," he said. "The love of God."

"The love of God is in this bread. Or in Jesus Christ, the gentle dog waiting outside the door for scraps. Or in Juan Talamantes when he comes to see me, an old woman about to make her journey into the next world."

Father Soledad began to rise from his chair. "How can I teach you anything when you—"

Juan Lobo stood behind him, breathing on his neck. "If you want to live another day, I suggest you accept our ways."

The priest whirled around and nearly lost his balance. "Getting Together was not part of our bargain, Juan Lobo. I cannot condone it."

The cacique shook his head and sat down. "The trouble with the religious is that they want to change things. What we do. What we eat. What we wear. What we learn. What we speak. Even our names. My name is not Juan Lobo, but Hand That Stops the Sun. Do we have rights, Padre?" A faint smile played across the old man's lips.

"Of course you have rights," Father Soledad said.

"Then why do you try and change us?"

"Because it is my duty as a priest." His words sounded hollow now.

"The padre has a troubled heart." Maria Lobo sighed. "Only one thing will cure him."

She said something in the Calabaza language that made Juan Lobo laugh uproariously. Then the old man got up. He had been out hunting, and he was tired. "If I were you, Padre," he said, "I wouldn't forget that people have the right to find happiness in whatever way they can." With that, he was gone.

For days after that, Soledad was unable to sleep. He consulted Bonito Lobo, who believed he hadn't slept in twenty years, about what to do. "Learn to . . . walk . . . among . . . the stars," said Bonito, "and count them. It . . . will . . . take your mind . . . off things."

Soledad took long, solitary walks into the mountains at night, but he remained wide awake. He noticed a huge, yellow dog following him, but when he tried to give it scraps, it ran away. "Are you Jesus Christ?" he called out, but no, it was larger than Jesus Christ. When he finally fell exhausted into bed, he thought he heard the dog howling on his porch; in the morning, he found muddy tracks on the boards. They were the size of a lion's.

One day, when Soledad was dozing by the river and thinking about La Luz, the huge dog jumped from a bank above his head and attacked him. Its fangs were long and sharp, and as Soledad rolled down toward the river with the dog on top of him, trying to sink its teeth into his throat, he feared he would be killed. "Help!" he cried, but no one came to rescue him. The dog bit his arm and drew blood. In his terror, the priest grabbed the one thing that could possibly be used as a weapon: his damaged cross. He yanked it from its chain and with a terrible cry, plunged it into the creature's neck. Then he fell back against the leaves and, for a moment, passed into unconsciousness.

When he came to, what stood above him was not the savage dog, but Pilar Mondragon in a long, black garment that came to her ankles. Around her eyes were painted two white diamond shapes; her mouth was outlined in red and black paint. She held the bloody cross in her hand. "You dropped this, Padre," she said as she helped him to his feet. "It has become a weapon."

His cassock was covered with mud; his arm and throat were sore to the touch. As Pilar helped him to Juan Lobo's house, he had an eerie suspicion. "You!" he gasped. "You were the dog who tried to kill me! I thought it was Jesus Christ, Juan's dog!"

But the dark, smelly woman only smiled. "I am the Custodian of Witchcraft," she said. "I can be anything I want."

With that, Pilar Mondragon disappeared. In her place was a badger with sharp teeth, who looked up at the priest with glassy eyes before it shambled off.

I believe nothing of what I have seen, Father Soledad thought as he sat painfully in Juan Lobo's kitchen and let the cacique put salve on his wounds. *If I believed it, I would have to say I had been attacked by a witch who can disguise herself as a dog. And then a badger.*

He laughed hysterically, but Juan Logo thought he was crying out. "Your wounds will heal, Padre," the old man said, gently bandaging his arm. "But the curse she has put upon you will not heal. Look, this was in your ear!" In his hand, Juan Lobo held a tiny black glass bead. "Pilar Mondragon is also known as the Snake Woman. She is very powerful."

"More powerful than you, Juan Lobo?"

"Her power is different," the cacique said. "It is evil." As he spoke, the old man poured a clear brown liquid into the padre's ear, meant to neutralize the power of Pilar Mondragon's spell.

It had the effect of transporting Soledad to the bottom of the sea. "Why don't you kill her then?" Soledad asked, trying to keep from passing out. "I tried to when she was a dog, but then she turned back into herself before she became a badger." The priest's words sounded peculiar even to himself, but the old man never changed his expression.

"If I were to kill her," he said, "the whole tribe would fall sick and die. Witches are very powerful. When I was a boy, a witch killed all the babies in the tribe. She rubbed their soft spots with snake venom, and they died. When I was learning the ways of the elders, a witch put a spell on me the year of the Great Famine. I fell in a deep sleep. The witch went around saying I would die."

Painfully, Soledad got up from the table and held on to the

chair. He could scarcely move. He felt feverish, sick to his stomach. "How did you get rid of that witch?" he managed to say.

Juan Lobo put away all his medicines before he answered. "An important person had to die," he said. "In this case, it was my grandfather, a great chief named Striped Wolf. On the day he died, the witch died also. From then on, no more babies died. And I woke up from my sleep."

With an effort, Soledad eased himself toward the door. "How did Striped Wolf die?"

"We ate him," the old man replied. "We were very hungry that year."

The priest saw the room spin around. "It's barbarous!" he gasped.

"You religious ate people long ago. My father told me. And his father told him."

Juan Lobo calmly began mending a pair of moccasins. "Some things are necessary if we are to survive," the cacique said evenly. "When Striped Wolf died, cooked in our big pots, sickness ended. Game returned. People stopped fighting. We were prosperous for a long time." Deftly, his fingers moved the bone needle, which was threaded with a length of sinew, along the edge of his torn moccasin. "When they cut off my ear, I was able to hear better. So you see."

"What else have you done, Juan Lobo?" The priest slid into a chair. He now knew why the monsignor had sent him here to Camposanto, where no priest had survived before. *Nor will I*, he thought wildly.

The old man paused. "We crucified my uncle, Elk Old Man," he said evenly, "so that the tribe could continue. It was revealed to us in the kiva what we must do. We thought about it long and hard."

"Why?" The priest realized he was close to hysteria.

The old man bent his head to his work. "Same reason they crucified your Christ," he said. "To improve life."

"It's not . . . not the same at all!" Soledad stammered. "Christ died to redeem sinners! To show us how to live. He died because he loved mankind!" He dropped his head in his hands.

"Same with Elk Old Man," Juan Lobo said. "Once he died, we

got better. How else do you think we could survive up here, with everything against us? He gave us what your Christ gave you! No different." He had never been able to understand the fuss over a ritual that was basically the same as their throwing virgins into the sacred lake during the time of the Animal People. People had their ways.

As usual, when he spoke to Juan Lobo, the priest felt he was getting nowhere. "Are you saying that you took a sacred Catholic belief and turned it into a pagan Indian ceremony?"

"Why not? You do not own it."

"No, but the crucifixion of our Lord Jesus Christ is the greatest sacrifice known to the world. With Christ's resurrection, mankind was redeemed—absolved of its sins. The Catholic faith was founded upon this belief. For nineteen centuries, we have worshipped the Son of God, not defiled Him!" He turned his head away. "Have you committed this ghastly sacrilege again, Juan Lobo?"

The old man put down his bone needle. His dark eyes bore into the padre's skull. "You believe a man can give his life to help others survive?"

"Of course I believe it, Juan Lobo," the priest replied. "*Deus vult.* God wills it. But this does not excuse cannibalism. Or crucifixion. Have there been others, eh?"

Juan Lobo shrugged. "Because you think only one way, you see only one way. And because you see only one way, you are blind." With that, he got up and walked out of his house.

Soledad realized he was shaking. What to believe or not to believe? If a lie was truth, then truth was a lie, just as he had learned so long ago, as a young man at the hands of a whore. Now he was wasting his time in a dissolute Indian village called the Place of the Dead, where people nursed a three-hundred-year-old grudge against the Catholic Church. Had the Calabazas really crucified Juan Lobo's uncle? Or eaten his grandfather to break the spell of a witch? Could Pilar turn herself into an animal at will? Why were human foot bones embedded in the wall of the ruined church? Why was a dog called Jesus Christ? Nothing in his lifetime, except the voices in the graveyards in Texas had prepared him for the bizarre events he was experiencing in Camposanto! And yet, he was strangely attracted to these people he had come to change.

THE SUMMER AIR was unusually brisk, though there had not yet been a frost. Soledad walked into the forest behind his casita. Birds called to him. A squirrel scampered past. Beautiful clouds sailed overhead. He stopped to look. An unfamiliar peace settled over him. Even Henrietta's face, which always was with him, receded into the fir branches. He was beginning to feel at home.

Later, Soledad found Juan Lobo making a pair of moccasins on his porch. "May I speak to you?" The old man nodded. Soledad sat down and looked across the plaza. "Do you know that I am a murderer, Juan Lobo?" The old man did not move a muscle. "My mother," Father Soledad went on. "I accidentally shot her. Ever since that moment, I have been a tormented man. I thought becoming a priest would ease my pain. It has only made it worse." The old man looked at some unseen object in the trees. "Here in Camposanto, I am beginning to find peace," the padre said. "The whole reason for my existence is your people. I love them."

Juan Lobo laid down his hunting knife and the strips of hide he was cutting. He got up. He had an angry look. "I can ask them to kill you," he said. "Or I can wait for you to kill yourself. Same end. Different means." And with that, he was gone.

SIXTEEN

SLOWLY, THE PRIEST began to relax. He spent a morning watching Canada geese migrate to the south, their shrill honking a counterpoint to his expanding delight. Another day, he tracked a bobcat through the forest, imaging himself inside the animal's skin. He became aware of every nuance, every smell, and every track in the dirt, the way Luis Madrone had taught him. Another world began to open, and it originated among the unpredictable Indians.

One evening, Sotero arrived with a basketful of carvings—the Animal People of his tribe, lovingly translated into wood. The priest's eyes filled with tears as he examined the beautiful pieces. "These are carved from your heart, Sotero," he said warmly, and he gave the boy a hug. "You have a rare talent." *Someday*, he thought, *the boy will carve the santos for my church. If there is ever to be a church.*

As always, whenever he was excited, the mute's head bobbed up and down. He wanted Soledad to like him; he wanted the padre to understand the wondrous things that lived inside his head. As the boy and the priest drank sweetish altar wine from the only two cups in the house, Soledad leaned back and looked at this bright, speechless lad. He might have had a son like this, had his life turned out differently. His heart went out to the boy.

"A long time ago, when I was your age," he said huskily, "I believed I could hear the dead speak just by lying in graveyards and pressing my ear to the ground. They talked to me! Yes, they did. So, you think that is funny? Well, I grew up in a little west Texas town, and all my friends were dead! But some others were what are called 'whores.' Oh, felix culpa!"

The boy clapped his hands together as if he understood; his twisted mouth struggled to make the Latin words the priest had just spoken. With a silent giggle, he began to carve a block of cedar he was holding in his lap. His hands could not keep still for very long.

Soledad stretched out on the bed and spread the folds of his cassock around him, his beloved cross, defiled through an act of selfishness, gleaming in the lamplight. "I had no friends to speak of back then because I was different from other boys, just as you are different. I was driven to do strange, unpredictable things. I have not had very good luck with women, either." Slowly, he began to unburden himself of all that had weighed him down.

The boy fiercely nodded his head. For the first time in his life, he had tasted wine, and he was feeling a little tipsy. Now, as he listened intently, he absorbed the fascinating stories and collected them in his head, with no means of expression save the figures he could carve. Ever since he was six years old, Sotero Madrone had carved what he felt most deeply. He pulled his chair closer to the priest. He wanted to get Soledad's nose and mouth just right. Although the mute did not understand everything the padre said, what found its way to his brain filled him with love. As he listened, the carving of the priest slowly took form.

Soledad sat up and looked at the piece. "So it is me?" he laughed. "I do not deserve such an honor." But he was clearly pleased. "What will happen to you?" he asked suddenly. "You have a talent too great for this place. You must leave Camposanto and go to school."

The mute stomped a small, moccasined foot on the floor. He threw down his carving knife as if to make a point. A hoarse cry of protest spilled from his lips. He seemed close to tears.

"Ah, Sotero," Soledad said huskily and tousled the boy's hair. "Life goes by in a moment. We all must leave something of ourselves behind. As for me, I'm not certain I'll leave anything of importance. But you are a genius. Like Michelangelo."

Sotero Madrone left Soledad's house late that night with a new-found belief in himself. The priest had made him see that the world was filled with new and wonderful possibilities. He looked up at the stars, so close that he reached up and tried to touch them. How beautiful everything was! Images churned in the child's brain. He was bursting with ideas. The small wood carvings were not enough. He had to think of a fitting way to honor his new friend.

Early the next morning, the mute scrambled up the mountain to the cave where the Anasazi had left their messages in stone so many centuries before. Over the years, he had studied these draw-ings carefully. Now he found a sharp rock with which he could cut into the cave surface himself on a blank spot so far to the back that he had to run home and fetch a coal oil lamp.

Carefully, Sotero started a drawing of the priest on the rock wall. It took him three days. In this drawing, the priest was lying on top of a dead person. In the next, he was sporting a penis much too long and was kissing a woman.

The boy stepped back and looked at his work. Not bad, but something was missing. The color red. Hematite. The Anasazi had used it on their drawings, so it had to be here somewhere. He searched outside and inside. Along the edge of the walls. With a curious grunt, he began to dig in the cold, coarse sand of the cave with his fingers, deeper and deeper. A foot beneath the surface, he stopped in amazement. Hundreds of bright coins were buried in the sand. He put one in his mouth, bit it, and placed it in his pouch. No hematite, but this, a shiny gold button.

Carefully, he covered the rest of the buttons with sand and scampered down the hillside. He wondered if the priest would be angry about the drawings. But at the last moment, he decided not to tell him. *No*, he thought. *Someday, when the drawings are done, I will show him the hidden buttons and see if he knows what to do with them.*

Soledad was not unhappy in this Place of the Dead, despite the fact that he had accomplished little of what the monsignor had sent him to do. Every day he could look at La Luz, bent over a rock by the river washing clothes, and admire her graceful body. He could speak Latin to Sotero and tell him more stories about his life until his mind felt thoroughly cleansed. He could let El Comanche shoot a tin can off his head, to show he was not afraid. Shedding his cassock for his workman's clothes, he could go to the forest and help Bonito and Delfine cut wood, holding on to one end of the crosscut saw as it bit into a tall, thick tree. He could follow the men—when he'd discovered their destination—to the kiva and stand there wondering what went on inside until someone climbed up the ladder and drove him away. He could help Maria Lobo and Catarina Madrone gather piñon nuts by shaking the tree while they spread out a blanket beneath it. The women laughed at his clumsiness, but Catarina shelled a bag of nuts for him, to show him she was grateful. But still there was no church, no matter how much he pleaded and cajoled.

As his body responded to the unaccustomed tasks, Soledad's muscles grew firm. A thick layer of calluses formed on his palms and fingertips. His endurance was such that he no longer puffed when he walked to the top of the mountain. Every morning, just as dawn broke over the low line of hills, the priest went out on his porch and stretched arms toward the rising sun. He gave a short, joyful cry, the two-note birdsong that Ansawaka had taught him. All over Camposanto, the Indian men were also greeting the dawn. "The padre is losing his vanity," they said, watching him. But this was not enough to suit the purpose they had in mind.

One afternoon, Papita the Dwarf came to Soledad's house and sat demurely on his bed, her hands clasped in her lap, while her uncle asked the priest to teach her to read. Narciso brought her there in hopes that Soledad could make her grow through the power of his Church. "If you do this, Padre," the woodcutter said, "I will give you everything that is mine."

"There are miracles, Narciso," Soledad said. "Pray for one."

Patiently, Soledad drew the letters on a slate he had found in Maria Lobo's old schoolhouse, but though Papita eventually mastered the alphabet, she didn't grow an inch.

When Juan Talamantes shyly asked Father Soledad to teach

him the elements of arithmetic, the priest was amazed at his quickness; he could add up a column of figures in less time than it took the padre. "You have a natural ability, Juan," he said admiringly.

The Custodian of Meekness was pleased to be singled out; at last he saw a way for him to forget his dead sweetheart and to make something of himself. With the pencil the padre had given him, the Custodian of Meekness made calculations on his wooden leg until at last he got the hang of it. Soon, he was ready for long division and, after that, fractions.

After listening to Luis Madrone's improbable stories, Soledad suggested he put them into a book to pass down to his grandchildren. "Through these stories, you will become immortal, Luis. It has always been so for writers, down through the ages. Five hundred years ago, a man named Chaucer wrote tales every bit as strange as yours."

"I cannot write," Luis confessed sheepishly. "Only Maria Lobo knows how. And Ermina and La Luz, a little bit, too, because they went away to convent school. The rest of us refused to go to the white man's school. We hid in the mountains. Our teachers were Eagles and Bears."

The padre persuaded him to sit in on his English class with the dwarf, who by this time was able to make words and, in time, simple sentences. Hermosa showed up, sat on the floor of the old schoolhouse, and begged the padre to teach her Latin. "So I can be ready for the world when it comes, unless my husband kills me first," she laughed, thinking of what El Comanche might do to her for defying his order to remain illiterate.

"*Absit invidia*," said the priest. "Let there be no ill will."

Sotero Madrone slipped in the door when the padre was speaking Latin to Hermosa, and listened intently. He managed to blow out a sound through his lips, a strange gurgling that made Soledad notice him.

"*Age quod agis*," he urged. "Do what you are doing."

But embarrassed by the attention, Sotero tore from the room and hid in the shed. He picked up his wood-carving knife and began another fine carving. Various Latin words kept running through his head like a chant. Although he could plainly hear the words, they refused to come out.

One day, while Soledad was practicing a Beethoven rondo on his squeaky violin, Ana Coyote came by with a sick rooster. Soledad doctored it as best he could before it died on his kitchen table, its red, rubbery legs thrust up in the air. "The rooster is inbred, Ana Coyote," the padre said. "Like this village. For years and years, you have married first cousins. Aunts. Uncles. Isn't that so? It's the same with your chickens. Your rooster died of old, tired blood. Now, I know a place where I can buy new roosters. A stronger kind. And some different hens. Resistant to disease. They'll be bigger and better than yours!"

The old woman in the feather coat simply stared at him, open mouthed. If the padre could come up with a better chicken or bigger eggs, she would overlook all his deficiencies.

Furtively, from secret hiding places, Pilar Mondragon watched everything that was happening. The people were beginning to accept the priest. He had a power over them that she found disturbing, for she feared it was greater than her own. She thought of ways to cast spells on him that would be more effective than the yellow dog or the bead had been.

Meanwhile, Peso Mondragon, as a result of an all-night political discussion with the priest, decided to run for governor again, on a platform of equality for his people. He kicked off his campaign by saddling his horse and making a tour of those Pueblo tribes along the Great River that had been so instrumental in achieving reform during the Great Revolt more than two hundred years before. This time, however, they wanted only to find a path through the ruins of their lives. "As for politicos," they said, "they are about as useful as rattlesnakes. Besides, we are unable to vote." When Peso returned home, it was to exchange political ambition for the formulation of a plot to overthrow the government of the United States of America, which had taken all their land, the center of their hearts. El Comanche made himself a general. He loaded his cannon and his rifles. He put on his battle regalia.

The villagers slowly warmed to their sad-eyed priest with the blazing comet on his cheek. Maria Lobo fed him roast elk and pinto beans spiced with hot red chile one night when he went there for supper. Ana Coyote brought him fresh eggs every morning, anxious to receive the poultry Soledad had ordered from Santa Fe. He found gifts of squash, beans, corn, and apples left anonymously on his doorstep. La Luz washed his clothes in the river, beating them clean on a rock, but she would not talk to him. Bonito Lobo came to the door with a load of firewood. "We do not . . . want you . . . to freeze, Padre," he said.

Juan Lobo appeared one morning with two well-tanned beaver pelts. "You will need these soon," the old man said, and dropped them on the floor. "I will show you how to make them into a coat." He looked around. "Are you ready to give up?" he asked. "I see no one is converted yet." The old man was stubborn and as cunning as a fox.

"I am learning about your people first, Juan Lobo," the priest replied. "I want them to help me build a church."

"Why should they? It is not their Church." He waved his arm toward the door. "Out there is our Church. The whole earth and sky. We do not need walls or roofs. Only the magic the Great Spirit gives." His eyes blazed.

"I understand," Soledad said. "But I don't admire the application of many of your religious beliefs."

"Bah! If you emptied out your head of false ideas, you could accept our ways, Padre. I will win our wager because my mind is open!"

Soledad watched him go, his blanket draped around his head, his steps as quick and agile as a young boy. The old man mounted his pony ground-tied in the plaza and rode away into the aspen trees. Something began to crack within the hard shell of Soledad's body, but he did not know what. Only that Juan Lobo had provoked him to a place he had not explored before. He spent four days in the wilderness, praying. When it was over, he felt just the same.

SEVENTEEN

YEARS LATER, WHEN *Father Antonio combed through Soledad's records for clues about his tenure in Camposanto, he would read that the martyred priest had held an open-air baptism in the plaza on the fifteenth day of August 1896. Only four people came forward to receive the sacrament. A one-legged man. A dwarf. A mute. A woman in love with chickens.* How very odd, *thought the Vatican priest, searching in vain for other converts in the skimpy pages of Soledad's ledgers. Soledad's mission seemed a failure by every standard required by Holy Mother Church. And yet.*

He began to understand Soledad in different terms, not the strict rules of his holy and apostolic Church. His heart went out to the martyred priest. What is true?, *he thought. For the first time in his life the old priest had doubts about his beliefs.* Why am I here?, *he wondered as he drank a cup of the Elixir of Dreams. He wasn't sure he knew.*

Father Bartholomew was by now thoroughly disgusted. He had no further interest in this foolish mission. He didn't care if Soledad became a saint or not. It would not affect his life. He stood on his porch watching the bustle in the plaza. The vendors. The false faithful throwing themselves at the base of what used to be the cross. It looked like a toothpick now. He went into the casita he shared with the older priest, much against his will. He found an open jug of the Elixir of Dreams and poured some into a cup. He drank it down. Then another. When he drifted off into a blessed sleep, he dreamed of the young Mexican boy he had met at the stable.

HIS CASSOCK FLAPPING *around his ankles, his scapular stained with the remains of his noonday meal, Father Antonio rooted himself in the plaza, his eyes turned toward a grassy place in the shadow of Luis Madrone's house where Soledad might have kissed La Luz. He looked toward the modest church where he said Mass. Married couples. Taught catechism. What had he preached? His own views or those of the Church? No one would say when he asked what Soledad actually did there, not even Juan Lobo. He said Soledad was a badger. A man an animal? Absurd. The old priest looked up at the sky and saw a red-tailed hawk soaring overhead. It seemed to grow larger and larger until it touched the clouds. He rubbed his eyes. The bird disappeared.* I don't care if Bartholomew is no longer interested, *he* thought. I am. I think I know what really happened here.

The notion fairly made his flesh tingle. At last Soledad's martyrdom made perfect sense. He wanted to show mankind something, *he thought.* The way Jesus Christ, Our Savior, did. *Father Antonio allowed himself a cry of joy as he hobbled to his casita and began to write down his findings.*

A simple truth had been there all along. He wondered why he had not seen it before. He looked at Father Bartholomew asleep on his cot, snoring.

If he doesn't see it my way . . . , *he thought.* It's time to look at things differently.

But into his confused mind crept Muy Contenta. Could a man love God and a woman at the same time, especially if the man was a Vatican priest and the woman had fallen from grace?

Bartholomew sat up and looked at him. "What are you thinking, Father?"

"Nothing, dear boy. Nothing," *the older man answered.* "Come outside. I want to show you the most marvelous thing. A bird that is half the size of Saint Peter's. Can you imagine?"

No, he could not. Bartholomew put on his sandals and walked out the door. It was starting to rain. "You are crazy, old man," *he said. But Antonio did not hear him. He had bent down to examine some pink flowers growing from under the porch. They were perfect.*

EIGHTEEN

SOLEDAD NEVER KNEW why he decided to hold baptism in the plaza that warm Sunday when most of the men were out hunting in the mountains. He did not believe in this sacrament anymore, not after what the early padres had done in its name. *Call it a whim*, he thought as he draped a clean white cloth over an improvised altar made from three boards Luis had nailed together.

The tabernacle gleamed golden in the sun, the tiny round hosts consecrated before a dozen curious Calabazas who waited for God to float out of the chalice like a butterfly. He delivered a homily about baptism being like a scouring rag, but that was not what he meant to say. He was going to talk about original sin, but he did not.

Juan Talamantes stepped forward and thrust his wooden leg out and begged the padre to pour water over it, in hopes his stump would materialize into a full-grown leg. "If that is magic water, show me what it can do."

Narciso came forth with Papita and made her kneel in the dust while the priest poured water over her head. "Now," the Custodian of Amends said confidently, "she will grow. You said it yourself." He helped himself to the bowl of holy water that the priest held in his hands and poured it over the dwarf's bare feet. "So she will run fast," he said, "up and down the mountains."

The dwarf squealed in delight.

Sotero Madrone looked up from the dirt where he had been drawing pictures of things that lived in his head and opened his mouth, trying to form a word in the Latin tongue that the priest was speaking. Getting up from the ground, he came forward and dropped to his knees, anxious to show his devotion to a man who had shared so many things. Around his neck, the boy wore the carcass of a young rabbit, tied on with a leather thong. The small, furry creature was stiff with blood and putrid with decay.

"What are you doing with this filthy thing, Sotero?" the priest whispered.

Luis Madrone, standing to one side, replied, "Because it is sacred to us, Padre. A rabbit, like Sotero, cannot speak. It makes them brothers, no?"

The priest sucked in his breath at the stench and, trying to control his displeasure, poured a measure of holy water over the boy's blue-black hair and said the blessed words, "E nomine Patris, et Filii, et Spiritus Sancti."

To Sotero, the feel of the magic water was like Papita's caress during those nights of Getting Together. Dripping wet, he reached into his pouch, took out the little gold button, and laid it in the padre's outstretched palm.

"A Spanish *real*," Soledad gasped, and felt its heaviness. "Pure gold. Where did you get it, young man?"

But Sotero only laughed his hoarse, labored laugh and backed away. *A pure gold* real, the priest thought excitedly, *is worth a great deal of money*. He stuffed it into the pocket of the trousers he wore beneath his alb, wondering whether there were more of Sotero's coins. With money, he could build a church. A school. Decent housing. With money, he could bring new meaning to the lives of the Calabazas. Would the mute tell him where he had found it? He shook his head when Soledad asked.

As the priest pondered the possibilities, Ana Coyote brought two sick hens along, one in either hand. Today she needed a special magic. Her beloved chickens were dying. Their gaunt little bodies littered the floor of the hen house. No eggs either, for more than two weeks. The hens were all dead, except for these two sick ones. The new roosters that Soledad had purchased were beginning to act sick, too. She suspected Pilar Mondragon, the witch who'd helped kill Balthazar, had put a spell on her chickens. "Baptize these poor, sick chickens, Padre," she said. "You must make them well. They are all I have in the world." She held the hens out by their scrawny necks.

"These hens aren't Catholic," he said. "They have never received instruction."

She scowled. "What does it matter? They need to be saved, if they are to have a place in the world."

With a sigh, the priest poured the cold water over the old woman's head and said the holy words. Dripping wet, Ana Coyote wondered if the magic water meant that now the priest expected something of her. In the old days, when she was only fourteen, she had had to give herself to an Apache warrior in exchange for a pony he brought to her.

He bent his dark head close to her white fuzzy one. "The gift you have received will help you to cure your chickens yourself. Pray for them, Ana Coyote, in whatever way you pray."

Peso Mondragon sauntered toward the priest. He was feeling rather bold, for he believed that, thanks to him, there would soon be another Great Revolt, just as there had been in 1680. Four pueblos had already signed up; he needed fifteen more, and runners fast enough to cover the whole vast territory of New Mexico in a single day. The Custodian of Good Intentions faced the priest, a disdainful look on his face. "The water does nothing, Padre," he said defiantly. "Where is your magic?"

The priest blinked. "My what?" he said. "Baptism is a holy sacrament instituted by Christ, Peso Mondragon. No magic, simply faith." He glanced behind him. The Calabazas were enjoying the debate, waiting for him to make a fool of himself. He shuddered and instinctively stepped away from this unpleasant man, tugging at his sleeve. "I have no magic, Peso, only the word of God."

El Comanche, dressed in his Confederate general's uniform especially for the occasion, shuffled to the baptismal table. He laid down his rifle beside the bowl, which the padre had filled with holy water drawn from the village well and blessed by himself early in the morning. "We want to see magic," he said. "That is all we believe in. War and magic." The old warrior dipped his hands into the bowl and rubbed his face with water. "Ah," he said. "I am ready for battle. Those flea-bitten soldiers will fall where I shoot them."

Soledad drew in his breath. "Stop!" he cried. "That is consecrated water, El Comanche."

The old warrior shrugged, picked up the bowl and drank from it, wiping his mouth on the sleeve of his threadbare Confederate jacket. He had seen a baptism once before, when Father Montez stood at this very spot and ordered the Calabazas to submit to his authority or he would cut off their winter supplies. "What matters is war," El Comanche said in his croaking voice. He glanced at Soledad. "If I had been in charge, there would have been no Spanish bastards shoving us into slavery." With that, he hobbled off, his rifle slung over his shoulder.

Angry with the old warrior, Soledad heard himself say, "Very well, I'll give you magic! I'll give you a miracle!" He took a flask of Communion wine from beneath his chasuble and poured it into the chalice. He asked for bread. Maria Lobo brought him a crusty loaf she'd baked the day before. Soledad asked Juan Talamantes for his blanket, and he placed the bread and a chalice filled with wine on top of it. "It is a symbol," he said. "Just as the dead rabbit Sotero wears around his neck is a symbol. It is a symbol of the Last Supper when Christ broke bread, gave it to His disciples, and said, 'Do this in memory of me.' The bread became a symbol of Christ's body; the wine became a symbol of His blood. At Mass, the priest changes the bread and wine into the body and blood of Christ. It is called transubstantiation."

This ancient, powerful ritual was what mattered most in Catholicism. The greatest sacrament of all. The transubstantiation of the bread and wine renewed him each time. At that moment, he saw, as men had for nearly two thousand years, the power and the holy mystery of his Church. Filled with humility and the desire to communicate this mystery to the skeptical Calabazas, Lorenzo

Soledad closed his eyes and began to say the Latin words of consecration over the bread and wine. But when he opened his eyes, the bread and wine were no longer there. Nor was his golden chalice, entrusted to him by the monsignor. He looked at Sotero Madrone, who stood beside him, fondling the dead rabbit.

"Did you take the body and blood of Christ?" he asked.

"Of course not, Padre," Luis replied. "We have enough to eat and drink."

The priest turned to Peso Mondragon, picking his teeth with the end of his hunting knife. "Did you?"

"Why would I steal such a thing, Padre? It is a miracle, no?" His smile looked guilty—at least it did to the angry priest.

The dark faces of the other Calabazas were impassive. The disappearance of the chalice lay with one of them, that much he knew. He said nothing as he finished Mass, then he walked back to his house with Luis, who carried the Missal and the altar cloth and the holy tabernacle.

The Custodian of Stories saw Pilar Mondragon, scuttling away ahead of him. "Who is that person in black up there?" he asked.

"That's Pilar Mondragon," the priest replied wearily.

"Does she look like a woman to you?"

"Of course she looks like a woman," Soledad snapped.

Luis Madrone stopped and spat in the dirt. "Well, she is not a woman."

"I'm tired of your jokes. I can see she is a woman."

But Luis thrust his face boldly into Soledad's. "You say she is a woman," Luis said. "You know she is a dog. What do you call that, Padre, if not a miracle?" He laughed. "If you want to know the truth, the Indian world is full of miracles. But we do not call attention to them!" The Custodian of Stories looked at the leaning cross, stubbornly less than vertical after all these years of trying to push it upright. "Before the last priest died, we tried to explain our way of miracles. But—"

"How did the last priest die, Luis?" Soledad asked sharply. "I want to know."

The older man remembered the day all too well. How the light fell around Father Montez like a halo. How all the four-legged animals came out of the forest to commiserate. How the birds stopped singing at the Moment of Passage. How the sky grew black at noon. How the people became very frightened and ran to their homes. "We crucified him, Padre, on that very cross you see before you." He shrugged his small shoulders. "It could not be helped."

Soledad stopped, his face dark with anger. "What do you mean, it could not be helped? Juan Lobo told me that your people crucified his uncle. And ate his grandfather. Are you all mad killers up here?"

His voice rose. Sotero and La Luz came out of their house to listen. So did Bonito and Maria Lobo.

Luis wasn't certain how to begin. He leaned against the wall and rubbed his chin. "You see, when the Catholics came in the old days, we liked some ideas they brought. One of these was crucifixion. A way for us to purify ourselves and become natural people once again. Juan Lobo's uncle, Elk Old Man, was the first. He recognized our fate long before it happened. He taught us to be brave. To prepare ourselves for the worst so that when it came, we would be ready. Then the priest came along. Father Montez. Not like you, but like a priest from the old days. We should have seen it coming. He ordered us locked in a dark, cold jail until we agreed to become Catholics. He had our fields burned because we would not build him a church. We lost all of our corn for the winter. Then he had one of our leaders, Soaring Eagle Heart, chained to a tree and whipped until we agreed to do what he wanted."

The Custodian of Stories had no wish to go on. He addressed the mountains, which had heard this tale before. "Padre Montez thought it was still the old days. So we went to the kiva and talked about how the priest made everybody feel bad. We decided to send him to his heaven. There is something dramatic about crucifixion. The minute we put him up on that cross, he died. Then the cross decided to lean to the east. We tried and tried, but the cross refused to go upright. 'It is a bad sign,' we said, but not even Juan

Lobo knew what to do." Luis wiped his mouth with the back of his hand. He wanted to go home and have supper, but the priest stopped him.

"I suppose I am next?" he said wryly.

Luis looked fearfully over his shoulder, then leaned toward the padre's ear and whispered, "They have considered it, believe me. But no, they say you are not good enough for the honor nor bad enough to deserve it. They say you will die of folly."

Soledad insisted he must know where Father Montez was buried.

Luis replied vaguely, "Up there in the mountains."

"You must take me there tomorrow," Soledad said firmly, almost at the end of whatever rope held him to sanity. "And please ask someone to help me straighten that cross!"

Luis Madrone shook his head. "I can do nothing," he said. "The cross has a mind of its own. It leans the way it wants. It has been that way a long time—another miracle?" He smiled bravely.

"No!" thundered the priest. "But it's something I can't explain." He shuddered. He looked around. What Father Montez had done to these people he would never do. Torture. Punishment. Humiliation. Because he believed they had a right to their ancient gods, just as he'd tried to explain to the monsignor.

Luis touched Soledad's sleeve as they went through the door. "Another thing. Father Montez was in love with Pilar Mondragon. And she with him. Peso went away to Lakota country for five years. Pilar thought he was dead. So she and the padre made a baby together. But do you know what happens if you make a baby with a witch? You get a Crow Dog. Born with four legs and a tail. A face like a beast. It can never sleep, but roams the world, looking for babies to eat." Luis knew that he would have to account for his words in the kiva. Yet he had a need to unburden himself to this sympathetic man in a long white robe. "But it was Pilar's fault. Because of what she is." He looked around nervously. "In case you think I am lying, Padre, the Crow Dog appears only on the full moon. It sets up such a howl that no one can sleep. The only one who can quiet it is its mother, the witch Pilar Mondragon. Perhaps tonight, in the full moon, you will see." Luis laid the cloth and the tabernacle and the Missal on the table.

"I don't believe in Crow Dogs," said the padre crossly. "I know Pilar can turn herself into a mad dog because she tried to kill me," he said. "And I struck the dog with this. A sacrilege." He held up the cracked cross, caked with blood that would not wash off. He rubbed his eyes. "Do you think I'm mad, Luis?" He rubbed his comet and felt it grow warm. "If you were to tell the monsignor what's happened here, he'd send me to an insane asylum."

"Pilar does not like you, Padre. She fears your magic is greater than hers." The storyteller started to go out the door, then he turned. "You tell us to believe in God coming out of a piece of bread and a cup of wine," he said. "Pilar says that she can turn people into owls or dogs or even snakes. Who is right?"

"Pilar believes in witchcraft. I believe in a merciful God."

Thoughtfully, Luis looked back at the crooked cross and the ruins of the church. "Then make the cross stand upright, Padre, and I will believe you."

Soledad hesitated, then with reckless abandon, he walked across the plaza and stared at the crooked cross. "Bring me water," he ordered tersely.

When Luis returned with a bowl of water, Soledad blessed it and, saying the Latin words of exorcism, sprinkled it on the cross. For a moment, nothing happened.

Luis waited, his arms folded across his chest, a smile of satisfaction on his lips. "What did I tell you, Padre? God has decided to leave the cross where it was." But even as he spoke, Soledad pushed against the cross until it stood upright again. Stupefied, Luis watched it straighten. With a slight bow, he turned to Soledad. "Padre, you are a very great man," he said. Already another story was forming in his mind.

LORENZO SOLEDAD STOOD uneasily on his porch, waiting for the moon to rise. When at last it soared above the eastern ridges, the color of copper and totally full, he reached his arms toward the sky. How beautiful everything was! Every detail of the village was illuminated, as if it were daylight.

As he turned to go inside, he saw a ghastly creature swaying along the narrow path through the trees beside his house. It was the size of a large dog, with a long tail, sharp teeth, and pointed ears. But its face was human. A human face, wrinkled and dehydrated like an old man's. The Crow Dog, more hideous than the dog who had attacked him earlier. The hideously deformed child of Pilar Mondragon and Father Montez opened its mouth and uttered a pitiful shriek loud enough to awaken the whole village. Voices shouted for Pilar to restore peace. Before Soledad's unbelieving eyes, Pilar hurried out of her house, tied a rope around the creature, and dragged it away.

Soledad did not believe in sorcery any more than he normally believed in miracles. Yet there the creature was, just as Luis had described. The padre looked up at the yellow moon. Camposanto was another world, spinning crazily, pulling him down toward the abyss. He stumbled up the steps to his house, opened another jug of the Elixir of Dreams, and drank it until he fell into a drugged sleep, dreaming of magic and miracles and awful creatures coming down from the moon.

That night, as Soledad slept, snoring like a freight train, two figures stood over him, making sure his slumbers were deep. They had noticed how frightened he had become at the appearance of the Crow Dog. How he had used his holy cross to attack the mongrel dog. The priest was a troublemaker. They had known it from the very first day. With a sigh, Pilar Mondragon cut off a lock of Soledad's hair. Peso pulled four sweat-soaked threads from the armpit of his cassock. They put the hair and the threads in a little chamois bag and disappeared into the night.

High above the village, in the cave where the Anasazi had sought refuge so many centuries before, and where Sotero had begun his depictions far to the back, Peso built a fire from sticks laid just so: four in the east-west position, four in the north-south position. Peso lighted the fire by rubbing a fire stick, the way his grandfather had taught him. He sang the old songs of witchcraft he'd learned from his mother's Zuni people. With his finger, Peso drew in the dirt a figure of Father Soledad. His arms were too long and his head was too big, but he wore a dishpan hat and a long, flowing garment. Into the middle of this figure, Peso inserted a tiny wooden cross he'd made from twigs in his yard. From a vial, he poured the still-warm blood of a rabbit on top of the cross; some of it dribbled down on the exaggerated figure of the priest. Then on top of the flickering yellow flames, Peso dropped the threads from the padre's cassock. They sizzled and disappeared. Pilar sprinkled the strands of the padre's hair on top of the coals. When the fire went out, Peso rubbed out the figure with the palm of his hand.

"The priest will not live long," he said confidently. Peso felt the strength of dead warriors flowing through his veins.

"No," said Pilar with a shrill laugh. "Soon, everything will be the same as it was before. Think how happy our lives will be then." Peso nodded.

Because of her magical power, Pilar was able to go back in time as easily as she was able to walk across the plaza. She had a connection to a pale, ancient time when animals mated with people and produced creatures that were invisible. In those days, nothing ever died. Nothing became worn out or old. The sun was the center of life, rising and setting with beauty and mystery. *It can be done*, she thought. *We have to get rid of the priest first.*

NINETEEN

*F*ATHER ANTONIO SAT *on his porch drinking a cup of the Elixir of Dreams. As always, when he drank it, his head became clouded. He actually felt himself transported back to the time of Michelangelo. He saw the crusaders with their slashing swords, heads of the heathens rolling in the dust. He no longer thought straight. Father Bartholomew sat opposite him, obviously agitated; his coarse brown cassock was pulled up around his knobby knees. His hair lay in damp strands across his rounded skull. The gold cross he wore around his neck gleamed in the sun. He stroked it absently.*

"These people are mad," he said. "And you, Father, believe everything they say. Look at you—you don't even dress like a priest anymore." And it was true. Father Antonio had shed his cassock for simple peasant attire. His face had turned brown in the sun. There was a giddy quality about him now. He no longer said Mass or conducted catechism.

"Better to understand them, my boy." His heart was full. Muy Contenta had visited recently. At eighty-three, he was fully alive, at last. Was there anything lovelier than the touch of her hand, the fullness of her lips on his? His long-forgotten passion had awakened. Who could explain the miracle? "We have to imagine ourselves in the sixteenth century," he said. "When these pagans, as you call them, were connected to all of life. They still are. Look at the trees, Bartholomew. Feel the wind." He smiled. "The Church does not know everything."

"Nonsense," Father Bartholomew said. "The Church is infallible."

His lips narrowed. He hated Father Antonio, the effete Florentine who could trace his roots back to a thirteenth-century dukedom, while he, Bartholomew, did not know who his parents were. He was a foundling, raised in an orphanage in Naples. Someday, he thought, I will kill the old man.

Father Antonio de Crepizi y Montefiore had seen much during the two years he'd spent on Soledad's trail, traveling all over the Southwest. At first, he'd detested him. His sins were great. But now, Father Antonio had begun to see that the sins of Father Soledad were the sins of every man. His martyr's death had redeemed him. There were the two miracles necessary for canonization; he'd affirmed these through the sworn testimony of the Indians. Could he deny the sanctifying grace of this poor fallen priest named Soledad, who had given his life so that others might live? Who was he to judge his affairs with women? Many had done so, even popes.

"Do you wish to walk with me a little, Bartholomew?" he asked softly.

The younger man shook his head. He had spent enough time on this fool's errand. "The Holy Father does not expect such duplicity. I am going to send a cable to Rome telling His Holiness what is happening." He drained his cup. The room spun around. "Especially to you."

"I would not do that if I were you," the old priest warned. He looked at the hustle and bustle of the plaza. Much had changed since Soledad died. There is meaning in it, *he thought.*

"It is my duty, so yes, I will do it. Your investigation will come to an end." Father Bartholomew had a smile of triumph as he got up and went inside.

FATHER ANTONIO THOUGHT his life as an ordained priest was over. And it was not altogether bad. He would renounce his vows and marry Muy Contenta. They'd raise fruit on a little farm she had in Colorado. He smiled at the sight of Camposanto basking in the sun. Here was something he had never known before. Antonio had come to love the deceased Father Soledad as much as he loved Jesus Christ. He did not trust Father Bartholomew, though. Too ambitious. Too insincere. He had caught him touching the Mexican boy's face down at the corral. It was simply too much. They would complete their assigned task and go their separate ways. They'd never see each other again. But first they had to write a convincing report to the Vatican council on Soledad's worthiness. Antonio would go to Rome himself and plead his case to the Supreme Pontiff.

Father Antonio poured himself a glass of the Elixir of Dreams and pulled up a chair. A mouse ran across the floor and up the table leg. He threw it a piece of dry cheese.

Father Bartholomew came in from his latest visit to the corral. His face was flushed. He pulled up a chair. "So what is your decision, Antonio? As if I didn't know. Or care."

The old priest looked out the small window. "Originally I said no, but something has happened to change my mind." He thought of Muy Contenta. He loved her, or felt what passed for love. "I am eighty-three years old," he said. "I never knew love before. Deus vult. *God wills it, Bartholomew." The younger priest stirred and crossed himself. He knew all too well what God willed. "I see a different kind of life out here," Antonio went on. "It's based on harmony and acceptance. No one is judged. Is that not what Our Lord Jesus Christ wanted?"*

Bartholomew got up and ran a hand through his thinning hair. "Surely you don't mean you've begun to believe their ways?"

Father Antonio was tired of Father Bartholomew and his incessant chattering.

"It's the truth, my boy." He crossed himself. "I have an open mind."

Every night, Father Antonio wrote his reports by the light of a kerosene lamp, while Father Bartholomew read the Latin breviary for guidance and wondered: When was a sin not a sin? When was a sinner not to be damned? When was God truly merciful?

"I HAVE LEARNED to become human here," Father Antonio said one evening as they ate their meal of tortillas and beans and drank the Elixir of Dreams, a fine beverage that transported them to another world. "And I have learned a great deal about the Indians. You know, Bartholomew, Soledad cured many Indians, and they still remember

him. *They call him Badger Man."* He remembered the old man who had handed him the talisman in the desert and how it had burned his hand.

From a small box, Father Antonio now extracted the eagle claw he had kept all this time, though Father Bartholomew had urged him to throw it away. He turned it over in his hand. The eagle claw had become his good luck talisman. He believed it had saved him from a flash flood. The bite of a rattlesnake. Heatstroke. A madwoman who had tried to kill him with a hunting knife. To say nothing about his arthritic hand that, with the help of a Navajo shaman, had been miraculously cured.

The Vatican priest looked closely at the eagle claw, with its sharp talons and strong bones, its look of absolute authority. "Badger Man," he said weakly.

Without thinking, the old priest dropped the eagle claw on the table. His golden cross lay beside it, gleaming in the lamplight. The priest turned away for a moment to draw a cup of water from a jug. When he turned back, the eagle claw had entwined itself around the cross. Father Antonio drew in his breath. With trembling fingers, he tried to separate one religious object from the other. Even Father Bartholomew, with his young muscles and strong fingers, could do nothing to separate this unholy talisman. A sense of fear came over them.

"What does it mean?" the younger priest asked. He had seen enough witchcraft in Camposanto to last him the rest of his life. He hoped his next posting was in a civilized place.

"Soledad," Father Antonio said. He walked to the door, opened it, and looked out. The moon was a pale green and nearly full; the stars gleamed brightly overhead. The pungent scent of burning cedar hung in the air. The mystery he felt here played with his disbelief. Far off, he heard chanting and drumming. Nothing has changed in a thousand years or more, he thought. The four seasons, the four directions, the sun, the moon, the stars, the plants, the animals, and the birds. All were connected, as Soledad had written in his journal. He was right.

Noticing that the moon was almost full and that Venus was racing along beneath it, he turned back into the cabin. He picked up the
eagle claw, now permanently entwined with the cross, from the table.
He rubbed it and felt a jolt.

"Help me get rid of it," he said to Bartholomew.

"I will not," said the younger priest. He walked out into the evening. Though he had no voting power at the Vatican, he was against
the beatification of this sinful priest. Somehow, he would make his
feelings known. He called over his shoulder. "I really am going to
send that cable to the Holy Father, Antonio. No more waiting. The
Supreme Pontiff needs to know the truth."

The next morning, Father Bartholomew went to the corral, wearing his cassock and sandals. The Mexican boy saddled a sorrel gelding similar to one he used to ride in Tucson when he was serving at
the mission church there. Off he went down the trail.

Father Antonio watched him go. Then he walked to the corral,
and the Mexican boy saddled a white horse for him. Father Antonio
was not a good rider. He had to hang on to the pommel to keep from
falling off. Ahead of him, the younger priest rode slowly, enjoying the
scenery he had begun to appreciate a little. Soon, Father Antonio
caught up with him.

"Get off your horse, Bartholomew," he puffed. "Give me your
sandals."

The older priest had authority the younger one did not. He obeyed.
"Now," Father Antonio said, "take that path through the trees. It leads
into the mountains."

The younger man looked around in terror. Wild animals lurked.
He was sure of it. Soon it would be dark. He hesitated. He could
easily outrun Father Antonio. He could knock him from his horse.
But he went meekly on the indicated path. Stones cut into his bare
feet. He hobbled along. "You will not get away with this, Father,"
Bartholomew cried over his shoulder.

"May God have mercy on your soul," the Vatican priest called. He
waited for perhaps an hour. Father Bartholomew did not come back.
Later, Father Antonio put on his vestments and offered a Mass in the

lost priest's name. He was sure the younger man's soul was in heaven. Possibly in hell, or somewhere in between.

And yet he caught himself looking into the trees for some sign of him. He peered into the well to see if he was there. At night, he thought he heard his voice crying out.

I sent him to his death, *he thought.*

Mea culpa. Mea maxima culpa.

PART FIVE

Camposanto, New Mexico Territory, 1896

TWENTY

B Y THE TIME summer had ripened into an indolent green and the wild plum trees were heavy with purple fruit, Soledad found himself starting to slip over the line that separated him from the Calabazas. In this crossing, imperceptible at first, he discovered a strength that he had not known before. He wanted to learn everything he could about them.

"We were once animals," Juan Talamantes told him. "Buffalo and deer and elk. We thought like them."

"We can go back in time," Juan Lobo said. "Even to the Beginning Time."

"I know how Coyote brought fire to our people," Pilar Mondragon said. "In his mouth." She had been there in her mind, she told her grandchildren.

ONE MORNING, Luis Madrone hitched the old mare to the wagon and took the padre up into the mountains to observe a family of bighorn sheep picking their way carefully among the rocks. How beautiful they were! He loved the way their horns curled. The priest sat motionless on the hard wooden seat, the sun warm on his bare arms and legs; the rich smell of earth rose to fill his nostrils. A bald eagle flew overhead, making a shrill sound. The priest laughed and extended his arms. "I wish I could go with you!" he cried.

The eagle had free will, but did it also possess a soul? *Yes,* he thought.

"A miracle, no?" Luis said. "Earth and sky coming together like a man and woman. That eagle. Those sheep. Each thing is sacred. Use your eyes, Padre. It's all there." The fat man with merry eyes was already writing a story in his mind about what the priest had done the first time he saw an eagle. He cried. Luis sighed. He reached behind the seat for the jug of the Elixir of Dreams. He took a swig, then passed it to the priest.

"Do you know how animals and men are alike?" the story-teller asked. The priest shook his head. "It is this ugly thing we have between our legs. It starts wars. Drives females crazy. Human females. Sheep females. Horse females. Even fish females, I suppose. How big is yours?"

Soledad felt his face grow red. "Really, Luis," he heard himself saying. "I am a priest. I don't think about such things."

Luis laughed, making mental note of the priest's discomfort. "Padre," he said, "I happen to know it's all you think about. Women are heaven on earth. I have bedded quite a few myself. And you?"

Soledad looked up. The bighorn sheep had reached the top of the rocks. They stood silhouetted against the sky like statues. He had never seen anything more beautiful. The eagle dipped above his head.

"Many," said the priest. The eagle flew straight at him, but Soledad did not move.

FOR THE FIRST time in his life, Soledad was truly happy. He listened to the songs of birds, warblers and jays, chickadees and mourning doves; he grew fond of the grouse and the white-topped quail who lived beneath the cedar tree to the east of his casita. A red-tailed hawk flew above him as he walked along. The bald eagle, perhaps the same one he had seen in the mountains with Luis, seemed to watch his every move. A mountain lion came by one evening, a dead rabbit in its mouth. A red fox walked with her kits in front of his porch while he squeaked out a tune on his violin. They stopped and looked at him.

"You like it, eh?" He played some more. Whoever would have expected foxes to like classical music?

FROM TIME TO time, the priest went on horseback to the mountains, where he helped the melancholy Narciso Ortega set beaver traps along the high country streams. He experienced something up there in the forest he had never felt before, though he could not define exactly what it was. Sensing his mood, Narciso said, "Ah, Padre, out here the world grows larger, while a man becomes a speck. In the long run, only these mountains will go on."

He had begun to believe this was so. For the Church to ignore nature was for it to ignore the very heart of God. He breathed deeply and uttered an Indian prayer, the way Luis had taught him: "Earth cure me. Earth receive my woe. Rock receive the anger from my heart."

The people gave him grudging acceptance and shared their simple meals, but they refused to build his church. Juan Lobo laughed at his frustration. "You see? We are pagans, as we have always been. You will lose the wager, Padre, and then?" Something in the old man's beady eyes made the priest shudder. In his mind's eye, he saw Striped Wolf. Elk Old Man. Father Montez. And he knew that, for all their outward charm, the Calabazas were as deadly as rattlesnakes.

He ached for La Luz. There was no other word to describe the tension in his body, the erection he inevitably had when he thought of her as he lay in his narrow bed at night. Sometimes he would pace up and down in front of her house, pretending to read his breviary, waiting for her to appear. Madness, he thought, yet he could not help himself. He began to find gifts from her in his house. Freshly baked bread. Wild plum jam. A dish of green chile. Tortillas. Beans. After his own simple fare, it tasted so good he would eat until he was full, grateful for even this much attention from a woman who would not let him rest.

One day, Soledad dragged himself home after helping Juan

Lobo cut vigas. His whole body ached. His door stood open, and inside La Luz was waiting for him in the dim coolness of the room, fingering the arrowheads he'd left on a low table beside the bed. He came through the door, trembling at the sight of her standing in his house as if she owned it. "La Luz," he said huskily. "What do you want?"

"I want to talk to you," she said, her face flushed, her hand on her breast. It had been more than a year since she'd made love, a year of frustrating days and lonely nights. She put the arrowheads back on the table, a tight smile on her lips. It had been very hard for her to overcome her fears and come to him. But she knew he was not immune to her charms. She looked at him, smiling.

"I did not expect to find you here," he said. "People don't usually just walk into my house." He looked away.

"It is Luis's house," she said shortly. "Besides, I used to live here when Rafael and I were first married." She looked around at the familiar walls, remembering how she and Rafael had made love in the flickering light and laughed at their copulating shadows. Almost every night for five years they had renewed their passion, until her girl's body rounded into the flower of womanhood.

"And now?" he asked. "Are you married now?"

She laughed a rich throaty laugh. "My husband is as good as dead. Why should I waste my life?" She tossed her head. Her hair was thick. He had a sudden urge to touch it.

He hesitated. "In the eyes of the Church, you are married until the day one of you dies." How strange these words sounded on his tongue, though he had repeated them often since his ordination.

"I do not care," she said, sitting down on the bed. "I do not like your Church, Padre. It makes me feel bad. What does that make me?"

He sat down in the chair and allowed himself to look directly into her eyes, their dark beauty catching at his throat, taking his breath away. "It makes you very challenging to a priest whose job it is to bring people into the Church," he said huskily. How foolish he felt, knowing how he had begun to understand their world.

"Well, I do not believe in the Church," La Luz said, getting up. "When I was twelve or thirteen, I went away to convent school. There I saw God in a vat of soap. I asked him for shoes. Stockings to keep my legs warm. A winter coat. Nothing happened. After a year, I ran away. Back here to the mountains. I do not belong to anything." She moved slowly across the room and stood by the window. "Or anyone."

"You cannot demand favors of God," he said irritably. "He is not a general store. God gives when people believe." How his heart ached when he looked at her! He was aroused.

She shrugged. "I believe in the mountains. And in the feathered creatures and the four-legged animals. I believe in the Great Spirit, who does not care if you are Catholic or not, as long as you live a harmonious life. I also believe in love," she said softly. Noticing his torment, she moved toward him and touched him lightly on the shoulder. "What are you afraid of, Padre? In two months' time, I have never seen you smile."

He felt his face grow hot. His comet throbbed painfully. "I don't know," he sighed. "I'm afraid of failing, I suppose. I've accomplished so little in my life." But he had seen the eagle and the bighorn sheep and been moved by them as an Indian would. It was something.

She shook her head. "That is why I have come here to see you, Padre. You should not have come to Camposanto. People are bitter. They do not need a priest. They need a way out. You see, this land belongs to the United States government. Next spring we will be gone. To a reservation in the desert, where many of us will die. We are mountain people. We do not belong there."

Soledad nodded numbly. That explained the strange things that were happening in the village. The way that people treated him— they were trying to cover up their fears. Why had the monsignor not warned him? "But why?" he asked softly, and took her hand in his. "I don't understand."

"The land has been made part of something called a 'forest reserve,'" she said. "The *federales* came and offered us money to give up the land. Juan Lobo threw it on the ground. He got a lawyer, and the lawyer told him what the *federales* said: the Calabazas do not own this land, the government does. As if anybody owns land."

The priest felt sick; he looked away from La Luz. "I'm sorry," he said.

"I am not going to the desert," she said. "I will take my children and go to San Juan Pueblo. I have relatives there."

Closing his eyes, Soledad could see the whole sad history of the Indians unfolding in his mind, tragedy after tragedy, until even the Calabazas—this fragile, forgotten tribe—would be destroyed. Rising from his chair, he clutched his damaged cross and rubbed it. "As God is my judge," he said in an almost inaudible voice, "I will find a way to help you!" He remembered his day with Luis. Had it not been planned? Had he not responded the way he was expected to?

La Luz squeezed his hand. She was afraid to believe in him, though his sincerity touched her heart. "Ah, Padre, what can you do?" she sighed. "We have tried many things, and now we must accept our fate. We are not the first ones to lose our homeland. My father-in-law says when we go to the desert, he will create a whole new set of stories." She smiled. "So you see, we will make the most of things."

The priest strode about the room, overcome with emotion. "You must not accept anything," he said. "You are stronger than the world out there will ever know. That's why you must try to resist them until I can figure out what to do!" Soledad's breath came in gasps, and he was sweating profusely, even though the room was cold. "Listen to me, La Luz. The white man was not ordained by God to have dominion over the red man. That's what the government says. That's what every priest and minister and newspaper editor in the country says. But it's wrong! You have every right to live here. I saw how the Comanche were killed in Texas, the buffalo slaughtered and left to rot. I was helpless to do anything."

She looked him straight in the eye. "I know that, Padre. It is what we are taught as children. We have a right to live as we always have. But they believe we are like ants."

He sat beside her and took her hand again. She moved against him. The pressure of her knee excited him, but he felt drained—as if he had walked a thousand miles. "What do you want me to do?"

She touched his unshaven cheek where the comet birthmark throbbed like a heartbeat. "You want to build a church. We do not need a church. We need you to make the *federales* go away and the surveyors and the people building roads and fences on our land, killing our deer and cutting down our trees. That is what we want you to do."

The flustered priest dropped his eyes to the floor, holding his head in his hands. "To do what you ask would take a miracle, La Luz." He sighed deeply. "Whatever happens here is part of my life, too. Your people have become like my own. I never had a home or any sort of normal life. Things are often bizarre here, yet I feel I belong."

Through the window, La Luz saw Delfine standing motionless in the twilight, staring at the house. She knew Delfine. He loved her. In a way, she loved him. But his brain was as dull as stone. Besides, he was Rafael's younger brother—jealous of him ever since he had married La Luz when she was sixteen years old and the most beautiful girl in the village; she had driven the boys crazy.

"There is no way out, Padre," she said quietly. "We have a little more time, then no more. People will die rather than pack up their things and go. It will be the end of our songs, no matter what Luis says." She looked up at him. Tears rolled down her cheeks.

The priest was deeply, powerfully moved. He rose and drew her to his chest, stroking her thick, dark hair. He brushed his lips across the top of her head. He told himself to stop, but by now he knew he could not. "Please don't cry," he said and offered her his handkerchief. She began to shiver, too scared to speak. Suddenly, she saw Delfine standing in the shadows outside. In his hand was a long-barreled revolver that belonged to Luis. She screamed and pushed Soledad to one side as a bullet tore into the whitewashed adobe wall. "You must leave Camposanto!" she cried. "He is drunk.

He will try again." She would never be happy or safe as long as Delfine was around.

"I will never leave," Soledad said calmly as he held her. He blew out the lamp. The room was almost totally dark. He shoved the dresser in front of the door, not realizing that Delfine could climb through the small window that had no latch. He pulled her against him. "I have always loved you," he said softly. "Since the very first day." She could not answer him, for she did not yet know how she felt. The sad-eyed priest was a man unlike any other. That much she knew. She felt drawn to him. He was strong, connected to an unfamiliar world that possessed him. *As I could possess him*, she thought.

La Luz lifted her head and kissed him. Softly, at first. Then full, hard until their deeply buried passions exploded together. Somehow she had expected it, as one expects the dawn. He pulled her head back and kissed her long neck, her chin, her full lips. Nothing else existed except La Luz and himself. He wanted to hold her forever, just as they were now, her body pressed tightly against the rough material of his cassock. Quickly, he took it off.

"Is it wrong, Padre?" La Luz breathed excitedly as she slid out of her dress and let it fall to the floor. She had nothing on underneath. With a gasp, he stumbled toward her with his usual erection.

"It's not wrong," he whispered. Her skin glowed in the moonlight. He kissed her firm, round breasts, then her protruding little tummy. She was even more beautiful than he had imagined. With a deep hunger, he ran his fingers up and down her body and felt its silken firmness. "You are flawless," he breathed. The love between a man and a woman was a sacrament as great as any instituted by his Church, he thought fleetingly. As he entered her, Soledad uttered a cry of pure ecstasy: "I love you, La Luz!"

She had not expected the way gentleness overtook him as the layers of her resistance fell away. Rafael was rough; he had his way, then rolled over and went to sleep. The other men she'd loved had never recognized her *tasoom*, a holy spirit, ready to fly through the air the moment they touched her. But Soledad knew all about *tasooms*; that was his business. Because he was a priest, he knew about love and tenderness; he sensed what it was a woman needed from him. Or so he told himself.

"I think I love you as well, Padre," La Luz whispered as she lay beside the priest on his hard, narrow bed, covered with a ragged quilt. She was part of him forever now. He had exploded in her; the bed was wet with their passion. With an excited little cry, he rolled on top of her and buried himself in her unresisting body once again. She thought she would die; his fury, his wild insistence as he kissed her, his cries of ecstasy somehow made her feel closer to God. "Yes, perhaps the priest was God," she would say years later, when Father Antonio came snooping around, wanting to know about the priest's sex life. For the rest of her life, La Luz would believe that the first night she and Father Soledad made love was the beginning of her eternal salvation.

Soledad awoke with a start. The place where La Luz had been was just a small, damp indentation in the bed. He turned over and smelled the rough muslin sheets. Her scent was there for him to enjoy until it faded. Flushed, he sat by the window, drinking cold coffee, watching the village stir to life. Once again, he had sinned with a woman, and this woman had become his in the process. Delfine could kill him if he wished, but La Luz was his. *Yes,* he thought, *but she is also married to Rafael, and she has just committed adultery.* He drummed his fingers on the table. He wanted her. Did he want her badly enough to give up the priesthood and see that she got a divorce from Rafael? What would he do for a living? He was not trained for anything else. Would he move to San Juan Pueblo with La Luz and her children and pretend to be an Indian, like so many white men nowadays? Or continue as a fallen priest, struggling to offer something the Indians never wanted in the first place? The situation was hopeless. Whatever happened between them last night could not—must not—happen again. Did he want to lose the one thing that connected him to respectability? Was he ready to have his name dragged from one end of the Church to the other? A wave of remorse washed over him. He fell to his knees and tried to pray, but the words stuck in his throat.

Soledad ate a meager breakfast of stale bread, moldy cheese, and withered apples, watching thin blue smoke from the chimneys curling around the small adobe houses like ghostly wreathes. He inhaled the pungent odor of burning wood. How could he help the Calabazas now, in a way that truly mattered? So far, his efforts had been a travesty. He was caught in lies, and lies would eventually kill him, he thought. He dropped his head in his hands. Outside his window, a mountain blue jay called, and the priest looked up. *I love her*, he thought in amazement. "Do you hear that, Mr. Blue Jay? I love her," he said. He was certain he had never been in love before. Yet this love, which began to change him in all sorts of unexpected ways, created a rift in his soul, deeper than any he had experienced before.

THERE WAS NO one to forgive Lorenzo Soledad of his ongoing sins except the mute Sotero, who listened patiently to all the priest's wrongdoings with the same neutral expression. Sotero was pure and uncorrupted, and he listened with his great inner silence to what that priest had to say.

"My life is difficult, Sotero," the priest sighed one morning after a sleepless night. He had no right to the woman, none at all. She was married with two children. But he could not live without her. He straddled a broken chair in the mute's little workroom and smoothed the folds of his cassock. His cross gleamed in the sunlight streaming in the cracked, grimy window, and the boy eyed it covetously, remembering the priest's promise. "You see, I have fallen in love with a woman. No ordinary woman, mind you. But a woman so beautiful that no other woman on earth can compare to her!"

As the priest talked, Sotero carved a statue of Saint Joseph from a drawing that Soledad had given him. "You know this woman because she lives in your house," Soledad continued. "I am not ashamed to tell you that I have sinned with La Luz," he blurted out. "Oh, she is God's gift, Sotero. But she is married to your brother, and I am a priest, bound by my vows to forsake women. Do you understand?"

The mute nodded and made his strange bleating noise as Soledad continued. "So this is a grievous sin I have committed. I must find a way to resist her. Yet in her, I find salvation. She is a holy woman, wise in many ways." He dropped his face in his hands. "I am a bad priest." The mute shook his head violently. "I am also a bad man because you see . . ." He stopped and ran his hands through his hair. "Ah, perhaps I should not tell you. It is something so terrible that I am afraid you won't like me anymore." The boy got up and threw his arms around the priest. He banged his head against his chest. The bleating grew louder. The boy could not imagine a circumstance under which he would not like the priest. He'd become an altar boy, though there was no altar—only a rough plank set between two stumps, covered with a pretty white cloth when Soledad said Sunday Mass. Though he could not utter the Latin responses, Sotero nonetheless quivered at the Latin words the priest said. They made the blood rush to his head. They made him think of doves and eagles and snow on the high peaks. For hours, Sotero would stand in front of his mother's tiny mirror, trying to get the Latin words to form.

Gently, the priest pushed the boy away. "All right, I will tell you about a very great sin. It happened a long time ago, when I was just a boy, not much older than you. I lived in Texas then, in a house filled with beautiful women, dressed in beautiful clothes. They were not bad women, mind you, simply women who could not help themselves. Men came to this house and paid these women to love them. Such women are called 'prostitutes,' my boy. Now, one of these women was my mother. Yes, she was a common whore, though it took me a long time to realize it." His head dropped to his chest, and for a moment it seemed he could not go on, until Sotero began to bleat and banged his wood-carving knife on a tin can.

Soledad rubbed his eyes. "There was a certain man—a rude, nasty man—who always came to see her. I hated him. He humiliated my mother, but she never tried to get away from him, even when he pushed her down. On the contrary, I think she liked her sinful work. One night, I couldn't stand it anymore. I took a revolver, intending to kill the man she was with. I aimed and fired. I shot my mother instead." Tears rolled down his cheeks, igniting his comet with sorrow. He scarcely knew what he was doing as he knelt beside the mute wood-carver with a bowed head. "For years I have said I meant to kill the man. But I am going to tell you a secret. I meant to kill my mother. For what she was, Sotero—don't you see? Wasting her life like that! I had no respect for her!"

With a cry, Soledad jumped up and began to pace the narrow room with the sawdust floor and the wind blowing through the cracks in the walls. "That's why I became a priest—thinking I would be free from guilt. But I am not free. My guilt is there all the time, eating me up like a cancer. I am not a holy man, Sotero."

How Sotero wished he could speak to comfort the sad priest when he needed it. He looked over the shelf of carved animals and selected the Bear and shoved it into his hands. "Thank you," said the priest, and he wiped his eyes with his handkerchief. For the first time in many years, his soul felt almost clean. He bent and kissed the top of the boy's head. "You have given me a priceless gift. This Bear. And the matter of your heart."

Sotero tugged on the padre's sleeve and held out his hand. In it was another *real*, gleaming in the light. Soledad took the coin and examined it closely. Where had it come from? Were there more? The priest pleaded with the boy. "I must know. For the love of God, Sotero! Where did you get this?" He shook him rather roughly. "Don't you understand? With this, your people might never have to move!"

With a shrill laugh, Sotero shook himself free and scampered through the door. He knew there were at least a hundred shiny coins, maybe more. The cave was not far away.

When the priest stepped outside in the sunlight, Luis was waiting at the door. Soledad knew he had heard every word. "Now you know about me, Luis," he said. "I am a murderer. A fornicator. A man who does not believe in his Church, except as it serves my end."

The Custodian of Stories shook his head. He was a practical man, who lived in a magical world he could create or suspend anytime he wished. What did it matter, when all was said and done? Life was the same. Death was the same. But he also had to live in Camposanto with a woman who mocked him and children who failed him and friends he did not trust. He took a deep breath. "You are a man, Padre," he said softly. "We are all men. Sometimes we do things that hurt other people. But it cannot be helped. What has this made you? A man who believes in something at long last? Or a man who is hollow inside, like a rotten log, eh?" With that, he strode up the hill and into the forest, where he would write a story in his mind about what had happened to the padre. He would invent a tale about how a comet had come from the sky to rest upon the padre's cheek.

TWENTY-ONE

*T*HE VATICAN PRIEST sat at the table drinking the Elixir of *Dreams. He began to feel dizzy. His heart was heavy.* He was certain *he had sent Father Bartholomew to his death, since several months had passed and no trace of him had been found. Guilt weighed heavily on his mind, but Bartholomew finally was out of his hair.* At my age to have committed murder, *he thought.* But was it really a sin considering how much had been gained? Soledad was as good as canonized.

In less than a fortnight he would leave for Rome. But there was business to attend to first.

There was a knock and a beautiful woman came in. Soledad's woman.

"You made him break his vows, La Luz," he said. She looked at him. An old man with an old man's dreams. Had Father Antonio ever had a woman? Did he ever know love? She gave him a crooked smile. A woman had visited not long ago. Stoutish. Dressed in long skirts. She had caught them holding hands. Muy Contenta, he called her.

"No, Padre," she said. "Because of me, Soledad found life."

"Copulation is not life," Father Antonio fumed. "It is the work of the Devil." His hands trembled. He forced himself to look at her. Though well past thirty, she was still beautiful, with a sensuality that made him think of a voluptuous peasant girl he had met in Amalfi the summer he was sixteen. Had he not fallen in love with her? Had he not lost his virginity behind the garden wall? He

brushed a tear from his eye. And now there was Muy Contenta. To have found her at his age was nothing short of a miracle. Before long, she would be back.

"You must apologize to the Blessed Virgin for tempting her son." He bit his tongue.

"I will not," she refused.

The old priest got up and tottered out the door. He blinked in the sunlight. There in the middle of the plaza was Muy Contenta and her wagon. She was a week ahead of schedule. He didn't mind.

"Climb up, Antonio," she said. He had been waiting for her, and now she was here. She wore a blue velvet cape and a plumed hat, white gloves, and lace-up boots. Oh, there was a wild beauty to her even now. He could not take his eyes off her. "I am taking you for a ride," she said and snapped the reins. The wagon rolled ahead.

He got in with a groan. "I have missed you," he said. "You have made an old man happy." He squeezed her hand. "My world is beautiful now."

"I missed you too, Antonio. That's why I'm early." she said.

La Luz watched through the window. The old priest is not immune to women, she thought. I think he may even be alive.

"It has been an interesting time," he said, hanging on as the wagon rolled along the narrow ruts. "Who was Soledad, after all? I see myself in him."

"It's time those stuffy old farts in the Vatican woke up," she said. "A man is a man no matter what." She drove to the ruins of the old church and got out. She had brought a picnic of bread and cheese. After they had eaten, she unbuttoned her shirtwaist. "It's never too late," she said. "Men are men. Come here and kiss me."

She had large breasts. He stared at them. They were as nice as he remembered.

I am too old, he thought. There is not enough time. I must go back to Rome. But he was already out of his trousers. His flesh sagged.

He kissed her on the mouth. He held her in his arms. Birds called to him. A coyote sauntered past.

"I am eighty-four years old," he panted. "I should be dead by now."

"In the eyes of God you are but a babe. The mountains are older than you."

Father Antonio struggled to his feet from the grass where they had been lying. "There is something you should know."

"I know I am crazy about you, Antonio. I want you to take me to Italy."

He shook his head. "That is not possible," he said. "Though I'd like to." He looked away to the snow-covered mountains. "I may have sent Father Bartholomew to his death. You see, he was going to inform the Holy Father about Soledad's true nature."

She burst out laughing. "True nature? His true nature was kindness."

"Yes, I know."

Muy Contenta put away the picnic things. "Father Bartholomew is in Batwing, living with a railroad engineer named Clarence," she said. "He found his way there after he found some letters from Henrietta to her son that were written long ago. Batwing sounded like a good place, so he made his way clear down to Texas. I don't know how. They are very happy in their little house. Father Bartholomew teaches Latin at the normal school. He helped to build the new church. He named it after Soledad. Clarence opened a bakery."

The old priest crossed himself. Tears ran down his cheeks. "Thanks be to God," he said.

TWENTY-TWO

PECULIAR THINGS BEGAN to happen in the village. Later, people would say they first noticed the changes around the time that La Luz fell in love with the priest and slept all night with him. Bonito Lobo discovered a way to cure his insomnia by becoming an aviator, long before airplanes had been invented. Luis Madrone decided to compose an epic poem in his mind about his tribe's long struggle to survive and took his verse to Santa Fe to have it published in the newspaper after Maria Lobo had written it out. Ana Coyote decided to try a genetic experiment, mating a Rhode Island Red rooster with a guinea hen El Comanche had stolen on one of his raids. In his crude, almost illegible hand, Delfine scratched out a letter to his brother, Rafael, telling him what La Luz had been doing while he was behind bars. El Comanche saddled up and headed north to commiserate with the Cheyenne, but they were no longer where he had seen them last; in their place, he found a city called Denver, spread out across their old camping grounds. Narciso Ortega climbed on top of his roof and sat there, day after day, beating the old blackened tribal drum until at last he'd drummed a cord between himself and the earth that would not break, even if he had to move to the desert.

Late in the Sun Going Away Moon, Peso departed on a combat strategy tour to the northern pueblos, believing it was only a matter of weeks before the Second Great Revolt would begin at Taos, where feelings still ran high against the religious after two hundred years. Pilar made straw padre dolls into which she stuck her pins. Though the padre slept a good bit of the time, he was not dead; Pilar watched him for signs of nascent decay, but all he exhibited was a giddiness associated with love. Juan Lobo made several trips to Santa Fe for last-ditch talks with the authorities. But each time he came home empty-handed, refusing to talk to anyone about what he had done. On his return, he would go deep into the mountains to fast and wait for a vision; he would sing all his old songs and appeal to all the old spirits. But all he heard was the silence of inevitability. On one of these pilgrimages, the cacique shot all his arrows into the ground, then picked them up and broke every one.

No work commenced on the church, though the priest went around from house to house, begging for help. The men went hunting; the women dried meat. "We are too busy," everyone said. Sotero developed cramps in his hands working so hard, carving the animals and the saints for the church and hammering the padre's biography on the stone walls of the cave. But he would not reveal where he had found the *reales*, no matter how many times the padre or Juan Lobo asked him. Juan Talamantes was studying multiplication tables, imagining making love to Ermina every chance he got, and trying to figure a way to apply his newfound knowledge to a practical end. He wanted to add up all their problems, divide them by practicality, and find the sum total of their courage. But Ermina discouraged him. "Fool," she said. "It is too late for that."

It was a busy fall, with everyone working hard to prepare for what they believed would be their last winter in Camposanto. A strong thread of gossip wove around the fool that La Luz was making of herself over the priest. She could not help herself. Nor could he. In a village of no more than a hundred people whose principal pastime was the observation and analysis of everyone else, the romance between the priest and La Luz was all anyone talked about. "We are a village of busybodies," Juan Lobo grumbled, disappointed that he no longer Got Together with La Luz, now that the padre had her. Instead, he Got Together with his own wife, Maria, and held her gently all night long, the way he used to when they were first married. "You are the shadow of my tree," the old man would say tenderly, the closest he would ever come to telling her that he loved her.

Other things happened, strange and unexplained. Isabela Talamantes's milk dried up, and her baby cried all night until Alvar found a goat to milk. Catarina Madrone's bread would not rise but turned into an enormous, tasteless tortilla. Maria Lobo's coffee boiled over, quickly covered the tabletop and then the floor, and just as quickly ran out the door. In the middle of the night, Juan Talamantes, dragging his wooden leg, dug up the old church bells, Gracia and Refugio, buried in the manure pile since the time of the last priest. With the help of Bonito and Narciso, he hung them from the deep, strong branches of El Abuelo. Then he rang them until the padre dressed and hurried down to the river where Juan stood, his face turned toward the stars. "I am ready for algebra!" he cried. "With algebra, I can tame the world!"

Soledad was in love. Nothing mattered except finding La Luz in his bed at the end of every day. He was aware of what people thought, and he didn't care. He only laughed when Maria Lobo warned him about the fool he was making of himself. Or when Luis took him to the waterfall, trying to talk sense into his head. Delfine, a scowl on his face, peered in the window one night and watched the priest and La Luz in wild copulation until Soledad, looking up, ran out into the cold night and shouted at him to stay away. La Luz laughed at the sight of him, naked and shivering, hopping about on the pebbles that hurt his feet. "You are crazy!" she laughed as he came back to her arms. She was happy with him. She had never been this happy before, and she was certain she would never be this happy again.

"What are we to do, Lorenzo?" she asked one evening, after she had cooked his supper and lay on the bed, her head on his lap. "Will I divorce Rafael and marry you?"

The priest frowned. "I only know I love you," he whispered, rubbing her scalp with his fingers. "Does anything else matter?" More and more he was certain that God was manifest in the sacred act of love, as surely as in any of the blessed sacraments. With her, he felt redeemed, cleansed of his sins—a man about to experience what eternity was all about.

He pulled away and looked at her. La Luz's face had become even lovelier; it had a mysterious luster that hadn't been there before. Her beauty crowded all other reality from his mind. He drew her to him and kissed her softly. "By all that is holy, I love you," he said. "This is what I was made for. Not even the love of Christ has offered me more."

"If you were not a priest, what would you be?" she asked thoughtfully.

"But I *am* a priest," he replied. "It's what I chose to become." The fabrication did not strike him. Playfully, he nibbled her ear. "But I am also a very great lover, don't you think?" For the first time, she heard him laugh.

"Yes," she said, "you are that." But a cloud had settled on her face, and in that instant, he saw her as she would be in old age, wrinkled but still beautiful, and he wondered if he would be around. "Tomorrow is Fuego's birthday," she said. "Seven years old. We will have a party in the afternoon. And you will come."

He nuzzled against her breasts. "I will," he said. "And I will bring him the most beautiful present of all. My pony, Amigo. Will he like my present, La Luz?" He danced across the hard-packed earth floor in his bare feet. He felt alive, fulfilled, peaceful. Surely his sins had been forgiven. He pulled her to him. "You know I love you." She nodded.

What else was there except this man? She kissed him. "He will love Amigo," she laughed, "as much as I love you."

Years later, when the details of her ill-starred affair with the priest became known to the Vatican priests, La Luz would think those few short months with Soledad turned her life around. She was the priest's woman. The center of his devotion. With her he'd forgotten his whole purpose. Or thought he had.

Maria Lobo confirmed what La Luz already thought. She was going to have the priest's baby. "There is something wrong," Maria Lobo said. When she listened for a heartbeat, she heard a terrible scream.

TWENTY-THREE

WHEN PAPITA THE Dwarf started having fits during the full moon, Pilar was summoned by Narciso to attend her. Dressed in black from head to toe and wailing as if to physically shatter the malaise that surrounded the girl, Pilar fed the dwarf a measure of lizard's blood and the urine of a mountain lion. She smeared her body with a paste of mashed worms and spiders and chanted as she danced around the bed with her witch's rattle. While Narciso paced up and down wringing his hands, Papita fell into unconsciousness, pale as a cloud. In the middle of the night, Isabela Talamantes, an apprentice medicine woman under the guidance of Maria Lobo, was summoned from her bed. She hurried over with her own particular potions—the heart of a freshly slaughtered lamb still pumping sticky blood in her hand and the bones of an eagle's foot ground into a fine, white powder. She laid the lamb's heart on top of Papita's own, then she rubbed the eagle foot powder on the girl's head, noticing that her eyes seemed focused on another world. While Pilar watched in brooding silence, Isabela went outside and built a fire of wet wood. When the fire was smoking heavily, she suspended Papita over the embers by her little ankles. When the girl was thoroughly smoked, Isabela carried her to the river and submerged all but her head in the icy water. She inserted spider webs in her ears and mouth to clear out the bad spirits.

But Isabel's magic was no more effective than Pilar's. When she brought Papita from the river, the girl's breath had stopped and her skin had turned blue. Sobbing, Isabela turned to the old witch. "She is dead, Pilar!" Her eyes were dark and accusing.

"It is your fault, you stupid girl," Pilar said, and she spat a substance like ink out of her mouth onto the ground. "If you had apprenticed to me instead of that foolish Maria Lobo, you might have saved her." In her black outfit, she looked as ominous as a rattlesnake. She looked around to see if the priest was watching them. Ever since she and Peso had their little ceremony in the cave, Father Soledad had seemed exhausted, but she did not connect this with his rampant love affair with La Luz, which deprived him of sleep.

"I am sorry," Isabela said over and over between sobs. She had loved Papita, for it was she who could make her baby laugh, she who could charm Alvar out of his rages. The whole village loved her. No one could imagine life without Papita.

Though Pilar tried her magic once again, it was no use. Weeping profusely, Narciso wrapped Papita in a blanket and, followed by the two medicine women, carried her toward the plaza. She was all he had left in the world, and now he had to dig a hole and bury her. Narciso wearily climbed the steps to Luis's house and stumbled toward Catarina Madrone. "She is gone," he sobbed, clutching the lifeless form in his arms. "So I will give her body to you to prepare for her journey to the World Beyond." Catarina's lip trembled. Papita had been the most beautiful baby in the village, with a happy laugh that made everyone around her smile. The Custodian of Lesser Causes resolved once Papita was laid in the ground to gather all the white stones she could find and arrange them in the shape of a ladder around the dwarf's head. In this way, Papita could climb back out of the earth whenever she wanted to.

Narciso tenderly laid the dwarf on the floor and smoothed her hair. When Catarina put her ear to the girl's chest, she thought she heard a faint heartbeat, but perhaps it was only the Death Spirit assuming control of the girl's destiny. The first thing she did was to rub Papita all over with sage. Next, she poured a warm, sweet oil over her smooth, soft skin. She took a flint and steel and struck them together until the sparks fell onto Papita's eyelids. Then

Catarina breathed into Papita's tight little mouth, forcing her lips apart with her fingers. "Accept my breath of life," she commanded, but nothing happened. She looked quite pale.

La Luz, who had come in to help, laid the still-warm body of a dove shot with an arrow and bird point by El Comanche on the dwarf's lifeless chest. She touched Papita's icy lips with her fingers and shook her head sadly.

When at last Catarina believed there was no longer a spark of life, she dressed the girl carefully and sent Fuego for the priest. Papita had been baptized, and she deserved whatever happened next in Catholic ritual. "I did what I could," she said to Narciso.

Catarina squeezed Luis's hand while she waited for the priest to arrive. She realized her husband was worried about weighty things these days, for he seemed to forget many of the stories that he had always known before. "It is a bad sign, the dwarf dying," she said. Luis only nodded and brushed a tear from his eyes. "She was sunlight," he said, remembering how she used to run barefoot around the plaza.

The Custodian of Lesser Causes looked at the walls of her house. Whitewashed more than twenty years before, they were now an unwholesome gray. She looked at the dirt floor, the tattered pieces of linoleum that covered it, the battered table and chairs, and the spinning wheel that El Comanche had appropriated from a wagon whose occupants he'd demolished on the Santa Fe Trail. An accumulated energy lay between these walls—births, deaths, passion, grief. Three generations of her family had lived and died here, and soon the walls would crumble, and the wind and the rain would take everything away. Catarina knew that the walls would soon absorb the death of the happy little dwarf who everyone in the village had loved.

When Father Soledad arrived, he scarcely looked at La Luz, pressed against one wall. With his surplice around his neck, he knelt beside the girl's still body, listened for a heartbeat, and opened her closed eyes with his fingers. Then to the amazement of the mourning Calabazas, he picked her up, kissed her on the forehead, and blessed her. "I believe you call this custom 'Getting Together,'" he said. "I don't want to be disturbed for any reason whatsoever." Then he carried the lifeless girl to the room that La Luz shared with her children and pulled aside the gunnysack curtains. He lay down beside Papita on the bed, arranged her dress, her hands, her hair as if for a funeral. He was not certain how this custom was done, so he lay, fully dressed, holding the girl in his arms. The smell of smoke was in the dwarf's clothing and hair, though the sage and sweet oil masked any smell of death. As he lay there, Soledad started to hum the Gloria from the Mass; then he sang the entire Mass straight through in his off-key, raspy tenor. He asked for his violin and played a Beethoven minuet. He was glad he had learned this music from Herr Lieber so many years ago in Batwing, but he would never play well.

He remembered the songs the Navajo man had taught him, and these he also hummed. He took two tail feathers of a blue jay from the pocket of his cassock and laid them across her eyes. He spoke soft words of encouragement, describing the rich fullness of sunsets she would miss and how the birds would grieve for her presence and how the animals would no longer have someone to talk to. "See here, Papita," he murmured, "it's not as if you've lived your life the way a young girl should. God does not want you in heaven yet. You must remember that." Holding her icy hands, he drifted off to sleep, dreaming of La Luz dancing on the top of the peaks and of red horses that carried him away to the stars, just as a Texas girl had predicted. All night long, one by one, the Calabazas tiptoed in to look at the priest Getting Together with the dead girl. In the darkest part of the night, Catarina thought she saw a change. She ran from the room to tell the others, and they waited anxiously for something definitive to happen.

In the morning, Soledad was awakened by the sound of Papita's laughter as she stood over him, clapping her small hands. "Get up, Padre," she said. "Uncle has something for you."

Narciso draped around the padre's shoulders a dark blue Pendleton, with a red stripe down the middle. "I am your friend for life," he whispered. "No harm will come to you as long as I am alive."

It was a miracle. Nothing else could be said about what happened that night in Luis Madrone's house. That morning, before Father Soledad even finished his coffee, the Custodian of Stories had composed a fable about it in his head. "You are a great man, Padre," he said in awe. "But you sing like a magpie," he laughed. "Look at her," he said as Papita scampered about, eating *biscochitos* and drinking goat's milk. "She remembers nothing, only the feeling of falling into a deep, dark hole. The hole was Death, and you pulled her out of it, amigo."

Around the village, the story of the padre's miracle grew; by the time the Vatican emissary, Father Antonio, arrived years later and related this miracle to the Holy Father, the Calabazas would say that the priest had snatched the dwarf from the jaws of death and given her the wings of life, an event that grew to such mythical proportions that Father Antonio had it entered in the Vatican's Book of Supernatural Occurrences. Even the Supreme Pontiff took note and ordered a special Saint's Day for Papita half a world away.

La Luz watched uncertainly from the kitchen. She loved the priest, but she was afraid for him. She tiptoed in while he slept and covered him with a blanket, her heart aching at the sight of him. A path of silver light shone from Papita and Soledad to the window. Seeing it, she understood that this sad-eyed priest had a power as great as Juan Lobo's. She kissed him while he slept and whispered, "I love you. But I will never know who you are, Lorenzo." Her fingers had rested lightly on his mouth; now she only touched his cassock as he passed her on his way out the door, preoccupied with the strange recovery of the dwarf.

"DID IT COUNT?" the padre asked Juan Lobo the next day, as he walked across the plaza. The sun was warm on his back, though the air was chill. "Bringing Papita back to life?"

The old Indian shook his head. "Of course not. She was already baptized. Besides, people often fall into trances. My daughter,

Florita, was in a trance for two weeks. Pilar brought her out by throwing her in the river and hanging her upside down from El Abuelo. It is what women here are trained to do."

"But they did all that," said the padre, "and it didn't work! Your daughter, Florita, died anyway. How can I convince you, Juan Lobo?" Soledad sighed.

"You could start by tearing yourself away from La Luz. Nothing good will come of it," Juan Lobo warned. "Our world is coming to an end. Your affair with La Luz will only make things worse!"

"I know about your troubles, Juan Lobo. La Luz told me. Why didn't you tell me before that you'll have to leave this place?"

The cacique scowled. "You religious are all alike. You want our *tasooms*. But you do not care if we dry up and blow away in the wind."

The priest walked along with the old man. "That's not true. I care very much. I don't know what to do, that's all. The government is very strong. Do you have the papers they gave you? If so, I want to see them. And I myself will go to Washington, if necessary." He touched the old man's buckskin-covered arm. "I want to help you."

The cacique pulled away. "You only see what you want to see, Padre," he said accusingly. "That is what is the matter with you!" He looked around. "The Great White Father is an evil man. That's what I've heard from many of our brothers. Indians cannot vote, so why should the president of the United States help us?"

The priest was silent for several minutes, then he said, "I've seen the deer in the plaza and how the people sing to them. I've watched the geese overhead, so thick you cannot see the sky. I've noticed how the bobcat lurks in the shadows. For an entire afternoon, I crawled inside his brain, just as he entered mine. At long last, I understood what connects me to him and him to me."

"It's called the Balance of Longevity," the old man said. "You live long enough, you know what an ant is thinking."

Together they entered the padre's house and sat at his rickety table while waiting for the coffee to boil. The old man was deep in thought, then he said, "Listen carefully to what I am about to tell you; it is the key to our survival. We believe there are two Worlds of Being. The First World of Being is the Outer World, where people wear the same faces, dress in the same clothes, live in the same houses, and think the same thoughts. It is a world without harmony. A world without balance. A world where everything looks alike because nothing rises above itself. The First World offers destruction and calls it progress. This world has power but no strength, ideas but no true knowledge. The First World is one of deception and greed that comes disguised as salvation. It is where my people were killed long ago for the sake of what we could never believe. The First World is you trying to make Catholics of us, even after so long a time."

Here the old man stopped and looked Soledad in the eyes. He seemed to be enjoying himself. "The First World is gringos doing good in their minds. Also politicians, and most of all, padres like yourself," he continued. "The Second World of Being is the Inner World. Anything can happen there because it is the World of Dreams. All things are in harmony in this world. Stories are born there. Ancestors inhabit this world and so do the spirits of birds and animals, clouds and insects. Time moves in a great circle in the Second World, on and on forever, so there is no beginning and no end. No yesterday and no tomorrow. In this world, there are no barriers—only pathways to peace and understanding. In the Second World, there is no death. No heaven or hell. No sin or salvation. Only an ever-changing world where the *tasoom* is part of every living thing. Which world do you seek, Padre? The time has come to choose."

The priest cut an apple and offered the old man a piece. He poured more coffee into their cups before he answered. "I seek God, Juan Lobo," he said at last.

"Same thing," Juan Lobo said, chewing carefully. "The Second World is where your spirit finds rest. But you are not there yet. In order to make this journey, you need to forget your self."

I am a priest, Soledad found himself thinking. *If I forget my self, what will I be?* He was afraid of his nothingness. He drew in his breath. "How do I forget my self, Juan Lobo?" he asked.

The old man looked at him; a strange, yellow light poured from his eyes. "Give your importance away."

THE PRIEST WAS shaken to his very core. He had brought a girl back to life, and the Calabazas started treating him differently, as if he were no longer their enemy. He was in love with a forbidden woman. He also had begun to see the way the Great Spirit breathed life into stones he once considered inanimate. The raven spoke to him, as did the chipmunks and the deer. He heard their words clearly, just as long ago he heard the dead speak. *So this was how the Indians had survived from Columbus onward to the present day*, he thought. They never let go of the Second World! They embraced a faith much older and deeper than his own, a faith that demanded little save individual responsibility. For hours, Soledad sat beneath El Abuelo, listening to the creak of its aged limbs, and when he thought he heard it speak, he flung his arms around its thick-ribbed trunk in gratitude. The interred Spaniards sang songs for him whenever he passed by, and he spoke to them out of old habit. *Am I a fool to expect this to last?*, he asked himself when La Luz told him she would bear his child late next spring. His unborn son floated deep in her womb, the size of a pinhead. Something of himself would continue long after he was gone. Continuity. Roots. Regeneration. Was this what the Calabazas had been trying to teach him? The priest was suspended above the First World concerns of his life, aware only of La Luz and the miracle of their unborn child.

SEEKING HIS OWN answers, Juan Lobo rode up into the mountains one cold fall day. He wore his heavy Pendleton with the red stripe around the middle, his buckskin leggings, and his high-topped moccasins. He did not feel the cold up there, where he'd hunted elk, sheep, bear, and mountain lion ever since Elk Old Man first took him hunting when he was seven years old. Resting on a rock, gazing eastward toward the old buffalo hunting grounds, Juan Lobo pondered the fate of his people. *Soon we will leave this place*, he thought, *but our tasooms will remain in these hills forever*. Because of the priest, he knew he could accept whatever happened. The priest was not wise, nor even very convincing. Still, he had shown the old man the need for adaptability in a First World time. He looked all around at the great land and committed the vastness to memory. *Never shall I leave the places that I love*, he thought, *even though my eyes are somewhere else*. Years ago, he had brought Maria Lobo to this very spot and tried to tell her how much she meant to him. "You are the moon," he had meant to say. But the words had become stuck in his throat, and now it was too late.

He rubbed his eyes and dropped his head. Maria was ill. Medicine men had come from San Juan and Taos, but no one could cure her. Her time was drawing down to a thin, dark shadow; soon she would leave him and travel to the World Beyond. So here he was, an old man with little power, a dying tribe, and disappearing land, wishing that his wife could understand the depth of his love before she died. He swung onto his old cavalry saddle with the high-rolled cantle and rode down through the snow toward the village. *What have I left behind so that people will remember me?*, he wondered.

He looked at the village below. Bluish smoke made wreathes above the chimneys. In their corrals, the horses fed on the hay put up during the summer. Venison hung to dry under the portals. His people—solid people of the earth—walked about, almost as if it were the old free days. The old man looked at the ruined church and the now-straightened cross, and he thought of the priest with the restless spirit and only half a heart. *Perhaps he could direct this spirit to some useful purpose*, he thought. *Perhaps there is a way for us to remain here after all*. His old heart beat faster; all his life he had lived on possibility. The cacique gently nudged his horse, Abundance, who understood the old man's mood and took him home the fast way.

WHILE JUAN LOBO was in the mountains, Maria Lobo made ready the things she would need for her journey to the World Beyond. A bag of pollen. Cornmeal. The eggs of a robin. A scarf to tie across her eyes. Her best beaded moccasins, made by her grandmother, White Cloud. As part of her preparation, she invited the padre for supper, and while he ate his chile and tortillas and drank strong coffee, she told him a story her grandmother had told her.

"In the old days, there was a bad time, when women had to be men," she said. "The Spanish had killed many of our warriors, so there was no one left to greet the sun. To hold council. To hunt for food. To fight the Arapahoe and the Navajo. The men that were left were weak. So the women dressed themselves as warriors and learned to shoot arrows as good as men. They painted their faces and rode out. In one battle, the Comanche had them surrounded, but the women warriors rode right through their lines. Not one among our women was killed or badly wounded. They took scalps and horses. When the women warriors came back to the village, one old man said, 'Now that you do the work of a man, you can do the work of a woman as well.' But the women warriors took their pots and baskets and corn and grinding tools, their children, and their hides waiting to be tanned, and gave them to the men. 'Here,' they said, 'if you learn to do our work, we will continue to do the work of a man.' And they left for another battleground. When they got back, the men were eager to hand back the children, the cooking, the tanning, and the washing, and to take up their men's work again. From that day on, there has always been the division of work. Some for men. Some for women." She laughed and, for the first time, looked directly at Soledad. "My work is almost finished, Padre. But I do not want to leave without knowing my people are safe." She reached out and rested her hand on his. "It will be up to you. I had a dream about it, so I know it must be true."

"What am I to do, Maria Lobo?" He saw that she looked very tired, that her skin was yellow and drawn tight against her cheekbones, and that she had not touched her food.

"Go and find the Second World, Padre," she said, "just as Juan

Lobo says. In it, you will find questions but no answers. Paths but no directions. May the Great Spirit guide you on your journey, as he has guided me." She paused. "I believe that horses with wings dance in the sky. I believe that your Christ was a medicine man, long ago, across the ocean. That is all he was, so why the fuss?"

"You believe both ways, Maria Lobo," he said, taking her cold hands in his.

She smiled. "I am the Custodian of Memory, Padre. I believe whatever belongs inside my basket. Everything in this world—this Catholic Church of yours, the Indian way we have practiced for so long—all is the same." Her head dropped, and she sighed sadly. "I saw in my dream how you will die. But out of this will come a new life for our people, part this and part that, and we will survive."

From that moment on, Soledad was torn. He still said Mass and baptized those who came to him, but it was not enough. At times he believed he could become a Calabaza, just as a couple of years ago, he believed he could become a Navajo. But his blood was half white, and the voice of Indian history didn't ring strongly in his ears. Torn and with a heavy heart, he studied the documents that Juan Lobo showed him. Maps. Deeds. Official-looking papers affixed with seals and flourishes. Nothing made sense to his inexperienced eyes. "I will do what I can," he promised, but he knew there was nothing he could really do except to pray with a half-hearted faith in his God.

EL COMANCHE WAS restless. The old brave had begun to think about his mortality, for he was certain he was more than one hundred years old, though he had no Wackamunga elders to tell him for sure. Someday, he would no longer be able to make love. Someday, he would no longer be able to make war on the locomotives. *If I am lucky,* he thought, *I have another hundred years to go. I wonder what the world will be like then.*

With that in mind, he dressed for battle, with his feathered headdress, his face painted in gruesome stripes, his rifle loaded and ready, and his tomahawk tied to his wrist. He went out of his little house to find his pig, General Sherman, rooting in the yard. He stopped to scratch its pink, pointed ears. "Goodbye, General," he said as he saluted. "The fort is yours." El Comanche rode down the mountain with a singular joy in his heart. He would do what he had to.

LUIS MADRONE, the Custodian of Stories, sensing literary potential in the unrest of Camposanto, decided to send for pencils and paper, even though he couldn't read or write. "There is something in the wind," he said to himself excitedly, trotting around the village in search of stories to pass down to his grandchildren, but he could not make sense of the convoluted state of affairs. "Write down what I tell you," he said to La Luz.

The priest was in love with Luis's daughter-in-law, a married woman with two children. After an argument with one-legged Juan Talamantes, his daughter Ermina had decided she was in love with the rich widower from San Sebastian and was packing her things. His long face disfigured with sorrow, Juan Talamantes dragged himself in and out of his house, trying to get Ermina to change her mind. Sotero had shut himself up in his little shed, carving who knows what strange kinds of things. Delfine, his red hair tangled and dirty, was drowning himself in the Elixir of Dreams, knowing La Luz would never be his. The priest had taken her from him, and his heart was broken. And Catarina, crushed by the weight of oncoming oblivion, went about her duties as the Custodian of Lesser Causes. She swept bird shit from the rooftops. She gathered pine needles from the ground. At night, she captured moonbeams and stored them in a box. Every morning, she presented this box to the priest, who emptied the moonbeams into his bed, saying they would give illumination to his dreams.

I live in a madhouse, Luis Madrone thought, as he tried to arrange all these developments in his mind. Stretched out along the river bank one day, he discovered blank verse as a way to tell his stories. Suddenly, he saw the possibility of arranging words in a simple way that he had never tried before. "Oh, my powerful village, weak," he said haltingly to a red squirrel in a nearby tree. "Oh, my troubled people, strong." For a moment, he could not go on. The Custodian of Stories had a lump in his throat brought on by an attack of nostalgia. "My people are a multitude of one," he began again. "Many voices are within them." Now he believed he was on to something, and he began to train himself to remember long passages of his work so he could repeat them to the priest, who could help him get his words on paper. "Why, you are a poet," Father Soledad would say in amazement. "The great Walt Whitman could not do better." He wrote down the poems as Luis told them to him, often helping him with grammar and construction. *A natural poet*, Soledad thought. *People will notice.*

Meanwhile, Juan Talamantes was clamoring to learn more math, and the priest was trying, without success, to remember how algebra went. He needed books, so he sent a letter to Richard Canopus, requesting certain texts. He also sent a letter outlining his missionary successes in a series of deliberate lies: twenty-nine souls baptized, one Catholic burial, a catechism class, and the successful completion of the church. He sent the letter to San Sebastian with Bonito Lobo to be mailed. So now falsification and fabrication were added to his list of sins, but Father Soledad was beginning to believe that, in the Second World of Being, the concept of sin was irrelevant.

ONE NIGHT, in the loneliness of his bed, which even the sheep had vacated, Juan Talamantes was startled awake. In the center of a pale blue light floated Florita Lobo, smiling as she extended her hand. "I forgive you," she said. "Now go and make your peace." Juan Talamantes sat up and rubbed his eyes. One day, long ago, Florita had run into a gun battle between himself and the widower, Narciso Ortega. Both young men were in love with Florita Lobo. She loved Juan Talamantes best, but she loved Narciso Ortega second best. When the two men climbed up the hill to argue over her hand, Florita Lobo had followed along. She did not care which man won, as long as one man claimed her. She was nineteen years old, and she wished to be married soon. Juan and Narciso drew their pistols and aimed. At that very moment, Florita jumped out from the bushes where she was watching them and too late heard the crack of the pistols. One bullet entered her body, the other hit a tree. Neither man ever knew which one had killed his sweetheart. Narciso retreated into the pain of a solitary life. In his agony, Juan Talamantes jumped off a cliff. He had not killed himself, but his right leg was hopelessly shattered. Juan Lobo cut it off himself, using his hunting knife and a flask of the Elixir of Dreams. Now Juan Talamantes strapped on his wooden leg and hobbled out of bed. If Florita Lobo forgave him, it meant that Ermina Madrone could finally be his. The Custodian of Meekness felt his lost courage return. *The padre*, he thought, *has made my life possible again.* He rubbed his wooden leg, no longer hard, but soft with moss.

FROM THE DAY she was revived from death, Papita Ortega, awakened and shaken by all the magical events that had happened to her, began to grow from the inside out. She put away her dolls. She refused to play with Sotero anymore. And subtly but surely, she grew in stature. People noticed her robust glow, the way she danced about as she had in the old days before her rape. One day, Papita crept into the priest's house in his absence and discovered the altar linens in his trunk. She felt each piece carefully—the embroidered crosses, graceful doves, delicate flowers, and winding ribbons of purity stretching around the sides of the cloth. She rubbed the beautiful pieces between her thumb and forefinger, feeling the fine texture of brocade and linen. Afterward, she borrowed material, thread, and needles from Maria Lobo. She stayed in her room, laboring furiously, until Narciso came in and made the discovery that one day would make Papita famous throughout the world. Colcha embroidery spilled across the room.

EL COMANCHE RETURNED, cut and bloody, from his latest assault against progress. He claimed to have killed a locomotive and three Mexicans who had attempted to ambush him as he was riding into town. The old warrior was exhausted; he stayed in bed for a week, with Hermosa and Tomasina tenderly administering to his wounds. They vowed not to let him fight again, but without war, what would El Comanche do? "He can join the circus," Hermosa said, thinking of the posters she'd seen for Buffalo Bill's Wild West show the last time she went to town. "He can shoot pigeons from Annie Oakley's head," said Tomasina. They thought Buffalo Bill's act might be a solution to their husband's homicidal inclinations, but in El Comanche's mind, his fighting career had only just begun.

Strange things continued to happen in Camposanto. A fine red powder fell from the ceilings, got into boiling pots of food, and caused diarrhea and vomiting. The deer disappeared over the mountain to the next valley. The food that had been harvested for winter began to rot. Even the grain developed rust and had to be thrown out. Horses became lame. The left feet of the ancestors disappeared from the ruined wall of the old church, and Peso Mondragon swore he saw them hopping up the hill, en route to a better life. The Crow Dog howled even when there was no full moon, and not even Pilar Mondragon could quiet it.

In the cornfield, the Spaniards began to sing some frightening new songs, left over from their days as conquistadores. They sang of invasion and enslavement. Ruined women and men whose manhood was cut off at the groin. Shattered warriors and starving children. Soledad shivered when he heard these words. To him, Camposanto seemed poised on the brink of disaster. Only La Luz, with her slightly rounded belly and her full breasts, reminded him that he had a purpose beyond himself. "Thy will be done," he whispered, as he walked down the hillside through the aspen trees, which were shedding the last of their yellow leaves. The child would be brought up somewhere near here, perhaps in Santa Fe. But he would be a Second World boy, learning the ways of his ancestors.

TWENTY-FOUR

THE PRIEST WALKED into the woods. A light snow had fallen. He said his rosary. So what if they wouldn't help him? He would build the church with his own two hands if he had to—a symbol of his convoluted devotion to a Catholic faith that no longer served him. Or he it. Out of his increasing doubt rose a determination to leave something of his faith behind. While Narciso mixed the mud in a trough, Soledad made it into bricks, using a wooden form that Luis had given him. He wore trousers and an old work shirt, scuffed boots, and his dishpan hat to keep the sun out of his eyes. He got an ugly gash on his knee that Ana Coyote treated with a smelly black ointment, and his back became so sore he could hardly stand up. La Luz brought tortillas and coffee; for several weeks, she had treated him like a husband. She fixed his meals. She laundered his clothes. She cleaned his casita and picked the last of the asters and put them in a jar of water beside his bed. She comforted him in the night, and when he was ill, she rubbed his head, his back, his feet. The padre leaned on his hoe and looked into her obsidian eyes. He didn't care if the whole world knew he loved her; she was his, and she was going to have his child. She was a married woman, but he didn't care, and she didn't either, he was sure. The priest kissed her full on the mouth, tasting the saltiness of her lips. Narciso smiled and looked away. Once, so many years ago that he could not count them, Florita Lobo had kissed him like that. And then, he'd shot her.

"I love you," said the priest, loud enough for everyone to hear. He no longer cared what anyone thought. Love had swept him off his feet. What would he do?

As he headed home through the trees, a beaver pelt slung over his shoulder, Delfine Madrone saw the priest kissing La Luz. *The padre is asking for trouble*, he thought, *acting like a fool*. Ever since the arrival of the priest, Delfine had felt ill. He kicked a stone with his moccasined foot. "You will never have her, Padre," Delfine whispered, his hands clenched into fists. "You are not Calabaza." *Neither am I*, he thought, as he went home and blew a dull skirl on his bagpipe. He thought of nothing else but the priest and La Luz; sometimes when he stood beneath their window, he caught the sound of their riotous lovemaking. At these unbearable moments, he was only stopped from using his knife by the presence of the ever-watchful Narciso, who had become the padre's self-appointed bodyguard ever since he'd brought Papita back to life.

Juan Lobo wandered over from his house, observing the padre's slow progress. The old man was the reason why no one in the village would help; one word from the cacique and the job would have been finished weeks ago. "Ah, Padre, what a waste of time," the old man said with quiet amazement. "The adobe will freeze. Those vigas are too green. Soon the heavy winter snow will come. You and Narciso will never get done." His voice was reedy, like an old man's, but the unmistakable aura of power that surrounded him was as ageless as the mountains. Juan Lobo could not help but smile. The poor padre, with a woman in his life, cared little for anything else. Just like Father Montez at the end, when he had flung himself at Pilar Mondragon, and half the village had fallen ill as a result. "Besides, I thought you were no longer interested in the white man's Church."

The priest turned to him. "I never said that, Juan Lobo. If I can be a Catholic and at the same time embrace certain of your Indian ways, why can't you do the same? It's the Second World. You said so yourself."

The old man looked around. "I was mistaken." He shook his

finger. "Your way. Or my way. That is what our wager is all about." He drew his blanket around his shoulders and thrust his face close to the priest's. "Will you marry La Luz?" he asked.

Soledad leaned on his hoe and wiped the sweat from his brow. "I love her with my whole being, and she loves me. But she is married and I am a priest. You see, there are things that even I cannot do."

The Custodian of Abundance was not a man to share his feelings, not even with his wife, who called him Old Stone Head. During meetings in the kiva, he would say almost nothing. Yet the men knew what he felt just by looking at his stoical face. "You say one thing and do another, Padre." Once, long ago, the old man had had a similar situation with an Acoma woman, who he thought he loved as much as his wife, Maria. He lived one whole winter with her, and then she died, the result of witchcraft in that village. "Our hearts play many tricks," Juan Lobo said. "But we can only be true to what we are. If you are a tree, you cannot be a stone. A bird is not a gopher. If you are clear on what you are, half your problems are solved."

"You think I am weak."

Juan Lobo drew closer. He'd eaten a great deal of garlic, and his breath was rank. "Not weak. Foolish. Where is your courage, Padre? How do you want to be known? As a lover of women? Or a man of strong beliefs?" He waited for his reply.

The padre dropped his eyes to the ground. "I don't know."

The cacique turned his face to the sun. "A long time ago, we had to believe two ways in order to survive. Father Montez wanted to prepare us for heaven. We wanted only to dance. And plant. And hunt. And worship the Animal People, same as before."

"I know Father Montez tried to turn back the clock two hundred years," the priest acknowledged. "And I know what you did to him." The old man's face was impassive. "I don't blame you for your anger, Juan Lobo. The job of a priest is not to take away the dignity of those he serves, but to bring them closer to God."

"Hah!" the old man grumbled and folded his arms across his chest. "Then help us keep this land! To us, that is God! Trees and birds and clouds. All God."

Soledad was aware that Narciso listened to everything they said while he pretended to mix adobe. "If I could, I would. Perhaps you will have to accept what you cannot change."

Juan Lobo stared into the padre's sunburned face. "I do not know you," he said sharply, then turned on his heel and left. Though Soledad called after him, the old man kept going, his blanket billowing behind him like a sail.

The padre resumed work, but a terrible ache clamped around his heart. Minutes later, a group of five armed men, stiff with self-importance, rode up to Juan Lobo's house. Hiding behind the church wall, the padre listened while they confronted the old cacique in his house. They were here to arrest El Comanche, they said, for the murder of the two homesteaders at Black Lake. "We know he is here," said an officious man who wore the big hat and the silver star of his profession. He looked around the forlorn little village. "Which house is his?" Flavio Trujillo, though part Indian, had been a federal officer for nine years; every time he had to arrest an Indian, he got heartburn, but he had a job to do.

Juan Lobo came down the two steps of his porch and faced the marshal. He had known Flavio since he was a small boy and came to fish with his middle son, Long Knives. How different Flavio was then.

In those days, he had returned to San Sebastian with arrowheads and a string of fish. Now he wanted a different kind of trophy. Out of the corner of his eye, Juan Lobo glanced at El Comanche's quiet house. Any moment now, he would be getting up from his nap with his wives. He'd stand on his porch and look at the sky, then he'd fire one of his antiquated guns because that's what he always did each afternoon at this time. The marshal or his men would kill him on the spot. "He is not here, Flavio. And if he were, what would you do with him?" Juan Lobo asked, trying to buy time. He knew that Indians taken away for murder did not come back.

The marshal stretched. The ride up the mountain had been long and cold. He had gotten up very early—at two o'clock in the morning—without making love to his wife. He yawned. "Maybe he will hang, Juan Lobo. I do not know. Maybe they will spare him because of his age. Maybe twenty or thirty years in prison. The charges are very serious. Murder in the first degree." He looked around. "We will search the houses." He directed his men to start at the top of the hill and work downward, one house at a time. Juan Lobo turned his head slightly so he could see the old man's house. A shadowy figure moved on the other side of the window. "He is not here, I tell you!" Juan Lobo said.

Flavio could not help but stare at the purple scar where the old man's ear had been. He shuddered.

Just then, the padre stepped out of the wreckage of the church. "I am Father Soledad. Perhaps I can be of assistance," he said pleasantly. He was dirty and disheveled, and he wore layman's clothes, but still he had the unmistakable air of a priest with his cross and his dishpan hat, worn at a rakish angle on his head. Instinctively, the men crossed themselves. "You are too late for El Comanche, my friends," Soledad said in the pious tones he normally reserved for the monsignor. "Last week, he had a seizure. He was, after all, a very old man. Now he is at peace with the Lord. He is buried up there on the hill. I conducted a funeral Mass for the repose of his soul." He looked away. Stretching the truth; that's all it was. He pressed his fingers together so they resembled a steeple.

The marshal and his deputies glanced dubiously at one another. Reports had circulated that El Comanche had been sighted blowing up the railroad bridge over Tecolote Creek just the day before. Still, if you could not believe a priest, who could you believe? Juan Lobo's face remained impassive as he walked leisurely along with the group while Soledad kept up a steady stream of conversation as he led the posse a short distance up the hill. Only last week, he had laid the Navajo outcast, Muladar, to rest at this very spot. For thirty years, the Navajo had sought refuge with the Calabazas, earning his keep by sharpening knives and mending torn clothes. Muladar was quite large and El Comanche was small, but the mound was believable, if you had stretched the old warrior out to his full length and buried his arsenal with him. "E nomine Patris, et Filii, et Spiritus Sancti," the priest said solemnly, as he made the sign of the cross over the Navajo's grave. He bowed his head. "May you rest in peace, El Comanche."

"I don't see any marker," said Flavio Trujillo suspiciously. He was accustomed to markers, if only the simplest wooden cross.

"No marker," the priest said evenly. "It's their custom. They know where they are. So do their relatives."

"The grave looks too small," Flavio said.

"He shrank. He was very old."

He opened his breviary and began to read. "*Domine, non sum dignus . . .*" He stopped. "Now, if you would care to search the houses, gentlemen." Juan Lobo stood at Soledad's elbow, as still as death. If he closed his eyes, he could see a catastrophe about to happen. He knew that El Comanche waited just inside his door, his finger on the trigger of his old Henry. If anyone tried to search his house, he would have killed them. "Fuck the law," El Comanche would have said, Hermosa and Tomasina weeping at his back before the policemen blew his head off. The cacique held his breath.

The marshal shook his head. "It is not necessary, Padre. We have your word." He looked around, a pained expression on his face. "In six months, we will be back to move you out, Juan Lobo. I am on your side. I hope you understand that I am only following orders." The tension had been too much. Flavio sat down suddenly and fumbled in his vest for the pills to control his heartburn. "I am going to have a heart attack," he said.

In his cluttered little house, the priest served cups of the Elixir of Dreams to all of the posse except Flavio, who didn't drink. By the time they rode down the mountain, they cared little for capturing Indian outlaws anymore. As their giddy laughter echoed through the trees, they remembered their own grandfathers, who, like El Comanche, had taught them to fish and to hunt and told them the kinds of stories they passed down to their children. They had not wanted to arrest the aged warrior in the first place, but orders were orders. El Comanche was a dangerous criminal, accused of killing more than a dozen men, blowing up trains and bridges, and attacking innocent settlers. They were glad he was dead.

But these lawmen would soon have reason to doubt their own sanity. Everywhere they went from that day on, they would see El Comanche. Astride his horse on a ridgetop, in his war bonnet and war paint. Waiting to ambush the trains they were assigned to protect. Lurking in the ruins of Fort Union, where they went to scavenge for old Civil War weapons. One deputy swore he saw him lighting a fuse under a railroad bridge the year that New Mexico became a state, some years later. This abortive expedition to catch El Comanche was the first inkling the people of the region would have that the old warrior was about to become a legend.

WHEN SOLEDAD GOT up the following morning, the sun was shining brightly through his window. His body ached from all the work he'd done the day before: his hands were blistered, his feet sore where his boots had rubbed them. There was even more to do today, but he was beginning to think his task was hopeless. He yawned, hobbled to the window, then stared in disbelief. Every man, woman, and child in the village was working on the church. Mixing adobe. Cutting up straw. Hauling water from the river. Making bricks. Bringing more logs down from the mountains. Juan Lobo stood to one side, directing everything. The padre dressed and hurried to the plaza. No one said anything, but he understood what had happened. And why El Comanche winked slyly as he walked past. The old man was peeling bark from logs to be used as vigas. Soledad rested his hand on the old warrior's shoulder.

"Death to the locomotives," the priest said, laughing.

"Death to the locomotives," the Custodian of War replied evenly, and he slipped the priest his favorite jasper arrowhead. At that moment, Soledad realized his acceptance in Camposanto had been achieved, not through the miracle of Papita, but through a bald-faced lie. Years later, Father Antonio would discover this lie in Soledad's journals and would tear out the page and crumple it, lest the church at Camposanto be considered invalid and Soledad along with it. Now, people nudged Soledad affectionately as he walked among them, hard at work. He said not his usual Latin blessing, but a new one, invented by himself. "May the Great Spirit make strong your arms, your legs, your hearts." He laughed, for he knew that old Ansawaka, the Indian he had known in Arizona Territory, approved.

IN LESS THAN three weeks' time, the people of Camposanto had built the padre's church. It was a rough little rectangle with one window, thick walls, a tamped earth floor, and two bell towers, so that Gracia and Refugio could be taken out of El Abuelo's stout branches, hung in the towers, and once again rung for special occasions. Soledad had worked long hours and had fallen into bed each night, too exhausted to do anything except sleep in La Luz's arms. When the work was done, the priest could only stand before his church, named Saint Pollo's after Ana Coyote's chickens, and wipe the tears from his eyes. The tiny adobe building gleamed in the sun, a silent testimony to the people who had weighed one thing against another in order to make amends. The foot bones of the ancestors played their part, too—mysteriously moving to become part of a new adobe wall. Soledad had observed the bones with amazement, but now he believed anything was possible, so he blessed them again, for good luck.

The golden chalice had miraculously reappeared on the altar, a rabbit's foot inside. The priest shook his head as he fished it out. Fragrant pine and cedar branches decorated the simple wooden altar. How beautiful everything was! The wooden reredos, painted by Sotero at the last minute, depicted none of the usual ecclesiastical subjects but showed scenes of the hills above Camposanto, filled with deer and elk and bear and birds, cavorting happily amidst wildflowers and waterfalls. Soledad found them exquisite. The boy had carved santos, too, but his painted wooden figures were not of saints but of the people of the village: Catarina sweeping bird droppings. Luis in his Civil War uniform, brandishing his musket. Delfine lying in bed with his bagpipe. Ana Coyote in her feathered coat. Juan Lobo astride his pony. Papita dancing in a little white dress. A sad-faced Juan Talamantes pointing his wooden leg like a weapon. Even Pilar, with her long doglike teeth. El Comanche wore feathers in his hair and held a bow and arrow. La Luz was depicted in a blue dress, kissing the priest. Soledad only laughed when he saw it and gave the boy a hug. Sotero had caught the essence of them all, and he had not the heart to fault the nature of these tributes, so lovingly and accurately carved by a mute who lived inside his silence, yet spoke to all through his great artistic gift.

Soledad glanced at all the carved animals and birds, for which Narciso had built special shelves on either side of the altar. "These are not the santos you wanted, Padre," Narciso said, appearing out of the church's gloom. "But they are part of us." He moved as close as he dared to the altar, where he believed the priest's God lived. "Everyone has been working very hard, ever since you saved Papita's life and kept El Comanche out of jail! It is a surprise, Padre. Are you pleased?" Soledad could not speak; he could only nod through his tears.

On the altar, the priest found a beautiful cloth, embroidered, he learned—to his astonishment—by Papita. It was breathtaking—a wonderful array of all the birds, flowers, and animals she'd ever seen, combining every color imaginable and reaching all the way to the floor. Papita had worked so long and hard on the cloth that her fingers were swollen and stiff. But to everyone in the village, including Soledad, Papita now looked five feet tall.

The next day, when the church was dedicated, El Comanche arrived on his stallion, dressed in full battle regalia, and rode boldly into the nave where the people were standing, waiting for Mass to begin. To show his gratitude to the padre for saving his life, he had brought Hermosa along as a gift. She clung to El Comanche's waist, her head lowered, as he presented her to the priest. When Soledad politely declined, the Custodian of War then offered his old Henry rifle, with which he had blazed a bloody path across the West. The priest shook his head.

"You will always make war, El Comanche," Soledad said fondly. "And you will always make love. So you will need the rifle and your wife, Hermosa. *Deo gratias.*" In all his life, he had never seen a horse inside a church, but he believed it a natural, heartfelt act of love, so he blessed both the warrior and his mount.

El Comanche pinched Hermosa's behind and let her slide to the floor. He was feeling unusually expansive, having escaped capture by the *federales*. But his heart had begun to ache with the knowledge that soon all that was meaningful in his life would disappear. The old raucous times of his youth were almost beyond the reach of his memory. He longed for something important to leave behind, now that the frontier was fading into the twilight of his dreams. "It is what I am, Padre," he said proudly. "A warrior and a lover. I cannot help myself. Soon I will go and make war before Old Man Winter comes and keeps me here for many moons." His horse raised its head and rolled its eyes.

"I don't want you to shoot any more locomotives," Soledad said firmly, returning to the altar, where he stood addressing the old man on horseback. "It's too dangerous for you around here. From now on, you must go out in the world and fight on the side of truth, justice, and peace. That is what I want you to do. Enlist in the army."

The old man blinked. He did not think he had heard the padre correctly. "I only know how to fight progress," he said.

"It's the same thing," the padre explained. "You see, all over the world, soldiers are fighting for good causes. It's been that way ever since David slew Goliath."

"Why?" said the Custodian of War, thinking David and Goliath were the Cheyenne warriors he'd met that time along the Arkansas. The Custodian of War was very tired, what with building the church and making love to his wives and shooting his last locomotive only the week before. "I am only one soldier," he said. "To go out in the world, I would have to be many." At this, the stallion perked up his ears. Because he was a Four-Legged Animal, he understood everything El Comanche said. He thought they were soon to leave on a journey.

"No," Soledad replied. "One solider can become many. It takes logic and cooperation."

"How, Padre?" It was amazing that the fine points of battle were being taught to him by a man trained only in the fine points of the Church. He supposed it was all right, though he wondered how he would fit into the padre's theory, accustomed as he was to doing things his way.

"Through believing in a cause, El Comanche."

My cause is to stop progress, the old warrior thought. Perhaps it cannot be done. Progress was approaching from all directions.

The old man seemed to grasp Soledad's message. So did the little knot of people assembled in the nave, waiting for the dedication to begin. They clapped politely at the padre's words, so different from what he had said before. La Luz was there. Narciso. Papita. Alvar Talamantes. Ana Coyote. Catarina. Pilar and Peso, back from his futile campaign for governor. He even saw Delfine, standing sullenly in the back, watching La Luz, the woman he was now certain he would never possess, though he dreamed of her all his waking and sleeping hours.

El Comanche sucked on his mail-order teeth and blew through his nostrils like a horse. He had faith in his Springfield and his Henry. His Remington and his three-inch field cannon. His matching pearl-handled Colts and his arrows. His strong shooting arm and his perfect aim. That was all. "I have killed many men in my life," he said. "It did no good. Wagons came over the Santa Fe Trail just the same. The locomotives came up the railroad tracks. Gringos covered the land."

"That's what I mean," the padre said. "All this killing and destruction, and nothing was ever accomplished. Violence begets more violence, and sooner or later, you will lose. But there are true enemies all over the world—evil men who would steal every human being's right to live as God intended. Those are the ones you must fight in the name of truth and justice. That's the cause I mean." His homily was meant to be apocryphal, but to El Comanche, the priest had issued a new kind of battle cry.

The old man let out a war whoop. He had waited for this kind of affirmation all his life. It made his job easier. With a cry of anticipation, he turned, nudged his horse out of the church, and galloped home to think how he might apply his skills to battles beyond the narrow confines of New Mexico. He laid out all his arrowheads and bullets, his tomahawks and scalping knives, trying to imagine where in the world he might begin his campaign against evil.

Soledad said the dedication Mass, with a happy Sotero serving as altar boy, even though he could not speak the Latin responses. Everyone in the village was proud of the Custodian of Silence; they said he was an artist who would bring great honor to the tribe, once his talents became known. His heart bursting with pride, Sotero looked at his beautiful reredos and all the carvings he had made, and he knew that these were the greatest gift to the priest that anyone would ever give. "Deo gratias," he tried to say. "Deo gratias," but all that came out was his usual bleat.

TWENTY-FIVE

AFTER MASS, Soledad tucked his violin under his chin and played a Mozart minuet from the altar. The people listened politely, but they made faces when they thought he wasn't looking. They preferred their traditional flutes and drums and rattles, echoing the natural rhythms of the earth. But La Luz smiled and clapped when he was through. Before Soledad came, she had never heard a violin. Now when he played, her heart turned over. She knew the music was for her. Whenever she looked at the padre, she realized that the Calabazas would never understand her love for a man unlike any other. He made her feel both weak and strong, and he gave her a sense of her own destiny as a woman. But deep inside she knew that in another year, perhaps less, he would not be hers at all.

"Play Beethoven, Padre," she said now, her voice filled with emotion. In his pure white vestments, he looked possessed of unearthly power, a god who was hers only part of the time. He bowed slightly and played a Beethoven rondo especially for her. How handsome was her lover, with his fine white teeth, his strong shoulders, his thick, dark hair cut by her so that it curled at the ends. She loved him, utterly and completely. In her dreams, La Luz still saw the vat of strong lye soap, but now, instead of the face of God, she saw her lover with his dark and brooding look.

When the church had emptied out, the priest walked slowly toward La Luz. He put his arms around her and mussed her hair. By now her pregnancy was beginning to show. "You are beautiful," he said, his heart expanding with love. "All during Mass, I could not take my eyes off you." She made him laugh. She made him quiver with happiness. He felt her hand on his shoulder—a small, gentle hand whose fingers he loved to kiss, one at a time. He put them to his mouth. "Ah, my love," he said huskily, "if only I were in a position to give you everything, then life would indeed be perfect." In six months, the child would come. What would he do?

La Luz had heard this excuse from men all her life. "Yes, and if life were perfect, we would have nothing to talk about. I do not want perfection, Lorenzo. I want life with you!" Yet she knew he belonged to his God; she belonged to no one. He had said so, time after time, as he held her in his arms, with an air of finality that diminished whatever happiness they'd achieved between them.

"I give you love, woman," he whispered as he pressed against the solid curve of her hip. "What else can I give?" Deep in her womb was his child, a fetus unaware of the world outside its watery prison. A child he might never see, yet would carry always in his heart, no matter where he went. He directed his love to this tiny being and prayed for its safe emergence into the world.

The rustle of his vestments, at once so appropriate and yet so ominous, made her think of his real commitment, not to her and their child, but to a Church that gave him the illusion of security. Soledad did nothing at all to relieve her anxiety—what with his moods and his pieties, his indecision and his guilt. "You take me for granted," she said angrily, and pushed his hand away. "I want more than your love, Lorenzo. I want a father for our child and a future for both of us!" Her dark eyes flashing, she tossed her raven hair and ran across the plaza.

Soledad understood only too well why La Luz was angry with him. As he walked toward his house, he confronted the contradiction between them. She loves me, as I love her. We are connected to one another, as earth to sky. Yet I cannot make her happy. She wants the one thing I cannot give. His mind tried to tear itself away from his body to better observe what was happening between them. If she expected marriage, she was wrong. He had told her that from the beginning. What they had now was all they would ever have. "Someday I'll leave you," he would say during their most intimate moments, causing her to hammer her small fists against his chest. "You must learn to care for yourself after I've gone." She was becoming increasingly demanding, even sending Luis to tell him what she wanted: a divorce from Rafael and marriage to him. "Myself, I would not do it, Padre," Luis had said, shrugging his round shoulders. "La Luz can be very difficult." Soledad realized a woman could not accept logic or reason either. She wanted ownership of him, as if he were a mule.

Soledad put his vestments away and poured himself a cup of the Elixir of Dreams. He drank it down. He washed his face and hands in the basin. La Luz was a stubborn but desirable woman who drove him mad sometimes. She took him to unimaginable heights and, just as predictably, sent him to the depths. Perhaps she would come to his bed tonight. Perhaps she would not. Could he live with the anguish of knowing he would eventually have to let her go? Was she a woman he was willing to die for? Probably not. But she'd brought him redemption, night after night in their bed of passion, his betrayal of his vows receding in the face of their ecstasy. Oh, it was rich, but he felt the same ache he had felt after Henrietta died, a deep ache that never entirely left him. *What have I become?*, he thought, as he rubbed his cross. *Mother of God, it is* they *who are converting* me *to their wanton, lustful ways*. He would do penance by lashing himself with a bagful of cacti, the way the Penitentes did. But in the end, would suffering make him become a better priest? Who would forgive his sins? Sotero? Richard Canopus?

He peered out the window to see who was in the plaza getting ready for fiesta. Juan Lobo had refused to attend the dedication of the church on religious grounds, but there he was, dressed for fiesta, speaking to El Comanche. Luis Madrone, who had done most of the work on the roof by himself, could not attend because he lay flat on his back at home, an enormous stone pressing his spine into alignment. Before the dedication was over, Alvar Talamantes, who had made the beautiful carved door, had ridden off in anger after an argument with the pregnant Isabela, who he'd caught holding hands and laughing with Zorrito the Orphan. Soledad resolved to look into the situation. Zorrito was a troublemaker. Insolent, vain, but with a genuine interest in the beliefs of the Roman Catholic Church. For one whole week, Zorrito had wanted to discuss nothing but the Blessed Trinity. Three in one. One in three. "How can it be?" Zorrito had queried. Now Alvar had come back in search of his wife and was threatening to shoot Zorrito unless he found her.

When Soledad came out of his house, dressed in a fresh cassock, his hair neatly combed, he saw that Ana Coyote and Catarina had decorated the once-crooked cross with fir branches. General Sherman, El Comanche's pig, wore a garland of faded asters around his neck as he ran around looking for something to eat. A tipsy Bonito Lobo clapped his hands and danced by himself to the sound of a flute drifting through the trees. It was an unusually warm day, so they could be outside. At a long table, La Luz and Isabela were arranging platters of food—beans, chile, posole, squash, fry bread, boiled potatoes, apple and raisin pies, and a roasted goat that Bonito had slaughtered in honor of the occasion. "Viva, Padre!" they cried, as they danced in a circle around him to the rhythm of the blackened old drum beaten by Narciso. From a bench set up expressly for her, Papita watched, flushed with her newfound acceptance. By now, she knew what she wanted to do with her life; Narciso had ridden to town and bought twenty-five yards of plain white material, some beautiful colored threads, and a silver thimble to protect her sewing finger. The padre went over and kissed her on the forehead. Watching his niece, Narciso's heart filled with love. *I am a new man*, he thought happily.

As the men drummed and sang, the people continued to dance. Soledad danced with them, around and around until his legs ached and he collapsed in a chair Catarina had brought from the house. He drank a cup of the Elixir of Dreams. Then another. He looked around for La Luz and saw her standing off in the trees, arm in arm with Delfine. He drew in his breath and turned his head away.

When he looked again, they were gone. His heart dropped, and he thought he would be ill. Ana Coyote seemed to read his mind.

"A spiteful girl, Padre," she said in her anemic, chicken-like voice, holding her favorite rooster in her arms. "You would be better off to forget her." Maria Lobo walked slowly toward him, leaning on a walking stick. In the last few weeks, her sickness had become worse, but she refused to let Juan Lobo take her to town. She accepted the chair the padre relinquished and clasped his hand. Her fingers were like ice.

"Listen to me, Padre. You are here to do a certain thing. You cannot do this thing with a woman around. Even you know that!" Her lower lip trembled, but her eyes were clear. "So you must forget yourself for once."

Soledad turned his eyes to the dancers. How deceptively happy they seemed, dancing around and around, as if fate were not about to strangle them. "I know that, Maria Lobo," he said slowly. "But what am I here to do?"

For a long time she did not answer, and then she said, "You are here to right a terrible wrong. We have known about you for years, from a sorcerer we met in Mexico. Why has it taken you so long to come?" She laughed. "This man said he was your father."

"I have no father," Soledad said. "My mother said so."

As the afternoon sun fell toward the horizon, Soledad dragged himself home. It had been a happy day, but La Luz had not shared it with him. What did she want with that silly Delfine? Her behavior was an affront to their love. How could she be so thoughtless? She might have considered how he had been willing to sacrifice an important principle in order to build the church for her people. "I lied, and they believed me," he said to the crucifix above his bed as he knelt before it. While he prayed for his sins to be forgiven, an amazing thing happened. The crucifix fell from the wall onto the bed and began to ooze blood from the sacred wounds of Christ. He stared at it. He put his finger into a drop of blood and held it to his tongue. It was real, all right. Taking this as a sign, he hurried to his dark, cold church, which still smelled of sweet earth and straw and the fresh wood of Sotero's carvings. He lit a candle and dropped to the dirt floor in front of the crude altar, where he could hear mice scurrying to find a home in the cold. *Lord, I am not worthy*, he thought, seeing all the women he had loved in his mind's eye. The matchless beauty of Christ's body rose in his mind. His weakness filled him with shame. He begged forgiveness.

So did the priest try to reinstate himself with God, unaware that his fate was sealed the moment he had lied to save El Comanche. Since then, the Calabazas had talked of little else than the con- duct of their priest. They knew he had become La Luz's lover. They knew he was the father of her unborn child. They remembered Rafael, her husband, an impetuous young man who had tried to help his people and would spend his life in prison for killing a man. Because it was a small village, they also knew when she came to the priest's bed at night and when she left at dawn. This was not Getting Together, but something reckless and profound. Yet, since this was Camposanto and not some regular Catholic village, where guilt and redemption went hand-in-hand, no one condemned the priest for what he had done with La Luz or for what he had had to do to save El Comanche. His half-hearted attempts to convert them had not made an impression. On the contrary, his weak- nesses endeared him to them. They knew he had come from an unfamiliar world, but they did not judge him for being different. Throughout Camposanto, a wave of affection rose, but this seemed not to reach him, either.

When Soledad left the church quite late, he knew he would always love her. No matter how La Luz behaved, he would forgive her. Part of him was in her, growing by the day. His blood would flow in his son's body and in his grandson's body, on and on, until the world ended. God approved. God forgave him. This much he knew. He looked up. The moon was high overhead; the stars spar- kled with an even greater brilliance than those he remembered from his youth.

He hurried up the path to his house. And stopped. The cloudy figure of a man sat on a bench, smoking a cigarette. The Stranger.

"Get out," Soledad said. He noticed the throbbing comet on the side of the man's face, exactly like his own, glowing like fire in the moonlight. Was this the sorcerer Maria Lobo had spoken about? Or the mysterious man he had seen on the train?

The Stranger appeared no older than before. In fact, he looked exactly the same as he had years before, the first time Soledad saw him at seminary, then recently on the train. A vague, dark face without expression. Eyes that were not eyes at all, but two dark smudges toward the top of his head. "Come with me," the Stranger said. "I have need of you elsewhere."

"I am a priest. I have a job to do here." Soledad was very tired, having risen two hours before dawn to prepare for the new baptisms he hoped for but never materialized. "I cannot leave until my work is finished."

"Nonetheless, you will not rest until you come with me," the Stranger insisted. "Your future had been decided, and you cannot refuse." The priest could not look into the apparition's face. When he tried to do so, he experienced a blinding pain. A cold wind blew down from the mountains, but the figure seemed not to notice.

The priest shivered. "How did you find me?"

The Stranger laughed, a strange, unearthly laugh that might have come from an old cemetery. "It does not matter how I found you. I have waited a long time to come to you again. You were not ready to receive me before."

Soledad stood beside the apparition. He felt a pulsating energy coming from him. He had a strong mouselike smell. The priest backed away. The night was quite cold, and he saw his breath in the air. "All these years, you have been with me at certain times in my life," Soledad said. "I realize you were there to protect me, though you've let me make my own mistakes."

The Stranger turned toward him and put out a formless hand. The priest recoiled; somehow, he could not bear to touch this apparition.

"You have been sent here for a reason," the Stranger said. "Do you know what it is?"

Soledad shook his head and looked closely. "You are dead, yet you speak and act as if you were alive. Who are you?"

The Stranger gurgled a reply. "Your father," he said. "I was a seaman on a cargo ship that carried tobacco to European ports. I was on shore leave and I wandered into the estate of a certain Colonel Farnsworth. The gate was open. And there she was strolling in the garden. The beautiful Henrietta. I made my way in. We looked at one another. I was a poor Mexican seaman and she was the daughter of a wealthy man. But we knew we were meant for each other. She led me to the stable. We became close in a very short time. I had to leave quickly because the Colonel arrived with his shotgun. I ran for my life. My ship left soon after. Somewhere off the coast of Florida it was caught in a hurricane. I drowned at sea, leaving Henrietta carrying you, my dear, troubled son. Now, may I come in?"

With trembling hands, Soledad opened the door and lighted the coal oil lamp. The Stranger unfurled himself into a chair as if he had no bones. He had no flesh; a loose material like gauze covered his form. The priest realized that the moment he looked away from the Stranger, he forgot what he looked like. Nor could he remember his words more than a moment after he spoke them, yet they became imprinted on his brain.

He took a bottle of altar wine from behind the wood box and set it on the table. He found two cups on the shelf and poured them each a drink. The Stranger sat in the one chair that was not broken. Soledad sat on the bed, noticing the Stranger's feet, long and wide like his own. He had the same big hands, long arms, and a hook to the bridge of his nose. Or what might have been his nose. Soledad rubbed his eyes. He realized he was no longer afraid.

"Why have you come?" the priest said.

The Stranger put down his cup. "To give you courage," he said. "No matter what happens, you are not alone."

Soledad took a deep breath. "But you are dead."

"I am not dead as long as there are music and flowers and fish in the sea." He nodded. "So you see, there is nothing to be afraid of." He made a terrible sound.

Soledad drew back. He looked out the window. "I killed her," he said slowly. "When I was sixteen years old. It was not an accident, but a deliberate act of fury. I hated her for wasting her life in a house of ill repute. It is your fault for taking her honor. For nearly twenty years, I've tried to make amends, yet the memory never leaves me, day or night."

"Yes," said the Stranger. "I am aware of it. Henrietta was the last thing I thought of when I drowned."

Soledad got up and moved closer. The Stranger looked as though he'd been buried a long time. "I was ashamed of her. I wanted to hurt somebody," the priest said.

"I have watched you," the Stranger said. "What a troubled young man!"

"I thought that becoming a priest would make up for killing her. But I cannot forget what I've done. I've tried to drown myself in this"—he raised the cup—"and in the pleasures of women. Nothing has helped." He turned and faced the Stranger. "I am a bad priest, Father. I no longer believe in God. Perhaps I never did." He took a long swallow from his cup. "Mostly, I believe in Beethoven, who is like God to me. I believe in making love to a woman. In trees and geese and rocks. In those Indians out there, who, through no fault of their own, will leave this land and go to the desert, where they'll surely die. I want to stop it. Yet what can I do?"

The Stranger shook his head. "So you have learned what it means to be human," he said. "To feel love, even for a moment, is to know what the world is all about. Your mother and I were together but a short time. Yet it was a blessed eternity for me."

With trembling hands, Soledad leaned over and refilled his cup.

"I am never far from you," the Stranger went on. "Because of the comet birthmark you wear upon your face. Certain men of Charcas, in San Luis Potosí, Mexico, where I come from, have it, and they are considered wise. Part fish, part animal, part bird. Because of us, the religion of our ancestors will never die out." Patiently, the Stranger told Soledad about Los Indios, who lived in the jungle, and how they had suffered since the time of Cortés.

"The Church thought they had wiped us out, but they did not," the Stranger said. "We go on, year after year."

Soledad's head was spinning. He swallowed the rest of his drink, noticing that the Stranger had not touched his. "Why do you tell me all this?"

"Where you are is not where you belong. But where you belong is not where you can go without passing through this world first." The Stranger paused, then continued. "When the time is right, I will take you to Charcas. You will become a teacher."

The priest was deeply troubled. "Are you telling me I must die?"

The Stranger reached out a shaggy hand, then drew it back. No fingers. "Everyone must die. But we come back."

"What do you want me to do?" Soledad cried and jumped up, spilling his wine down the front of his cassock. It left a dark stain.

"Nothing!" the Stranger said. "Events will come to you." He drifted up from the chair.

"What is your name?" Soledad asked.

"Sierra Ruiz, in the life when she knew me. I am something else now."

Soledad took a step toward this shadowy figure, but the Stranger backed away. "You may not touch me in this world," he said as he went through the door without opening it. Soledad flung open the door and ran after him, across the frozen earth, toward the thick, black trees swaying in the wind, crying for his father who was dead, and yet fully, wondrously alive.

PART SIX

Camposanto, New Mexico,
1896–1897

TWENTY-SIX

ONE NIGHT, when the Dog Star was breathing in the sky, Juan Lobo wrapped his blanket around his shoulders and headed up a narrow path that led to the kiva. Two figures came along the path and joined him. Other men came, silently finding their way by moonlight. They stopped and picked out familiar stars, brothers to their wandering souls. Each man felt the biting chill in the air. Spring was still a long way off. A great melancholy descended on them, for each one knew in his heart that at this same time next year, they would be in the Arizona desert next to their hated enemies, the Navajo. They came to the kiva to share their common fears, to commiserate, and to make certain they had exhausted every possibility for preserving their cherished way of life. It now seemed that it was not possible.

The kiva was partly aboveground—a circular room about fifteen feet in diameter that they reached by way of a ladder through the roof. Soledad had already stumbled upon this temple of Indian worship, forbidden by his Church for three hundred years and still outlawed. He had not gone in. He'd merely listened to the sound of voices coming through the hole in the roof, inhaled the smell of piñon smoke, and resumed walking. *Let them have their rituals*, he'd thought, with only a twinge of regret. *They believe in them. It does no harm.*

Inside the kiva, the fire cast its glow on the plastered walls built by Elk Old Man and his sons. Twenty men sat cross-legged on the floor—all except El Comanche who, in deference to his age, was allowed to sit on an old board placed between two rocks. Juan Lobo stood up. Although small in stature, he loomed large in the firelight.

"It is finished," he said. "There is nothing more we can do."

"We are entitled to a fair trial," Luis Madrone said, trying to remember the last time an Indian received a fair trial. "We should have known this would happen!"

Juan Lobo looked away. "You are a wise man, Luis," he said. "Yes, we should have known." Now he had a responsibility to tell them everything, straight from the beginning two years ago, when some government men came and talked about eminent domain. "What does it mean?" he'd asked. The government man had smiled. "What it means, chief," he'd said, "is that we have the right to take your land."

"Shoot the bastards," El Comanche said, the only response he knew. He banged the butt of his rifle on the floor. "I will ride to Santa Fe and kill them."

"You cannot," Juan Lobo said evenly. "They think you are dead." Everyone laughed, a hollow laugh meant to mask their fears.

Juan Talamantes, his eyes on the hard mud floor, tried to imagine life someplace else. Because of his foolishness, he had lost Ermina. She'd already left for San Sebastian and a new life with the widower. Now he would lose the only other thing he loved, besides his newfound passion for long division. His lower lip trembled. Lately the Custodian of Meekness had begun to see the faces of his ancestors swirling beneath his feet. "How can they take what has always belonged to us?"

Narciso Ortega spoke up. "Well, it is like this, Clay Pipe," he said, using one of Juan's Indian names. Others were bestowed upon him at birth by the elders. "They do not need our rocks. They do not need our flowers. They do not need our animals to talk to. Some are farmers, but they cannot farm in these mountains. But they do want our trees and the gold in the rocks. What does that make them, then?"

Alvar Talamantes waved his hand. "Maggots," he said furiously. "They are maggots on a piece of rotting flesh." He thought of a thousand things to do to Camposanto's enemies. After all, he was the Custodian of Madness, inclined to doing mad things, just as he had that time he'd carried home the head of an Apache warrior he'd cut off in battle, and used it to play stickball in the plaza.

Juan Lobo spoke. He had one more idea, and they listened, but without enthusiasm, for they knew they were facing a force greater than their own. "In Colorado, I saw Utes moved out at gunpoint. Their lodges were burned, their children captured and sent away to the white man's school. I have heard the same thing about all our brothers. So let them try to do that to us. We will sit right here and dare them to shoot us. We will drive them out with fire." The men cheered, but that was only because they wanted to appear fearless. As for Juan Lobo, he had already decided he would never leave this place. They would find him here, and they would have to kill him before they dragged him out.

The situation seemed so desperate that they voted to do nothing except practice the resistance Juan Lobo had suggested. El Comanche cast a vote to declare war on the government of the United States of America. He would go to Washington and shoot the Great White Father himself.

Peso Mondragon sat alone, his back pressed against the wall of the kiva. Nothing had turned out right, not the spell he and Pilar had put on the priest. Not the deal he'd made with certain officials who had remembered him from his days as governor. He'd been promised numerous presents in exchange for helping them acquire the title to the Calabaza land, but when he went to Santa Fe, all he'd received were a sack of cornmeal and a set of horseshoes. Now he was caught in the middle of an unpleasant situation. "All we have to do," Peso Mondragon said, as he struggled to his feet, "is give the right people enough money, and they will see it our way!" The men nodded in dubious agreement, but every one of them knew there wasn't enough money in all of Camposanto to accomplish Peso's plan.

Juan Lobo sniffed the air and smelled something rotten. He went around and cut off an inch from the ends of each man's braids with his hunting knife and threw each piece into the fire as a means of purification. When he came to Peso Mondragon, the Custodian of Good Intentions pulled away. "Do not cut my hair, Hand That Stops the Sun. It will go bad for you." The old man hesitated. Then he took his knife and cut off the end of Peso's braid anyway. He could feel a change almost immediately. The air became heavier. A blast of cold air rose from the sipapu, fanned the fire, and swirled up the ladder, where it startled a skunk who was peering down the hole. A look of blank terror turned Peso's face to a caricature.

Peso was the one who had brought bad medicine to the village—he and his witch-wife Pilar! The cacique brushed his hand across his eyes. Suddenly, everything made sense. The government documents the padre had read aloud. The visits from the *federales*. Juan Lobo had wondered at the time how they'd known so much about places they could not have gone, even in their dreams. Juan Lobo had seen what witchcraft could do. Had not his middle son, Long Knives, become violently ill after a dispute with Pilar? Later, had he not found in Long Knives's bed a mud figure stuffed with cactus needles? Not even Juan Lobo, with all his powers, had been able to save his son. Or his two uncles. Or his young niece, Blue Feather. The witches were often more powerful than the medicine men, though on his side, Juan Lobo had a thousand years of tradition that he believed would save him from their spells. He pointed a finger at Peso Mondragon.

"You!" he said in a deep voice that reflected both earth and sky. "You have betrayed your people!" The old man beckoned the traitor forward to stand before him in front of the flickering fire. As was the custom, Juan Lobo recited all of Peso Mondragon's offenses, from the first spell he had cast on the village long ago, to the present time when he had betrayed a hundred generations of Calabazas with his selfishness. It was within Juan Lobo's power to order the fat man killed, but instead, he banished him from the kiva, never more to participate in those rituals which kept hope and tradition alive. In his shame, Peso Mondragon climbed out of the kiva, thinking of suicide. But he would live well into the twentieth century and die of natural causes.

No sooner had Peso left than Delfine Madrone got unsteadily to his feet. For weeks, he had been trying to impress La Luz with his love, but she had only laughed and refused to lie with him or even kiss him the way she used to. She was in love with the priest; she would soon have his child. "The padre does nothing," he said. "Ever since he came, there has been trouble. I say, let's kill him, Hand That Stops the Sun. That way, one problem will be solved."

The cacique shook his head. Delfine had always been like one of the tribe, though his father was a Scotsman, but now he saw that Delfine knew nothing, despite a lifetime spent in the kiva.

Because of his foreign bagpiper blood, the cacique thought. Blood was everything. It made you strong or weak. Connected to the earth or not. A part of a long unbroken cord of tradition stretching back to the time the Calabazas came out of the lake and looked around. *What have I taught him*, he wondered, *that he talks like this? Blowing his bagpipe is not the same.*

"We will not kill the padre," Juan Lobo said firmly. "He saved El Comanche. He brought Papita back to life. Just because he loves La Luz is no reason to kill him. Yet."

Delfine sat down, hot with shame. The men all laughed, for they knew what a fool Delfine had made of himself, creeping around the village after Soledad and La Luz. "Well, at least we will get money from the *federales* for the land."

"Money means nothing. I know where some more of it is. How long do you think it will last, Mountain Boy?" the Custodian of Abundance thundered, using Delfine's Calabaza name. Each Indian was to receive two hundred dollars in silver when the *federales* returned. "The money will be gone in no time! Then what will you do?"

El Comanche had been dozing on the bench. He jumped up with astonishing agility. "You stupid bastards," he said, waving the rifle he always carried with him. "Without the land, what have you got left? My people, the Wackamungas, used to own land from horizon to horizon, as far as the eye could see. Plenty buffalo. Water. Grass. Now the Wackamungas are all dead but me. Buffalo all gone. Land belongs to gringos. No real warriors left, Hand That Stops the Sun, except you and me." He was ready to shoot a round into the beamed ceiling when Juan Lobo stopped him.

"And me," Luis Madrone piped up. "I do not want to leave this land either. I want my grandchildren and their grandchildren to grow up here." He turned and glared at Delfine. "You are no son of mine, talking like that! If you do not like it here, why don't you leave right now?"

Alvar Talamantes had a headache. And his stomach hurt. As if his troubles with Isabela and Zorrito were not enough! "I used to own all the land on the north side of the river," he said, stretching his arms above his head. "My father gave it to me. I was a rich man until gringos stole it. Now I am poor like the rest of you." He sat down, not feeling any better. There stood Zorrito, wrapped in a blanket. Only his two dark eyes peeked out. *That son of a bitch,* Alvar thought wearily. *He's fucking my wife. With her, he made a baby, and I am too tired to kill him.* His big hands trembled. What was he to do? Underneath his clothes, Zorrito was a man, and Isabela was all woman.

Juan Talamantes banged his wooden leg on the floor. It made a hollow-sounding thud. Despite the promise of baptism, a real leg had not yet formed; only the moss grew on his artificial leg. He spoke in a slow, hesitant voice, filled with all his old fears and doubts. Ever since Florita died, he'd had trouble addressing her father directly, remembering the day he'd amputated his shattered leg and given him enough Elixir of Dreams to numb the pain. "I think we should tell the priest our problems. Maybe he could help us." There was a chorus of negative response. Juan Talamantes shrank back into his blanket. Something was happening though. He looked down. A vine was growing around his wooden leg. A miracle, no?

"The priest already knows," Narciso said, seated on the other side of the circle. "He asked me what I would do in the desert. I said I would build a house of sand and live there with Papita. I said I would learn about life in a different place."

Juan Lobo listened to their disconnected arguments, none of which offered any real solutions. *We are afraid*, he thought, sensing that before long his people would splinter. He had no more power over them. The Calabazas would vanish just like many other tribes all over the country. *Progress has done it*, he thought bitterly. *And greed*. All that was dear and familiar to him was disappearing before his eyes. Four of his children were gone. His wife was dying. The great leader known as Hand That Stops the Sun stood before them, a man of dignity and experience. "I am an old man who does not have much time left," he said. "Soon I will travel up the Hanging Road. But before I go, I want certain things to happen."

He looked around at the items in the room, a mixture of their Indian faith and the Catholic one. There were the foot-high stone fetishes that had been in the old kiva before it flooded and drowned the two boys who were guarding the spirits—one of the Turtle, the other of the Bear clan. There was a chipped plaster statue of the Virgin Mary because they liked her, especially during planting season when they took her out, placed her in their cornfields, and prayed for rain. A wooden cross because it represented the Four Directions. There was even an oversized set of rosary beads—which they had removed from the body of Father Montez—draped across a beam. Three sacred jars contained pollen, cornmeal, and tobacco. Another contained eagle feathers used in certain ceremonies. In the corner, locked in a trunk, were the ceremonial blankets. Feathered headdresses. Beaded moccasins pried from the feet of a dead Lakota. On the wall above his head loomed the solemn face of a buffalo. Next to it hung the shield found in the cave where the Anasazis hid out from their enemies five centuries before and drew on the rock walls their inherited recollections of the misty time when men were still animals.

The kiva was the repository of the best ideas that had come their way since the beginning. Symbols of both religions were here, and none among the Calabazas were bothered by the contradiction of placing the Catholic ones there alongside their own icons. Bringing his attention back to the men around him, Juan Lobo said, "We have been a part of the white man's way a long time. What we say. What we do. What we eat. Even what we believe. We cannot go back to the time of our ancestors. We cannot live in the white man's world either. So we will create a Seam of Accommodation between the First World and the Second World. And in this Seam of Accommodation we will live, one foot placed in each world. This is what we will do, as long as one Calabaza is alive in these mountains."

After Juan Lobo had spoken, they sat and argued and talked and talked and argued for many hours. *How was it possible to live in two Worlds at the same time?*, they wondered. Was a Seam of Accommodation like a bridge? Or was it a hole, into which they would fall like stones? They sang and banged their old drum, hoping that the ancestors would tell them what to do. All they heard was the wind whistling down the hole and the fire crackling when Zorrito put more wood on it. Still, no one understood what the cacique meant, and he told them nothing further.

The men came out of the kiva well after midnight. The stars glittered overhead, as bright as diamonds. Juan Lobo drew in his breath, filling his lungs with the mountain air his ancestors had breathed. How he loved this place! How he would miss the lessons he learned from each thing he saw—ravens and eagles, clouds and lightning! The cacique walked briskly down the path. In his heart he knew the men thought he had failed them. They would resist change, yes. All any of them really wanted was the right to enjoy those stars overhead, unencumbered. How were they to create a Seam of Accommodation without sacrificing their principles? He did not know the answers.

As he went up the steps to his house, the old man realized that they lived on borrowed time—time borrowed from the Catholics, from the gringos, from destiny itself. What of little Agua Madrone, La Luz's pretty daughter? *When she is my age*, he thought, *it will be the year 1965. What would the world be like then? Would my people have any place in it, even with the Seam of Accommodation?*

Suddenly, Juan Lobo felt very tired. His wife was sick. His son believed he could fly. What precious little time was left he wanted to savor like a piece of rich meat roasted over the fire. *What can I do?*, he wondered. *I am a man betrayed by time.*

AFTER THE MEN had returned from the kiva, Lorenzo Soledad paced around the plaza, wrapped in his woolen cloak. He had not slept in several nights, worrying about a woman who pretended he no longer existed. La Luz was breaking his heart. She would not speak to him when he came to her house, offering to make amends. "What have I done?" he'd asked, yearning to put his arms around her once again. He noticed the dark circles under her eyes and how she was putting on a little weight. How he missed her beside him in his narrow, lonely bed! She'd turned to him and said, "I do not want to talk to you, Lorenzo. And you know what you have done!"

She wanted what he could not give, but was he certain he could not give it? He'd written a letter of resignation to the monsignor and another to La Luz, which he slipped under her door. He'd sat all day and watched her house, hoping for a glimpse of her when she went in or out. She was carrying his child, and he believed he had a right to see her. He would marry her, if that's what she wanted. He'd renounce his vows and follow these poor people to the desert, and there he'd spend his life tending sheep like a Navajo.

Sensing his misery, Luis had come over one day with a twenty-year-old jug of the Elixir of Dreams, which had the effect of an anesthetic. "She is not feeling well, Padre. You know how it is with women when they are this way," the Custodian of Stories said solicitously. "When my wife was that way, she went to live with a bunch of mountain lions." He expelled a breath. "Delfine wrote to Rafael about you. Rafael wrote back. He says he is going to get out of the *pinta* and kill you. So naturally she is upset."

Luis was his friend. He understood the sorts of things a woman did to a man. He had gone through a crisis or two himself. He'd shared his experience with the priest, as if in confession. "I made love to Siamese twins," he said. "In Denver."

"I have no right to her," Soledad said. "Why can't I just forget her?"

"Why does a man need the right to love a woman?" Luis replied. "It is in our balls, Padre. We are going to love women until the sun falls out of the sky! Or our balls fall out from between our legs."

Slightly tipsy from the Elixir of Dreams, Soledad had been walking up and down for some time in the frigid night, trying to calm his nerves. He blew on his hands to warm them. It was dark; there was no moon or stars, and a chill wind rushed down from the peaks as the inexorable fingers of winter gripped the land. He sighed. It was not just his futile love for La Luz that had upset him, but pondering the enigmatic words of the Stranger: "Your purpose is not here, but elsewhere." Where was he to go?

"Why do you torment me, La Luz?" Soledad cried and looked up at the velvety sky. He had never felt lonelier in his life—nor more worthless. What would he do once the monsignor accepted his resignation? He remembered a line from Saint Augustine: "Thou hast made us in thy image, Oh Lord, and we are restless."

Around him, the ponderosas swayed. An owl cried from the depth of the forest. He heard coyotes, just over the ridge. He shivered. *My life is nothing*, he thought. *I am a selfish man, who has given little. Now I have ruined her life*. He would leave in the morning and not give her another thought.

Slowly, the priest walked up the path, his head bent against the cold wind. As usual, Narciso crept along discreetly behind him. He had sworn to protect this man for as long as he lived, and he had worn himself out, standing guard both night and day. He was armed with a six-inch knife that was as sharp as a razor. As Soledad mounted the two short steps to his porch, a figure lunged out of the shadows and pulled him to the ground with a terrible cry. They rolled over and over, Soledad trying to defend himself as best he could from a blade that sought his heart. But Narciso, moving swiftly and silently, forced himself between them. Soledad's assailant staggered backward and fell to the ground with a hoarse cry. Narciso stumbled away, scarcely able to breathe, then stopped to vomit on the ground. He had never killed a man before; he had only killed the beautiful Florita.

His breath coming in short, labored gasps, Soledad knelt beside the motionless form of the man who had tried to kill him. He rolled him over and felt the warm, sticky blood pumping out of his heart. He gave him last rites.

"Delfine!" the priest cried, and blessed whatever life remained in him. Then, his cassock torn and bloody, he ran as fast as his legs would carry him to Luis Madrone's house. The Custodian of Stories only shook his head. "I have been expecting it," he said. "He was a half-blood, after all." La Luz stared sleepily at Soledad. Then, with a little animal cry, she threw herself into his arms.

TWENTY-SEVEN

*W*HERE HAS THE *time gone?*, Maria Lobo wondered as she lay in her stale bed in a house grown cold from sorrow. She remembered her childhood in the old pueblo, where her mother had taught her courage by bathing her in the Pecos River in the winter. Her grandmothers had given her names. One for each moon. So she was Dry Flower. Walking Rain. Antelope Dreaming. And nine others. She was also Maria Teresa, a name conferred by the Spanish priests, anxious to legitimize her wavering conversion to the Catholic faith. In the old days, she had eaten with her fingers straight from the cooking pot her mother set in the middle of the floor of the one room in which seven people lived. When the food ran out, she had gnawed on bark or captured spiders and caterpillars and mice and cooked them in bear grease. There had been no furniture in that pueblo house, no beds except a pile of skins under which she slept with her three sisters until Juan Lobo had brought her to his mother's house. She used to think that life was forever, she had felt no different from one year to the next. Her eyes saw the same blue sky, the same red earth, the same birds and animals. Now in old age, she felt inside the same as she had in the flower of her youth. But now her heart was heavier. And her body and her mind had begun to ache. Her Time of Departure had come, and she did not want to go.

What have I learned over all these years?, she wondered. The names of things. The way the sun breaks the night into tiny shadows and brings the fresh, sweet songs of birds. The way the river washes away sorrow. How you are able to see the other half of the rainbow in your dreams. How men and women are different, and how women are warriors, too. *I learned my own time*, Maria thought, *which is different from any other time and which will not come again.*

Her children had not lived long. One had died of a curse put on him by an Apache sorcerer. Another of smallpox. Her beautiful Florita, only nineteen years old, was shot by two men pretending to be fierce warriors in a battle for her hand. Her next beautiful daughter, Birdsong, was washed away by a flash flood in the canyon. She had grieved for her children, but you could not grieve too much, or their *tasooms* would never rest. She had only Bonito left, but he stood outside life, looking in. She wondered what would become of him when she was gone. Perhaps he would become a white man and wear shoes and regular clothes and take a job in town. He was determined to make something of himself, she knew. So maybe he would succeed in making his machine and flying through the air, and everyone in the village would laugh because you could not play with nature that way and pretend you were born with wings.

Painfully, Maria Lobo eased herself out of bed and put on her buckskin Corn Dance dress with the woven red sash and her tall white boots made of softest doeskin; she fixed her hair in a *chongo* and wore her best jewelry—the turquoise necklace that Muladar, the Navajo, had given her that time she Got Together with him and a pair of silver earrings that Juan Lobo had brought back the winter he spent with the Acoma woman. Last night, Juan Lobo had said he would come to her in time and that they would have in the World Beyond what they never had in the Middle World. "Oh, you mean you will love me then?" she'd asked hopefully. "I only mean I will have time to look into your eyes," he'd said.

Today is a very good day to die, she thought. Juan Lobo was hunting in the mountains. Bonito had taken the wagon to town to get parts for his flying machine before the weather got too cold. The Owl of Death had perched at the foot of her bed, urging her on to the next world. The day was cold but sunny, with a slight breeze making the trees dance. She walked out of the house and up the trail to the mountains. She did not look back.

Overhead, the ravens flew in a circle until at last they came down and hovered around Maria, as if to help her climb the mountain. When she neared the cave entrance, she turned and looked at the valley below. She had memorized every last contour of it. The breaks in the hills where a stream had pushed through the rock. The canyons where she had gone to pick berries. The trees where she'd lain in the shade and dreamed of her life as a woman of knowledge. She remembered where the waterfall was and how she and Catarina had taken off their clothes and splashed each other. Each tree and bush and rock was familiar to her, the changing moods of mountains and streams and flowers. She remembered where a family of skunks had lived in a log and where a grumpy old badger had played with the eggs of a grouse before he ate them. She knew the direction of the geese when they brought seeds and dropped them in the earth. She recognized the songs of all the different birds when she heard them, a whole symphony of sound that made her happy. She had watched certain trees grow up from tiny saplings to their full mature height. These were the important things. She reached out to the wind and told everything good-bye.

With bunches of sage and sweetgrass clutched tightly in her hands, Maria Lobo pushed her way through the bushes and entered the cave. She saw the petroglyphs the Anasazi had scratched long ago, and she saw the drawings Sotero had made of the priest with an erection. She smiled. How like the boy to want to remember Soledad that way. Then she saw the great sleeping bear, curled up at the rear of the cave. He had a strong, rich odor.

"Will you be my companion on my journey?" she asked. The bear continued snoring, but she saw that he raised one huge paw in the air. He had long, sharp claws. Wrapped in her best blue shawl, Maria Lobo snuggled beside the bear and made herself comfortable. His fur was thick and warm. She took his outstretched paw and held it firmly. "Be kind to me," she said.

And then, she went to sleep.

TWENTY-EIGHT

THE OLD MAN was alone in his sorrow. The death of Maria he kept in his heart, surrounded by memory. He saw her as a young girl, as a robin, as a deer. He burned her clothing, destroyed her few possessions, and conversed with her *tasoom* during the three-day mourning period, as was the custom. She came to him while he sat alone in the kiva, trying to understand the Great Circle that he had taught to the young for many years. Juan Lobo was very tired, yet the fresh energy of Maria flowed into his veins, the way she'd promised. How differently everything looked with Maria gone. Things he never saw before, he saw now. Things that he remembered seeing had disappeared.

"Ah, Padre, this is the Second World time," Juan Lobo said. He had joined the priest in his little house, where a fire was blazing away in the stove. Soledad was mending his torn cassock with green thread, brought to him by Papita, who had grown one whole inch since he'd brought her back from the dead.

Soledad bit the thread in two. "Your wife is at peace, old man." When Sotero found her, she was curled up with the bear, holding his paw. "Maria Lobo is not in heaven, for I believe there is no heaven. She's here among us. I have felt her presence for days."

The old man was pleased. The padre saw many things their way now. "Yes, she is here," he said slowly. He had spent the day watching a large, thick-coated coyote circle his house. It had raised its head and howled. Then it darted into the trees. He believed it was

Maria, for the three-day period of the *tasoom* trying to find a new home was over. He was able to smile, knowing she was nearby, ready to comfort him. "I have seen her several times."

Soledad fixed coffee and offered Juan Lobo the last of Isabela's apple pie. She'd baked it as a present after the priest had a long talk with Zorrito concerning the Ten Commandments, which, for the moment, had seemed to cure the boy's obsession with Alvar's wife.

"If she is here, then she will help us, Juan Lobo," Soledad said softly, eating the pie with his fingers. He had not been allowed to conduct Maria Lobo's funeral. Juan Lobo had done that himself, offering only Calabaza prayers and rituals.

"I have asked her," the old man said. He stared forlornly out the window. He was not supposed to grieve, but today he could not help himself. He felt utterly drained. First, the murder of Delfine by Narciso. Then, the death of his wife. Two burials in less than a week. Bad medicine. Yesterday, Bonito had tried to launch his flying machine from the top of the hill in a wind strong enough to uproot trees. The machine resembled a wasp, with a long, thin body and two stubby wings covered this time in stout muslin cloth. The padre found him crumpled on a grassy slope—the machine torn to pieces—and carried him to Juan Lobo's house in his arms. It was a wonder Bonito hadn't killed himself. The cacique laid him out on the floor and one by one set his fractured bones— one leg, two arms, and a collarbone. The three ribs would have to heal by themselves; Bonito would be immobilized for a long time. Afterward, Soledad laid two Spanish *reales* on the table in front of the cacique, who, raising his head, smiled and tossed them in the palm of his hand.

"When we first came here, we found gold all over the place," the cacique said, unimpressed. "It is nothing new. We had little use for gold, Padre. Once a year, my wife and I would go to El Paso on the train and sell the coins because we were afraid to sell them here. Then we'd buy what we needed for the year. Flour. Sugar. Coffee. Boots. Each family got the same amount of money." The old man seemed to relax. "These coins are Spanish. Left here a long time ago. There are supposed to be more hidden around. No one knows where."

"Sotero knows where," the priest said. "Don't you see, if there were enough gold, maybe we could buy back this land from the government. You would never have to move." Soledad's face, already gaunt, reflected his concern.

The old man fastened his bony fingers around the padre's wrist. "No," he said quietly. "That is the white man's way. We have our own way." He gave him a long, meaningful look and pushed aside his plate. "We have a belief that has to do with apple trees. Every spring, the apple tree is filled with beautiful blossoms. They smell sweet. Soon they turn into apples. The apples ripen. We pick them and eat them. Pretty soon not even one is left. We look at the empty tree and think, soon there will be blossoms, then apples, then we will eat. Around and around it goes, in the same way always. Spring follows winter, no matter what. That is the way it is with our village. Gringos will never own our land. We look dead, but soon, we will be blossoms, then apples. Do you understand?"

The padre laughed. He loved this man's simple wisdom derived from the natural world around him. Soledad realized that his own education, though formal, had been very limited. "You are wise, Juan Lobo, wiser than I'll ever be."

The Custodian of Abundance waved him away. "I know little," he said. "I am only now beginning to learn, now that it is nearly time for me to leave this world." But many years would pass before he actually went.

Soledad took the old man's hand and squeezed it; it was still a tough and sinewy hand, accustomed to the bow, the rifle, the reins. What the old man had seen in his lifetime would never come again. "As for me, I have learned nothing of real value," the priest said, "until now."

LA LUZ RETURNED to him the wintry day before he was to leave for Santa Fe to plead the Calabazas' case in front of the authorities.

It was a last-ditch attempt, but Soledad was obsessed; he had the *reales*—a small coffee can full that Sotero had unexpectedly dumped on his table. It seemed like a lot of money, enough perhaps to buy this little corner of the world. And there were more *reales*, Sotero, in his muteness, had given him to understand, but he would not say where. The priest was rereading all the old documents pertaining to the Calabazas' land when La Luz opened the door and walked in. He caught his breath at the sight of her, her shawl covered with light, fluffy flakes of snow. He had never seen her look more beautiful. She stood above him, unsure how to begin. "I want you to hear my confession, Padre," she said, and she dropped to her knees in front of him.

"I cannot," he said as his comet began to throb the way it always did when he was embarrassed or afraid. But she had already started to tell him what was on her mind.

"I am the reason Delfine died," she said. "Oh, yes. I tempted him. I showed him my body with your child inside. I lay down beside him when he was sleeping. But I never let him make love to me. On the day he died, I told him to come to my bed that night. I said I did not love Rafael anymore, and I did not love you either. Poor Delfine was beside himself. That night he thought he saw his chance at long last. I did not know he meant to kill you, or I would have tried to stop him. You must believe me, Lorenzo."

The priest shook his head. "Why would you do such a thing, woman?"

"Because I love you," she said. "I thought that if you saw me with Delfine, you would . . . you would—"

"Become jealous enough to marry you? Get up!" he said angrily, and he pulled her to her feet. She fell into his arms and buried her face in his cassock. He held her away at first, struggling with his anger. Then he pulled her to him and kissed the top of her head. "God does not hold you responsible for Delfine's death. You mustn't worry." He found himself stroking her shoulders. Her arms. Her face. He bent and kissed her, tenderly. She pulled away and wiped her lips with the back of her hand. "Don't," she said, "I am not a good woman, Lorenzo. Because of me, a man is dead. I am filled with sin."

He drew her to him. "I am not a good priest either," he said. "Because of me, a woman is dead. My own mother. Oh, yes, I killed her when I was young. I never meant to, but there she was, dead on the bed." He covered his eyes. "That was almost twenty years ago. Not a day goes by that I don't see her face. Or hear her voice telling me I have not suffered enough." He turned his long, sad face away. "Guilt will eat you alive, if you let it. Tear apart everything you're made of. Destroy your hopes, your idea of your-self. You can't run away because guilt is always there. That's how I've lived all these years. I pray it won't happen to you."

She put her arms around his neck and kissed him. But when he started to unbutton the front of her dress, she gently pushed him away. "Not now, Lorenzo. I cannot get Delfine out of my mind, cannot stop thinking that I was, in some way, responsible for what happened." She noticed the stricken look in his eyes. "Do I love you? Yes, more than life itself."

He smoothed back her hair. "I knew it as well," he murmured, "but I was afraid." He hugged her to him. In the summer, he would have a son—flesh of his flesh, soul of his soul, blood of the jungle ancestors that he had come from. Perhaps he had a purpose at last. Him. La Luz. The children. "Suppose I could arrange for a divorce, La Luz?" he said, cupping one hand around her breast. "It's not unheard of. I could use some of the *reales*." Even as he said these words, he knew they were wrong. He would be disgraced more than he already was.

"No, Lorenzo," she said stubbornly, her body aching at his touch. "I do not want to marry anyone." Sensing his disappoint-ment, La Luz drew him down to the bed and lay beside him before she spoke. "What we have is more than any marriage, my love. We will make the most of it for as long as we have together." She turned her tear-streaked face to him. "When the child comes, you will be gone," she said. "I had a dream about it. But I promise he will grow up like you." Then she got up and was

gone, leaving Soledad alone but somehow exalted by the knowledge that she was his.

At daybreak, Soledad dressed warmly, packed food and water,
and rode down the mountain, heavy snowflakes stinging his
cheeks. In the lining of his little dishpan hat, tied securely under
his chin, La Luz had sewn the fifteen gold *reales* given to him by
the mute boy. Sotero had brought the coins in a deerskin pouch,
delighted with himself. The priest was convinced there were more
and that with more he could make a deal with the government, no
matter what Juan Lobo said. "Please," he had begged Sotero, "Tell
me where these came from." But the boy only ran away. La Luz
tried to reason with her brother-in-law, but Sotero was firm. This
was his own special secret; he would reveal it in his own good time.

In San Sebastian, Soledad spent a restless night in a small room
that Colonel Pazote let him have behind the stable. "Ah, Padre,"
he said, wiping the remains of breakfast from the corners of his
mouth with his hand. "There is a rumor going around. All that
land up there in the mountains they are taking illegally from the
Calabazas. Only some money is going to them. Much is going in
the lawyers' pockets, if you know what I mean. In Mexico, it was
the same thing."

Soledad finished the strong, black coffee, rolls, and fresh eggs
cooked with cheese and chile before he spoke. "Do you think it possible to win a war against the United States government, Colonel?"
He was beginning to sound like El Comanche.

Colonel Pazote's round face, with its mouthful of gold teeth,
broke into a huge grin. "That is like the mouse killing the cat,
Padre." He looked around the cluttered room. "Can you sprout
wings and fly? Well, those are your chances."

Soledad walked to the train station and stood shivering on the
platform. His head felt the weight of the cervezas he had drank the
night before when he and the colonel stayed up late playing monte.
He removed his hat and scratched his scalp with a quick, rough
motion. A cold wind blew from the north, and he glanced down the
platform where one other passenger—a dark, ragged man—waited.

Thirty minutes late, the train puffed in from the north and shuddered to a halt. Soledad smiled as he looked at the hissing locomotive; he half expected El Comanche to attack it, though the old man had foresworn such futile gestures. He sat in the last car, as he always did, and he gave his usual blessing when people asked him to. But his heart was not in benediction anymore, but in the sort of battle for justice that El Comanche craved. Out of the corner of his eye, he saw the dark man from San Sebastian staring at him from down the aisle. He appeared to be a mestizo, very dirty, apparently drunk on a bottle of cheap wine that he carried inside his jacket. An expression of pure malice spread across his face as he looked at the priest. Soledad turned to the window and tried to concentrate on the frozen landscape flashing past, but the man's eyes bore into the back of his head. What did he want? There was something so ominous in his glance that Lorenzo sank lower into his seat, his hat tied securely under his chin. He tried to read, but it was no use. The man's gaze was relentless. After a while the priest made his way to the observation platform to get some air. It was very cold, with a sharp wind. He stared idly into space; the shiny tracks fell away in front of him, a cold wind ripped across the snow-covered land and revived him a little. He deeply inhaled the pure, thin air. As he turned to go back inside, he saw the mestizo crouched, a knife in his hand. "Give me your money," the mestizo said. His face was contorted and odd.

"I have no money," the priest said, feeling some loose change in the pocket of his cassock.

"You got money," the man said, "and I don't mean pesetas." He pressed closer.

Soledad remembered the gold *reales* he was carrying in his dishpan hat. He pulled the strings tighter as if to secure his treasure. "I will never give it to you," he said. He stood with his back to the railing that separated him from the tracks. He felt strangely calm. Even as the man lunged at him, he did not panic; he merely stepped to one side. As the man lurched against the railing, the knife dropped out of his hands onto the tracks. The priest saw his opportunity to escape, but the man turned like a flash and pulled him back in a powerful grip. Though small, the man was many times stronger than himself, and he had the advantage of youth.

"Help!" the priest cried as he felt himself being lifted into the air. Then the train swerved around a curve and the man lost his footing; Soledad saw the tracks below him and in a superhuman burst of energy, he reached back for the steel pole that supported the roof of the observation platform. For a split second it seemed that the two of them would topple over the edge together. Then the priest felt the man's hands give way. The mestizo uttered an unearthly cry and toppled backward, grabbing as he did, the hat that had slipped across Lorenzo's eyes.

The padre slumped over the rail, half in and half out of the train. He clutched his familiar cross. "Mother of God," he gasped, "I've killed him." He squinted through the blowing cinders. Behind him, lying in a crumpled heap on the receding tracks, was the mestizo. Soledad's hat, filled with gold, was lying to one side, a brown blotch on the drifted snow. There was no way to get it without jumping off the train.

Wearing his torn and dirty cassock, his face scratched and swollen, Soledad arrived in Santa Fe around midmorning on the Lamy stage and went directly to see Juan Lobo's sometime lawyer, José Guerra. He was a black-eyed, sallow-skinned man with four strands of hair on top of his head and a drooping mustache that he stroked as he talked. He sat behind a big mahogany desk, imported—he proudly claimed—from Spain. The priest tried to look important, as befitted an emissary from the Calabazas, but in his present condition, he resembled a derelict. He glanced around the richly appointed office and knew his case was hopeless before he even opened his mouth. Guerra was not the sort of man to defend clients like the Calabazas without an exorbitant fee paid up front. The priest despised him on sight. A slick, oily man with a drooping mustache. Bulging eyes that focused on shelves of books.

The lawyer in the expensive black suit and fine Cordova boots proceeded to explain to Soledad the legality of the land transaction.

The government's right of eminent domain. The theory of Manifest Destiny, which governed everything these days. He claimed the department, at his urging, was offering money to the Calabazas in exchange for more than one hundred thousand acres of land.

"The *federales* don't have to pay them anything, not a dime," Guerra said with faint disdain. This bedraggled, uncertain priest was obviously not the sort who could swing much weight with the governor or the federal officers. He sniffed. "It would be perfectly legal to condemn the land and move the Indians out, Padre, since they have no statutory claim. But I myself am a true Spaniard, with roots in the valley that go back to the time of don Diego de Vargas. So I have compassion for these savages. Ten thousand dollars for that worthless land is not a precedent, believe me. It is a privilege. The Calabazas don't realize how lucky they are. Get them to sign the papers, Padre, before the government throws them out." Guerra took a Turkish cigarette from a silver case and offered one to the priest. "You have ninety days."

Soledad declined, then appraised this self-important lawyer. "I'm afraid you don't understand, Señor Guerra. It's not just land we're talking about. It's the lives of these people. They'll die out there in the desert. And you know it. You cannot let this happen."

Guerra flicked a whisper of ash into a silver ashtray. The priest was getting on his nerves. Guerra had some influence with the monsignor; perhaps an inquiry could be made into the right of this priest to mix religion with politics. "See here, my dear Padre, your job may be to save souls. Mine is to facilitate progress. Now, in the course of facilitation, certain sacrifices must be made. The loss of these savages is one of them. Do I make myself clear?"

Soledad's heart sank. Here was a man accustomed to viewing his cases in the mirror of his prejudices. Sadly, he realized that the Calabazas would never win their battle to keep their sacred land. What Soledad didn't know was that Guerra, as a practical businessman, had struck a deal with the federal government for ten sections of Calabaza land on which to run his cattle, in exchange for altering certain boundary documents that included rivers and forests where the Calabazas now lived. He'd acquired timber and water rights as well, which would make him rich beyond his wildest dreams.

Soledad stared at his grimy nails, his blistered hands, and he smelled his own dirt. He knew he looked disreputable. "Señor Guerra," he said patiently, "did it ever occur to you that these savages, as you call them, were here first? Long before your people came, long before Columbus, the Indians were here, living in harmony with nature. Then people like you began to exploit them. You wanted their land. Their women. Their souls. Now you want them to go away so you can steal what's left." Soledad stood up and leaned over the mahogany desk, piled high with the documents of the lawyer's trade. "You are a lawyer, Señor Guerra. You know every mean trick there is. So you and your government friends will win, I am sure. You'll send the Calabazas to the desert, where they'll become sick and die." He pounded the desk and shouted, "May God have mercy on your miserable soul!"

Guerra's mouth dropped open. He looked closely at the scruffy priest. Not true Spanish, but mestizo. Poorly educated. No real bloodlines. He speaks like a fanatic when he ought to be instructing the poor on the inevitability of their lot. The lawyer crossed himself and looked to the crucifix on the opposite wall. He had a pure Castilian wife and six children, as well as a great hacienda with peons like this lowly priest to maintain his vast lands and livestock.

"My dear Padre," the lawyer said slowly, "even you must realize that some classes of people are above others. The Indian, for all his attempts to better himself, remains inferior." He tapped his skull with his forefinger. "Their brains are quite small, and they do not work normally. Believe me, you will be better off to forget them." He extended his hand, but the priest would not take it.

Soledad felt his comet throb and his temperature rise. "I will never forget them," he said, his lips drawn tight against his teeth. "As for you, Señor Guerra, you are a crook. You belong in the *pinta* along with Rafael Madrone. You were representing Juan Lobo, I thought."

Only because Soledad was a priest did the lawyer not take exception to his remarks. "I also represent the government," he said. "Because they are the winning side." He rose and bowed stiffly. "You are free to appeal, Padre," he said. He was a lifelong Catholic, as were twenty generations of his family. But still, he was unable to trust the clergy, especially when they were involved with politics. He ushered Soledad out with a false sympathy that the priest found annoying. "I'm sorry about all this, Padre," Guerra said, baring his little white teeth. "There is nothing I can do. The world moves on!"

Wearily, Soledad dragged himself across the plaza and collapsed in the office of his friend, Monsignor Richard Canopus. "I have failed miserably, Richard," he said to the monsignor, who had temporarily assumed the duties of the archbishop, who died of consumption a few weeks before.

"Nonsense, dear Lorenzo," said Richard Canopus. He knew that something profound was troubling his friend, who was slouched in a chair, his dark hair tousled from the wind and his cassock looking as if it had been dragged through the street. "You have made some friends. Built a church. Baptized nearly thirty souls. What more do you want?"

Soledad waved his hand impatiently. "Do you think those things matter? When they are going to lose their land and become homeless wanderers, do you think anything counts?" He was exhausted. His whole body ached. He wanted to go to bed and sleep for a week. He bit his lower lip. "On top of everything, I am in love with a married woman. She is to have my child. And this morning on the train, I may have killed a man who was trying to kill me." He mopped his head with his handkerchief and went on. "Also, there is this dog called Jesus Christ. Every night the people fornicate with anyone they please. A jealous man tried to kill me because I am in love with his sister-in-law, but he was killed by a man whose niece I brought back from the dead." His look was dazed. "Ah, what does it matter, Richard? My pain is nothing beside what they will have to endure. They will *die* out there, damn it!"

The monsignor gripped the arms of his chair. "A girl brought back from the dead?" he said, thinking of Lazarus. "Tell me about that, Lorenzo!" Nothing like that had happened in many years. What crossed his mind might become useful later on. He scribbled a few notes on a piece of paper. He folded his hands on his desk.

"One of my few successes," Soledad mumbled. "A dwarf who, for all intents and purposes, was dead. My faith in God awakened her when everyone else was ready to bury her. But what good is one success when everything else is a failure? I am here to tell you that wherever they go, I will go with them. Not as a priest, but as one committed to their way." More scribbling. Was he to believe these stories?

Richard Canopus raised his eyebrows. For many years, he had protected Soledad, put up with his lapses, made excuses for his flagrant disobedience. Not long ago, he'd destroyed the damaging file on Soledad the archbishop before him had collected before he died. But he could not go on shielding a bad priest forever. "You are a sick man, my friend. You must go far from here and get well. I will fill out the necessary papers. But now, I want you to make a confession. Kneel down."

Soledad shook his head. "I want only to help them, Richard. Don't you see? By all that is holy, I want them to keep their land. And I will do anything to keep them there!" In his mind, he saw the drunk mestizo toppling onto the tracks. La Luz naked on the bed. He saw the satisfaction on El Comanche's face when he found out the priest had lied to save him. Little Papita, when he'd raised her from the dead. Sotero, when the priest had confessed his sins. All this he haltingly told to his astonished friend. But he did not kneel.

"Are you truly sorry for these sins, Lorenzo?" the monsignor asked. Never in his life had he heard such a confession; never before had he granted absolution to such an unrepentant sinner. "That's just it, Richard," Soledad said. "I'm sorry for many sins. But being there in Camposanto, doing what I've done, is not one of them. Surely God allows a man to serve Him in different ways. I must remain a priest, for it's only within that context that I can fulfill certain prophecies." And he told the monsignor what the

Stranger had told him the last time. "I've seen this apparition for years, Richard. It's my father, Sierra Ruiz, who died before I was born! Not long ago he appeared again to warn me I must be careful. He looked like something from the grave."

The monsignor stared at him. Soledad was crazy. He was certain of this now. Was his duty to protect him or to uphold the holy laws of his Church? He played with a letter opener on his desk. "Don't ask me to help you anymore, Lorenzo. You've sent no collection money. The Church is in dire straits. Missions are closing for lack of funds. And Camposanto, well, it's not long for this world. Stay here with me, I beg of you, until I can find a retreat where you can rest until you're well again."

Soledad went to the window. Palace Avenue was decorated in anticipation of Christmas, with wreathes and *farolitos*. A scattering of snowflakes drifted through the bare tree limbs. "For the first time in my life, I'm happy," he said. "I feel closer to God. As for La Luz, she is part of me. When she has our child, I will renounce my sacred vows and marry her. I hope you will arrange for an annulment of her current marriage. But until then, I have much work to do."

The priest looked quite deranged as he stood at the window, his black hair standing on end, his comet livid, a twisted smile on his lips.

"Do you believe in God, Lorenzo?" the monsignor asked kindly.

Soledad laughed a thin, cynical laugh and started for the door. "What is God, Richard? I have seen him in a eucalyptus tree. La Luz saw him in a vat of soap. Juan Lobo says God is an eagle. Does anybody know?" With that, he closed the door and was gone. The monsignor rested his head in his hands. Much later, he would remember every word of this conversation. It would help him to prove that even then the door to sainthood was opening just a crack.

TWENTY-NINE

WHEN HE GOT off the train at San Sebastian, Lorenzo Soledad hurried to the cantina and sat at a table by the window. Despite the snow that lay on the ground and the threatening clouds, he thought he might still reach Camposanto by nightfall. But what would he tell Juan Lobo? That he had failed the one last chance to save the village? That his gold-lined hat had disappeared? Yet he knew in his heart that even that much gold would not have impressed Guerra, nor changed the outcome.

He was drinking a cerveza and finishing the last of his green chile enchiladas when a dark-skinned Indian man, about thirty-five years old, sat down opposite him. He had in his hands the padre's old hat, dirty and torn. "Good morning, Padre," he said brightly. "Someone found this hat along the tracks beside a dead body. They brought it in, thinking you'd be back." The man broke into a wide, unnatural grin. Most of his teeth were missing. His hair was badly cut, clipped close to his head. He had flabby cheeks.

Soledad's heart pounded. He reached for the hat and casually turned it over so he could see the band. It was empty of the *reales*. "Thank you," he said. He crossed the street to the stable, the man following close on his heels. There was something odd about him. The Indian came up and pulled insistently on Soledad's cloak. "You are going to Camposanto?" he asked.

"Yes," said the priest, looking around for Colonel Pazote so that he could reclaim his horse.

"I am going to Camposanto, too," the man said. "May I ride along with you? I am Rafael Madrone."

Soledad felt the blood drain from his face as he whirled around. "I . . . I thought you were in the *pinta*," he blurted. He leaned against the side of the building, afraid he would fall down. *It cannot be*, he thought, not daring to wonder what effect this would have on his life with La Luz. And what this man, who was her husband, might do to him.

"I escaped from the *pinta*, Padre, two weeks ago. I missed my wife, my children. I did not want to stay behind bars the rest of my life. So I have been hiding all over. In barns. In ditches. Even in a church, where the padre gave me food and a blanket. Also money from the collection box." His laugh was deep and hearty. "What is the matter? You look like you have seen a ghost. Let us go. I borrowed a horse from a gringo down the road. He is tied to a tree over there. I was waiting for you, Padre." He looked the priest squarely in the eyes. *So this is the man who has been fucking my wife*, he thought, remembering Delfine's letters. *I will kill him before long.* He had a sharp knife tucked in his belt.

"But how did you know I was coming, Rafael?" asked the priest. The Mexican colonel strode up and whispered that Rafael had come in last night wanting food, a saddle, some clothing, and a place to sleep. Rafael worried Soledad. How long before someone came looking for this convict? How long before he would hear the truth from La Luz? Sensing that something was wrong, Colonel Pazote went into the hacienda and came out with a pistol, wrapped in a cloth. "Take it, Padre," he begged.

Soledad shook his head. "I am not afraid," he said, mounting his horse. But he *was* afraid. More than he cared to admit.

Rafael Madrone watched the priest intently. He had learned certain techniques in prison. How to cover your tracks. How to live longer than anyone else by being smarter. How to kill a man with his bare hands. He swung himself into the saddle with a murderous look that made the priest's stomach turn over. Rafael dug his new spurs into his pony's flanks and saluted the colonel slyly with one finger at his hat brim.

"You know my wife, La Luz?" Rafael asked casually, guiding his horse across the snowy field and onto the trail to Camposanto. "I have heard that you do."

"Only at a distance," the nervous priest lied. "She is busy tending to the children. Cleaning house. Helping her relatives." *And she is beginning to look pregnant*, he thought.

Rafael Madrone took a deep breath of the pure mountain air, the first he'd enjoyed in more than three years. "My wife is a good woman," he said bitterly. "She will be glad I have come home."

The priest said nothing as he rode up the mountain, where the snow drifted in a foot-deep blanket. Afraid that Rafael would try and kill him, Soledad tried to hang back and let the Indian go first. But Rafael was too smart for that, so he made the priest ride single file ahead of him. As he rode up the steep trail, Rafael sang an old Calabaza song he had almost forgotten in the *pinta*.

Lorenzo Soledad arrived after dark with Rafael Madrone, to no one's surprise. They had always expected the convict to escape, for his Indian name was Coyote Dreaming; when he was a boy and Luis had nailed him in boxes for fun, he had always gotten free. Rafael was the one to find a way out of the wilderness or from the kiva to the village on the darkest night, without so much as missing a step. La Luz was not happy to see her husband, and for several nights, she refused to sleep with him, saying she was sick. The priest kept to himself, restlessly pacing up and down in his casita, dreading the eventual outcome of Rafael's return. The snow piled up, deeper and deeper, outside his door. *I do not want to die like this*, he thought.

Luis came by to offer his condolences. "She does not love my son anymore," he said sadly. "She loves you. What will you do?" Soledad shook his head. "I don't know," he murmured. "Then I will make a story," Luis said brightly. "With a story, everything will be all right." He patted the priest on the shoulder. "Believe me, Padre, you are better off without La Luz. She is not true Calabaza, but partly Spanish. We traded a good horse to the Apache for her, but we still do not know if it was a good trade!"

Soledad went to see Juan Lobo, who said he was not concerned about what had happened to the *reales*. He only laughed. "What did I tell you? Our way is the best for us!" He said he would spend the winter making moccasins and conversing with his wife's spirit, who hung around the house most of the day in her coyote form. When spring came, he would be ready for whatever happened next. "You try too hard, friend Soledad. Run here, run there, expecting to change people's minds." With a sweep of his hand, he indicated the snow-covered mountains outside his door. "See those mountains, Padre? They will never belong to the white man. I had a dream about it. My coyote-wife told me how something will happen and the mountains will stay with us forever."

Soledad sat forlornly at Juan Lobo's linoleum-covered table. The house was cluttered and dirty without Maria to take care of it. "How can you be sure?" he asked.

"I am never wrong," Juan Lobo said.

One night, La Luz slipped into Soledad's house after Rafael had fallen asleep, drunk on the Elixir of Dreams. He had beaten her a little, before Luis stopped him and told him about the child in her belly. "So now he knows," she said, brushing the snow from her hair. She put her arms around his neck and tried to kiss him, but he turned away. "But he thinks it is Delfine's child," she said. "And Delfine is dead."

He shook his head and held her gently away. "He knows it is mine. If I knew what was good for me—and you—I would leave and never come back. In a day, I could be in Santa Fe." But he knew what awaited him there. Besides, the snow was too deep for travel now.

He saw that because of her pregnancy, a robust glow had started to illuminate her face. She looked around. The whitewashed room was hallowed by the intensity of their passion all those months.

"I do not love Rafael," she said sadly. "There is something strange about him. I will never be happy except with you."

"It is the will of God that we live apart," he said gently.

She touched her belly. "What of the child? Our child?"

He turned away quickly so she would not see his tears. "Raise him as Rafael's child, La Luz. And someday, tell him about me. That I loved him when he was nothing but a butterfly in your belly."

"FOR THE LOVE of God, you must tell me where the rest of the gold is, Sotero. I know there's more. It's the only way your people can be saved, do you understand?" Soledad shook the boy gently. For two hours he had tried to persuade him, first with chocolates, then with a fine new wood-carving knife, then with the logic of Latin. "Gloria Patris, et Filii, et Spiritus Sancti," he said, knowing these words might move the mute. Finally, Sotero handed him a few more *reales* from the cave, then ran out the door through the knee-deep snow to fetch a new carving from his shop. This carving was much larger than the ones he had made before. As Soledad unwrapped it from a blanket, he gasped. The carving was of him, with a large, erect penis protruding from his cassock. He sat down on the bed and held the carving. "This is a work of art, Sotero, my boy," the padre said evenly, patting the mute's dark head. "May I keep it?" Eagerly, Sotero nodded. No sooner was the mute out of the house than the padre took his own knife and began the ludicrous task of cutting off the statue's embarrassing appendage.

THIRTY

O N A CLEAR, cold day in December, when the snow had melted a little, Marshal Flavio Trujillo and his deputies struggled up through the deep snow with what they called "formalities." Papers for the Calabazas to sign with a little pot of ink into which they were to dip their thumbs and make their marks upon the paper. Guerra had sent them. They came with two heavy saddle-bags full of silver dollars, in exchange for the thumb prints. This time, Juan Lobo invited the men into his warm house, and they crowded around the stove, rubbing their chapped hands. They had been riding since before daybreak, and tonight they would have to camp in the bitter cold, for the way back was long and the trail nearly drifted shut.

"A hundred silver dollars each, Juan Lobo," Flavio said, his nose dripping onto his Mackinaw. "Every man, woman, and child gets his pile. It's your last chance. After this, no money. You'll be moved out anyway." He noticed the old man's hesitation. "Look, chief, I used to play with your son, remember? But I got a job to do. What Señor Guerra told me was to get these papers signed." He had a helpless look.

Juan Lobo stood in the middle of the room, his hands behind his back. How he missed Maria at times like these, with her practical wisdom and strength. He said nothing, but surveyed the marshal's men. Weak men. No spines. No balls. Only big ears through which their thoughts ran out. Nearby, Soledad sat at the table, calmly studying the sheaf of papers. Several thoughts were running through his mind. He got up and whispered in Juan Lobo's ear, "Sign nothing." He turned to Trujillo. "See here, Marshal, you and I understand each other. Do we not? What I am asking for is more time."

"It's not my decision, Padre," Flavio Trujillo said with an air of importance. "The law says the white race is ordained by God to rule the world. The red man has to give up his land to the white man. It's not my rule. But the West will never get developed without it."

"Preposterous," said Soledad. "Go back to Señor Guerra. Take all the silver dollars with you. Tell him the padre is making miracles in this place!"

The marshal blinked. "What kind of miracles?" Being a devout Catholic, miracles were a very serious matter to him. He turned his eyes to the ceiling as if he expected one to materialize right there. He crossed himself and squeezed his hands together.

"Miracles are miracles," Soledad said, catching Juan Lobo's bewildered expression. "The greatest miracle is yet to come. Everyone will be famous, even you."

"But . . . but we've come a long way, Padre," Flavio Trujillo complained, wiping his nose on his sleeve. "It is winter now. Another storm is coming. I can't go back without those signatures. I'll lose my job."

The priest took the sheaf of papers, tore them in two, and handed them back to the marshal. "Tell Señor Guerra that when he gets every bear and every deer and every bird and every tree to sign, then the Calabazas will, too," Rather roughly, he took Flavio Trujillo by the arm and escorted him and his deputies out the door. Outside was a big coyote with a thick coat standing in the snow, an expression of cunning on its face. A flicker of recognition passed between it and Soledad.

Inside, Juan Lobo sat in his chair, his chin cupped in his hands. He appeared to be thinking. "They will be back," he said softly, "no matter what you do." The old man's thoughts drifted back to the time of the buffalo. He saw them in his mind's eyes, spread out across the plains as far as the distant horizon. His grandfather, Striped Wolf, had predicted that one day the plains would be empty of buffalo. And that houses would cover the land. Now Juan Lobo's wife was dead. So were four of his children. His village was crumbling. And the *federales* were taking his land. "It is all over, Padre," he sighed. "You won the wager, so now we will not kill you. I never wanted to anyway."

The padre smiled. "Who was converted, Juan Lobo?"

"Me." The Custodian of Abundance folded his arms across his chest. "I saw your magic with my wife, the Custodian of Memory. She came back in three days as a coyote. I saw it with Papita, the Custodian of Innocence, who died as a child and returned as a woman. I saw it when you gave the mute Sotero Madrone, the Custodian of Silence, the gift of encouragement so he could express himself in his statues. I was there when you saved Bonito, my foolish son, the Custodian of Unfinished Thoughts, when he drove his flying machine into the rocks. You taught Juan Talamantes, the Custodian of Meekness, arithmetic so that now he believes numbers will save our lives. Luis Madrone, a blowhard who always kept us entertained with his stories, is working on a way to put his thoughts to paper. He wants to be a writer, Padre, with the idea of enticing the world to come to us, in hopes that we will enlighten them. He is learning to write whole sentences. And Narciso, who killed my daughter when he was young, has been your bodyguard, though you did not know it at first. He killed Delfine because Delfine was going to kill you. Now he is building Papita a little workroom where she can make her tapestries, and he will make rugs out of Juan Talamantes's wool.

"The first day you were here, you made it rain by leaving that cross in the ground. We prayed in the kiva, but by then it had already started to rain. I did not want to admit this to you so early in the game. Yes, and I noticed your clever way of lying to the authorities so that El Comanche, the Custodian of War, could go on fighting his foolish battles. You destroyed the power of Pilar

Mondragon, the Custodian of Witchcraft, and Peso, the Custodian of Good Intentions, so that they can no longer put any spells on people. Ana Coyote, a woman I used to Get Together with when Balthazar was not around, no longer whines and complains about her life. The Custodian of Oblivion believes she has discovered a chicken that will outsmart a fox and survive drought, plague, and earthquakes. Night and day she works in the henhouse to produce the perfect hen. What you did with La Luz, the Custodian of Desire, may have a bad outcome now that her husband has returned home. But her son will be raised a Calabaza, as long as I am still alive. What you have given me, the Custodian of Abundance, is to make me see that the world does not stop because I want it to. If these things you have done are Catholic things, then I am a Catholic now, at least in my mind. I must let go, Padre, but it is very hard to do."

Soledad did not know what to say. He stood beside the old man, wanting to touch him yet afraid to do so. He could hardly speak. "Do you still believe in your Indian religion?" he asked softly, realizing it no longer mattered.

Juan Lobo threw his hands in the air. "What is the matter with you?" he asked impatiently. "I can have two religions if I want. Or ten or twenty. They are nothing but layers, Padre. Like that rock out there. One layer for Catholics. One layer for Indians. On and on. Who is to say one layer is better than the other? You?"

"We have not exactly been friends, Juan Lobo," Soledad said. "But I have come to respect your ways. I've come to see the beauty of your religion. And how, in certain ways, it surpasses my own. You told me that one day I would see eagles come out of the mountains, and so I have. Just this morning, before the sun came up. What does it mean?"

"It means you have learned humility, Padre." Juan Lobo got up and went into the kitchen to make coffee and get something to eat. Without his wife, he was at a loss how to do these simple chores. He simply took a fistful of coffee, threw it in the coffee pot, added water, and waited until it boiled. He put some cold, half-cooked beans in a pot and placed them and some chile on the stove to heat. Then he sat down at the kitchen table while he waited and smoked a cigarette he had rolled between his nimble fingers. He breathed a wreath of smoke in the air. "Whatever the Great Spirit wants to happen will happen. Neither you nor I can change it. Pain is part of the lesson, Padre. Even you know that."

The priest slowly drank his coffee, a thick residue of grounds at the bottom of the cup; he chewed on the half-cooked beans until his teeth hurt, then shoved them aside. By comparison, a pot of green chile looked good, so he scooped it out onto his tin plate and helped himself to a stale tortilla. He chewed slowly.

"My pain is in knowing that I've failed. Not in making Catholics of you, but in not being able to find some way to keep you here, where you belong." He looked out the one small window; the sun had already set. "I realize I've been very selfish. I did not love anyone or anything. Not even my Church. But up here, in the Second World—as you call it—I've come to love many things. La Luz. These mountains. And you, old man. You have taught me more in six short months than I've learned in nearly thirty-five years of life. So I thank you for your gift."

The cacique sat motionless as the priest said this. No one had ever told him he was loved before. Not his mother. Not his wife. Not his children. He took the padre's hand and held it for a long moment. If only there were more time.

LORENZO SOLEDAD ACHIEVED a sort of peace within himself during the long winter months at Camposanto. When storms howled down out of the Sangre de Cristo Mountains and snow reached the top of his window, he stayed indoors, reading or playing his violin. On Sundays, he struggled through the snow and tried to say Mass in the new church, but hardly anyone came. At times he saw La Luz, wrapped in a blanket, walking wearily across the plaza. She would say little to him anymore, but her eyes told him all he wished to know.

Always, he was aware of Rafael, slinking along behind wherever he went, but Rafael did nothing except look daggers at his back. Then, suddenly, La Luz's husband stopped tailing the priest and began to care for the shattered Bonito, still recovering from his ill-fated flight. In the *pinta*, Rafael had found his true nature as a man. Now he had found another man to care for, and he was happy with him in the way he had been behind bars with someone named Victor, a murderer from Las Cruces.

The mountains slept under a deep blanket of snow, and the people were subdued by the silent heaviness of winter. It was bitterly cold. Fresh food became scarce, and almost every day the men pushed out through the snow to look for meat, asking the deer and the elk for their deaths in order for the people to eat. There was still flour and cornmeal, so there were tortillas and bread. There also were beans, soaked and cooked and eaten seven days a week. People were hungry, but no one complained. They had seen much worse.

Father Soledad dreaded the thought of Christmas, but when it arrived, the Calabazas surprised him once again. They decorated the church with pine boughs, crude candles, and wreathes of kinnikinnick. Sotero had lovingly painted a new Cristo, and Papita had made a special altar cloth, bordered with green forest trees against a snowy white background. The priest smiled; never was the church more beautiful.

It seemed as though the whole village had trudged through the knee-deep snow to attend Christmas Mass. Even Rafael came with La Luz and the children; El Comanche stood in the back of the crowd dressed for battle, and Juan Lobo, secure in his newfound tolerance, stood close to the priest, silently blessing him in his Calabaza way. Pilar and Peso came, too, carrying fir branches that they laid around the altar. Ana Coyote edged up close to the priest so he could see her latest hen—a sturdy, white-feathered fowl, apparently impervious to disease and climate. Juan Talamantes, his head whirling like an adding machine, stood with Ermina, who had returned to Camposanto after her failed relationship with the widower in San Sebastian, and banged his wooden leg on the dirt floor to show his appreciation. Then Luis, flapping his arms like a great marooned bird, led the informal congregation in an off-key but deeply felt rendition of "Silent Night." It had taken two weeks to teach them this and other Christmas carols, but the Custodian of Stories knew that at last he had given the padre a fitting surprise.

Strangely touched by the outpouring from these people who only a few short months ago had seemed his enemies, Soledad conducted the most impassioned Holy Mass of his life. It was almost as if he believed! During the Introit, he happened to glance up among the church's new beams, and there he saw the same sad and kindly face that he had seen in the eucalyptus tree at seminary. He was somehow not surprised to find God staring at him thus. And when the same resonant voice spoke to him about what he must do, he only nodded and pressed his lips to the holy Missal opened in his hands.

So God had not forsaken him after all! How strange was God's command, yet entirely within the framework of what he'd always known he must do. "Ete, missa est," he said at the end of the service and bowed to the people. Sotero, dressed especially for the Mass, bleated in his usual way, but a single word escaped his lips. "*E-e-te,*" he stammered, so softly that only the priest heard him. *At last*, he thought, *the mute's tongue is at least partially loosened.* "*Missa,*" the priest said, but the mute said no more.

After Mass and the brief Communion administered to anyone who wanted it, the men beat out a flat place in the snow of the plaza, donned the heads of some newly-killed deer, and danced, two sticks serving as improvised front legs. The Deer Dance was old—as old as the inherited memory of the Calabazas, who believed that the First Deer had given it to them long ago. While Narciso beat on the old blackened drum, the men's voices rose in a chant, higher and higher, that was like the soft moaning of a mortally wounded deer. As the men did a shuffling dance, small boys shot toy arrows at them. When a man-deer fell, a hunter came and carried it away, slung over his shoulders like an animal.

The priest watched as Juan Lobo placed a piece of raw deer meat on the tongues of the deer dancers, who stood stoically, almost naked in the cold. This was a holy ritual, perhaps as old as any on earth, and the men received the offering with a quiet, forceful dignity. Then the cacique came to Soledad, who drew back, hesitant at being part of this pagan ritual. The old man waited, absolutely still, his fingers numb with cold as he held a small piece of meat between them. His eyes held something primordial—the old chants, the old beliefs, the old visions of the past floating in them.

The priest took a deep breath. He looked from this pagan communion to Juan Lobo's serene, stoical face. He took a step forward. Little was left of what he had been, nor was there more than a shadow of what he might become. Eternity was this one excruciating moment of humility, when the essence of both his worlds met, here in Camposanto. The priest closed his eyes and clutched his cross, which shone in the cold sunlight. Then he opened his mouth and took the meat on his tongue. A rich, bitter, full flavor. He chewed slowly. He felt no shame, only a deep and blessed unity with whatever world was finally to be his.

THIRTY-ONE

Y EARS LATER, *when Juan Lobo was a very old man and about to travel on the Hanging Road, Father Antonio went to see him in his casita—a place cluttered with the richness of his existence: Navajo blankets. Pueblo pots. Drums. Arrows. Father Antonio had put off this encounter as long as he could, but in a few days he would be leaving for the Vatican. The old man was an integral part of Father Antonio's mission, for he knew now that no one had been closer to Soledad than Juan Lobo. The cacique made him nervous. He seemed to float a few inches above the ground; he spoke to birds and the birds spoke back. The Vatican priest had heard these conversations, and they made him afraid. The whole village seemed bewitched with a faith he did not understand, yet for all the months he had been in Camposanto, he was aware of it every day.* Three hundred years and we have not made a dent, *Father Antonio thought, sitting uncomfortably on the floor where Juan Lobo preferred to sit these day, his legs tucked beneath him. Perhaps so much authority has not been good.*

"Was Father Soledad a pagan, Juan Lobo? Did he believe your ways?"

"Answers do not put an end to questions," *Juan Lobo said in a reedy voice that still rang with authority. Between his fingers he held a small black stone. As he rubbed it, the stone seemed to grow bigger. The priest stared at what was happening.*

"I see," *said Father Antonio.* "In a few years, Father Soledad may become a saint. Do you think he's worthy?" *Ever since Muy Contenta came into his life, the concept of worthiness troubled Father Antonio.* Ah, worthiness, *he thought.* Am I not worthy of a woman like her?

Juan Lobo raised his hand. The stone was now quite large and was changing shape. Father Antonio tried not to look, for the supernatural disturbed him, except when it had to do with his own Church.

"How do I know?" *the cacique asked crossly. His face was deeply lined, and his eyes, which had seen so much, were filmy with old age. Because his time to travel to the World Beyond had nearly come, he had no patience with small talk.* "This moment, right now, is all there is. Animals, birds, plants, air, rocks, trees, flowers—all live in the moment. When we live in the future, we die in the future. When we live in the past, we die in the past. I tried to teach Father Soledad that."

The Italian priest was writing excitedly in his notebook, a combination of English and Italian and Spanish that only he could decipher. "So, you tried to convert him?"

By this time the stone had become too heavy to hold, so Juan Lobo set it down on the floor. The priest stared. A small mouse scampered across his feet. The stone was gone. "I did nothing," *the cacique said.* "He made his own decisions. He lived his own way. Maybe we helped him a little." *He shrugged.* "Why is it important?"

Father Antonio felt he was getting nowhere. "Did he receive a pagan communion from you, Juan Lobo? I have been told that you placed a piece of deer meat on his tongue, as if it were the Body of Christ. Think carefully. It's very important. On this single sacrilegious point, I will rest my case." *Father Antonio knew, however, which way he would vote. Still, there were reports to be filled out. He had to make it seem as if he'd confirmed Soledad's allegiance to Holy Mother Church, even at the end. Rome had to see he deserved to become a saint.*

Juan Lobo closed his eyes. "You and the old woman will marry. I have seen her. She sleeps in your bed. Is that not true? And why not?" *The Vatican priest could not conceal his embarrassment.* "So the priest ate raw meat," *the cacique said.* "He was being polite. Just like you when you help that old lady into the wagon." *He laughed and laughed.*

Father Antonio struggled to his feet. Both his legs had gone to sleep. Juan Lobo said, "In our way, there is no judgment; you did this right . . . you did this wrong . . . I am going to punish you. We live by our own conscience. Whatever Father Soledad did, he did by looking into his own heart. He decided to die, and so he did. We did not try and stop him. We only wished him well on his journey." The Indian glared at the priest.

Father Antonio gave up on ever eliciting what he wanted to know from this old man. "Why can't you answer my questions, Juan Lobo?" How happy he would be to leave Camposanto and build his life with Muy Contenta. "Why did Soledad want to die?," he said.

With considerable effort, the Custodian of Abundance got up from the floor. In his old age, he always wore leggings, a buckskin shirt, and his old, patched moccasins. His long hair, streaked with white, was braided with long, red felt strips. From a dark corner of his room, the cacique brought out a bundle containing the totems Soledad had collected during his lifetime: a kachina meant to ward off evil spirits. The obsidian bear that an old Indian had pressed upon him when he was a boy. A leather pouch, filled with medicinal herbs that Maria Lobo had collected. A good luck charm from La Luz, made of quartzite and shaped like a penis. And Juan Lobo's most prized possession: a scalp taken by El Comanche on his last raid. Carefully, he laid everything out on the table, then he turned to the puzzled priest. "These are the same as your rosary beads. Your cross. Each totem has the power of the Great Spirit—greater than your Church power. Soledad saw what these totems can do. What they have always done since the Animal People became men. He died for us—poor, stupid Indians who believe in magic such as these. That was the reason, Padre. He wanted to."

The old man's eyes looked unfocused, but Father Antonio nonetheless felt them bore into his head. "It's not true," he said flatly. "A priest cannot worship these . . . these idols!"

Juan Lobo laughed a thin, coarse laugh. "Make him a saint, if you want. We have made him into a badger. Look." He pointed out the window to a fat badger, foraging in the yard.

Father Antonio looked out the window. He saw nothing but two boys playing stickball in the plaza. After the old man left, the Vatican priest went outside and stood in the sun. His eyes swept across the busy plaza where tourists swarmed. He heard a noise in the bushes. He turned. A badger was looking at him. "You are not Soledad," Father Antonio said. The creature came closer. It suddenly materialized into a man. The old priest had seen photographs of Soledad taken in Santa Fe when he went to see the monsignor. The badger looked like him.

"Mother of God," Father Antonio said, crossing himself before he sank to the ground.

THIRTY-TWO

T HE WINTER SUN had finished its long journey to the south and now began to roll northward along the horizon, expanding those moments of daylight that lightened the melancholy that had fallen over the village. But winter still cast its shadow on the land, and the people stayed indoors, and there they burrowed inside themselves, like owls or badgers. It was a period of introspection that the Calabazas called Quiet Time. The men spent long nights in the kiva, speaking of things that would not come again and summoning, through song and prayer, the power of the Great Spirit to keep them from their fate, even though everyone knew it was too late. They sang and drummed until dawn, their disconsolate voices drifting out the smoke hole so that the Four-Legged Animals and the Winged Creatures heard them and knew that something was wrong.

The Calabaza women took this Quiet Time for themselves. Often they just sat and watched the snowflakes coming down. They noticed the color and size of shadows on the walls. They looked into their hearts and, in this winter, found them cracked in two. They mended clothes, prepared pemmican, and made durable clothing from deer hide; they also began to pack, discarding those items that would not fit in the wagons that would take them to their new home in the desert. Little piles of belongings appeared in the houses, reminders of their destiny.

"It is all right," Catarina Madrone, the Custodian of Lesser

Causes, said with a curious twist of her head. "We will never be cold in the desert. And we will make new friends with the Animal People who live there." Her nature was to make the best of things. But in her heart, she did not want to leave Camposanto. It was home; it was where she wanted her bones to lie and her thoughts to remain for generations yet to come.

For the tribe as a whole, Quiet Time was when everyone reflected on his Second World life and tried to accept what the First World was doing to it. This was a time of emptying out evil, cowardly thoughts and replacing them with kindness and courage. No one danced or sang or talked very much during Quiet Time; their *tasooms* came out and looked around to see if people were living right.

Even Pilar Mondragon became human during this period, and she busied herself with all her dead relatives lying in the cemetery west of town. She asked forgiveness for what she'd done to them, and then she scraped aside the snow and laid cornmeal and sage on the frozen ground above the graves as an offering for peace.

For his part, Peso Mondragon, banished from the kiva because of his betrayal of his people, nonetheless sought the propitiation of the Calabazas. He went from house to house with a petition that the padre wrote out for him. He wanted Camposanto to secede from New Mexico Territory and become an independent nation. "Why not?" said Luis Madrone, and he affixed his *X* to the paper. All the others followed. "I will become headman," he announced.

During Quiet Time, Soledad spent his days doing what he liked to do best: studying, teaching, and talking with the villagers when they came to him for advice. He had mellowed greatly since he had come to Camposanto; a new and unfamiliar serenity had entered his heart and stayed there. When he could not get out, he read or played his violin; his fingers became more nimble again, and he was able to master the few pieces of music he'd brought with him. He found an atlas and pointed out to El Comanche where he might find wars worth fighting. Strange lands called the Transvaal, Sudan, and Ethiopia, colored brown and yellow on the map.

How will I cross the ocean?, El Comanche wondered; he was terrified of ships, which he knew would separate him from solid earth.
But he readied all his weapons and ammunition anyway. Hermosa
and Tomasina spent a month making him a set of beaded, fringed
warrior clothes of finest buckskin, just in case. As El Comanche
looked to the padre for suggestions about the best possible wars for
him to fight, he wondered if they would understand his language
in a foreign land.

"No," the padre said, affectionately. "All you need to say is 'death
to the locomotives,' the way you always have."

By March, Soledad had finished teaching fractions to Juan
Talamantes and was engrossed in trying to teach him what trigo-
nometry he remembered from his seminary days. Twice a week
he held reading classes in his tiny house, and Papita, Peso, and
Luis came, struggling with the McGuffey's Readers Soledad had
unearthed in Maria Lobo's abandoned schoolhouse.

Peso Mondragon, who as governor had had to content himself with Xs when marking official documents, learned to write
his name. PESO MONDRAGON. And two words: "the" and "so." He
believed he would soon become an educated man.

One snowy afternoon, Soledad performed a marriage in
the church. Ermina Madrone had finally agreed to marry Juan
Talamantes, if he would keep his sheep out of their bed. She looked
beautiful in her buckskin dress and high-topped boots, and the
priest knew she would make Juan a good wife. After that, Soledad
had settled the potentially murderous triangle among Isabela, Alvar,
and Zorrito by convincing the boy he was meant for better things.
When the snow melted, the upstart would enter a Catholic boarding school in Albuquerque in preparation for seminary and a lifetime dedicated to the power and the glory of Holy Mother Church.

Alvar, the Custodian of Madness, became as meek as a kitten as
he awaited the birth of a child who eventually would become his
favorite son, even though he was not the father. Alvar and Isabela
were like new lovers; they waded through the snow arm in arm,
having forgotten their previous bitterness.

"If you ask me," Alvar said, "Zorrito, that horse with one nut, got in over his head. A boy is not a man, Isabela, no matter what you thought." As for Isabela, she had talked herself into happiness with this man, but in her heart, she would always love Zorrito the Orphan, Custodian of False Affections.

"Yes, Alvar," she said contritely. "I know that now."

Pilar showed up one day during a blizzard and dumped all her effigies on the padre's bed. A fat man made of clay, meant to be Luis Madrone. An old woman made of straw, meant to be Maria Lobo. A gaunt figure in a brown dress, meant to be the priest. And a box of magic pins designed to create pain and sickness when she stuck them in certain spots on the effigies.

"I am no longer able to place spells on people, Padre," Pilar said in a civil tone. "When you attacked the dog with your cross, you also killed my power. Without my power, I am just another old woman. And my husband, without his power, is just another old man, dreaming of the old days. We are packed and ready to leave for the new place. Perhaps there our power will return." Already she knew that she would align herself with the Hopi and Navajo witches in order to learn their secrets.

Others came to give him gifts—a ritual of appreciation that was in their blood and had been ever since they had repaid the Animal People for teaching them how to gather food. Papita presented him with another embroidered altar cloth, a magnificent, brightly colored panel. By now the Custodian of Innocence had grown two inches and had begun to develop the curves and stature of a woman. She was quite pretty, with an innocent look still in her eyes; a sweet, honest smile; and the delightful habit of laughing whenever she felt like it.

Papita was twenty-two years old, and Soledad knew as he looked at her that one day a man would come to love her and that he would give her an adult life. "You are very talented," he said huskily, and kissed her softly on the cheek. One day Papita Ortega would become famous for the sort of unique embroidery that Soledad held in his hands.

Narciso came and stood, shifting from one foot to the other. He had given the priest a gift far greater than any other. All his life he would carry the burden of having killed Delfine, but he also had the comfort of having saved the padre's life. Soledad was a holy man, destined, Narciso was sure, to leave his mark on the world. Hadn't he seen Soledad's *tasoom* hovering over his house as the sun went down, proof that the priest held strange and mystical powers beyond this poor village?

The Custodian of Amends took off his hat and lowered his chin. "When you are far away, think of us, Padre," he said. "Think what you made of us. We are not the cowards of before, but a people who can accept whatever happens. We are not afraid to leave now, and we believe we can be satisfied in the desert, no matter what it is like." The priest looked deep into Narciso's black eyes. "You saved my life, Narciso. Greater love hath no man. What will become of you?"

"I am a simple woodcutter, Padre," Narciso said. "There are no trees in the desert. So Papita and I will make a new life in the mountains to the west with the Jemez, who are relatives on my mother's side. Because of you, I am no longer afraid to face the future." Shyly, Narciso gave the priest his most treasured possession—a beaded case that contained his umbilical cord.

When Juan Talamantes pushed his way through the snow and pounded on the porch with his wooden leg, the padre was not surprised. A rich glow spread across the face of the Custodian of Meekness; already Ermina was with child. Juan had known the night she opened her legs and tiny blue butterflies flew out in a moist, sweet haze. In the spring, when he could get down the mountain, Juan Talamantes was going to study mathematics in a regular school. "I am not really a Catholic, Padre," he said, "for in my heart, I will always believe a different way. But thanks to your teaching, I know now that the world comes down to mathematical equations. All I think about is how the planets are a certain distance apart that never changes. How the sun comes up and goes down in a different place each day. How apples or nuts or a rock from a cliff will always fall straight to the earth. Are you aware of that?"

"Yes," said Soledad. "Great men named Galileo and Newton came up with those ideas a long time ago. Perhaps you should study physics once you've learned mathematics."

Juan Talamantes burst out laughing. "Physics?" he said. "I cannot read or write; how could I study physics? Or mathematics, for that matter!"

Catarina, his next visitor, took the priest to task for what had happened to La Luz, but nonetheless she forgave him. "It is no secret," the Custodian of Lesser Causes said in her strange, halting way. "You and La Luz making a baby in front of everyone. At first, Rafael wanted to kill you, like Pilar and Delfine did. But Luis talked him out of it. He said, 'Do you want to go back to the *pinta* for two lifetimes?' Now Luis is making a story about how a priest became a father. How a girl became a woman. Ah, the same thing happened to me the summer Luis went away and MacGregor the Scot arrived with his charms. I was eighteen, already the mother of Rafael. The surveyor paid attention to me. He listened to what I had to say. He let me play the bagpipe he had brought along. Delfine was MacGregor's son, but MacGregor did not live long enough to see him. The Calabazas killed him before Luis got back. They cut his head off."

Catarina sighed. Her village was not whole anymore, and she feared what the future would bring. "You have turned my family upside down," she complained. "My poor lost Delfine is dead. Rafael drinks too much because he knows La Luz does not love him, and he has found love with a man! The mute still carves more things for the church. La Luz weeps because you are not with her. My husband thinks that stories and poems will save us."

He took her hand. "And you, Catarina?" he said softly. "What will you do in the new place?"

"I, Padre? I have learned to waltz. Look." She danced around his small, cluttered room with surprising grace, performing the steps that Luis had taught her when he was feeling amorous.

The priest clapped. "Brava, Catarina!"

She blushed. "In the new place, I am going to waltz across the sand and turn it into grass. I am going to make trees sprout. Streams and rocks. Make it just like home. The deer have promised to come along." She turned her round, pinched face toward him. "Do you think we will be happy there?"

Soledad glanced out the window at the snow-covered ground. If he wanted to, he could see flowers beginning to bloom there in the late-March snow. "In the Second World of Being, anything is possible. True?" She nodded. Catarina could see that the padre had begun to learn some things at long last, and in the process, he had become a man who walked in their moccasins.

The village still lay deep in snow, yet the days were sunny and mild, with a blinding blue sky and white clouds scudding off over the plains to the east. Snowmelt dripped from the canales and ran across the plaza, making small canyons in the mud. In his shirt-sleeves, Soledad climbed a ladder to shovel off the roof of the church, which had begun to sag from the weight of the winter snow. He helped Juan Lobo shore up an adobe wall of his house, which was caving in for the same reason. He tried to gut and skin a rabbit that El Comanche had shot for supper, but he gagged at the sight and the smell, and he had to settle for his usual beans and tortillas and dried meat.

On the warmest days, Soledad would open the window of his house, pick up his violin, and let the soft, sweet sounds of a Beethoven rondo drift out across the awakening land. No one knew what Beethoven was, but they stopped to listen to his magic.

Lorenzo Soledad's life would have settled into a happy, contented rhythm, had it not been for the constant encounters with La Luz. Every morning, he watched as she stood in the plaza, lifted her dress, and exposed her bare belly to the sun, believing that this would help her baby grow. She was becoming quite large, and she walked with a bowlegged gait that belied her former gracefulness. His heart leapt each time he saw her, and it was all he could do not to run out and embrace her. He prayed that her beauty and goodness would be passed on to their child.

"I love you," was all he could say, breathlessly, one day when he passed her in the plaza and saw their passion manifest in her swollen form. But her sad, dark eyes stripped him of all illusion.

"What do you know of love, Lorenzo?" she said coldly, shading her eyes against the early spring sun. "You are not with me anymore."

"I will always be with you," he said, and he held out his hands to her, but she moved away. "What have you told Rafael about me?"

"He knows I love you," she said. "He no longer loves me."

"Nothing will ever make me love you less," he whispered. "For one brief moment, you made me believe in God." La Luz turned on her heel and began to walk away from him. He shook his head. How could he make it right with her?

"God is a mouse," she said as she continued walking.

ONE MORNING, when the earth was beginning to stir with the seeds dropped by the Canada geese long months before, when the red-winged blackbirds and the meadowlarks had begun to sing their passionate songs, when pussy willows sprouted along the riverbanks and the faintest green blush began to paint the limbs of El Abuelo, the sacred tree that was older than El Comanche, Soledad got up and dressed with particular care. He inhaled the early spring air deeply; a fresh, clean smell filled his lungs. The sun was not yet up over the low eastern hills, and the room was filled with a lovely pewter light that bathed him in its gentleness. He felt fully, keenly alive as he dressed in a clean, mended cassock and then stretched his arms to the sky. He had had a dream three nights in a row containing the same message that God had sent him in the church at Christmas Mass, and even before that in seminary. This was a dream about his destiny.

At long last, he knew what he'd been put on earth to do. During the last six months, he'd recorded his feelings in his journal, writing down his reasons for wanting to become a man worthy of his God.

Then, his reasons for abandoning the traditional God. He hoped his sleepless nights were now over; whatever doubts he might have had vanished with the surge of life he felt as spring approached.

La Luz herself must also feel new life at this time, he thought. Resurrection. A way to begin anew. A way to save those he lived with, most of all. A way to ensure that those in the past had not died in vain.

I am not afraid, he told himself as he trudged up the hill through the mud and snow toward the kiva. A fresh wind blew from the east and he shivered. *At first, they will not understand my being there. They'll think me a fool. No one will speak on my behalf, yet I need no spokesman. Only agreement. Of course they will object, but I will make them see the wisdom*, he thought. The history is there for anyone to read. Ten million Indians dead. *Because of my Church. My Church's laws.* Three hundred years of religious persecution in New Mexico rolled up in a ball and dropped at his feet. Dare he kick it away merely to satisfy himself?

When the right moment came, he would strip off his cassock and would not wear it again. But for now, he fingered his cross, and it felt not like cold metal, but warm flesh. So he still believed. And would go on believing. Not only in God as the unifying thread among all living things, but in the right of people to accept what form they wanted God to take. Nature, without question. But also the deep, wondrous mystery of human love. He stopped to crush a fistful of pine needles and smell them. Had his Church recognized the other side of God when they murdered the Indians in the New World? Had the hierarchy seen fit to accept a valid, holy, aboriginal faith, much older than their own? A simple faith that did not judge, condemn, or reward? That required no buildings?

Lorenzo Soledad reached the kiva and stopped. His own pain would be a temporary discomfort. In sacrifice, he would find release and in release, not salvation but renewal, as each of the religions he now embraced had taught him. Juan Lobo had explained that in the Second World of Being lay the foundation for the practicalities of the First World, not the other way around. The Second

World was simply a long cord of experience, connecting every thought that had ever been and every voice and every experience with the thoughts and voices and experiences of today and future todays, without end. Holding this cord among them, each generation went on, one footstep at a time.

The priest stood at the rooftop entrance to the kiva and lifted his head. The raven blessed him. So did the tall fir trees, gently swaying in the wind. "Yes," he said to himself.

Down in the kiva, the men had been meeting all night. Stiff from sitting in the same position for so long, they were numb in body and in mind. Within days, the *federales* would throw them off their land. They had talked about the inevitability of it all, but none of them could come up with a solution. Luis Madrone said he would go on telling stories in hopes that the people would remember their lives. El Comanche said he would go on making war. Juan Talamantes said he would figure a way out of their predicament through mathematics, which could measure the distance between planets and could therefore measure the road out of their misery.

Rafael Madrone's mind was not on the problems of his people. For three years, he'd been locked up in prison. The village he had once longed for was decrepit; the people were weak and disheartened. He no longer wanted his wife, La Luz. He wanted to get out as soon as the snow melted and forget this part of his life. So Rafael sat against the wall, saying nothing. He thought of Bonito.

Alvar Talamantes stood up and solemnly announced that it was time they realized they were not alone. Just the other day, a Lakota had ridden through deep snow, bringing news of his people—many of them were shot to death at Wounded Knee, only seven years ago. They were starving. Homeless. Ill.

The Lakota warrior had brought with him some peyote buttons, and all but Juan Lobo and Sotero had taken it. Father Peyote had made them less afraid but had brought nothing new to their minds.

Now, as they sat in the kiva, chewing the bitter peyote buttons, not one man was able to see a way out. They were ready to look at

the mountains for the last time. To say good-bye to their ancestors. To tell the embedded feet where they were going and see if
they wanted to come along. To say good-bye to El Abuelo, their
guardian tree. To listen to the songs of the Spaniards one last time.
To destroy the kiva and all their houses. But not the church. No,
the church would remain standing, a symbol of all their hopeless-
ness. When everything was done, they would climb in the wagons
for the long journey west. Even Juan Lobo, who had wanted to die
where he was, had finally agreed to ride with Bonito, at least as far
as San Sebastian. Perhaps later he would join his relatives at Jemez.
He was unable to think.

"At least you are alive, brothers," the Lakota warrior had said
before he rode back the way he had come. "Most of us are dead,
except for me. The world has ended."

The men said nothing for a long time. They sat wrapped in their
blankets, staring at the orange coals of the fire. They inhaled the
fragrant smell of juniper and bathed themselves in the purifying
smoke. Their heads were down, and they were as still as statues. A
wisp of blue smoke curled up from the floor of the kiva through
the smoke hole. Outside, the sun had just risen. Sensing the silence
below, the priest hesitated. Then he walked across the roof of the
kiva and lowered himself down the ladder hole into the round, dim
room, saturated with the fears of tired men.

The Calabazas, sleepy-eyed and silent, greeted the priest with
unbelieving stares, then they shouted at him in the old language
of their ancestors. Improbably, Soledad understood almost every
word. Juan Lobo's face flushed with anger. "Get out," he said darkly.
"You have no business here." Both Juan Lobo and Father Soledad
knew that. The last priest, Father Montez, had invaded the kiva and
destroyed it. So the Calabazas had killed him. But Soledad stood
his ground and calmly looked around—at the life-size santos, the
large crucifix, the plaster statue of the Virgin Mary, the buffalo head,
the medicine bundle, the stone fetishes, the feathers, and sacred
corn dolls stolen from the Kiowa. So there it was, the First World
of Being connected with the Second World, yet the Indians did not

even realize it: the Catholic Church, or at least its symbols, and their own ancient beliefs had been inextricably mingled for a very long time. At last, Soledad understood how two disparate religions could become compatible. How paganism could enrich the Catholic faith. How the Church of Rome could forfeit dogma long enough to find a common ground. The priest looked at the dying embers of the fire. Each man's face shone in the light. He realized he loved them all. He swallowed and made his offer. The men were stunned.

"You cannot," Luis Madrone said. "We are not murderers, Padre. We already decided to send you home."

"This is my home," the priest said.

Juan Lobo looked at him. "Your offer is refused. Now go."

"I will not die, my friends. I promise you. But I will make it possible for you to stay here where you belong." The priest came closer to the fire. He fingered his gleaming cross.

El Comanche cleared his throat. "There will be trouble," he said. He banged the butt of his Henry on the hard dirt floor. "No crucifixion, you idiots."

"He says he will not die," said Luis Madrone, making careful mental note of how the priest's face looked in the flickering light.

"Maybe we could crucify him a little bit," said Juan Talamantes. "Not all the way."

"Crucify him," Rafael said maliciously.

"I am the one to decide," Juan Lobo said. "The last priest to die in such a manner brought sickness to our village. The game went away."

"I am going," Soledad said, climbing up the kiva ladder. "Tomorrow I will be ready. Make sure the cross will not fall down, Juan Lobo. It's been there a long time."

He went to his casita to pray. La Luz visited him one last time. "Do not do this," she begged, pulling on the sleeve of his cassock. "You are mad."

"I must," he said. He stroked her long, silky hair.

He listened to the song of the Owl Spirit, who was coming to claim him. He staggered to his bed and threw himself down. "Hold me," he said to La Luz.

THIRTY-THREE

THE PEOPLE, gathered in the plaza in the predawn cold, drew their blankets around their shoulders. A ladder stood against the old cross. Ravens perched on the cross pieces. The cross stood upright, as solid as a rock. The moment the sun came up, Soledad walked slowly from his house dressed in his usual brown cassock and gold cross. He was barefoot. The crowd parted to let him pass. Some people reached out to touch him. Soledad stepped out of his cassock at the base of the cross, naked except for his underdrawers and his gleaming cross. A murmur arose. "Don't do it, Padre!" someone shouted. Seeming not to hear, the priest climbed the ladder and stood, arms outstretched, while the men tied him to the crosspieces with strong leather thongs. People were crying. El Comanche stood to one side. He was sure the priest would save himself at the end. "I never meant to offend you, Padre," he said. "I am very sorry."

Juan Lobo placed two eagle feathers in the priest's dark hair. He said nothing. Soledad's eyes bored into him. His hands were fastened to the crosspieces. His overlapping feet were lashed together. They rested on a little block of wood. Pain swept across his shoulders and down his legs. He turned his head from side to side. He shivered. He heard the sound of drums. A flute. The death songs the Calabazas sang whenever a spirit departed for the next world.

"I am ready," the padre said hoarsely. He closed his eyes. The ravens flapped their wings.

PART SEVEN

Camposanto, New Mexico Territory, 1897–

THIRTY-FOUR

NEWS OF THE Soledad crucifixion spread quickly. The deputies saw to it that everyone knew of the bizarre event. They rode to town scarcely able to contain themselves. Telegrams went out. A BARBARIC ACT OUT OF THE SIXTEENTH CENTURY, the newspapers said in blazing headlines. Graphic illustrations showed Soledad torn apart by lions. Almost immediately, tourists began to stream up the mountain by whatever means they could. They paid ten cents to see the cross. Another ten cents to hear the Custodian of Stories give his version of the crucifixion. "A lost tribe did it," he said. "Crazy animals. Merciless. They escaped into the mountains."

The tourists stood in reverential silence in the middle of the plaza. Ravens soared and dipped their wings and watched. A strange hush fell. The tourists bought souvenirs from Juan Talamantes and got to sign his wooden leg.

There were the usual investigations by the local authorities. The murder of the priest—and that's what the deputies said it was—was a cold-blooded act and they witnessed it themselves. They arrested Juan Lobo and dragged him off to jail, his hands tied behind his back. There he sat for six months, carving pictographs of the story of his life into the thick adobe walls with an arrowhead. Later, the museum would cut them out and put them in a display case. Every day the cacique looked out the barred window of his tiny cell. He watched the sun make its slow journey across the sky. He spoke to it. Officials of the federal government came in to talk to him. "Tell us what you know," they said. "We'll let you go."

"I know nothing," he said. "One day Father Soledad was alive. The next day he was on the cross. A black ghost carried him away. We do not know where he went."

One of the *federales* kicked him. Another banged his head against the wall. Still, he said nothing because he knew nothing. He fed a little gray mouse part of his daily ration of posole and beans.

"Badger Man," he said. The mouse sat up on its hind legs and looked at him.

THIRTY-FIVE

AFTER THE DEATH of Soledad, Camposanto was reborn. It was no longer fitting that this thriving village be called a graveyard, which is what the word "Camposanto" means in Spanish. With state and national dignitaries attending the ceremony while Juan Lobo beat his drum, the village was christened Paradiso. The residents, long known as Calabazas, or Squash, a lowly vegetable, legally became the Angelos. Angels living in Paradise. Yes.

By this time, the United States government had signed a treaty awarding the Angelos the deed to the two hundred thousand disputed acres. This was what Soledad had fought for. It was the only time in U.S. history that a treaty with the Indians had never been broken, even to the present day. Sotero Madrone, speaking the words of the Latin Mass, gave the president of the United States a sack containing the gold *reales* he had found in the cave. The president was there to make a speech praising his government's humanitarian efforts.

"Gloria tibi, Domine," Sotero said, scampering off. With this money the Angelos were able to purchase an additional hundred thousand acres. The feet came out of the wall for a week-long celebration. The reserve supply of the Elixir of Dreams was drunk.

FATHER ANTONIO, by this time living in Grand Junction, Colorado, with his wife, the still-lovely Muy Contenta, had something to do with Paradiso's fame. Thanks to him the canonization process was speeded up. It was unusual, of course, but the Holy Father had been persuaded by members of the Curia to make an early decision before reporters dug too deeply and spoiled everything. The Pope, who had suffered several recent setbacks on a global scale, needed something to offset his defeats.

Father Antonio started a nondenominational church on the banks of the Colorado River amidst his thriving apple orchard. He called it Saint Jude's after the patron saint of lost causes. All were welcome—Protestants, Jews, Mormons, and freed slaves. Muy Contenta bought an old house and refurbished it with the finest antiques. She hired girls from Denver and Salt Lake City to entertain the distinguished gentlemen who came in on the D and RGW train. She served high tea and read the part of Juliet in Shakespeare's famous play. A senator applauded.

PARADISO WAS HUMMING. It had never had such attention in its history. El Abuelo, the giant cottonwood from which the cross had been made years ago, was cut into small strips and sold as souvenirs. When the old tree finally died, another tree was planted in its place. Indian dances took place nightly in front of a crackling fire. Juan Talamantes, with his wooden leg stuck straight out, jumped up and down on the real one. He was a sensation. So was Papita, who, thanks to Saint Soledad's miraculous intervention years before, was now almost six feet tall. She draped herself in her colcha embroidery and sold pieces to the appreciative visitors. After a few years, Ermina and Juan Talamantes made their way to Princeton, where he worked on revolutionary mathematics equations with esteemed scientists. He was given an office with a German physicist named Albert Einstein. Together they made an amazing scientific discovery which is famous to this day.

Colonel Pazote built a cantina in San Sebastian near the old train station, where thirsty tourists could stop for margaritas and nachos before the long haul up the mountain via open-air tour buses. His wife, Luisa, now older and heavier, set up a stage in the parlor where she and her seven children reenacted Soledad's tragic fate. The colonel himself played Luis Madrone. He wore a loincloth, and his skin was painted brick red. One of the Pazote children beat a tom-tom and decorated himself with feathers and red and yellow paint.

LA LUZ WAS accepted at Harvard Medical School, though she did not have a high school diploma. When university officials read about her extraordinary life in the *Boston Globe*, they wanted her among their student body. She took her three children to Cambridge, including Mundo Ruiz Soledad, the priest's precocious son, who was his identical image. La Luz graduated at the top of her class. During the Great War, she became a field surgeon. After Indians were given the vote, Mundo Ruiz Soledad, a graduate of the University of New Mexico School of Law, became a three-term congressman and the father of six children by a beautiful Navajo woman.

Luis Madrone gathered his tribal stories with the help of a student from Highlands University. They were published in a popular book called *Black Deer Seldom Speaks*. He was given an honorary doctorate degree from Yale University.

Edward Curtis, a photographer on his way to photograph the Cheyenne, stopped at Paradiso long enough to take a picture of Juan Lobo dressed in a headdress and a J. C. Penney blanket. The cacique held a scalping knife in one hand and assumed a warlike look. The picture was published in one of the leading magazines, where it caught the attention of a Hollywood producer who rushed to Paradiso to get the old Indian to sign on the dotted line. Juan Lobo traveled to Hollywood and made a movie, *Painted Moccasins*, before he became homesick. He never went anywhere again. He sat on his porch talking with Jesus Christ, Jr., the son of Juan Talamantes's old yellow dog, Jesus Christ. The dog was his responsibility now that Juan Talamantes had left for that fancy university in New Jersey.

El Comanche no longer killed locomotives. It wasn't practical. But the fighting spirit was in his blood, so one day he packed his

Springfield, his Henry, and his Colt .45. He said good-bye to his wives, applied his gruesome war paint, adjusted his eagle-feather war bonnet, and made sure the fringe on his beaded buckskin shirt and leggings was just so. He rode his dependable old sorrel gelding Kit Carson through the plaza. People stepped aside, terrified. He raised a gnarled fist and shouted, "Death to the locomotives!" The tourists shouted back, "Death to the locomotives!" They had no idea what the epithet meant, but they repeated it many times as progress took over.

El Comanche rode his horse, Kit Carson, through the forest toward Las Vegas, noticing how barbed-wire fences and dirt roads were cutting up the land he loved. Ranches, schools, churches, and villages dotted the land. Black coal smoke billowed out.

Once El Comanche got to Las Vegas, he signed up with the Rough Riders because he'd heard there was a war going on in some far-off place called Cuba. He led the charge up San Juan Hill, though a pudgy gringo named Teddy Roosevelt tried to take credit. Foot soldiers heard the old mounted warrior yelling, "Hurry up, Kit Carson, you bastard!" The legendary Indian fighter had been dead for many years.

People claimed to see El Comanche everywhere, even many years later at El Alamein when the Second World War was raging. Reporters said they heard the Allies shouting, "Death to the locomotives!" Exhausted troops swore they saw an Indian chief in full battle regalia riding a prancing horse behind enemy lines.

ARCHAEOLOGISTS SWAGGERED into Paradiso and dug holes. They claimed to have found evidence of an Indian civilization that predated the Clovis entry, which made it eight thousand years old, or more. They found pieces of jasper and flint, bones of creatures thought extinct, and strange hieroglyphics carved on a flat rock. Scientists from the Field Museum in Chicago proclaimed these crude drawings had great worth. They offered clues to a distant time before roads or factories. More sites were excavated. The leftover dirt was blessed by the new priest, Father Bernard, and made available for a small donation. The holy dirt was said to cure rheumatism, boils, impotence, cancer, and mental depression. There was never enough of it.

Tour buses disgorged visitors by the dozens. They gawked at the Indians sitting on their blankets, selling turquoise jewelry made in Mexico. When Kodak cameras came in, tourists took souvenir pictures. The Angelos dressed as they might have a century before, in war paint and feathers and beaded clothes, posed patiently for their guests. Quaint restaurants sprang up, featuring the fiery hot food of northern New Mexico. From their old enemies, the Navajo, the Angelos learned how to make fry bread and caused digestive disturbance in everyone because of the lard they cooked it in. When motor cars began to wind up the steep road from San Sebastian, Bonito Lobo, at last able to finish his thoughts, said, "These stupid gringos will pay anything to park their stupid cars." He opened a parking lot for the wheezing, overheated automobiles. His partner, Rafael, learned how to be a mechanic. They were a happy couple.

Eventually, a Paradiso Hilton was built. A museum went up to house the artifacts the archaeologists had dug up. Much later, a golf course was built and next to it a casino. Even then, submerged in the realities of the twentieth century, the Angelos remained true to the ways of their ancestors. Boys still trained in the kivas. The ancient language was still spoken. Ceremonial dances, for natives only, were held at night, away from the prying eyes of tourists. The Indians were still Getting Together, still drinking the Elixir of Dreams. As time threatened to strip away what had cost them dearly, the Angelos retreated into the mountains, there to converse with their trusted animal spirits and to observe the dependable journeys of the sun, the moon, and the stars.

JUAN LOBO WAS a very old man, half blind. As the end of his circle approached, he gathered his sacred bundle, put on his special beaded moccasins, and put two eagle feathers in his hair. Luis Madrone approached. He bowed his head and pressed a bear fetish into the cacique's hand. "Great leader and Keeper of Tradition, I wish to know one thing." He looked to the sky. "What were Father Soledad's last words? You were the only one to hear them when he was hanging on the cross."

The old man hesitated. He had never repeated Soledad's last words to anyone, but now he felt obliged to speak so that future generations might know the truth.

"His last words were these: 'There are no answers,'" Juan Lobo said. He caught the surprised look on Luis's face. "That's what he said. 'There are no answers.' Remember it, Luis." With that, he was gone.

There are no answers. Luis looked at the activity in the plaza. He looked at two deer sauntering out of the trees. He heard the scream of an eagle high overhead. At last, everything made sense.

THIRTY-SIX

Despite the success of Paradiso and its residents, one mystery remained. What had happened to Father Soledad, the martyred priest who at last became a saint? Church historians scoured the route he might have taken with the spectre who removed him from the cross. Down through the badlands they went, searching for clues. No one in the poor Catholic villages remembered a dead man being carried along by a ghost on horseback. "Muy loco," the villagers said, crossing themselves.

Then, just about the time that El Comanche was charging up San Juan Hill, a young novitiate found a dried-out leather thong along the banks of the Rio Grande. It appeared to have blood on it. He showed it to his superior, who threw it in the water.

"Do not disturb the flow," the older priest said.

EPILOGUE

I N THE HOT, slick jungle, where the turquoise sea laps against
the fine-grained sand, a solitary figure in a white robe stares at
the gently moving water. He pictures the day when, almost four
hundred and fifty years ago, the first shiploads of Spanish priests
and soldiers landed. The aged man, slightly stooped, presses his
lips together. What had the Spaniards brought in their evangeli-
cal fervor? The wheel. The handshake. Cheese. Leavened bread. A
European language. Disease. Horses. Steel. The religion of Rome.
Genocide. His mind whirls with the myths and actualities of history. How little he was able to change things.

The village of Charcas has changed, thanks to the sainthood of
a man whose father, a poor seaman, once lived here. A few years
back, Charcas was transformed into a shrine to the saint and to his
paternal family, the dirt-poor Ruizes, who had worked in the fields
on a rich man's mescal plantation in the hills above the village.
Others, like one named Sierra Ruiz, did not want to be miserable
field slaves. They had taken to the sea where they were miserable
ship slaves. Legions of genealogists were employed by the Vatican
to establish bloodlines, which putatively traced the saint's ancestry
back to a Spanish nobleman said to have come ashore with the first
boatload of conquistadores. But this was not true.

The old man is content to live where he is, receiving the
warmth of people who seek him out. There is a peacefulness about

it. In Mexico City, a petition is before the president to make the saint's birthday a national holiday. "So much fuss over a martyred Franciscan," the old man says to himself as he watches more pilgrims emerge from a dilapidated bus and race along the beach to the beautiful white church and the shrine of this first American saint. Summer or winter, the influx never ceases.

The aged man in the long white robe watches the waves break on the sand, nodding to their gentle rhythm. He looks up. He does not like what he sees.

In response to the ever-growing pilgrim traffic, the Charcas city fathers constructed a long wharf, where debarking passengers can eat *camarones* and *langostas* while reading the pamphlets on the patron saint of loneliness, as he has become known. They can purchase relics, certified to have come from the site of the saint's crucifixion in New Mexico. Since he was crucified so far away, a lucrative trade connection was established—in the name of reciprocal sanctity—between Charcas and Paradiso. Huge crates of holy relics are shipped monthly to Charcas from the north, and Charcas ships to Paradiso heavy crates of sand from the beaches where El Maestro's ancestors walked. It has been blessed by the parish priest, so it is holy sand.

The old man rests in the shade of a palm tree. His hair is completely white and reaches his shoulders. His beard bears the traces of the sangria and *pollo con arroz* he had for lunch. His face, accustomed to the raw sun and steady wind of Charcas, is as tough and brown as leather. For some time, El Maestro has been teaching the young Mayas about the ways of their ancestors, which churchmen and academics have purposefully repressed. He walks from village to village, inquiring after the origins of the oldest men. Although these villages have been deep Catholic for four centuries, El Maestro finds grains of the old Mayan religion everywhere he goes. He deciphers the mythic secrets of the javelinas and the tortoises, the ospreys and the jaguars.

Armed with this rich legacy, El Maestro teaches the ancestral wisdom of the region, and slowly, his fame spreads. Before long, few of the young are attending Mass. Instead they explore the jungle for the stone idols of their ancestors and learn to dance the ancient dances. On moonlit nights, they shed their clothing and dance naked on the beach, alive with the possibility of natural love and passion.

One day, the aged teacher walks slowly toward the plaza. A cool breeze blows through the palm trees, creating a soft clicking sound. The village is bustling. Traffic moves clockwise around the plaza—cars and trucks that he can never quite get used to. In the plaza in front of the church, a work crew is installing a life-size statue. He cannot resist having a look at it. The bronze figure is tall and dignified, with birds perched on either shoulder and rabbits at its feet, in the manner of another saint whose name he revered. He shakes his head. *As if the world doesn't have enough saints without adding another*, he thinks. Besides, it doesn't look like him. The nose is too long.

The hunched, slow, middle-aged sculptor in charge of the crew stands back, admiring his work. The statue is exactly how he remembers the priest. The brown cassock. The dishpan hat. The Missal clutched in his hand. The cross, the original of which he himself now wears around his neck. The rosary beads that hung from his belt like a lasso. The sculptor runs his hands lovingly over the smooth bronze finish. The padre saved his life. Now he, Sotero Madrone, is world famous. Even though he can't speak in a way that anyone can understand him, he has magic in his fingers. Perhaps the chin is not quite right, but the comet on the saint's cheek looks alive. The sculptor stares at the old man standing close by, watching intently. There is something familiar about him.

"Gloria Patris, et Filii, et Spiritus Sancti," the sculptor says in the old, dead language he learned to speak as a boy. It's still all he knows.

El Maestro stands, watching quietly for several minutes, his hands behind his back. The sculptor looks familiar to him also, but he doesn't know why. He gazes intently from the sculptor to the statue and back again. A smile flickers across his face.

"Sicut erat in principio, et nunc, et semper, et in saecula saeculorum," he murmurs.

The sculptor would recognize those sad eyes anywhere. But no, it cannot be. Soledad died on the cross more than forty years earlier. "Adjutorium nostrum in nominee Domini!" he cries, and he takes a halting step toward the old man in white.

"Qui fecit caelum et terram." El Maestro shakes his head and raises his hand. He doesn't want anyone to touch him.

Sotero Madrone covers his ears and closes his eyes, moaning with the pain and joy of his discovery. But when he open his eyes again, the old man is walking toward the beach. The sculptor starts to run after him, then stops. The Church does not make saints of living men. He turns back to his statue. He did not get the nose quite right.

He has seen a miracle, but he will be unable to tell anyone. He watches the old man disappear. He hugs the statue as if it were alive. "Deo gratias," he weeps.

Later, in the *palapa*, the sea breeze cooling him, El Maestro sits comfortably in a bamboo chair, facing his class. Beside him is a table containing a pitcher of water, a glass, and a number of books. The class is mixed. A doctor from Venezuela. A lawyer from Columbia. A playwright from Peru. Two graduate students from the University of Chicago. A magistrate from Madrid. Some bohemian-looking women from California. A frightened young Jewish couple who have recently fled Austria to escape the Nazis.

"We are on the verge of war, Maestro," says the young Jewish man, "What is going to happen to the world? Hitler has invaded our homeland. Many have been sent to concentration camps." For a moment, the professor is overcome, then he says, "Reason means nothing. Justice is gone. Humanity is dead. What can the world believe in anymore?"

The class begins to murmur. The world *was* in chaos. That much they knew. And each of them knew that, in one way or another, life would not be the same for any of them, ever again. Turning to their teacher, they start to clamor for answers, pressing closer for a look at the old man's ankles, which are as curiously scarred as his wrists. They wonder what happened to him.

"The world is in ruins," the professor reiterates. "Is there anything left to believe in?" The sun is hot. He fans himself with a straw hat.

From the bottom shelf of the table, El Maestro takes out a battered violin similar to the one he played long ago. He picks up a bow. Then he begins to play a squeaky tune, off-key at first, then stronger.

"Believe in Beethoven," he says.

When people look again, El Maestro's chair is empty.

OTHER BOOKS BY NANCY WOOD

POETRY

We Became as Mountains
Sacred Fire
Shaman's Circle
Dancing Moons
Spirit Walker
War Cry on a Prayer Feather
Many Winters
Hollering Sun

COLLECTIONS

The Serpent's Tongue

FICTION

Thunderwoman
The Man Who Gave Thunder to the Earth
The King of Liberty Bend
The Last Five Dollar Baby